The BIG BANG

a novel

Linda Joffe Hull

TYRUS BOOKS

F+W Media, Inc.

Published by
TYRUS BOOKS
an imprint of F+W Media, Inc.
10151 Carver Road, Suite 200
Blue Ash, Ohio 45242
www.tyrusbooks.com

ISBN 10: 1-4405-4415-8
ISBN 13: 978-1-4405-4415-6
eISBN 10: 1-4405-4522-7
eISBN 13: 978-1-4405-4522-1

Printed in the United States of America.

10   9   8   7   6   5   4   3   2   1

This is a work of fiction. Names, characters, corporations, institutions, organizations, events, or locales in this novel are either the product of the author's imagination or, if real, used fictitiously. The resemblance of any character to actual persons (living or dead) is entirely coincidental.

Many of the designations used by manufacturers and sellers to distinguish their product are claimed as trademarks. Where those designations appear in this book and F+W Media was aware of a trademark claim, the designations have been printed with initial capital letters.

This book is available at quantity discounts for bulk purchases.
For information, please call 1-800-289-0963.

Dedication

For Brandon,
No such thing as a better half any better than you.

Acknowledgments

$\mathcal{T}$hank you, first and foremost, to my editor, publisher, fellow writer, and dear friend, Ben LeRoy. Your spirit, guidance, intelligence, and friendship are a daily blessing.

Thanks to Josh Getzler for believing in me and being an all-around mensch.

I am forever indebted to Monica Poole for showing me the way from the very start. To Kay Bergstrom, Joel Reiff, and Terri Bischoff for your friendship and constant support. To Alison Dasho for your superior editing skills. To Cary Cazzanigi for making everything work so I can. To Becky Stevens, Carleen Evanoff, and Julie Goldsmith for a million reasons.

I could not have written, much less finished this or any other book, were it not for the help of Rocky Mountain Fiction Writers, the Hand Hotel gang, and especially the Capital Hill critique group, including (but not at all limited to) Scott Brendel, Robert Buettner, Janet Lane, Chris Jorgenson, Terry Wright, Alex Kalinchuk, Jedeane McDonald, Steve Reinsma, Dave Jackson, Luke Dutka, Brianna Martray, Jan Gurney, and Mark Stevens.

To Piper Stevens, Ellen Rosenblum, Wendy Kelly, Doug Webster, Caryn McClelland, Rick Anderson, Angie Lancaster, Judy Bloomberg Schenkein, Rachel Greenwald, Sue Aaronson, Beth Hooper, Marc Kerman, Susan Hennes, Ruchi Brunvand, and the gang at OMHD for being there in a variety of ways, some of you for a long time.

To Bill Joffe, Elizabeth Heller, Bob Moskowitz, Ron Hull, Naomi Hull, Kathryn Hull, Brian Hull, Kevin Hull, Dan Mitchell, Donavon Mitchell, Jacob Hendrickson, and Elliot Springer. Love you guys!

To my sisters Nancy Mitchell, Laura Hendrickson, Jenny Springer, and Rachel Moskowitz—thanks for always agreeing to listen, read, give feedback, and play sisterly shrinks.

Special thanks to my mom, Marjorie Moskowitz—your enthusiasm, input, and insight have been beyond invaluable.

To Andrew, Evan, and Eliza for believing in me through it all. I can't believe how lucky I am to be your mom.

And, finally to Brandon. Thank you for the years of love, encouragement, patience, unflagging optimism, and never, ever buying into Lawndale as the path of development.

A breathtaking Rocky Mountain vista sets the backdrop for your dreams at Melody Mountain Ranch, a Henderson Homes master-planned community. Choose from six dazzling floor plans in the Colorado Birdsong Collection and revel in arresting architectural features including dramatic foyers, standard-plus living rooms, gourmet-style kitchens, and expansive master suites.* With a state-of-the-art family recreation center, ample green space, and tree-lined parks,** there is no better place to call home.

Melody Mountain Ranch—Life in Harmony with Your Dreams

*Upgrades available at additional cost

** Planned

Part I

RABBITS

CHAPTER ONE

Melody Mountain Ranch Covenants, Conditions, and Restrictions: Restriction 8.7.41. Window Coverings: All windows shall be covered with curtains, drapes, or other acceptable coverings necessary to maintain privacy.

From the moment Hope first looked into Jim Jordan's blue eyes, all she could think about were the gorgeous, flaxen-haired children he'd make.

They'd make together.

The tongue-tied awe he inspired in everyone, from her sorority sisters to store clerks to even her mother's friends on their wedding day, kept her from admitting the one thing she suspected from their first conversation: God had been so taken by the sheer magnificence of Her creation, She figured there wasn't much more needed in the way of filler.

If only he had a little more in the way of get-the-job-done sperm.

Hope Jordan capped the ovulation prediction test and carried it from her bathroom toward her walk-in closet. Lifting the false drawer at the back of her dresser, she opened her keepsake box and replaced last month's disappointment with this one's promise. The most promising yet, thanks to the optimal dosage of Clomid now flowing through her system.

In the drawer above, wrapped in a cushion of lavender tissue, was the most potent fertility-enhancing lingerie in her arsenal. She lifted the La Perla sticker without causing so much as a hairline tear in the paper and removed the black silk and lace babydoll top and matching panties.

Clipping the tags with a snip of her nail scissors, she lifted the top over her head, settled into the lace cups, set the spaghetti straps atop each shoulder, and stepped into the tiny triangle of panty. Before she turned for the mirror, she closed her eyes, and as she'd done for the last nine ovulation cycles, visualized the onslaught of robust candidates all vying for her big, healthy, ripe egg.

She opened her eyes, turned for the mirrored bathroom wall, and smiled at the overall effect. In a year, she'd happily weather the extra pounds, loose skin, and stretch marks. But for now, if she couldn't get pregnant wearing this . . .

She grabbed some roses from the bouquet on her nightstand, plucked the petals, spread a handful on the bed, and left a multicolored breadcrumb path behind her as she started toward the open bedroom door.

* * *

Will Pierce-Cohn scraped a stray chunk of Mini-Wheat from the front of his shirt, zipped his Patagonia fleece, and headed for a house identical to his own, except for the Sunset Taupe accent trim.

And the woman who lived inside.

For once, Will Pierce-Cohn wished Hope Jordan lived anywhere else but across the street. The thought of her forced smile made his guts churn, but he had to get his playground petition in front of every neighbor in the development before the April homeowner's board meeting. Before reverend-cum-homeowner's-board-president Frank Griffin waxed too eloquent and the HOB rubber-stamped his environmentally questionable, proposed location change.

Will took a deep breath.

Starting with Hope.

Before he stepped onto the top step to equalize any height disadvantage, Will allowed himself a quick peek through the potted plant on her front steps and into her accent window.

He made a point not to look at other women in *that* way.

Especially her.

If he spotted Hope across the grocery store in low-rise jeans, he waved and diverted his cart in the other direction. At aerobics class, he only allowed himself a split-second glance at the silhouette of her butt in yoga pants before dropping his Bosu Ball and weights behind hers. He even saved friendly conversation for the odd morning when she appeared at the community mailboxes in loose sweats.

Before he could knock, he spotted her on the landing at the top of the steps.

He gasped silently.

She definitely wasn't wearing sweats.

Backlit, with her golden hair billowing around her head like a halo, Hope wore nothing but a flowing, sheer black top.

And matching panties.

He thought about averting his eyes.

Should have.

Couldn't.

Clearly, she was dressed for a fertility day *coffee break* with her husband. She'd told him months ago they were trying to get pregnant. Still, how many times had he accidentally imagined her creamy skin and the pale blush of her nipples, perky through her sweat-dampened sports bra? To see her, all of her, in near touching distance—more spectacular than he'd ever dared imagine.

Sheer lace clung to her narrow waist.

Her flat belly.

If Meg ever wore anything to bed besides a t-shirt . . . if, every so often, she came home from work thinking about his needs instead of her own . . . if, for once, she let him make the first move before reaching for his . . .

He let his gaze drop to Hope's downy landing strip.

His clipboard slipped from his hand and clattered on the concrete stoop.

Hello echoed through the hallway.

There was no time to duck. It was too late to make a run for it. If he didn't do something quickly, she was going to find him standing there like a garden-variety peeper with an erection. Beads of sweat dribbled down his back.

Astros, Mariners, Cardinals, Rockies . . .

He stood like a statue, unable to force his knuckle to the door.

The dead bolt flipped open with a familiar hollow metal *plink.*

In a surge of arousal-deadening panic, he managed a split-second trouser adjustment, placed his clipboard at a strategic angle, and attempted a casual expression.

The door opened a crack.

Hope's lips, pink, pouty, and full, shimmered in the morning sun. Her sweet floral scent intermingled with the early spring air and the heady aroma of warm, baked goods.

"H . . . Hope. I . . ." He hadn't stuttered since elementary school. "You answered before I had a chance to knock."

"This isn't a great time, Will."

"Sorry," he said. The thought of her body pressed against the opposite side of the hollow door separating them sent a heat wave across his face. "I'll only take a second."

His face felt engulfed in flames.

"Is this about the ice cream truck ban?"

"No, no." Thanks to Frank Griffin and his mini-sermon on vanishing Americana, Will's solution to sobering statistics about ice-cream truck operator DMV and criminal records was voted down at the last homeowner's board meeting. Will turned away toward the empty parcel of land next to the Estridge home to compose himself as much as to make his point. "The playground."

"I see," she said, not looking.

11

Will's practiced talking points about his concerns for the environmental impact and the reason for the developer's lack of plans to develop prime residential sites at both Songbird Canyon and Warbler Valley Drive vanished from his brain. He couldn't form an intelligible sentence questioning the sudden switch from the planned super-playground proposal on the vacant, commercial land at Wonderland Vista Way and Melody Mountain Ranch Parkway.

A white-tailed rabbit scurried across the pavers separating the Jordan and Estridge properties and loped toward a snow-dusted mound of dirt on his or her proposed former home.

"The bunnies," he uttered.

"The bunnies?"

"Rabbit habitat." He took a silent breath to compose himself. "Too marshy to accommodate—"

"You want me to sign something?"

"Please." He handed her the petition bearing, so far, only his name. "I know for a fact I have support on both Weeping Willow Way and . . ."

As Hope reached for the clipboard, her fingernail scraped the tip of his thumb and sent another surge of desire through him.

Astros, Mariners, Cardinals, Rockies . . .

She signed on the first line and handed back the petition. "See you at aerobics."

Before he could say thanks, the door closed and she was gone.

So was he.

* * *

From her bathroom window, Maryellen Griffin watched Will Pierce-Cohn, clipboard in hand, head from Hope Jordan's house toward the empty lot where he leaned over to inspect a patch of dirt. The futility gave her an anxious pang, causing her to shift and throw off her daily weigh-in.

Maryellen stepped off the scale, reset the button, and stepped on again to the same dismal *102*. Before the blasphemous flashing faded to black, she grabbed her robe and cinched the waist tightly around her middle. She crossed the master bath and plucked the honey-do list from the usual spot on the mirror above her sink.

> *Morning Mel,*
> *Help us face the day with gladness, O Lord, for today comes*
> *as a fresh new page.*
> *Before you embark on what is sure to be a blessed day, please take care*
> *of the following:*

1. *We are nearly out of orange juice.*
2. *I am low on Avon Derek Jeter shave lotion. Please call Laney Estridge to reorder.*
3. *Check to see if Young Christian Leaders received summer camp nomination for Evangeline.*

The dull ache at the base of her neck radiated upward as she scanned the rest of Frank's fussy scrawl. *Need more X-14 for mold in basement shower. . . . Speak to Evangeline re: missed youth choir practice . . .*

Eva might not show up for choir again if he didn't stop calling her Evangeline. Never mind her reaction when he so much as suggested she go to a leadership camp this summer. Maryellen took a breath and skipped to the last item on the list:

> *I'm meeting with Henderson Homes late afternoon to finalize playground details. Would love to celebrate with a pot roast for dinner!*
>
> *Yours,*
> *Frank*

Her stomach turned at the thought of loading cow rump into the Crockpot at 7 A.M. If he wanted her to celebrate the big land swap he'd been negotiating with Henderson Homes, why couldn't he spring for take-out? Eva was on a vegetarian kick and wouldn't eat a bite anyway. Besides, he knew she had to close at the library.

She folded the note, stuffed it into her pocket with a week's worth of others, and started her morning routine with a flip of the faucet.

The base of her electric toothbrush fell onto its side as she yanked a little too hard and squirted on a blob of Colgate. As the bristles met her front teeth, she savored the mint flavor on her tongue like peppermint candy. There'd be no real sweets until the scale bestowed a double-digit number. No dab of ice cream would pass her lips, no cookie crumb, and no sugar of any kind. She certainly couldn't eat a dinner of fatty meat and grease-soaked vegetables.

After the dentist-recommended two minutes, she spit into her sink, rinsed with a handful of water, righted the overturned base, and set her Sonic Care carefully within.

Then, she grabbed Frank's toothbrush.

Warmth encircled her toes as she padded across the heated floor to the toilet.

She paused for a moment to picture him, running his hands through his dark, gelled hair, still hopped up like Napoleon from one-upping poor Will

Pierce-Cohn over the playground. In anticipation of climbing into bed to *celebrate* some more, he'd pick up his toothbrush and brush the pot roast with carrots, potatoes, and pearl onions from his teeth.

No doubt he'd be extra talkative tonight but at least the chatter would keep the overexuberant kissing to a minimum.

She opened the door, leaned over the bowl, and dipped in his toothbrush.

* * *

Laney Estridge parked her Land Rover at a strategic angle to both highlight the FOR SALE sign featuring her professional glamour shot and block the view next door. Her head, aching from an impending sinus infection, began to throb as she exited the car and started up the front walk. It was bad enough her sellers insisted on pricing their wildly overdecorated, almost two-year-old home nearly on par with the brand new models in the Melody Mountain Collection. Now, to add insult to injury, the neighbor's driveway featured a room's worth of wall-to-wall carpet lying on the concrete like a soapy gray beard.

As small streams trickled from the edges and joined the river of bubbles emptying into the storm drain beside her car, she grabbed her cell, autodialed the community violations hotline, and left a detailed message.

She tucked a stray strand of newly copper-and-honey highlighted hair behind her ear and straightened her plum-hued jacket. She'd managed to sell the property on Winding Valley Circle by downplaying the *minor* explosion that resulted in $30,000 of meth lab cleanup costs. No reason she couldn't do the same for a listing that included the charm of do-it-yourselfers for neighbors.

With her home equity line hovering at the limit, she had to.

A car neared the entrance to the cul-de-sac.

She hurried up the front steps and clicked open the lock box.

Closing her eyes, she took a congested, but Chi-restoring, inhale and exhale and willed these buyers to be appreciative of the artistic value inherent in a basement mural of Paris.

And velvet wall accents.

And black bath fixtures.

She stationed herself to best blur the adjacent scene before the hybrid Tahoe with temporary tags approached the driveway. A big, new SUV signaled either hefty car payments or readily available cash, but it wouldn't matter which if the wife got out, scrunched her nose, and inquired politely about *the neighbors.*

The passenger window slid down and, to Laney's relief, the wife waved warmly.

Laney waved back and proffered a practiced smile.

The husband exited the driver's side. Forty, plus or minus, and five foot seven give or take, with dark hair, prominent nose, and a mid-priced suit, he fell firmly into the borderline handsome category.

His loafers squeaked with possibility as he ambled up the walk.

A house with "dramatic appointments" would surely provide any swagger he lacked.

Laney slunk down so as not to eclipse him with her almost six feet and offered her hand. "Laney Estridge, Mountain Realty."

"Tim Trautman."

His handshake bore a promising overfirmness.

"I'm Theresa." The wife waddled toward them in crisp maternity slacks and a floral print top that was more A Pea in the Pod than Target, but her tennis bracelet sparkled with the flat light of cubic zirconium. "We were so excited to find your listing."

"I'm delighted you came by," Laney said with a measured calm to mask a blossoming sense of too-good-to-be-true.

Theresa looked past her toward the carpeting.

Laney pointed at the greenbelt to the north and away from the foaming eyesore. "Just behind those houses, beside the open space, a state-of-the-art play structure's slated to go in soon."

Or, would be, once Frank Griffin quashed Will Pierce-Cohn's ridiculous anti-playground jihad.

"A block over?" Theresa's voice rose by an octave.

"We're so excited to finally have a place for our little ones in this corner of the development."

"You live nearby?"

"Next cul-de-sac."

Theresa looked hopefully at Tim.

"Meg Pierce-Cohn lives on our block, too."

"The state rep?" Tim asked.

Laney nodded.

Theresa's nose twitched like an enthusiastic rabbit as she turned toward the front door. "What model is it? It looks like a Red Robin."

"Close, it's a Blue Jay." The endorphin rush melted the lump that had threatened to close her throat. "A full step up from the Robin."

"A friend of mine has this house in a Henderson Homes development in Northglenn." Theresa tucked her hair behind her ear. "It's called a Shiraz there, but it's the exact same floor plan."

"The Blue Jay has the same great layout, only it's larger." Laney paused. "And this particular home is *beyond* upgraded." Her voice echoed as she entered the oversized foyer, which made up the only significant difference between the two models—that and a main floor laundry room.

"I can feel the difference." Theresa spread her arms out.

"Kind of pricey, though," Tim said.

"It's negotiable," Laney said. With an imminent job transfer and a McMansion set for closing outside of Dallas, her sellers needed the proceeds from the sale almost as badly as she did. Talking them into a slightly lower price wasn't out of the question, particularly since the husband had already expressed interest in additional *advice* in the form of a hand job. "But new Blue Jay models, with no upgrades other than a stone façade, are going for $15,000 more in the MM Collection."

"That's what I told Tim," Theresa said. "I never thought something would pop up in this part of the development near our price point."

Laney's heart skipped a delighted beat.

Theresa eyed the gold drapes Laney had the owners tie back to obscure some hairline cracks fanning out like crow's feet on either side of the bay window. "Of course, we'd need to factor in some sort of redecorating budget before we could possibly write a bid."

"Just got our current house how we want it." Tim ducked into the living room.

"Tim's a little hesitant to leave Eagle's Nest Vista," Theresa whispered. "He's president-elect of our homeowner's board."

"Our HOB president, Frank Griffin, lives across the street from me," Laney said. "I'll be glad to put in a good word about Tim."

"That would be great." Theresa rubbed her belly. "Tim has to face the fact that with three kids already, we've outgrown anything available in our neighborhood."

"When are you due?"

"Early June." Theresa ran her fingers along the gold-foiled, lavender faux-finish wall.

"The walls are hand-done." Laney touched Theresa, but carefully so as not to depress the substantial padding on her upper arm while she up-sold the existing décor. She looked into the mirror above the gold cherub sculpture. Tim seemed to have no aversion to the bordello red living room. "The artist lives over on Melody Mountain Court and gives a great break to Ranchers."

"Ranchers, huh?" Tim raised an eyebrow and opened the coat closet.

"We're a very friendly community." She headed down the hallway to unveil the first male-oriented weapon in her arsenal. "You have to see the study, Tim. The owners added triple insulation so you'll be assured quiet even when the baby is running up and down the outer hall."

"Babies." Tim ducked into the cherry study, the one room devoid of the wife's garish touch.

"Twins?" Laney asked.

Theresa glanced at the oriental runner running up the curved stairway. "A double surprise."

"Been there." She patted Theresa.

"You have twins, too?"

"Seems like everyone does these days." Laney smiled. "Mine are identical girls."

Theresa's eyes sparkled with a potential play-date radar gleam.

"They started high school this year."

Theresa's enthusiasm only seemed to grow. "Our Lauren is in ninth grade, too." I'm not sure how she's going to feel about switching schools when we—"

Tim edged past them. "If we . . ."

Laney grasped Theresa's hand and led her toward the back of the house with a practiced realtor run that looked like a strut. Other than the odd husband with an unnatural interest in fashion magazines and interior décor, they were all the same—Tim was headed for the backyard.

She deposited Theresa in the kitchen by the commercial-style refrigerator and reached him just before he opened the sliding door that didn't quite run on its tracks. With an effortless looking shove that sent a shock through her shoulder, she lifted the panel. "The deck is new."

There was no need to disclose that the original had sunk.

"Hmm." He didn't stop to examine the new redwood, scan the yard, or take a single step toward the oversized hot tub. Tim Trautman's full attention was focused on the kitchen window of the house on the other side of the back fence.

More accurately, the neighbor inside.

Wearing a sheer babydoll top and matching panties, Hope Jordan was too caught up in her baking to notice the blinds were cracked.

She bent over to retrieve a tray from her lower oven.

"Who's that?" Tim asked.

There was no need to turn around and check on Theresa's whereabouts. Before she even heard the rustle of the blinds, she could feel the poor, bloated thing behind her.

Fuck. The last thing she needed was blond, stunning Hope Jordan prancing around with the windows open in her get-me-pregnant frillies. Her Playboy Bunny body was enough to make the most secure of wives reconsider the value of a property in such close proximity.

"Hope Jordan." Laney shook her head. "Her husband's been coming home for ovulation day lunch for almost a year." She waited a beat. "With any luck, it won't be too long before your twins will have a set of playmates."

An hour-long second passed until Theresa appeared on the deck, rubbing what was presumably her naturally bountiful womb. "Tim, did you see the painted vines above the cabinets?"

His eyes lingered on Hope until she moved out of sight.

"Look, honey." Theresa grasped Tim's hand. She pointed to the ivy pattern stenciled along the wall as though the fake flowers had actually grown and spread out across the trellis painted above the cabinetry.

Tim gave a cursory glance at one of the wicker baskets filled with plastic greenery. "Let's check out the bedrooms."

* * *

Hope removed the chocolate dipped strawberries from the refrigerator and arranged them in a semicircle around a wedge of Brie. Grabbing the platter and a plate of freshly baked chocolate chip cookies, she left the kitchen and walked into the great room. She set the silver trays on the hearth beside the sweating ice bucket in which a split of Dom Perignon, her last splurge until after Birth Day, was chilling.

With the flip of a switch, she had a roaring fire and the perfect picnic à deux.

As she lay on the Karastan area rug awaiting the sound of Jim's car, she checked her watch again. Twenty minutes had passed since he'd called to say he'd be leaving soon.

Nine months since they'd started trying to get pregnant.

Just to be sure the timing was still ideal, she grabbed the thermometer she'd set next to the ice bucket, placed the metal bulb under her tongue, closed her eyes, and visualized the bold red plus that had eluded her so far.

The tick of the grandfather clock in the entry hall echoed and faded into the vaulted ceiling. Even with rooms full of handpicked furniture, rugs, wallpaper, and window treatments, their semi-custom still felt like a model.

It took the scattered mess of baby gear to make a house into a home.

She pulled the thermometer from her mouth and let her gaze settle at the hash mark where the silver line ended.

Elevated.

She picked up the phone and dialed Jim's office number once again.

"You've reached the office of Jim Jordan. He is unavailable to answer your call. Please leave a message and . . ."

She pressed the off button, set the phone down, and readjusted a strap that had slipped down her shoulder. Jim would die if he knew so little lace and silk cost almost $200, but if Will Pierce-Cohn's ashen face was any indication, the combination of lingerie and fertility drugs were sure-fire. Under normal circumstances she'd be horrified by the thought of him sneaking a peek from behind his petition, but his dumbfounded awe only made her more certain of the effect of the lingerie on the enthusiasm of Jim.

And his potent, but so far unsuccessful, little swimmers.

She popped the cork, poured herself some champagne, and settled into throw pillows where she'd spend thirty post-coital minutes with her legs in the air to ensure the sperm couldn't miss her ripe, awaiting egg.

The garage door finally rolled open.

She ran her fingers through her hair, assumed a Ms. February pose complete with licked lips, and checked her reflection in the fireplace doors. "In here, honey," she said over the clink of his keys in the bowl on the hall table. As he rounded the corner, she filled his glass. "I made us a picnic."

As he reached for the Dom and emptied the glass, his pants, already unzipped, dropped to the floor. Without a comment on the spread, much less hers, he dropped to his knees and tugged at the crotch of her panties. "I have to be back at the office in fifteen minutes."

CHAPTER TWO

With a nostalgic Main Street filled with retail shops,
restaurants, and services, there's no place you'll ever need to
be but home—
From the Melody Mountain Ranch sales brochure.

*H*ope dabbed her eyes with a handful of crinkled exam table paper and looked out the window overlooking the parking lot of the Melody Valley Medical Plaza.

"Any hot flashes, headaches, mood disorders, or visual problems since starting the Clomid?" the doctor asked.

Hope shook her head.

"Other side effects?"

"Besides feeling like a total failure?"

The doctor's kind smile made the ache all the worse. "Patience can be the toughest side effect of all."

How much more patient could she be?

She and Jim had been together since college when a girl she didn't know appeared out of nowhere, grabbed her by the hand, and walked her across the quad where he stood with a group of buddies. *The two of you are too beautiful together not to belong together*, the girl had said. Jim smiled his killer smile and they'd pretty much been *that one couple* from that moment on. She wanted to start trying for a baby right after the wedding, but he wanted to wait until he had his MBA, got a job, and rose to a *family safe* level of career security at his consulting firm. She'd never once complained, in fact enjoyed their double-income-no-kids lifestyle in their tiny Washington Park bungalow, even if they were in Denver and not an interior design mecca like NY or L.A. Finally, he agreed to put a deposit down on a *family* home. She spent a year watching the house take shape amid the rolling hills of Melody Mountain Ranch and then another decorating the perfect space in the ideal kid neighborhood waiting for

Jim's travel schedule to die down enough to start filling it with children. She hadn't grown her business much beyond holiday decor, flowerbed design, and the occasional room redo so she could slip seamlessly into the role of mother. In fact, she'd spent the better part of yet another year patiently trying every guaranteed how-to pregnancy hint.

And still, nothing.

"I always thought I'd have three children by now."

"Hope, there's nothing medically to suggest you won't."

Tears dripped down her cheeks as fast as she could wipe them away. Despite a negative home pee-on-a-stick test, three actually, she was two days late with both breast sensitivity and, she could swear, slight morning sickness. "I really thought I was pregnant this time."

The bleeding started on the drive over.

"You've possibly suffered what's known as a chemical pregnancy. If so, it bodes even better for your chances of a successful future pregnancy."

Question was, how far into the future?

"You've been at this for, what, eight months?"

"Nine." The irony only intensified the cramping. "And I've tried everything from wild yams to Chinese herbs to cough syrup."

The doctor shook his head. "None of the old wives' tales work as well as relaxing about the whole process."

Endless sessions with her therapist, the acupuncturist, and Reverend Frank were supposed to have covered that base. "Jim doesn't know if he's willing to go the artificial insemination, much less the in vitro, route, but I'm starting to worry we'll have to and—"

"Hope, you've only been on fertility meds for one cycle."

"One unsuccessful cycle."

"Forty to sixty percent of patients conceive on Clomid within six months." He jotted on his prescription pad, tore off the top sheet, and handed it to her. "A month and a refill."

"Meaning you think I'll be pregnant by the beginning of summer?"

He patted her knee. "Meaning you're still a long way off from considering yourself a failure."

CHAPTER THREE

Melody Mountain Ranch Rules and Regulations: Section 4.
Board of Directors: The Board of Directors shall have the powers
and duties necessary for the operation and maintenance
of a first-class community.

Frank Griffin rapped his gavel on the podium. "Let the April meeting of the Melody Mountain Ranch Homeowner's Board come to order."

As residents found seats and board members filed toward chairs he'd arranged in an arc, à là city council meetings he'd seen on the public access channel, Frank eyed the gold inscription plate on his prized wormwood mallet: *Exercise Influence through Higher Power. Presented to Judge Mortimer Callahan for Twenty-Five Years of Devoted Service.*

Of all the yard sale gems Maryellen had found, none felt as divinely inspired as this treasure she'd uncovered for him in a widow's garage. If not for The Calling, and a dozen successful years in pharmaceutical sales, he'd have made an excellent judge.

Or so he'd been told.

The rec center multipurpose room was filled to capacity. Apparently, his Sunday sermon on paths to finding the Lord through community had resonated through the Melody Rancher rank and file. "I want to thank you all for coming this evening."

He made eye contact around the room, stopping to smile in the direction of his new neighbor, Tim Trautman. According to Laney Estridge, Trautman's previous HOB experience made him a good candidate for the next open position.

Will Pierce-Cohn's position.

Even with the comeuppance of his failed presidential bid, P-C took on Covenant Violations chair, as far as Frank could tell, to disrupt the monthly meeting with a heartfelt plea for banning ice cream trucks, reexamining approved air conditioning systems in light of global warming, or whatever pointless issue was stuck in his unemployed, took-his-wife's-name-with-a-hyphen, Jewish-liberal, househusband craw. He was sure to shit another pointless brick when he found out his current cause célèbre, the mega-playground land, had already been earmarked for a more lofty purpose: The Melody Mountain Community Church.

Having dreamed of, planned for, and then uprooted his family from Colorado Springs specifically for the spiritual leadership opportunity in South Metro Denver, the mere idea of finally breaking ground on a real live brick and mortar (or stucco for that matter) dream church sent a chill through him more intense than any desire of the flesh.

Despite P-C's objections, the plan was a true win-win. After double-digit months of commercial zoning issues on the super-playground land Henderson Homes mandated in the original covenant documents, they would get what they wanted—an amendment that allowed for multiple smaller playgrounds in satellite locations. In return, Henderson Homes agreed to sell the now vacant property to the Melody Mountain Church at a price well under market. The sweetheart deal included builder financing and was sealed with the twenty-three grand in the church building fund as earnest money. Frank even managed to finagle a ninety-day closing to rustle the remaining seventeen thousand he needed from his flock.

By that time, the neighborhood children would be happily ensconced in summer play and no one but his delighted parishioners and Pierce-Cohn would care anymore about the switch.

"Roll call," Frank said, to get the proceedings moving along before the honorable Mrs. Pierce-Cohn came home to spring her man from household Hades. If she really cared about family and community as much as she claimed, she'd resign from the state legislature and send her desperate househusband back to work.

Not that Frank was worried.

Once the community saw the new recreation space arrangement they'd hammered out, ratification, technically a formality since he'd already signed the paperwork, would be a foregone conclusion. "Chair is, of course, present."

A handful of covenant breakers and complainers already had their hands in the air.

He looked past a repeat offender from Allegro Meadow Drive, fined again for leaving his boat in excess of forty-eight hours in front of the house, and nodded to the first-time violator to the man's right.

"I received a citation for shampooing the carpet on my front driveway and . . ."

"To my knowledge, wall-to-wall is typically cleaned inside the house."

"Not when the padding's moldy and has to be replaced while the carpet's being treated."

"Wouldn't a mold problem override covenant restrictions?" Roseanne Goldberg, neighborhood expert on all things scientifically dubious, added.

"I'm not sure there is a section that refers to indoor carpet cleaning done outdoors," Frank said. He couldn't allow one of her diatribes to give Pierce-Cohn time to arrive and derail the evening's important business. "But I agree an exemption may be in order until we investigate further."

Both the violator and Mrs. Goldberg nodded and took their seats.

"In fact, I've decided to pardon all of tonight's attendees from fines associated with their infractions—assuming proof of compliance is provided within ninety days."

Hands went down and sighs of unanticipated grace filled the room.

He pretended to scan for other raised hands. "As there appear to be no further questions, I'll continue with roll call. Officers?"

Over a chorus of present, Frank nodded to his energetic, industrious treasurer. With her Christian spirit and can-do attitude, Jane Hunt was a bright spot on the board. Why her ex-husband decided to become a woman on her was a true mystery. "Ms. Hunt, would you please review the minutes from the last meeting?"

He hopped off the riser behind the podium and sat before she could stand to full height.

With an upward adjustment of the microphone, Jane began to cite the previous month's minutes. "Our last meeting was called to order at six P.M. on March first. Notices were sent out for the following covenant infractions: 12354 Melody Way for installing a basketball hoop without painting the backboard to match the trim work; 31724 Songbird Mountain Circle for . . ."

The double doors banged open.

Will Pierce-Cohn paused for a moment in the doorway, scanned the room—for allies, no doubt—and then entered looking his usual diminutive, unkempt self. The damp pits of his faded polo shirt threatened the paperwork tucked under his arm.

Frank looked pointedly at his Bulova.

"Sorry. My wife was tied up in a legislative session."

"Not a problem." Despite irritation over the inevitable scuffle ahead, it was probably to his benefit to have Pierce-Cohn show up late, looking like the disheveled distraction everyone knew him to be, than absent and filing objections after the fact. If nothing else, Frank would get to see P-C's reaction as the playground surprises unfolded.

"I recall this meeting to order at seven past six."

Jane shook her head in what was surely a show of annoyance solidarity. "A $100 fine was assessed to 19432 Meadow View Drive for repeatedly violating the *no nudity in backyard hot tubs* clause . . ."

Frank chuckled along with everyone else.

P-C sat expressionless, arms folded.

"Under discussion," Jane continued, "was a stray cat problem in the neighborhood. An inquiry committee has been appointed. Also announced was Henderson Homes' offer to extend warranty coverage for driveway cracking and selected issues related to expansive soils in the Phase One cul-de-sacs. It was voted on and passed that the toilet tissue in the rec center be downgraded to reduce costs and impede spitball formation. The savings from this and other cost saving measures instituted over the past year allowed the board to consider and approve . . ."

Frank nodded along as Jane detailed the increase in suburban crime and the security system she'd negotiated for the community center to combat said dangers. Melody Meadow Ranch didn't have webcams to keep tabs on the kiddies as they frolicked in the fountain like the Stapleton development or to ensure safe shopping like the Bel Mar Main Street, but at least the assets of the rec center would now be secure.

On his cue, his wife, Maryellen, padded silently toward the art supply closet.

Frank smiled watching P-C watch Maryellen disappear among the easels and paints. While Frank preferred his slim, schoolgirl pretty wife in colors, he'd had her wear an earth-toned skirt and blouse tonight so she wouldn't distract anyone from the oversized metal cart she extracted from the closet.

Jane finished discussing the details of the security install, threw in a subtle but preapproved pitch for her home security business, and uttered the word *playground.* Maryellen rolled the cart into the center of the room and halted in front of the podium, as planned.

Not part of the plan was the floral scarf she'd added to her ensemble.

Frank strode around from behind the board members, stopped beside the cart, and shot Maryellen a quick look before she returned to her seat.

"Ranchers . . ." He pinched the coarse linen cloth covering the contents of the cart between his fingers. "I present to you the prototype for our new community playgrounds."

He tugged the sheet.

In the center of an open Plexiglas box, a diorama of a tri-level play structure nestled in a soft bed of pale sand. Plastic children smiled mid-swing from the monkey bars. Smiling mothers tended to plump babies on cozy benches beneath the shade of towering shade trees.

The enthusiastic oohs and aahs hardly did his display justice.

"Frank." Pierce-Cohn's voice warbled like he was in the throes of puberty.

"Discussion hasn't been called yet," Jane said.

"I'll allow it." With the warm response of the crowd, Frank didn't have to force his smile. "Mr. Pierce-?"

P-C was on his feet before Frank could get out the post-hyphen segment of his name. "Are the fully grown trees part and parcel of the project, too?"

"We'll have to plant young trees for cost effectiveness." The man's desperation was palpable. "I'm sure you all realize this is merely an artist's rendering of the two projected playgrounds."

"Frank, there's no denying the appeal of your model or the idea of our children finally enjoying a new playground." Temporarily silenced by another round of applause, he continued, "but I have concerns about the location changes as well as the new locations themselves."

Frank nodded thoughtfully as though considering P-C's position.

Will set the petition on the podium. "So do a number of members of this community."

"I see," Frank said, pretending to scan the legalese. His eyes dropped down to the only section of interest: the handful of signatures on the lines below.

He never made it past the loopy, feminine signature on the first line.

Hope Jordan.

He looked at the name again in disbelief.

Hope was his neighbor. His parishioner. He'd not only excused her last two covenant violations, but also made changes to the landscaping regulations when she'd argued for a more inclusive approved planting list. "I'm concerned, too," he finally managed, turning to whisk a grain of sand from the flag adorning the enclosed fort atop the third level. "Concerned the residents of this community get that which they were promised. And more."

"Frank, you know I want what's best for this community and that includes a new playground for our children." Will shook his head dramatically. "Neighbors and friends, I stand to benefit more than most of you since one of the proposed relocation sites is on my, Frank's, own street." He paused. "But I can't help but wonder why Henderson Homes left prime lots, one on our cul-de-sac, undeveloped in the first place."

How could Hope have depended on him for friendship, guidance, and support these last months with her infertility problems and then gone and signed that rabble-rouser's petition?

Against him.

"Henderson Homes is the premier planned community developer in the Front Range. They are all about quality, which is one of the primary reasons I chose Melody Mountain Ranch for my family and ministry." Frank cleared his throat. "Not to mention the promise of ample green space and parks."

The applause rolled through him like a soothing wave.

"I'm telling you, there is something off, at least with the Songbird Canyon Court plot of green space," Pierce-Cohn said. "The soil is too soggy."

"Making it the perfect site for a neighborhood park," Frank said.

"The original site at the corner of Wonderland Valley Road and Wonderland Valley Court was perfect—set on land that's homestead adjacent, but zoned commercial to keep strip malls and gas stations from dotting hillside views and . . . "

"Which is why Henderson Homes got tangled up with the zoning board for so long. Besides, the property faces east and is only accessible by foot for the neighbors on the adjacent cul-de-sacs."

"So is the Songbird Canyon Court site."

"The walking path will be extended to the green belt beside it."

"It's a rabbit habitat."

"We're overrun by the end of summer as it is." He glanced out onto the audience of bobbing heads. "I think we can all agree on that."

"Then you plan to exterminate the rabbits?"

"Relocate."

"No need. The play structure will sink."

"Not if it's moored in concrete."

Perspiration dampened Pierce-Cohn's forehead. "And there's the size of the land relative to the original."

Frank stood taller than his five feet eight inches, set his shoulders back. The shock of seeing Hope's name had distracted him. He'd let P-C go on too long. "We stand to gain nearly a third more acreage."

"You mean a third less, don't you?"

Frank smiled. Almost winked at Tim Trautman to show him how it was done in Melody Mountain Ranch. "Because some of the land is admittedly flawed, but eminently fixable, I was able to negotiate with Henderson Homes for an unprecedented deal." He paused for an extra-long beat for the room to quiet down. "We'll not only have identical playgrounds on Songbird Canyon Court and Warbler Way, but I also managed to wrangle a mini-sports park for the older kids in the southernmost cul-de-sac of Phase Four."

"On Hummingbird Cove?" someone asked.

"Exactly," Frank said over the applause.

Pierce-Cohn's face was priceless.

If only Hope were there to look as contrite.

He allowed implications to echo through the room. Before Will could ask about the fate of the soon-to-be-forgotten-by-everyone-but-Pierce-Cohn former parcel of playground land in question, the answer to which was a secret known only to himself and the top brass at Henderson Homes, he added, "In addition, the play equipment manufacturer discounted the second structure by nearly thirty percent because we're doing two sets." Over the cheers he allowed himself a smile of victory. "With the approval of my fellow board, the children of Melody Mountain Ranch will have not one, but three new playgrounds by the start of summer."

* * *

Eva Griffin stroked her velvet cape and looked out at the group of kids circling her basement ping-pong table. If she could get everyone out of the house by eight, there'd be plenty of time to mask the smell of burning candles and weed with a Glade plug-in before her parents came home from their homeowner's board meeting.

Following the rules of order in her bible, *Covens Made Simple*, she bowed her head at Tyler Pierce-Cohn, her head warlock and BFF-with-benefits. "Eagle feather and raven's claw, our coven meeting is now called."

While Tyler technically *discovered* Witchcraft in a library book, Eva ran with it, bringing the sacred peace to their suburban Hell. She handpicked prospects from the halls of Melody Mountain High and around the neighborhood. She designed their capes from curtain fabric. She uncovered a real Athame in a bin of rusty hardware and unearthed a bag of initiation charms while she was stuck on one of her mom's wretched yard sale expeditions.

Working as prop master in the school theater department provided the perfect cover. If her dad let her act in anything other than the church Easter pageant or silly Sunday morality one-acts, she might never have envisioned the tableau spread before her.

> *Christian girls don't overindulge.*
> *Christian girls don't dress like whores.*
> *Christian girls don't do secular theater.*

Eva smiled at her growing flock.

They led covens.

She nodded at her crew before turning to the two newbies standing together in the back of the room. The first, Heather McDaniel, a sophomore wanna-be black girl was outcast from the real African-American kids and needed a new gang of homies. The other, Lauren Trautman, was new at Melody Mountain High. Disney teen star pretty, with shoulder-length black curls and blue eyes, she looked like she'd shown up at the wrong after-school club. It was a wonder the cheerleader crowd hadn't already snapped her up.

Lauren smiled like she was at a pep rally.

Apparently, girlfriend was fated for more important things than Saturday night keggers and guys with letter jackets.

They all were.

As soon as she initiated these two, they would have the thirteen official members she needed to start casting real spells.

Eva waved her wand over the elaborate altar of feathers, seashells, incense, and candles. "High-ranking warlock, I call upon thee for the altar blessing."

Tyler stepped forward, the hood of his robe pulled over his wavy brown hair. His eyebrow piercing, a tiny hoop with a treble charm, reflected in the flickering candlelight. Glassy-eyed from the preceremony bong they'd shared, he began to recite the opening chant:

Blessed be the precious and preserving air, the breath of life, of inspiration and delight . . .

Tyler's words echoed through the basement.

One of the Estridge twins sniffled.

The other sneezed.

Eva made a mental note to look up a potion to keep their allergies or whatever from disrupting the ceremonies.

Blessed be the precious, preserving Earth, the flesh of life, our sustainer and our wisdom.

"Praise the Goddess." The silver curl of moon she'd painted above her brow pulsed with power as she raised her hands to quiet the rustle of voices in the room. She turned toward Heather and Lauren. "I hereby pronounce you to be Dedicants."

"Whoa!" Tyler looked confused. "We didn't even have new member orientation, yet."

"Special events allow for special circumstances." She allowed a smile. "We now have the divine power of thirteen."

"True that," he admitted.

"Time to try a spell."

"Don't you think we're kind of rushing?"

"No." Eva ran the edge of a black-painted Bowie knife across the surface of the chimes suspended above the altar. "And so it is done."

She returned to the altar and turned to Libby Estridge. "Mistress Elizabeth, please read from the Witch Book."

Libby bowed and picked up a leather-bound journal with a removable pentagram sticker affixed to the front. "Our last meeting coincided with the crescent moon. After the memorial service for our sacred feline, Chalice, a committee was appointed to locate a new coven cat."

Eva wiped a tear with her robe sleeve. When her secret stray disappeared from under the patio, she couldn't help but think her father was somehow involved. At holiday time, she'd written KITTEN in block letters at the top of her list. On Christmas Day, when she cried because there was no purr of a furry little creature, he'd said, "Your mother is allergic," which wasn't true. Worse, he added like he was joking, "Cats come from and go to Hell."

What about cat killers?

He was so fucking controlling about everything in *his* house, she definitely wouldn't put offing a poor kitten living under the deck past him.

"The following incantations were deemed promising: the pool area lock opening spell and the extended snow-day spell. A committee was appointed to work on the love potion after Hannah Hunt accidentally attracted that freak math teacher. Also, we will only hold *youth group* meetings at the rec center until the new security system is installed. Since we won't have any more privacy after that, future meetings will be held—"

"At my house. Thank you, Libby." She had to keep the pacing up so the energy peaked at the perfect moment. "New business."

"Didn't think we were finished with old business, yet," Tyler said.

"Time constraints. Besides, our coven has achieved the divine number. It's time to test our casting abilities."

Tyler furrowed his brow. "Tonight?"

Apparently he wasn't as stoned as she'd hoped. "I found a cool spell we have to try."

"And what would that be?"

"Something I think might time out perfectly with the upcoming Easter holiday."

"What are we going to do to your dad?" Tyler asked.

She flashed him the no-more-benefits-to-our-friendship-if-you-keep-this-up look. "Why do you assume it's about my dad?"

He shrugged. "Just a guess."

Margaret Estridge, Libby's identical twin, down to the flaming red hair and freckles, giggled. "Our mom thinks he's hot."

"I know, right," Libby added.

Gingers were always a little tweaked. Eva shook her head. "Sick."

"My dad says he's cool," one of the Goth kids added. "For a minister."

"So cool, he forces my mom and me to start working on that stupid Easter egg hunt like two months in advance."

"I knew this was about your dad," Tyler said.

Eva's nose burned with impending tears. "You don't get it."

Hannah Hunt stepped forward. "If Mistress Eva wants to try a spell, why don't we just go for it and see what happens?"

Around the room, headpieces jangled with nods of assent.

Tyler glanced nervously at the two new initiates.

At least the rest of them were with her.

"All I want to do is make sure Easter isn't such a total pain in the ass.

"Don't you think it's a little weird mixing the Christian thing with Witchcraft?"

"Depends on how you look at it." Eva lifted her Athame skyward. "It's all about faith."

* * *

Everyone loved the soon-to-be reality of two new playgrounds.

Loved him.

Frank held his cheeks together to restrain a sudden urge to pass gas.

Hope Jordan had a right to her opinion and, really, her signature didn't make any difference . . .

A queasy feeling rolled through his gut.

Must have been something he ate.

He belched silently, stood, and smiled. "Do I have a motion in favor of the playground?"

"I motion that we approve the costs for both construction and playground equipment at rates and sites outlined by our president," Jane Hunt said.

Beads of sweat broke out across his brow.

"Second."

"All in favor?"

The room began to spin.

As hands sailed into the air, a wave of nausea crashed on the shores of his esophagus. Before the foul taste of bile could roar up his throat and spill into his mouth, he tried but couldn't manage to utter the two final words, "All opposed?"

CHAPTER FOUR

Melody Mountain Ranch Covenants, Conditions, and
Restrictions: Section 1.2. Owner: "Owner" shall mean any person
or entity at any time owning the lot. The terms "Owner" and
"Member" may be used interchangeably herein.

After a sleepless night of rapid-cycling through the further research he could have done, the signatures he should have collected, and the points he might have made, no matter how pointless, in light of Griffin's dazzling land grab, Will felt sick himself. Frank's sudden illness made it impossible to ask for a delayed vote or make any further inquiries whatsoever without looking like a total ass. "I feel like I'm between a rock and a hard place."

Meg spooned against him and nuzzled his neck. "I'll be the judge of that."

"I'm serious." He shifted positions to block his wife's hand from its imminent path toward his clammy, flaccid dick. He'd clearly been out-orated and out-strategized. Griffin had to know his three-for-one land deal would be a slam-dunk, so why had he gone to the trouble of putting together that diorama? Revenge? Ego? "I spent half the night coming up with excuses for why we have to pack up and move out to Saddle Rock like we should have done in the first place."

"That's ridiculous."

"No more ridiculous than Griffin imposing his will on everyone."

"Honey, you need to accept you're the only one who's feeling that way."

"Ouch."

"Welcome to my world." She twisted one of the hairs circling his belly button. "I vote today on a construction bill that will either limit my constituents' ability to sue culpable homebuilders or end upscale, affordable living as we know it."

He sighed. "What are you going to do?"

"I want to vote against it, but I have to go with the polls." She rested her fingers just beneath the waistband of his boxers. "And try to get my mind off any possible ramifications with a little stress relief."

"I don't know if I can focus enough to . . ."

She took his hand and placed it on her right breast. "I'm confident you can."

Her nipple hardened beneath the silk-screened countenance of some forgotten candidate on her oversized T-shirt. At least there was something willing to be swayed toward his cause.

As he reached under Meg's shirt with his other hand, he glanced over her at the digital clock on his nightstand. "It's almost seven. I should get the kids up or they'll miss the bus."

"Drive them." She reached into his boxers.

He drove them most mornings, anyway. After rousing Tyler from his teenage death-sleep and hustling him out the door, there were the twins to contend with. It was almost impossible to coax them into clothes, stuff cereal into their mouths, and rush them down the street before the bus huffed up the hill. The dog, cat, and guinea pig simply had to wait for breakfast until he got home.

Meg ran her tongue from his jaw toward his mouth. "Give the people what they want."

He feathered his fingers through his wife's short take-me-seriously haircut. Once Meg finally made governor, maybe she'd grow it again. With the thought of her silky chestnut mane spread across the gubernatorial pillowcases, a rush of blood finally surged southward.

A stray thought of Hope Jordan in sheer black lace made him rock hard.

He burrowed his lips into the warm crook of Meg's neck, lifted her shirt, and quickly removed her lavender Jockey for Her panties.

"It's been so long," Meg moaned.

Only a month.

He entered her.

And a week.

As he began to move inside her, forgetting, if only momentarily, everything but the amazing warmth of her, the house felt like it began to tremble beneath them.

Will peered over Meg's head and out the window.

A truck passed the Jordans' house and stopped at the end of the cul-de-sac. Workers with surveying equipment piled out the back of the flatbed. The foreman tipped his thermos and seemed to smile toward Will's bay window.

"Damn it." He pulled the covers up over himself and Meg. "How can they be—?"

"Ignore it," Meg pressed against him.

A hiss of hydraulic brakes echoed through the neighborhood, followed by the rattle of a rear door unrolling.

"How can I ignore them?"

Meg grabbed his ass.

A tidal wave of rage swept through him as backhoes, excavators, and assorted Earth-moving equipment rolled off the back of the truck. "The vote just passed last night."

"You did what you could, Will."

"They can't start construction before seven o'clock A.M. It's against the covenants."

Meg's clock radio blared with the nonsense of the morning shock team.

Seven exactly.

Will slammed his hand on the snooze.

"I'm calling him right . . ." His words were muffled by the *meep-meep-meep* of a truck backing into their driveway.

"Let it go, Will."

* * *

Maryellen Griffin had been extra good yesterday: half a grapefruit for breakfast, romaine with tomatoes and balsamic for lunch, chicken breast for dinner. She'd had her eight glasses of water, three pieces of sugarless gum, and killed the urge to splurge with two dried apricots and a peppermint, which she'd spit out just before the little holes began to form.

The diorama to-do, followed by Frank's bout of whatever having made him so ill he could barely whimper his approval at the playground trucks rolling into the neighborhood, kept any hunger pangs at bay.

Frank groaned.

Yesterday had been a good day for her, anyway.

She looked at the reflection of her vanity mirror from the mirror behind the scale. With no honey-do list, today looked equally promising.

She stepped on the scale.

The phone rang as the digital red blur whirled beneath feet. She managed a quick glance at the flashing scale readout.

99.5.

With no time to savor her triumphant return to the double digits, she flew across the bathroom and picked up the cordless before it rolled into voice mail.

"Hello?" She reached into the sleeve of her robe with her free hand.

"Will Pierce-Cohn here."

Her stomach flip-flopped as she put her other arm into her other sleeve. The poor man had worked so hard on his petition, having no idea Frank had the deal already wrapped up. "Hi, Will."

"Frank available?"

Maryellen glanced out the window. The playground site was as spongy as Will claimed, but Frank said it wouldn't make any difference once the concrete went in. A win-win for Henderson Homes, the church, everyone—everyone but Will, that was. "Frank was up all night and he's finally resting."

"Sorry to hear that." His conviction sounded dubious.

"Who is it?" Frank asked weakly from the other room.

"Be right there," she said, and then lowered her voice. "He really is sick."

"And I really am sorry to impose," he said. "It's just I couldn't help but notice the trucks stopped at the end of the cul-de-sac."

She wanted to tell him she agreed the playground should have been located elsewhere, that she hated seeing all those innocent bunnies displaced, that Frank had steamrolled him, even if it was for the good of the community.

From the next room, Frank coughed.

Not that Will had a chance in the first place. Long before Frank put up his first yard sign advertising the new congregation or began to conduct Sunday services at the high school, he had plans drawn up for the Melody Mountain Community Church. Just like the pronouncement he'd made halfway through their first date—they'd be married in a year and have their one and only daughter the following, Frank always got what he wanted. No one else's opinions really seemed to factor in. Not hers, anyway. "He planned ahead."

"Apparently so."

Luckily, she didn't have to lie about that. Will was such a nice man and a good father, never seeming to mind the role of younger, stay-at-home husband to his ambitious wife. He reminded her of a tousled, dark-haired Hugh Grant as he hurried his girls off to the bus or beamed from the audience at one of his stepson Tyler's plays. To protect his feelings she added, "With all the various site possibilities, he wanted to make sure there wouldn't be any delays that would keep the kids from enjoying the equipment as soon as possible."

"I see," he said.

"The crew's been lined up for a while," she added. "On whatever land got the go-ahead."

During the awkward pause that followed, she pinched herself for the white lie. "Should I have Frank call you back when he can?"

"No." He paused. "I guess I'll just catch up with him later this week or something."

"Okay. Thanks for calling."

She replaced the phone on the wall stand.

"Maryellen?" Frank's croak seeped into the room under the bathroom door. "Mel?"

She cinched up her robe and started back toward their room. "Coming."

"That wasn't Hope Jordan by any chance, was it?"

* * *

"Black fixtures are nearly impossible to keep clean," Theresa Trautman said.

"I see what you mean," Tim said, watching a white blob of shaving cream slide down the side of the ebony colored sink. He spread the rest of the shaving cream across his cheeks. "But considering the new mortgage payment, I'm sure you can find something that works."

"It's not about getting it clean." Her hand looked toddler-sized as she rubbed the vast expanse of her growing belly. "It's a matter of keeping it clean."

Tim ran the razor down his face. "The old house had white fixtures and all you wanted was a new house."

"Needed," she said.

"Have to admit, I do like the new neighborhood, though."

"The homeowner's association certainly seems dynamic," she said.

"Sure does," he said.

"Laney told me she put in a good word for you with Frank Griffin."

"Hopefully it'll pay off." Tim nodded.

"I was thinking we should check out his church this Sunday," she added.

"I was thinking the same," he said, delighted to discover that by looking in the mirror and through the reflection of the open blinds, he could see into Hope Jordan's master bath behind them. Too bad the shades weren't up. "Quickest way to get to know our new neighbors."

* * *

Jim never whispered how beautiful she was, or how right a couple they were like he used to when they made love or happened to pass a mirror together. He hadn't acknowledged last month's black lace much beyond tearing the panties as he pushed the seam aside. Really, he hadn't given any more than an appreciative nod to the parade of teddies and see-thru tank tops that now overflowed Hope's lingerie drawer and had taken up residence in her sock drawer. Only when she'd worn his silk boxers and nothing else had his response resulted in the virile baby-making romp she'd hoped for.

Of course, that was during the first month.

Ten months later, could she blame him for his waning enthusiasm?

With a dismissive snip of her nail scissors, Hope clipped the tags on this month's ovulation day peach lace bra and g-string combo. As she fastened the bra hook, the phone rang.

Before she could make it down the hall to her office where she'd left the handset, the message machine picked up.

"You've reached the Jordans and Hope for Your Home Design. Please leave a—"

"Hope, it's Jim . . ."

His message was partially blurred by the noise of a passing truck, but his last sentence was all she needed to hear.

"Be there in ten."

She was being paranoid. Jim was on his way home. If not eager to make passionate love for the umpteenth time every other day in a row, he was certainly a willing participant in their shared goal. Before she got back into bed in preparation, she grabbed a few roses from the peach bouquet she'd picked up to match her lingerie and plucked the petals.

Halfway down the curved staircase, she stopped and closed her eyes. Mid her monthly visualization of the onslaught of robust candidates all vying for her big, healthy, ripe egg, a chill came over her like she was being watched. Half-expecting to catch Will Pierce-Cohn gazing at her through her front door accent windows, she opened her eyes.

No one was there, of course.

Yet another example of paranoia.

The Clomid was doing its job.

Hope smiled.

Everything was okay.

More than okay.

CHAPTER FIVE

*Section 2.3. Miscellaneous Use Site: Miscellaneous Use Site shall
mean any Privately Owned Site within the Community Association
Area designated in the Supplemental Declaration covering that site
for agricultural, mixed residential, and office or other uses.*

"How long have you been symptomatic?" the doctor, nerdy cute, but younger than Laney Estridge preferred, both medically and recreationally, asked.

"Long enough to be sick of feeling sick." If her utter lack of interest in flirting with him regardless was any indication, she was getting worse.

"Any other symptoms besides sinus congestion?"

"Headaches, cough, phlegm, intermittent body aches." She shivered from the cold tip of the scope in her ear.

"It's been a rough cold and flu season." The doctor looked up her left and then her right nostril. "Especially for you."

"I've gone from one virus to another since fall," Laney said. "What do you think is going on with me?"

"Your sinuses are definitely inflamed," he said. "And your recent medical history indicates some mild immune-suppression."

"Meaning what?"

"How would you characterize your recent stress levels?"

"No worse than usual."

"Are you taking anything else besides Zoloft on a daily basis?"

"A multi, calcium, vitamin D, fish oil, and B complex."

"Any herbal supplements?"

"Juice Plus, which I sell, and have tremendous faith in."

He began to jot down a prescription. "In the absence of any underlying pathology, chronic low-grade illness is commonly brought on by the combination of stressors and increased anxiety levels."

"Stress?" Laney's relieved sigh came out as a snort. "With the real estate and retail markets spiraling downward as fast as the cost of gas goes up—not to mention my husband's job prospects, I'm lucky I haven't been deathly ill."

"I think we all feel that way." He smiled kindly. "Let's try Augmentin this time and up your current dosage of Zoloft by twenty-five milligrams. I'd also like for you to focus on stress-reduction, happy thoughts, and activities that promote relaxation whenever possible."

The closest thing she had to a happy thought, thanks to the Trautman closing and an unexpectedly robust Avon reorder month, were two out of six credit cards with zero balances.

"If the sinus symptoms persist, we'll give you a referral to an allergist." He handed her the antibiotic prescription. "In the meantime, saline nasal baths and a good steam or two will help clear the mucus."

CHAPTER SIX

Covenant Section 2.48. Recreation Function:
"Recreation Functions" shall mean providing for active and
passive recreational activities.

*W*ill Pierce-Cohn leaned against the cul-de-sac mailboxes, took a deep whiff of spring, and did a few lunges. With his back to the overturned pile of soggy dirt behind him, he upped the volume on his iPod and started down the parkway. Eyes on the tulips sprouting along the north side of the west-facing homes and the green buds on the wire-supported saplings, he vowed to *let it go*, just like his wife said. Shift his attention from the will of the Melody Mountain Ranch community to the things he, Will, loved about living here—like running down clean, wide streets filled with attractive, uniform homes.

And Saturday fitness class. The combination boot camp, mat Pilates, and step aerobics had returned definition to his chest and quads. Better, his total initial inability to dance, much less step up and down on a bench to music, was corrected on the first day by Hope Jordan.

With a legitimate reason to stare, he noted her careful, lithe movements. Following her footwork, he lifted his arms and clapped over his head in time with the music. Before he knew it, he had a flawless hamstring-pivot-adductor routine.

Hope rarely missed the Saturday class.

Other than the occasional ski day, he hadn't either.

He sprinted the remaining seven-tenths of a mile to the rec center. His lungs burned and perspiration dripped down his back, but the endorphin rush left him feeling better than he had in months. If he kept it up, his abs would be at three-pack status in time for their summer vacation.

The endorphin high dropped off with his first step into the building.

The diorama, now decorated with iridescent balloons, was stationed in the center of the lobby. Griffin, recovered and Saturday casual in an untucked shirt, jeans, and sneakers, was parked beside his plastic fantasy, an elbow resting jauntily on the edge of the Plexiglas corner.

Will eyed the white board propped between the diorama and Maryellen Griffin, who, with glazed grin, looked like a wilting, anorexic flower despite the word Juicy emblazoned across her daffodil-yellow sweats.

COUPON CLIPPERS!
TWELVE STEPS TO A NEW LIFE!
SAVE AND BE SAVED TODAY AND EVERY SATURDAY!

If only the Griffins would find a new life somewhere else.

"Joining us for our class today?" Griffin smiled.

A jolt of indigestion, at least he hoped it was indigestion, radiated across his chest. "Sorry. My weights class is starting."

Frank eyed Will's already damp T-shirt. "Looks like you've already worked up a sweat."

Nothing like the sweat he could work up with a few well-placed questions about the suspicious lack of time between the HOB vote and the playground groundbreaking. He avoided eye contact with an unfocused glance at the diorama swing set. "Just getting started."

Griffin patted his belly, which despite his illness, seemed to have risen like a mini-bread loaf. "I planned to hit the weights, but I'm so behind after being down with that flu, the workout is going to have to wait until after Easter."

"Sounds like a plan," Will managed. "Got to run."

As if in confirmation, a bicycle-shorts-and-cycling-shoes-clad group click-clacked downstairs toward the spinning studio for their class.

"I want you to know," Griffin's face morphed from his usual good-humor-from-the-abundance-of-blessings expression into an almost convincing attempt at humility, "I really do respect your commitment to this community."

"Thanks."

Frank put a pinkie to the white board and erased a portion of the extra-long tail on the *S* at the end of *COUPON CLIPPERS*. "No hard feelings?"

The first bars of a Lady Gaga song filtered up the stairs from the aerobics studio and helped Will push back a burbling urge to ram Frank's face into the Plexiglas lid of the diorama. Truth was, Frank hadn't done anything but give the people what they thought they wanted.

"No hard feelings." Will managed a feeble wave and escaped toward the steps as Frank turned to address a pair of women who'd wandered in the front door.

"Ladies, would you believe the sweats my wife's wearing retail for well over a hundred but only set me back $24.95? Come to Coupon Clippers and I'll teach you how it's done."

Will bounded down the stairs. In seconds, he'd be in aerobics, alongside the one person on his block who'd believed in his cause. And, he couldn't help but note, she'd likely be wearing a much more appealing ensemble than anything Maryellen or Frank could dig up on sale. He conjured a quick memory of how Hope looked in much less before Roseanne Goldberg blocked his view like a human pylon in a tangerine T-shirt and compression shorts that pressed her cellulite toward her knees. "You missed some interesting covenant violations on Monday."

"I have the notes from Jane." Unable to see around her, he looked through the triangle formed by her hand on her hip for a glimpse of a blond ponytail.

"Did you read about the family on Wonderland Valley Court who got cited for trying to clean carpeting on their driveway?"

"I haven't had a chance to look anything over, yet." He spotted Hope, standing in her usual place, stretching her quads with the graceful, light-footed stride of a ballerina.

"Frank let it slide, but there could be an underlying issue that—"

"I'm afraid my class is about to start."

"No problem," she said. "I'm leaving some books you need to read in your milk box."

"Great," he said, lacking the nerve or the time to tell her he was probably done fighting the futile fight anyway. "We'll chat later."

Before Roseanne tried to pin him down to a discussion coffee time, he slid around her, bolted down the hallway, and made his way to the door of the aerobics studio.

Hope, standing in her usual spot, stopped, bent over, grabbed her water bottle, and unscrewed the top.

Time slowed along with her long, drawn-out sip.

He watched a water droplet dribble down her chin and disappear between her breasts.

She spotted him, smiled in his direction.

He sauntered into the room.

She motioned him toward the empty step behind her, where a ten-pound set of weights, a body bar, and an extra-tight band sat beside the step.

She'd set up his equipment for him!

Was it possible that she'd ever, even for a second, thought about him in the same way that he couldn't help but think about her? "I'm a married man," he'd have to say. "I can't deny my attraction to you either, but I stood before my wife and vowed to . . ."

"I figured you were running late," she said as he put his towel down and took his spot.

"Thanks." His dorky, stammered *you're the best* was drowned out by the instructor, Sarah Fowler's, amplified voice. "Ladies," she slapped her perfect round bottom, "we're starting with squats, so remember to be sure and stick out your rear like you're sitting in a chair."

As Will squatted in time to "It's Raining Men," he gnawed on the inside of his cheek so he wouldn't smile as a pleasing spandex spectacle unfolded around him.

Letting it go didn't seem so hard after all.

* * *

"You wouldn't believe how many great savings tips the Griffins gave this morning." Laney Estridge plopped down beside her best friend, Sarah Fowler, on the steam room bench and took a deep sinus-cleansing breath. "I have a page full of notes on everything from buying expired cereal in bulk to getting $4 generic prescriptions."

"This means you're going to ditch my aerobics class from now on?" Sarah asked.

"Only until my sinuses clear up." Laney massaged the sides of her nose. "Frank's easy enough on the eyes, but Maryellen's thinner, thriftier, and holier routine is gonna wear thin."

"I don't think I'd have made it through the first hour."

"I had to do something," Laney said. "The doctor's diagnosis of *stressed-out* sent me on an online peace-and-harmony-regaining shopping spree."

"And did it make you feel any better?"

"Until I got my statement."

Sarah's new C cups barely moved as she knotted her naturally auburn hair behind her head. "No offense, but do you think you might be working a little too hard at trying to relax?"

Easy for her to say. Sarah, tiny, fair, and pretty, had tall, very dark, and handsome Randall's NFL paycheck, albeit third string, to stay that way. Laney resisted the urge to feel for twangy grays in her highlights or shove a thumb sideways and check her real set of breasts' further gravity changes. By the time the real estate market bounced back and/or Steve decided he'd recovered from Chronic Fatigue, or whatever it was he was calling the malaise that kept him from looking for a new job until his severance package ran out, her jowls could hang where her breasts used to be. "I suppose I could up the Zoloft even more than the doctor suggested."

"Or you could get that book I recommended."

A few Costco runs back, Sarah picked up a copy of her latest favorite self-help title and was threatening to toss it over a pile of Kirkland men's jeans and into their shared cart. Laney managed to intercept, promising she'd pick it up at the library.

"Seriously, Laney. If you see yourself living in health and abundance, believe you deserve it, and envision for yourself exactly what you want . . ."

"I know, I know." Laney eyes wandered along the length of Sarah's toned curves, stopping at the dragonfly tattoo at her hip. Though identical in size, color, and location to her own, Sarah's somehow looked more delicate. "I'll attract everything I truly need and desire."

"Get the book and you'll believe it."

"I'll do it this week. In the meantime I still need to figure out how to make some more money before I have to flip burgers in Lakewood or somewhere where no one knows me."

Sarah ran her nails lightly down Laney's arm. "Surely, we can come up with something more promising to supplement your income until another listing sells."

"Like what?"

Sarah pulled Laney to her and kissed her softly, then not so softly. "Maybe there's something we can do together."

CHAPTER SEVEN

*Melody Mountain High School rental clause I C 7: Rental
group agrees to assume responsibility for all liabilities arising
incident to the occupancy of the facility.*

*H*ope breathed in the heady mixture of fresh rain, spring blooms, and
chocolate. Even in a high school auditorium made humid from the steady patter of rain and an overflow of people seated in folding chairs, Easter, with its
message of renewal and new life, was, by far, her favorite holiday.

"God did not spare His own Son, but delivered Him up for us. How shall
He who would do that, not also freely give us all things?" Frank Griffin, boyishly
handsome with his dark hair and broad smile, yet somehow larger than life in a
velvet-trimmed robe, closed the Bible with a regal thump. He looked out from
his pulpit onto the capacity crowd. "So, here we are, enjoying the abundant
blessings our Lord has provided on this special day."

And she was.

Jim, dozing beside her, had made it home on the red-eye from New York in
time for the service. She rested her head on his shoulder and visualized the two
of them at next year's Easter, newborn in tow, among the sea of pastel-suited
families.

"We're all looking and feeling our Easter best," Frank continued, as though
reading her mind. "We've welcomed with open arms our old friends, the new
faces in the Meadow Mountain Ranch community, and those of you whose
schedules only allow a visit on the big ticket holidays."

The crowd chuckled.

"We've reveled in the processional parade, rejoiced in our beloved Easter
hymns, and relished the holy words." Frank gave a thumbs-up to the choir and
burst into a joyous smile. "Easter with all the trimmings!"

Hope's *Amen* joined the eruption of praise, like vocal fireworks, exploding
throughout the room.

"Amen is right, because today is just the beginning of God's blessings for you!" Frank raised a hand skyward. "God loves you so much, He'll keep handing out good things to all of us."

She already had so many good things. Was it so wrong to ache for her 2.5 children more?

"God did not stop His Son from going to the cross," Frank continued. "In fact, God showed that He loves us by giving His Son over for the judgment you and I deserve. Why? So God could lavish His abundant love on us. God demonstrated His love by giving us freedom from sin and eternal life. And these acts are not the end of His love. God still wants to hand out His blessings to you."

As *Amens* from the crowd accentuated his every sentence, Hope spotted her impossibly big-with-child(ren) new neighbor, seated amid her cornucopia of offspring. The proud papa caught Hope's glance and smiled with what was surely smug satisfaction.

A pang of envy forced her to look down at her persimmon colored skirt as he draped an arm around his wife's and then his daughter's shoulder.

"God spared His Son nothing in the way of pain that He might spare us no pleasure or bounty."

What did she have to be jealous of, really? She wasn't looking to have a passel of kids, though her neighbors' were beautiful—especially the daughter, a lovely combination of her housewife-next-door pretty mom and the husband, who looked a little like Al Pacino's not-quite-ready-for-primetime kid brother.

The wife rubbed her belly.

His unquestionably virile little brother.

"But God didn't let His Son stay there. God lifted Jesus up from the grave to show His love to the world. After the resurrection, God said: 'Now that act of love has been done and I can spend my love on my children. I can give them whatever they need.'" Frank paused. "Folks, for you, this could be renewed good health, extra bucks to furnish the house, finding that special someone . . ." He scanned the room, his gaze on the center section where Hope was seated. "Maybe adding a beloved soul to your family."

Two rows ahead, a darling little girl of about six blew a bubble. She had blond ringlets the color Hope and Jim would surely make. She wore a powder-blue polka dot dress and white patent leather Mary Janes, just like she'd have dressed a daughter in for Easter.

The bubble popped and the little girl giggled.

Tears Hope swore she wouldn't allow on this day of renewed dreams, spilled down her cheeks anyway.

"Maybe you're thinking, God hasn't given me what I want . . ."

Hope felt a rush of blood to her cheeks. After all the teary conversations she had with Frank, maybe he *was* talking directly to her.

"If so, maybe you've forgotten a thing or two about your relationship with God. Some of the ways he hands out his love may in fact be different than you would expect, but God is there, waiting to give to you." He stopped to smile. "If you are ready, get your hands out, and look forward to receiving everything you need and more than you ever wanted . . ."

Jim stirred and grasped her hand.

"Because, our Lord wants you to have what you want."

Why wouldn't the Lord want her to have what she, what she and Jim, wanted too?

"In return, all He wants is your devotion and appreciation."

A "*Thank you, Jesus*" rang from the audience, followed by a handful more.

"That's a nice start." Frank smiled. "Follow that up by throwing a few extra bucks onto the plate today and I think we may be on to something."

The crowd chuckled with him.

"Seriously, I challenge all of you to dig a little deeper this Easter. Thank Him for the beautiful home and safe, family-friendly lifestyle he's provided." Frank grasped the heavy velvet drape behind him. "This humble servant wants to do for the Lord what he has already done for me—give him a home and a community to be proud of." He rustled the collection plate next to the microphone. "There will be plenty of good surprises in store if you do the same."

He motioned Maryellen from the front row to the side steps and leaned into the microphone one last time before she took over with the weekly announcements. "Say it with me folks," he said over the end-of-sermon rustle. "The Lord wants me to have what I want!"

Hope's voice joined the great multitoned voice that echoed through the room. "The Lord wants me to have what I want!"

And the choir burst into song.

Alleluia! Alleluia!

* * *

If the Lord wanted Tim Trautman to have what he desired, he wouldn't have created Hope Jordan's husband in the image of a Nordic god.

The amp screeched with feedback as Reverend Frank's attractive, but breakable-looking, wife craned the mike to mouth height and unfolded her announcement list. "Tuesday night, *Cooking with Christ* will be hosted by Janet Jamison."

Hope's husband smoothed his thick, wheat-hued, nonreceding hair.

Not that ridiculous good looks could scare him off.

"Thursday night at six P.M., weather permitting," Maryellen Griffin's nervous falsetto trilled through the auditorium as Rev. Frank, another member of the no-need-for-the-Hair-Club-for-Men, disappeared backstage, "any and all pet owners should bring their leashed and/or caged pets and meet at the community dog park for our annual Pet Blessing service."

Usually, guys as good looking as Hope's husband had no idea how to put out—especially in the personality department.

"I know you're all planning to join our indoor egg hunt and raffle," Maryellen Griffin said over the rustle of the crowd. "But if I don't get a chance in the midst of all the hustle and bustle, I wish you a happy, healthy Easter."

The Jordan aisle rose en masse.

Problem was, the dude had to be six foot four slouching.

Tim's idea of a friendly, post-service hi-we're-the-new-neighbors, hatched the moment Hope caught his eye from beside her *seated* husband, had to be scrapped for a more calculated hello on an evened playing field.

Before he began to scramble for a workable plan B, Theresa, God love her, reached a swollen hand into her purse and handed him the greatest of all height equalizers—his checkbook.

His daughter, Lauren, tugged his arm as their row stood. "I need to meet up with my friends in the cafeteria."

Tim brushed a stray hair from her face and looked past her in time to catch a glimpse of Hope's silk-covered ass. What he needed to do was time his meet-and-greet so the Jordans, already headed in that direction, were nearby to appreciate Reverend Frank appreciating the generosity of a Trautman Easter donation. "I want to introduce you to Reverend Griffin first."

"Already know him. His daughter's a friend."

"As a family," Tim said.

"But I'm supposed to help with the Easter egg hunt."

"And you will, as soon as we present our family Easter donation."

Lauren sighed.

Theresa, who loved public displays of financial affection, squeezed his shoulder and smiled. "How much are we going to give?"

* * *

The Lord definitely wanted Frank to have what he wanted.

Even with a rain-soaked Easter and the ongoing challenge of squeezing funds from a house-poor flock, the Melody Mountain Community Church collection plate overflowed. All he had to do was keep donations up 20 percent for the next six weeks, do another push fueled by the excitement of the Memorial Weekend playground ribbon cutting, and continue to collect at 10 percent above normal to meet the fifteen thousand he still needed to get title in hand.

Two, or at the very most, three years from today, instead of being stationed outside high school cafeteria doors, he'd greet parishioners at the entrance to a social pavilion in the northwest corner of the main lobby of his new church—a church complete with bell tower, religious school classrooms, and a pulpit/stage area large enough for the choir and the band. The Parker Pines Community Church was in the framing stage, and his buddy, Roger Manning, was insufferable since christening the Harmony Hills Neighborhood Church, but neither had, nor would have, both a mini-chapel and a gymnasium.

"Lovely sermon," Samantha Torgenson said, and like the five people he'd greeted before her, added, "I made my donation online."

It hadn't taken too many underwhelming collection plate totals or fervent prayers for assistance before he'd had an inspired vision: The Melody Mountain Ranch Community Church needed to take Visa, MasterCard, and Discover.

"The Lord gives thanks to those who give thanks to Him." He nudged Samantha gently toward the cafeteria so he wouldn't miss the Estridges, whose daughters had already slipped through the doors to join Evangeline.

He gave Laney Estridge a friendly wink and shook hands with Steve. What they lacked in liquid assets Laney made up for in elbow grease and community spirit. Having organized the last two Memorial Weekend potlucks and the Halloween Haunt, not to mention the Community Chrisanukwanzaa, her donation, in the form of her party-planning abilities, would ensure the success of the playground dedication celebration. "In the interest of separation of church and state, I won't pester you today, but we need to talk."

Laney smiled. "You know I'm glad to help out in any way I can."

"Good to know," he said, indulging her need for a little harmless flirtation. "Because I think you know what I want."

She batted her eyes. "This wouldn't involve a little something you're planning over Memorial Weekend?"

"I can't imagine putting the event in anyone else's hands."

"I assume Maryellen's already on board to run the potluck?"

"You know my wife—she wouldn't have it any other way."

"Perfect, because I've already printed up the spreadsheets and planning notes from the last three events."

"That's why I pay you the big bucks." He patted her shoulder, did the same to her bosom buddy, Sarah Fowler, and reached out to shake with Randall Fowler. Somehow, the sight of fair Sarah and her ebony-skinned husband, Randall, always gave Frank a start. Maybe it was more a thrill. Not every minister could claim a local sports celebrity as his parishioner. "For your first official duty I'm hoping you'll talk this guy into handling ribbon cutting honors at the playground dedication."

"My pleasure," Randall said, offering a blinding smile, a meaty hand, and a check to the pile on the collection plate.

A *Praise Jesus* was definitely in order.

Frank bowed his head, but before he could utter a word of prayer, the door to the girls' bathroom squealed open and Hope Jordan, displaying her God-given assets in a red silk dress, disappeared into the bathroom.

He was left feeling like a bull taunted by a flag. Easter, no matter how glorious, couldn't be called a success until the two of them had a Come-to-Jesus.

As it were.

"I still can't imagine what prompted her to sign Pierce-Cohn's petition."

Laney and Sarah's knowing looks sent prickles across his cheeks and forehead.

"We heard she signed to get him off her doorstep," Sarah finally said.

"As in he coerced her? If that's the case, it's totally unacceptable and—"

"By coerced, I think Sarah means he stood tongue-tied and drooling at her door, fantasizing that his *Unknown Dangers* rant would somehow make her want to throw herself at him."

"Oh," Frank said. "I didn't realize—"

"He follows her around like a lovesick teenager?"

"Pierce-Cohn?"

They nodded in unison.

"I see," Frank said. His irritation with the already vanquished P-C began to rise once again.

"But even if she did sign to get him to leave her alone, it still has to be hard to watch a playground go up across the street from your empty nest," Sarah said.

"Particularly when hopped up on fertility drugs," Laney added. "They made me nutty."

"If you ask me, Hope needs to do something beyond working out and dabbling in home décor while she's waiting to be pregnant."

"She taught the youth group kids how to make jewelry."

"That's a start."

"Everyone I know has her doing their Christmas décor."

"But that's not until the holidays. In the meantime, she seems to be at that so-obsessed-by-getting-pregnant stage everything else is just a blur."

"Great sermon." Rhonda Miller horned in and grasped Frank's hand. "Glad you're feeling better."

"Thank you." He nudged Rhonda gently toward the cafeteria. Had Hope signed just to get P-C off her doorstep, or had he himself inadvertently offended her by relocating the playground across the cul-de-sac from her house? He had just enough time before the next family approached. Closing his eyes, Frank silently asked for some enlightenment, opened to a random page in his pocket Bible, and looked inside.

Job 28:12. And where is the place of understanding?

He looked toward the ladies' room but the Trautman brood blocked the door. Tim seemed to hesitate while the wife continued on toward the greetings line, kids trailing behind.

Tim eventually followed.

Frank smiled in their direction, his gaze fixed on the bathroom door and his thoughts on understanding. He could easily understand her wanting to get pitiful Pierce-Cohn off her doorstep. Still, she could have agreed to think about it, or not opened the door in the first place.

He closed his eyes again.

He couldn't help but understand how she might feel watching a playground go up across the street from her empty nest, but why hadn't she said anything, referenced the playground issue at all during any of the myriad counseling sessions they'd had over the last few months? Was she afraid he wouldn't understand her objections to the playground given his enthusiasm about the project? Then again, maybe riding the roller coaster of fertility, often absent of her husband, had made her temporarily crazy.

Frank bowed his head and meditated on understanding.

"Happy Easter." Tim Trautman made his way to the front of the line and extended his hand. "This is Theresa; our daughter, Lauren; and the boys, Timmy and Jacob."

"Nice to meet you." Frank shook with the wife and all three children. "How are you enjoying our Easter festivities?"

"Wonderful," the wife said.

"We're impressed with just about everything we've seen around here so far," Tim said. "I'm anxious to get involved in the community."

"So I'm told. I plan to hold you to that." Frank smiled and turned to the Trautman kids. "You three ready to get involved in an Easter egg hunt?"

"Can we go in?" the bouncier of the two boys asked.

"Can I go, Dad?" The daughter looked longingly toward the teens clustered around Evangeline in the corner. "I'm already supposed to be helping."

Frank patted the daughter's shoulder. "Can you tell Evangeline to start handing out baskets and to make sure the big kids don't hog everything when things get rolling."

"Sure." Their pretty, raven-haired daughter disappeared into the crowd.

"Can we go too?" the other boy asked.

"We probably should give him our check," Theresa said. "The kids are anxious." The bathroom door squealed open.

Frank turned to watch Hope emerge and join her husband.

"Tim?" Theresa said to her husband, who also seemed distracted by the Jordans.

"Of course." Tim reached into his suit coat without looking down.

With the Jordans in near handshaking distance, Frank found himself torn as to whether he should greet them before accepting the Trautman donation, or hold off until just after. He settled on a friendly, no-hard feelings wave while Tim fumbled for the check.

"I think we're holding up the line, honey," Theresa said.

Hope and Jim made their way over and stopped directly behind the Trautmans.

A folded slip of safety-blue paper appeared between Tim's fingers. "Got it. A token of our commitment to our new community," Tim said, loudly enough for Frank to anticipate a healthy number.

"Hope." Leslie Pepper appeared beside the Jordans. "I have a friend you need to meet. She loved the furniture you picked out for our family room and patio and she wants to talk to you about doing some work in their master."

Before Frank could either catch a glance at the check, or give an approving smile to Hope, she was being led away.

Trautman, who was holding his check and seemed about to hand it over, turned and instead placed it atop the collection pile.

Face up.

* * *

Eva Griffin leaned against the cool tile corner of the cafeteria and inhaled the last of her second donut before her dad spotted her and called her out for gluttony. The tangy jelly threatened to congeal in the back of her throat while she watched him shake people down for money. "I can't believe the spell didn't work."

"My mom told me that your dad told her he was super sick and stuff." Libby Estridge grabbed a chocolate egg from its hiding place on the windowsill, unwrapped the foil, and popped it in her mouth. "I say that counts for something."

Her dad's booming, fake-friendly laugh bounced across the room as he glad-handed Lauren Trautman's parents and pushed them through the cafeteria doors so he could move on to his next victim.

"Not enough," Eva said.

They all watched as Lauren, fully working it, with straightened hair, a killer black skirt, and ballet flats, appeared from behind her mountain of a mother and scanned the room.

"Her top totally rocks," Hannah said.

"So does her skirt," Margaret said. "It's Abercrombie."

Eva waved her over.

"Do you think Tyler was right about the new people not being ready or powerful enough or whatever?" Libby asked as Lauren started toward them.

"The book said all we needed were thirteen willing souls." Eva shrugged. "We definitely had them."

"Maybe it was a full moon problem," Margaret said.

"The moon phase shouldn't affect nuisance abatement spells."

"Maybe we missed a chant or an ingredient or something?" Hannah asked.

Eva gave her the evil eye.

"Well it did rain."

"Made it worse. Mom and I had to redo like everything for an indoor Easter egg hunt."

Hannah took another candy from the kiddie stash. "Just saying . . ."

"Hey." Lauren joined the group. "Your dad wants us to start handing out baskets to the little kids and stuff."

Eva rolled her eyes.

"Eva's bumming about the spell," Hannah said.

"At the moment, I'm bumming more about dealing with all the booger-nosed monsters all hopped up on sugar."

"Speaking of which, are you wearing Pink Sugar?" Margaret asked.

Lauren nodded and stuck out her wrist.

"Smells like strawberry candy on you."

And popularity. With her shiny hair and sweet dimples, Lauren was so anti-witch, her presence alone should have been enough of a catalyst for the spell to work.

Across the room, while her poor mom slaved away selling raffle tickets and baked goods she made but wouldn't eat, her father was practically drooling all over Hope Jordan and that smokin' husband of hers.

"Tyler was right about one thing; the spell definitely didn't go how it was supposed to."

Lauren looked up and around the room. "Have you guys seen him yet, today?"

"Tyler?" Hannah asked.

"Like here?" Margaret asked.

Lauren's cheeks seemed to color. "Since it's Easter and all, I figured . . ."

"Reverend Griffin and Mr. Pierce-Cohn are full-on enemies," Libby said.

"He's also half-Jewish," Eva said.

"My bad." Lauren opened the napkin she was clutching in her palm and began to chow down on a chocolate bunny like she hadn't eaten in a week.

Eva sighed and started toward an unmanned table full of Easter baskets. "My dad's going to bite my head off if we don't get to work."

* * *

Frank shook hands with Jim Jordan, but looked past him at the collection plate.

He hadn't imagined that extra zero on the Trautman check.

One Thousand and xx/100.

Despite the statement inherent in leaving a big check faceup for all to see, the sudden, exhilarating boost in funds made it that much easier for Frank to slip a friendly arm around Hope. "I think I may owe you an apology."

Never mind that Pierce-Cohn owed her the bigger apology for being a desperate letch in the first place. Or that no matter what her current state of mind, the Jordans would one day thank him when they had children who spent countless hours enjoying blissful outdoor play in plain sight of home. And, if by some sad twist of The Lord's plan, Hope was never blessed with the offspring she so wanted, the real estate appreciation, especially with a never-to-be obstructed view, would certainly ease the pain of a move to a loft in LoDo or some other trendy, more adult-oriented community. "About the playground going in across the street . . ."

It took everything he had to merely hand her a Kleenex and not wipe away the stray tear that drifted down her cheek as she looked up at him with her clear, blue, already contrite eyes.

Surely, her apology would follow.

"I want you to know I do understand the construction process may be stressful in the midst of your attempts to start a family. And, for that, I'm sorry."

"Thank you," she said. "I'm sure it'll be nice when it's done."

Jim, who seemed unmoved in one direction or the other, nodded.

"I prayed on this and I've been assured that, in the long run, you'll enjoy all the benefits of having such a strategically placed playground across the street."

Hope's pretty face still seemed awash in pain.

He reached out, gently placed his hand atop her silk headband, and bowed his head. "Lord, help Hope to conceive a healthy baby. She asks for your intervention in everything she tries and has faith in you, for you said none shall be barren, may your will be done. Amen."

Both Hope and Jim smiled.

"The Lord wants you to have what you want," Frank said, anticipating the apology for her shortsightedness in signing P-C's ill-fated petition that would soon follow.

She merely nodded in agreement.

CHAPTER EIGHT

*With new, state-of-the-art top-flight schools, libraries, and
educational facilities you'll rest even easier knowing your children
are getting the education of a lifetime.—From the Melody
Mountain Ranch initial offerings brochure.*

*L*aney reclined in her Jacuzzi tub, a library copy of *Bring It On* in hand, Celine Dion on the CD player, and her head on a lavender-scented aromatherapy pillow.

Happy thoughts or your favorite tunes can instantly transform your well-being.
She added a capful of organic bubble bath to the water.

If you want to change your life, think positive!
She'd opened the book before bed. The idea of drawing happiness, good health, and abundance through positive thought hooked her on page one, and she couldn't put it down. Instead of her usual irritation over being congested, overweight, short of cash, and relegated to mat Pilates at the rec center, she'd fallen asleep picturing herself with clear sinuses, taut and toned as Hope Jordan, and working out at the private studio on Parker Road. Her hot-yet-enlightened instructor, complete with washboard abs and tan legs, would flash his approving grin as she stretched across the Reformer machine. From there, who knew what exercises were in store?

For the first time in months, she awoke in the morning before her alarm. She went downstairs, fully expecting to find Steve slurping his coffee like he was in a hurry to go somewhere besides the recliner, and the girls foraging for their usual breakfast of a Red Bull and a PowerBar. Instead, they'd all left early: Steve probably for an early tee time he'd sleep off the rest of the day, and the girls for a makeup test or bring-your-grade-up extra-credit session.

Still . . .

She decided to show The Universe she meant business by substituting her morning toast for egg whites and heading to the gym for a workout during the 8 A.M. time slot she planned to someday enjoy with Justin.

Or, maybe, his name would be Julian.

Start with something small, like willing a checker to open up the line for you on a busy day at the grocery store and see what happens.

Of course, Justin/Julian wouldn't be small.

As she eased into her well-deserved, post-workout bubble bath, she turned the page to a chapter entitled, "Money! Money! Money!"

Half an hour later, filled with *gratitude* for what she already had and what would soon be hers, having *imagined* closings in the pipeline, checks in the mail for real estate and all her sideline businesses, and feeling truly *happy*, knowing that was the fastest way to bring in as much money as she could imagine, she put the book down and closed her eyes again.

"Bring it on."

With a contented sigh, she refreshed her bath with more hot water, grabbed the remote, and flipped on the tub deck TV while she awaited her good fortune.

Martha Stewart's face filled the screen.

An omen for business acumen and financial redemption if ever there was one.

* * *

Maryellen Griffin loved Mondays.

She loved pulling into the lot of the Melody Mountain annex branch of the public library, walking past the Quiznos, veterinary clinic, and U-Frame-It that shared the L-shaped strip mall. She loved the sound of her key in the lock, the click of the lights, the colorful blip as she turned on the computers, and the overflowing return bin she needed to reshelf. She loved that budget cuts stipulated only one senior staffer for the first two, gloriously quiet, nearly patron-free hours at the start of the week.

Stowing her purse and a post-Easter brown bag lunch of celery sticks, grapefruit wedges, and half a chicken breast in the drawer beneath the circulation desk, she sat down and turned on the staff computer.

Maryellen especially loved the Monday after Easter. Another year would pass before the stress of organizing an egg hunt, shopping for a dress to complement Frank's purple robe, or listening to his *the Lord wants you to have what you want if you give money* sermon she'd committed to memory six Easters ago when he was called to make the leap from full-time parishioner to part-time pastor. By scheduling herself for the opening shift, she'd not only miss this year's rundown of each check amount and who from, but possibly the initial transition into Memorial Day planning mode. Best of all, she managed to slip out of bed, shower, dress, and get out of the house before Frank woke up and rubbed up against her for morning sex. He'd be more insistent, rougher, and certainly more vocal than usual tonight. . . .

Tell me how good I was yesterday.

Tell me how bad you want me.

Tell me you want it as much as they want me to build them a big church.

Tell me how big and hard I am.

Tell me . . .

She sighed.

Even though she was alone, she did a quick scan of the tables and stacks filling the space once slated to be a Dress Barn. Satisfied no one was looking over her shoulder, she double-clicked on Internet Explorer and, like every Monday, typed in the website for the Denver Public Library. She clicked on *about the library* for the scroll-down menu and went to *jobs.*

She liked the suburban public library system, and the convenience of living and working in the same neighborhood couldn't be overestimated.

She closed her eyes.

But what if she didn't live in the suburbs at all, but in a little bungalow on a shady tree-lined street in Congress Park or Sloan's Lake?

Frank would never live in a bungalow, or anywhere as diverse as Sloan's Lake.

She scanned the listings.

Shelver, Ross-Barnum Branch (20 hours)

Shelver, Hampden Branch Library (20 hours)

Education Program Assistant, Various Branch Libraries (40 hours)

She was far too senior for a shelving position, and the longer hours, reduced pay, and status of an education program assistant wasn't for her.

Library Security Supervisor, Central Library (40 hours)

Facilities security was of no interest, but the location gave her a shudder of pleasure.

Central Library.

Whenever she made the trek into downtown or even to the Cherry Creek Mall, she always allowed time for a detour to the Central Library. Set like a contemporary, sophisticated cousin beside the ultramodern art museum and kitty-corner to the state capital, she could spend forever in the open atrium, soaking in the smell of periodicals and well-worn hard covers. She'd watch the steady stream of students, readers, even vagrants, as they traveled en masse up and down the open elevators, in and out of the three floors' worth of genre-specific galleries.

It was nothing short of amazing how patrons lined up in front of the bank of self-serve computers and knew exactly how to check out their books.

She glanced at the last listing.

Head Reference Librarian, Branch location

As she started to double-click for a more detailed description, the front door jangled open.

Will Pierce-Cohn popped his head in. "You open?"

Her stomach flip-flopped with the sight of him, but she smiled. "Come on in."

He did and placed a small stack of books on the Formica counter almost before she'd switched back to the circulation screen.

"I think these might be a day or two overdue," he said.

"Let's look." She grabbed a book and scanned the barcode. "Three days, I'm afraid."

He reached into his back pocket and pulled out his wallet.

"You want to renew any of these?"

"Nope. Not mine."

Roseanne Goldberg's name populated the borrower screen. "I can note the charge and Roseanne can pay the fine next time she's in."

"I got it," he mumbled, handing her a five.

"That's awfully nice of you." An icky recognition he probably thought of her as Frank's coconspirator flitted in her gut.

"I told her I'd look these over, but I only had a chance to glance through the first book."

"How was it?" she asked, to be friendly and conversational.

"Interesting." He drummed his fingers on the book atop the remaining pile. "I guess."

Whether it was his expression, the sense he held back around her, or curiosity about the reading he was doing at Roseanne's behest, Maryellen set the book aside as she checked in the other titles. Instead of putting it with the others on the reshelving cart, she opened the drawer below her desk and glanced at the title before stowing it next to her lunch for noontime reading.

ToxiCity.

CHAPTER NINE

Melody Mountain Ranch General Provision 9.6.
Certain areas are designated as common property intended for the
common use and enjoyment of the owners for their recreation
and other related activities.

"*I* mean, my dad was supposed to get out of my hair, and he did in a way, just not for Easter, like I wanted." Eva placed the last of the onyx and seed pearl amulets on the length of purple velvet she'd draped over the multipurpose room podium and started for the art supply closet to put away the pilfered jewelry-making supplies. "But I think I figured out why."

Tyler, who'd been maddeningly chill about the whole thing, stood there looking smug. "Why's that?"

"We're just not powerful enough, yet."

"It's also pretty unpredictable to attempt black magic with green members."

"You know you sound like a full-on witch geek."

"Tyler could have a point," Margaret Estridge said from the door of the all-purpose room where she stood as "youth group" sentry. "Mom says the playground deal made Reverend Griffin like the hero of the neighborhood. Everyone totally loves him even more than usual."

"Love energy can cause problems," Hannah Hunt, who'd spent another week avoiding the math teacher, added.

"Tyler's stepdad doesn't exactly love him." Eva smirked. "I wonder what kind of power an adult would bring to our . . ."

Drills from the security system installers drowned out her final words.

"Don't even think about it," Tyler said.

Hannah ran into the room and whisper-screamed, "Black alert!"

Tyler quickly rolled the remaining jewelry into the velvet drape and stuffed it beneath the podium while Eva unrolled a banner from the end of one of the tables facing the audience. Just as the bottom of *Welcome Rancher Youth* brushed the linoleum, her father popped into the room holding a tray of cookies.

"Afternoon." Her dad nodded, smoothed a crease in his ironed jeans with his free hand, and started toward her. "What's in the offing for today?"

"Busy, busy, busy!" Eva said in her most chipper lilt.

"The Lord provides the wind, but man must raise the sails."

Not that her dad would notice, but Eva flashed what had to be the most ungodly fake smile ever.

"I just dropped in to apologize for the noise disturbance around here this afternoon," Reverend Griffin said. "I'm hoping warm Snickerdoodles will make up for the inconvenience."

"Thanks, Reverend Frank," Margaret said.

"You're welcome," he said. "I have to admit I do have ulterior motives."

Eva managed a nearly imperceptible eye roll. "What is it you want us to do?"

"I'd like your group to help out with the Memorial Weekend festivities."

"Help out how?" She grabbed a cookie of her own and waited for him to knit his brow in disapproval.

"I've asked the homeowner's board to double your current operating budget if your group participates," he said instead.

Murmurs filled the room.

She took a bite. "I'm not sure that's workable for us."

"Evangeline," he said.

"Eva," she said, mid-chew.

"I've also arranged things so that those of you who are interested will have first priority for lifeguard positions and other rec center summer jobs."

"Including me?"

"That's interesting," her father said, grasping the spiral charm of the Goddess amulet she'd forgotten to tuck into her shirt.

"Mrs. Jordan helped me make it," she said quickly. "Pretty, huh?"

"Very." He smiled. "Talk things over kids and let me know as soon as you make a decision."

"Really?"

He gave a cursory wave and started for the door. "Be sure and write YOUTH GROUP MEMBER at the top of any job applications you decide to submit."

"Will do," Tyler said.

"You know what they say," he turned. "If you want children to keep their feet on the ground, put some responsibility on their shoulders."

Eva flipped him the bird as soon as he was gone. "I hope you all realize *maybe* means yes to him."

"I agree your dad's kind of railroading us," Tyler said.

Was there any chance he'd actually let her work at the rec center? "I know, right?"

"It's kinda hard to imagine the Goths in jobs that involve constant sunshine and little red Speedos, but it will double the money in the youth club treasury/ spell fund for a couple days of work," Tyler said.

Everyone laughed.

"He'll work us to the bone that weekend."

"But we'll be able to do more practice spells so the new people will catch up faster."

"The devil's in the details." Reverend Griffin's deep voice boomed through the room of whomever he'd moved on to chatting up as he headed down the hall.

"More money would allow us to do some really tight spells," Heather said.

"As in?" Tyler and Eva said in unison.

At least no one said *jinx*.

"Maybe we could make weed pop up in the community flower beds," one of the Goths said.

"I was sort of thinking it could be cool if we made the model of the playground sink, just like Mr. Pierce-Cohn says it will," Lauren Trautman said.

"That's an awesome idea," Tyler said.

Lauren smiled in his direction.

Eva tried to ignore the hollow feeling that seemed to be growing by the second.

Other than the high-pitched squeal of electric drills, the room fell silent.

"What do you think, Eva?"

"I don't know." She shook her head. "But, I wish they'd stop that damned drilling so we could figure it out in peace."

* * *

"I have cameras set up at the entrances, exits, and high-traffic locations throughout—"

Frank nodded along as if he were listening while the installer from the security company rattled off the specifics of operating the system. His thoughts, however, were on Hope.

He shouldn't be so bugged that his apology wasn't enough for her to apologize in return, and he couldn't seem to let go of the niggling feeling he'd somehow pissed her off. Luckily, she wouldn't continue to harbor whatever it was she was feeling for long. Thanks to Laney Estridge's comment about Hope getting involved in something bigger than herself, he'd come up with a *give and it shall be given to you* solution for whatever strain stood between them.

Banking that she'd show up for the Saturday afternoon aerobics class, he planned a strategic hello for the moment she passed the playground diorama, whereupon he'd teasingly shake a finger in her direction. "I haven't seen your name on anything having to do with the Memorial Weekend playground dedication festivities."

This time, her look of contrition would be unmistakable. "To be honest, I didn't consider getting involved because . . ."

"No worries," he'd say and smile benevolently. "I understand completely."

"I'm sorry," she'd say, a stray tear travelling down her face.

"No need to apologize." He'd look straight into her clear, deep blue eyes.

"I'm just not myself these days. You have to forgive—"

He'd hold up a hand. "Just tell me you'll agree to look over the playground design before it's finalized."

"Wow." She'd look down so he wouldn't see her blush. "I'm honored."

"From everything I hear, you've got quite an eye for both indoor and outdoor design."

The attitude of her gratitude would charge the air around them.

Frank smiled expectantly and looked toward the front door of the rec center in anticipation of her imminent arrival while the security installation technician prattled on. "We just need a decision on final placements for the interior surveillance cameras."

The front door swung open.

"Where would you suggest?" Frank asked.

Hope, dressed in snug workout pants and a sweatshirt, entered the building.

"We should place a camera in the fitness hallway in case of vandalism or theft."

She passed the diorama without a glance and continued on to the drinking fountain.

"Great." Frank took a conversation-ending step in Hope's direction.

"And another one in that blind hallway outside the second floor restrooms."

"Sounds like a plan."

Before he could take another step, Tim Trautman flew past both of them and stopped directly behind Hope.

As Hope bent over to take a drink, Frank was left with his unspoken plan and an unfortunate view of Trautman's backside instead.

* * *

Tim Trautman managed a split second inventory: toned quads, nice slice of tan lower back peeking out between her red workout top and waistband, perfect little butt. God, how he'd love to cup his hands around those round cheeks and . . .

Hope looked up from the water fountain and turned toward him.

With her hair pulled back into a ponytail, her face was even more stunning up close than he'd imagined.

So was her rack.

She was taller than he liked—at least five foot six—but he still had an inch or two on her.

Seven inches in her would be even better.

He struggled to keep his eyes on the deep blue of hers.

"Sorry, I didn't realize you were waiting," she said.

For weeks.

He'd only been a second away from an introduction at church when she'd turned and took off to meet whomever it was that had enticed her away with the promise of a bedroom redo.

"No worries," he said, fighting the urge to dry a stray bead of water from her lower lip with his tongue. Instead, he smiled a sheepish guy-next-door smile, which, conveniently, was true. "I believe we're neighbors."

"Hope Jordan."

He extended his hand. "Tim Trautman."

"Nice to meet you."

Her smile sent his cock to war within the confines of his jock.

"You just moved in to the Smithers' place, right?"

She knew who he was. Maybe the check he'd left on the donation plate had worked its magic after all?

"I finally met your wife, Theresa, over our shared fence yesterday," she said.

Or not.

"Great," he said with a little too much enthusiasm. Nothing like pissing away a grand when Theresa would have felt just as generous and worthy of neighborhood attention with a $500 donation.

"New house and the babies." Her eyes misted over. "You must be thrilled."

"Looking forward to a sharp increase in the chaos, anyway."

"I can only imagine."

With no good way to *not* ask about her family situation, he decided to get it over with. "You have kids?"

Her look of pain was unmistakable. "We're trying."

"Took us almost two years to get pregnant with Lauren." He chuckled and shook his head. "Hard to believe we have numbers four and five on deck."

Her face brightened.

"Enjoy the process because once it happens, you go from drinking wine to drinking from a fire hose."

"Haven't heard that particular analogy before." Her giggle was surprisingly deep and, not surprisingly, sexy. "Makes me feel better than you know."

Before he could manage a *my pleasure*, the power flickered on and off.

"That doesn't bode too well," she said, looking overhead.

He glanced over at Frank who stood by the front desk scowling as he consulted a clipboard held by a security workman. "I think they're putting in the security system."

"Frank's doing quite a job of making sure everyone's safe around here."

Hope Jordan was anything but safe.

She checked her watch. "I'd better get going to my workout class before they cut the power indefinitely."

"I'm headed that direction myself."

"Spinning?" She smiled as they started down the staircase leading to the workout rooms.

If that's where you're going. "I thought I'd check out what's available."

"At two, it's either spinning or muscle madness."

"What do you recommend?"

"That you hurry and grab a bike before they're all gone."

"What about this muscle whatever class?"

As they reached the bottom of the stairs she stopped in front of a set of glass doors. "That's where I'm off to."

He looked into a room filled with enough housewives to give him estrogen poisoning.

Intriguing as it was to spend an hour sweating and breathing alongside Hope, he wasn't about to ruin his chance to do the same on top, or better yet beneath her, by hanging with the girls like Will the petition guy, the only guy in the room. "I think I'll be scooting across the hall."

"Good choice." She turned for the throng of women. "See you later."

"Definitely."

He made it into the spinning studio and staked his claim to a bike by throwing a towel over the handlebars. As he headed for the drink of water he'd missed, he managed to catch another glimpse of that fine ass.

He'd definitely see her later.

* * *

Frank watched Hope and Trautman as they disappeared down the stairs together.

"Mr. Griffin?" the security installation guy asked. "I asked if you had any specific surveillance preferences?"

Frank stepped over to the rail overlooking the basement fitness wing. He needed to catch her so he could at least tell her he wanted to talk to her about the playground plans later. "I'll trust you to place the camera where you feel surveillance is most valuable."

The security workman checked off a box on the paperwork. "Sign off at the bottom for me, then?"

"Back in two seconds." Frank grabbed the clipboard and bolted toward the stairs, but before he'd even reached the landing, Trautman left Hope at the door.

And watched her disappear into the fitness studio.

* * *

Hope deliberately walked past the bathrooms and over to the locker area. She'd sweated way more than usual during class. The dampness between her legs was surely perspiration.

Besides, she wasn't due for nearly a week.

She removed her tank top and felt for the reassuring moisture along the lower elastic of her workout bra before peeling it over her head and tossing it in her locker. As she unhooked the heart rate monitor—her pulse had at no time risen higher than the recommended 150 beats per minute—she felt the pull of a slight cramp.

She swallowed away the sudden thickness in the back of her throat. The cramps were exercise related. Menstrual discomfort was to be expected the week before the period was due. Even when her period wasn't coming at all.

Without bending in any way that might irritate her uterus, she steadied the heel of her left Nike with the other and slid her foot out of the shoe. Using her toe, she removed the right Nike.

Not that she could determine anything definitive with the kind of lightning-quick glance that went unnoticed in a public locker room, but still, as she finished undressing, she avoided the black lining of her yoga pants altogether.

Wrapped in a towel, she carried her toiletries past the hot tub where the post-pregnancy crowd gabbed unselfconsciously about preschools and chicken pox as their surgically renewed breasts bobbed in the Jacuzzi bubbles. She pretended to readjust her towel, but touched the sides of her own breasts for the reassuring tenderness. Careful not to turn the hot spigot too high, Hope put her towel on the hook and stepped into the shower. She shampooed, conditioned, and completed careful circles up and down her legs with the loofah before soaping her body.

Lord, help me to conceive a healthy baby. . . .

The power went out.

The last thing she saw before everything went dark was the crimson streak on her washcloth.

CHAPTER TEN

Section 5.2. No noxious or offensive activity shall be carried on within any property in the Community Association Area, nor shall anything be done that may become a nuisance or cause unreasonable embarrassment or annoyance to others.

"If Jesus didn't want us to be happy and successful, why would he put us in the suburbs and give us this blessed life?" Frank's voice echoed through the auditorium but reverberated through Laney's head.

"A tax day Amen to that," she said to Sarah, seated beside her and wedged between their respective husbands. Then, she sneezed.

"Bless you." Sarah handed her a tissue.

"Next time we meet," Frank said, "we'll discuss our place in the bosom of the Lord . . ."

"Which reminds me," Sarah whispered. "I have something for you."

"A present?"

"Better." Sarah reached into the side pouch of her Coach handbag. "I've found the perfect home-based business for you."

"I've already got a storeroom full of Tupperware, Pampered Chef, and Avon overstock," Laney said. "I'm not sure I can stuff my shelves with any more paraphernalia."

"I promise you won't be stuffing it in your shelves."

"Before you embark upon the glorious week our Lord has planned for you, we have some announcements," Frank continued, "but first, a little treat."

"That's what you said about the ionic foot detoxification system."

"This is different." Sarah handed her a pamphlet. "Very different."

Laney opened the tri-fold to the words *Enticing* and *Compensation.* "Mother's Helpers?"

The choir stood and opened their hymnals.

"This could be a hoot, but—"

"But what?"

Eva Griffin stepped forward. Her dark hair shimmered like a halo under the lights as she began her solo.

"Who would I invite?"

"The regulars—Stacy Simon, Samantha Torgenson, and Jenny Thompson will love it. And you know Will Pierce-Cohn—"

"Loves anything home shopping." Laney tilted her head in Hope Jordan's direction. "But Hope's not going to show up for a party called Mother's Helpers."

"Send her an Evite and tell her it's called Household Helpers. She'll never know the difference until she gets to your house."

"I suppose."

Across the aisle, Theresa Trautman shifted uncomfortably in her seat.

"And how about your very pregnant client over there?"

"In her condition?"

"Neighborhood newbies always buy, no matter what's for sale."

"True." Laney examined the brochure more closely as the choir rejoined Eva and they belted out the chorus.

With the final claps of the crowd, Laney watched Maryellen saunter across the stage in the tiniest of wraparound dresses. She craned the mike to face height and unfolded her announcement list. "On Wednesday, the Mothers of Preschoolers are going on a field trip to the Englewood petting zoo . . ."

"I could make up a flyer and get it to the MOPS moms," Laney whispered. "They're always desperate for get-away-from-the-kiddies activities."

"Yup."

"And if you'll make sure word gets around your rec center classes . . ."

"Done."

Lights illuminated the portable golden cross, showering light onto Maryellen. "But, what do I do about Maryellen?"

"What about her?"

"If she sees everyone pulling up across the street for a party she isn't invited to—"

"Why wouldn't she be invited?"

"Tuesday night," Maryellen's voice trilled through the room, "I'll be moderating the women's club discussion on incorporating Proverbs thirty-one into modern life."

"You're kidding, right?"

"Of course, I'm not kidding."

"But she's a minister's wife."

"Not just any minister." She glanced at Frank, who was whispering intently into the ear of the choir director.

"Meaning what?"

"Meaning, I heard an interesting tidbit about our fair Frank the other day."

"As in?"

Sarah's smile was anything but coy. "Apparently, he's something of a dirty talker."

"Seriously?" Laney couldn't be sure whether the sudden rush came from the idea of Frank's X-rated chatter or Sarah's warm breath in her ear. Other than a few men with the distracting need to announce they were coming, she'd never been with a full-on dirty talker—that she could remember, anyway. "Where did you hear that?"

Sarah pointed her head in the direction of Jane Hunt, who was seated in the front row. "The Griffins' bedroom window faces the Connors' bedroom wall. Jane said Julie Connor hears them going at it all the time."

Jane nodded, as though in confirmation.

Thin walls, closely spaced homes, and sound-conductive siding made for dubious privacy. Luckily her bedroom overlooked the playground and her neighbors to the north were older and didn't socialize with anyone she knew.

"I can't believe . . ."

"Doesn't fit your fantasy about the Rev.?"

"I don't fantasize about Frank." Not regularly, anyway.

"Good, 'cause apparently he's something of a growler, too."

"This week, Cooking with Christ will be at Sue Perkins's home . . ." said Maryellen.

"I can't even picture Maryellen and dirty talk in the same thought."

"Our theme will be the cuisine of Tuscany." Enthusiasm spiked Maryellen's otherwise measured monotone. "Which, I have to say, I'm very excited about and I'm sure you will be too."

Sarah brushed the toe of her pump against Laney's ankle. "Never can tell what turns people on."

* * *

Twenty-four hours had passed since the rec center incident and Eva was still in total shock. One minute her head throbbed from her father's carrot dangling and the squeal of electric drills. The next, she had one overwhelming, all-consuming wish:

Make the noise stop.

Before Tyler had a chance to suggest they think through things, object to the color of the spell, or otherwise mess things up, everyone materialized in a circle around her.

And she was practically speaking in tongues.

Chanting, anyway.

The air charged as the rest of the group joined along.

The rec center lights flickered once.

Went dark.

Totally freaking dark.

Hours after everyone in the coven scampered off and her father returned home from waiting for the Excel energy truck to repair the *transformer blowout*, she buzzed with electricity she could swear transferred straight from the rec center into her body. The second her parents closed their bedroom door for the night, she overrode the parental controls on her computer and Googled anything and everything she'd made up instead of looked up about Witchcraft. By the time she pretended to wake for church, she knew as much about circle casting, voodoo, and White Magick as any of the sanctimonious do-gooders at teenwitch.com.

As far as the darker elements and coven management, she knew more.

A cool breeze rustled Eva's hair and the afternoon sun warmed her face as she stood on the playground gravel pile reveling in the *anything was possible* of it all.

She sang her heart out at church. Afterward, when her father started in on his Sunday *every last page of your homework must be complete before you can so much text a friend* sermon, she simply mentioned that the transformer blowout kept the youth group from officially voting yes on his proposal and, like magic, he did an instant (two-faced) about face. He not only let her call everyone for a meeting, but located her American Eagle hoodie for her before she left the house.

"The Goddess is with us." Eva looked out at the gang seated in front of her on the newly poured concrete pavilion. "So our spells will be successful from now on."

"If we focus our energies and pay attention to the details," Tyler added.

Before yesterday, his I-told-you-so smirk would have pissed her off beyond words. Now, she got how much she needed him to be totally into it for the spells to work right. According to a website called warlockwarriors, *a second-in-command warlock, treated with the proper respect, can and will guarantee the success of every aspect of coven practice.* Eva dug her toe into the hard-packed dirt beneath her feet, looked up, and smiled. "From now on, we won't cast a spell without making sure we do everything right."

"Sounds like a plan." Tyler nodded.

"Tyler was also right about needing extra bucks for spell supplies," she added.

"So we're going to do the Memorial Weekend thing?" Hannah Hunt asked.

"The idea of giving in to my dad kinda makes me want to slit my wrists, but he is offering us the chance to get our spells on faster and better."

Hannah Hunt raised her hand. "Second."

"Everyone else agree?" She held her breath waiting for some objection from Tyler.

All hands went up.

Eva bit the inside of her cheek to keep from grinning. "Okay, in Numerology, the number four stands for success, so, counting yesterday, we need to do three increasingly difficult spells to build up our combined power." She reached into her backpack and pulled out the handout she'd compiled of possible choices. "If you turn the paper over, you'll find the spell I think will be the best to kick things off."

With everyone's agreement, she pulled black feathers and matches from her pocket and joined the group on the concrete. "Lauren, your idea to make the diorama sink matched a spell I found on a website for newer practitioners of the craft, so I'd like you to assist."

"Nice." Tyler pushed Lauren gently toward the center of the circle.

Eva gave her a black feather and a pat on the shoulder. "State your intention."

Lauren stepped forward and bowed her head. Her voice, sugary with a slight lisp, carried in the wind. "I will the playground to sink."

"We now restate Lauren's intention together and repeat the chant three times." Eva reached out her hands, one to Tyler and the other to Lauren. She had to move things along before her dad stuck his head out the door to let her know the comradeship timer had gone off.

As everyone shuffled into a tight circle, Eva found herself holding hands with Lauren on her left and one of the Goths to her right. Tyler had taken it upon himself to move around her and grasp Lauren's other hand.

Eva managed not to bitch about not following directions or flash him a look. *A second-in-command warlock, treated with the proper respect, can and will guarantee the success of every aspect of coven practice.* Instead, she smiled sweetly in his direction. "Ready to go for it?"

A feather slipped from her hand and brushed her face as it floated upward in the wind.

The Goddess clearly approved.

* * *

The beep of the oven timer distracted Maryellen from fully digesting the sentence she'd already reread twice: *Stachybotrys is another fungi that has the ability to produce mycotoxins, ones that are extremely toxic, suspected carcinogens, and immunosuppressive.*

"God love her." Frank peered out through the side window blinds. "Evangeline has those kids in a prayer circle."

Maryellen opened the drawer on the table beside her reading chair, pulled a Post-it off the pad, and marked the passage from the book Will had returned for Roseanne Goldberg. "She really does want to be called Eva."

He turned toward the kitchen and the infernal timer. "Have we heard back from the summer leadership program yet?"

"Not yet." She didn't add that she might have accidentally mistaken the information for a mortgage refinance inquiry and shredded it along with a pile of Money Mailers and catalogs. "She mentioned something about wanting to work at the rec center with her friends this summer."

"Our girl's a Chief." He reached into the refrigerator and grabbed one of the diet Red Bulls she stocked for his afternoon pick-me-up. "Those jobs are for the Indians."

Maryellen fumbled for her glasses, leaned sideways, and glanced out the window at their *chief*. "I don't think she's going to want to go away to that camp."

"Don't worry about Eva," he said. "She'll thank us someday for honing her natural skill."

Maryellen glanced at the photo atop the piano of three-year-old Eva with her sweet smile and angelic blond curls. As she looked back outside and watched the kids let go of each other's hands, the same low dread came over her that she felt when she caught the faint aroma of burnt wax and incense in the basement after their meetings.

The same bad feeling she'd had when Tyler had checked out that book on Witchcraft as research for a history project.

She took a calming breath. Whatever they were doing at the playground, in addition to voting about Frank's committee, they were doing in plain view of the house. Besides, everything she'd read said rebelliousness and experimentation were part and parcel of the teenage experience. Unfortunately, Frank, who started across the entry hall toward the front door, was unlikely to agree. If he so much as spotted Eva holding that feathered whatever it was they seemed to be passing around, he'd ship her off to Christian military school so fast it would be like Maryellen never had a daughter in the first place.

The only daughter she'd ever have.

Maryellen waved her book to distract Frank. "Roseanne Goldberg's been reading up about mold."

"Mold is the Fibromyalgia of the new millennium," he said, but kept walking.

Maryellen lifted her readers from her neck and opened to the page she'd marked. "It says here that a family in Texas—"

"Probably wasn't leaving food and pouring drinks on the family room carpet."

She snuck another peek out the window. The kids hadn't started to disperse. "I just hope Roseanne's not collecting information to build some case against the homeowner's board."

"HOB isn't on the hook." He reached the door. "We suspended all fines this month."

"Couldn't she be overzealous and file a nuisance suit?"

He grasped the door handle. "If she does, I'll file a counter-suit for all the pain and suffering I deal with around here over hocus-pocus."

"I'll round Eva up." Maryellen stood.

"I'm already right here," he said.

"I need her to help me carry in some yard sale goodies I left in the trunk of the car," she said on her way down the hall. She was in the garage and had the door rolling upward before Frank opened the front door.

Eva turned toward the house with the sound of the front door and garage opening simultaneously. Luckily, she was both empty handed and smiling.

Maryellen waited by the open trunk of the car while she said good-bye to her friends and sauntered back over.

"I knew I had to come home and everything." Eva exhaled heavily as she reached the garage. "You didn't both have to stand there and wait."

Maryellen picked up an antique cookie jar and handed it to her daughter. "I needed a hand with some of this stuff."

As Eva examined the hand-painted Three Little Pigs scene, an airplane passed overhead.

"Does this mean you're actually going to eat some of the cookies you're constantly making for everyone else?"

With the extraneous noise, Maryellen wasn't sure she'd heard the question correctly.

"Won't it be darling in the kitchen?" she said by way of answer.

CHAPTER ELEVEN

Section 9.1. Declarant's Rights to Grant and Create Easements:
Declarant hereby reserves the right to grant and create temporary
or permanent easements provided such easements do not create a
permanent, unreasonable interference with the rights of the owners.

*H*ope passed a Super Target, a Safeway, and countless gas-station mini-marts. She was halfway into Denver proper and still couldn't bring herself to stop. It was hard enough to get out of bed and make herself presentable enough to go grocery shopping. The effort involved in getting out of the car for a gallon of milk before Jim came home from Dallas or Detroit or wherever he'd been for however many days—three or four—seemed insurmountable.

Maybe it was time to face the fact there might never be milk in the house.

Maybe they should never have bought a family house in the first place.

Even though she'd cried more tears in the last three days than she could possibly produce, a whole new batch began to drip down her cheeks. Approaching Leetsdale and Monaco, she grabbed a handful of tissue and tried to pull herself together enough to stop in at the King Soopers on the southeast corner.

A misshapen stucco building caught her eye first.

Set back at an angle, on an inconvenient bend in the road, the structure appeared to be a house, re-fronted and refaced at some point to look commercial. With a Broncos purple front door and matching windowsills, she couldn't believe she'd never noticed the place before.

Or the sign:

Readings by Renata
Walk-ins Welcome

Hope made a questionable U-turn from a left-only lane for a drive-thru Starbucks and found herself in the tiny lot parking beside a dented Explorer. The view to whatever chicanery awaited inside was obscured by stained-glass decals covering the front window. A turban-headed woman gazed into her mist-filled crystal ball from the hand-drawn sign propped in the window in front of her.

Hope climbed out of her car, stepped up the rickety wooden steps, and opened the door.

"Have a look at the menu." Renata, ostensibly, said over the jangling bells twisted around the inside doorknob. "I'll be right out."

Trying not to read too much into the Muzak version of "You Can't Always Get What You Want," Hope stepped into the crimson wallpapered front room filled with antique parlor furniture. She sat on the edge of a worn velvet, high-backed couch and looked up at a gilt-edged mirror on which an elaborate list of offerings were written in gold ink.

The Tea and Tarot package caught her eye.

So did the unsettling lack of prices next to the various services.

Before she had time to consider the psychic ramifications of getting fleeced, the inner door opened and Renata, requisite red hair, abundant bosom, and flowing caftan, appeared in a stereotypical mist of incense and rose perfume.

Had the woman not been carrying a tray with a teapot and two cups, Hope assured herself, she'd already be in a rush home, with or without her half-gallon of milk.

"I just went out to get some groceries," Hope said. "I'm not exactly the type to . . . I mean I've never stopped in at a psychic before, but . . ."

"But here you are," Renata said.

She felt both more relaxed and tense at the same time. "Here I am."

"I don't feel Tarot is going to be necessary today." Renata seemed disarmingly kind as she sat and set the tea service on the coffee table in front of them. "I think your leaves will tell us enough."

Had she even said she was looking at the Tea and Tarot package?

Renata poured the tea into two white cups and pushed one over to Hope. "Wait a minute for the tea to cool, drink, but leave a tiny bit of liquid and the leaves in the bottom of the cup."

Hope watched the leaves swirl then settle in her cup. "How much will the reading be?"

Renata lifted her cup and blew lightly across the top. "Not more than you can afford."

A tea reading minus the Tarot couldn't be any more than an hour with the masseuse or, at worst, a day at the spa. If the woman was a total charlatan wouldn't she have tried to add services, not subtract? Besides, she could always refuse to pay if Renata saw fit to charge some outrageous amount, or better yet, she could say nothing, pay with a credit card, and then dispute the amount later if . . .

"Clear your mind of all extraneous thoughts and concerns," Renata said. "And concentrate on whatever it is that brought you in to see me."

For the next few minutes, they sat next to each other in an oddly peaceful silence punctuated only by the sounds of polite sipping until everything else fell away and only one question remained:

Will I ever get pregnant and when?

Renata reached for the cup as Hope finished her second-to-last sip. She held the handle in her left hand, covered the top with her right, and swirled clockwise three times.

"How do the leaves . . . ?"

"The tea leaves form images." Renata peered into the cup at the brown clumps on the sides and bottom of the cup. "I see in yours that one great desire has overtaken all others."

Hope took a deep breath to calm her pounding heart. Didn't everyone who walked into the roadside psychic have some burning question they needed answered?

"Many women come to me with the ache that can only be relieved by the divine pain of childbirth." She shook her head. "And so often I see a long, difficult path ahead."

"I thought it would be so easy." The black sinking feeling Hope knew so well settled deeper into her soul. "I get my period like clockwork every four weeks and I eat right and I exercise. There aren't any issues the doctor can find wrong with either of us that would keep us from getting pregnant . . ."

"But in your cup, I see an open book with an oar and a leaf upon it."

"Meaning?"

"A new life is ready to come through very soon."

Crazy as it was to buy into the words of a woman who'd just read the muck in the bottom of her cup, the heaviness of a second ago and the last ten months gave way to a lightness so intense, she put a hand on the armrest as if to keep from floating away. "Really?"

Renata, still staring into the cup, shook her head. "But, I also see ants."

"Ants?"

"And a forked line." Renata looked up.

"Meaning?"

"Impending difficulties and a coming decision."

A fog of terror snuffed out the light. "Like there might be something wrong with the baby?"

Renata tilted her head sideways and examined a leaf configuration stuck to the side of the cup. "I don't think so. There's an oak tree—which means robust health."

The fog, thick and unforgiving, lifted again. "We would love any baby we were blessed with, I guess it's just that in all the effort involved in trying to get pregnant, I guess I never considered the possibility that something could be . . ."

"Your marriage."

"What about it?"

"Is it a happy one?"

"Happy?"

Renata nodded.

Before she met Jim, her definition of a happy marriage would have included living somewhere like Soho, owning a funky little mid-century modern furniture store, and spending evenings and weekends with her soul mate debating the merits of the film or play they'd managed to take in despite the shared demands of their growing family. The parameters necessarily changed when they married and he got a job in Denver, but how could she complain about what could only be called a comfortable existence? There were times when she did wonder why, when they looked and seemed so well-suited, were from such similar backgrounds, and had the same long-term goals, they didn't have more in common to talk about? She wished she felt more out-of-control, madly in love instead of just meant to be, but maybe that was too Hollywood to expect, given their even temperaments. "I'm not unhappy."

"That's not what I asked."

The answer, that she really believed once they had a baby, were a real family, the inadequacies would fade and they would truly be happy, was too trite to actually utter aloud. "I mean, the stress of trying to get pregnant and Jim's work schedule make things a little more trying, but I'd say we're content."

"I see." Renata paused for an overlong moment. "Well, that could explain the boiling kettle. There is also a wheel, which indicates business advancement."

"My husband is something of a workaholic, which is challenging in the short run, but in the long run is good, I think."

"I don't typically find answers for one spouse by looking into the other's tea leaves."

"I do have my own business. It's small, but I plan to grow it once I have kids and they are in school and stuff."

"The garden and anchor must relate to that."

Hope shifted in her seat, suddenly itchy to get to the grocery store. "Meaning what?"

"A party and an awkward situation."

"Weird," Hope said. "I'm not really sure how those symbols relate to me."

"You will."

"And will I be pregnant, soon?"

"That is definitely one of the paths that lies directly before you."

* * *

The psychic otherworld of low lighting, velvet draperies, and a future foretold in wet leaves faded into the mundane reality of strip malls and box stores as Hope headed home with milk. Still, the paltry $25 she'd paid for what anyone in their right mind would say was a brilliantly orchestrated parlor game, was more satisfying, more healing to her aching psyche, than any hour she'd spent with a therapist, or listening to Frank's soothing but ultimately unsatisfying message.

A new life is ready to come through very soon.

She set her grocery bags on the counter next to her flashing phone. Three days had passed since she'd answered a call from anyone but Jim. Even then, she had to summon all her strength to mask her devastation. She grabbed the milk jug and a block of cheddar from the bag and started for the refrigerator. On the way back to get the orange juice and a few containers of yogurt, she jiggled the mouse beside the computer on the built-in kitchen desk.

She hadn't checked e-mail at all.

After rooting through and deleting the junk, she opened her Yahoo fertility and interior decorator chat groups, glanced at the conversation thread topics, and printed out an e-mail for filing away from someone who wanted to be added to her holiday décor list. Despite the warmth of traipsing around the kitchen putting away groceries, a chill rushed through her when she spotted the last remaining message. An Evite:

EVERYONE NEEDS A HOUSEHOLD HELPER!
GET YOURS WHEN YOU COME!
THURSDAY, APRIL 26th
10 AM
DON'T MISS THIS ONE!!!!!!
BIG REGRETS ONLY!
laney@laneyenterprises.com

Much as she dreaded oohing and aahing over stuff she didn't need or want at a multilevel, home-shopping party, *big regrets*, particularly in light of Renata's mention of a *party,* seemed too ominous a warning to ignore.

So did the red message alert blinking on the phone.

She pressed the button.

Hope, Frank Griffin here . . .

CHAPTER TWELVE

Section 4.4.17. Landscaping: A maximum of 25 percent
of the unimproved area of each Lot may be landscaped
with a combination of short-lived landscape materials as approved
by the HOA and maintained in a neat, attractive, sightly,
and well-kept condition.

"*I* really needed another pair of eyes on this." Frank unrolled the landscape design blueprints on the table beside the diorama. He paused to look earnestly into the ocean blue of Hope's eyes. "Yours."

Hope's smile was as genuine as he'd ever seen it.

"I'm glad you called," she said.

Glad hardly covered his feelings. After the near-miss with her at the rec center, he'd kept an eye on her house for nearly three days, waiting for Hope to go on a run, take out the trash—anything that would give him a chance to start up the conversation that would culminate in her agreement to oversee the playground planting.

"After I got your message, I ran by the sites and looked around." Hope glanced at the outstretched plans. "I'm eager to see the plans."

The Lord, in his grace and wisdom, finally led him to a window just as Hope's garage door rolled open. The minute she drove away, he went to the phone and left a more-humble-than-in-person, *favor to ask* message.

She called back by early afternoon, not only positive, but also eager to meet with him.

"Hope." His shoulder brushed hers as he joined her in looking at the already near-perfect design. "I appreciate your professionalism in light of what I realize are objections to the project."

She looked away. "I never really had a problem with the proposal per se."

Laney and Sarah's comment about the effect of fertility drugs on the psyche helped him swallow the acid burbling in the back of his throat. "But you did sign Will's petition?"

Her cheeks colored. "He sort of caught me at a bad time."

"I see," he said, hoping for something more along the lines of, *I couldn't face looking at the playground with my empty womb,* or *Will wouldn't leave until I signed,* or even a far-fetched, *the fertility drugs made me do it.* "Well, I'm glad you're on board, now," he said, to break a looming awkward silence. "As I've said, I know you'll enjoy *all* the benefits of a playground across the street soon."

"Thanks." Her face, beautiful to begin with, glowed with what seemed to be a new confidence. "I'm in a much better place about everything related to that now."

"Good," he said, and sensing the lack of need for an additional platitude or word of advice by the way she dug into the plans, said nothing more.

"Have plant materials been ordered?" she asked.

"Not yet."

"So there's flexibility on substitutions?"

"Shouldn't be a problem. Why?"

"The half-court plan looks great," she said. "But I'm afraid the flowers slated to go alongside could get trampled."

"I see what you mean." Much as he would have preferred a more personal interchange, what more could he hope for than Hope, standing beside him, visualizing the soon-to-be flowers on his playgrounds. "Good call."

And smelling of lilac.

"I'm thinking a hearty grass or a pea gravel would wear better," she said.

He glanced at the area in question. With Hope on board, couldn't the *sorry* he thought he wanted be considered an unnecessary technicality? Furthermore, if she did a good job, who was to say where their partnership might lead, particularly once the church began to take shape?

He pointed to a corner of the diorama. "How about moving the pea gravel slated to go behind the retaining wall and swap it with flowers—at least for the northerly playground."

"Hmm." Hope scrunched her nose as she examined the diorama.

"If you want to take the plans home and look them over before—"

"Definitely," she said. "But . . ."

"But what?"

Hope narrowed her eyes. "Does that leg of the play structure look a little bit crooked to you?"

CHAPTER THIRTEEN

Careful landscape planning and detailed design of your site will greatly enhance the ultimate appearance of our Blue Ribbon Community—From the Melody Mountain Ranch Homeowner's Welcome Packet.

Tim Trautman spotted a silver Volvo at the intersection of Melody Highlands Road and Songbird Canyon Court. What were the chances the driver, blond, with the same car and coming out of Hope Jordan's street, wasn't her?

He slowed to allow the car, to make a right turn ahead of him.

Definitely her.

The groceries and dry cleaning he'd picked up for Theresa would keep. Considering he'd brought home lunch every day since the doctor put her on semi-bed rest last week, so would her sandwich.

Maintaining a safe distance, he followed Hope's Volvo past the treble clef pillars at the development entrance and out onto Parker Road. He tailed her for a few miles, trailing to the right and a car back, until she merged into the left lane and turned into Home Depot.

He high-fived the dashboard. There was always something he wanted or needed at the hardware store.

He pulled into the turn lane for the second entrance and swung into the lot. She parked. He grabbed a space two rows away, facing Hope's car, but partially blocked from view by a PT Cruiser. With an unobstructed view of Hope's perfect heart of an ass, he dialed home and left a *last minute deal* message.

She got out of her car, walked across the lot, passed the main entrance, and headed for the greenhouse on the side of the building. The second she disappeared through the sliding doors, he popped a mint, hopped out of his Acura, and dragged a flat cart across the lot.

The doors slid open and he stepped into the humid loamy garden department.

Before he'd cleared the registers, or began to navigate the maze of potting soil and fertilizer, he spotted her. Like a jeans-clad Aphrodite, she stood against a backdrop of terra-cotta planters, patio furniture, and cascading backyard fountains amid a rainbow of multicolored blooms.

He rolled his cart next to a table of flowering cacti.

"We meet again," he said, keeping his eyes on her face, more specifically her lips. Full and gloss-shiny, they could only look more sensual if they were, say, wrapped around his cock.

"Tim." Her smile ranged somewhere between perfunctory and neighborly, but she remembered his name. "With a new house, I guess I should expect to run into you here."

"And the grocery store, the drug store, the cleaners," he said, in case she were inclined to have a chance encounter elsewhere. "Theresa needs to take it easy for the next little while, so I've stepped in as the family gofer."

"That's sweet of you."

With the word *sweet*, any sour thoughts he may have harbored about his upcoming months of post-, and now prebirth, indentured servitude vanished in the floral mist. The dutiful father routine, played right, could possibly kill two birdies, Theresa and Hope, with one stone. "We're all pitching in, but really, Theresa's doing the hard part of this deal."

Hope's smile warmed.

Score.

"And running to the hardware store isn't exactly a hardship for me."

She eyed a table of fledgling bushes with a reverence that gave him the seeds of a possibly perfect idea. "Did I hear something about you doing landscaping?"

"Mostly I do interiors." She ran her fingers along the branches of a potted fir. "But Frank Griffin asked me to consult on the final landscaping for the new playgrounds."

The man was clearly no dummy, hiring her instead of some leathery, grizzled landscaper.

"Perfect." He turned to examine a table covered in flats of purple blooms. "Because I came in thinking I might surprise Theresa by planting the flower beds."

"I'm sure she'll love that."

He shoots. He scores again.

"Problem is, I don't know the first thing about what to get." He did his best befuddled look at the never-ending racks of flowers. "I've heard something about not planting before Memorial Day but . . ."

"Depends on what you're looking for. The hearty annuals should be okay, and the common varieties are on the covenant-approved list. It's the perennials where things get sticky."

The word *sticky* hung in the loamy air between them.

"Annuals, perennials—I wouldn't know the difference." He smiled. "I just need the flowers to be pink."

"All pink?"

"We're having girls, so I thought that might be a fun touch for Theresa."

Her eyes, blue and glassy, misted over.

Hat trick.

"I noticed some healthy looking lobelia on the way in," she said wistfully. "Pansies are always nice. And petunias . . ."

"Petunias," he said. "I know she likes petunias."

"Right behind us." Hope turned toward a tiered rack overflowing with flowers.

He smiled as he grabbed a few grow packs filled with pink and white striped blooms. "What's your favorite flower?"

"I love lilies, but I wouldn't recommend them if you're not much of a gardener." She handed him two flats filled with some sort of scarlet blooms. Her flushed cheeks matched the flowers in her hand. "When are you planning to plant?"

"As soon as possible."

"You'll need to." She stuck a finger into an eight-pack of pink and white flowers. "The soil and roots are dry."

Resisting a comment as to how dry his root really was, he said, "Theresa's going out tomorrow morning for a couple hours, so I was thinking I'd sneak home and get it done."

Hope glanced into his cart, which was quickly filling with a variety of pink blooms. "Where are you going to keep them in the meantime?"

"I thought I might stow them along the north side of the house."

"Can't she see them from the family room window?"

"If she looks."

"If she does, the surprise will be ruined."

"True," he said. "I guess I could keep them in my car."

"They'll never make it."

"Or—"

"Or, you're welcome to hide your flowers in my yard."

Tim bit the inside of his cheek to keep from grinning. "That would be amazing."

CHAPTER FOURTEEN

Section 3.2. Nuisance: The owner of any Lot shall not suffer or permit any noxious or offensive activity to be conducted, carried on, or practiced in any residence or for any purpose.

*W*ill gave Laney Estridge an air kiss to avoid a crimson smudge of her party hostess war paint and stepped into her front hall. The short leather skirt, stilettos, and tight top she wore, a far cry from her usual business casual sweater set and pearl ensemble, boded an interesting morning, whatever Mother's Helpers turned out to be.

"We'll get started, soon." Laney flashed a flirty smile, handed him a pink-stemmed champagne flute, and disappeared behind the French doors into the vestigial living room cum staging area for ever-sharp knives, allergenic vacuum cleaners, or whatever it was she was trying to hawk.

He never expected to stomach, much less appreciate, multilevel marketing in the context of a social get-together, but there was no denying the convenience in picking up reasonably priced jewelry, clothing, and culinary gadgets at a neighbor's house instead of having to brave the mall.

Will took a sip of a mimosa, savored the warm kick in his throat, and sniffed the air for a hint of Pampered Chef or something with taste testing. In his hurry to get everyone off and the house straightened, he'd forgotten to grab breakfast. Other than the cinnamon and vanilla from pillar candles, there was no distinctive aroma intermingling with the perfumed air.

Probably a home décor deal.

If so, he'd stick around for whatever Costco munchies were to be had, pick up a few aromatherapy candles or whatever, and say his good-byes. With any luck, he'd have time to squeeze in a quick workout before he was due in the twins' class to help make stone soup.

He headed for the great room.

Laney's obtuse invitation seemed to have sparked the curiosity of just about everyone. The usual suspects were clustered together on the sectional, but the rest of the room was nearly packed. The aerobics class regulars were there in force. A group of younger mothers were seated on the ledge along the double-sided gas log fireplace. Maryellen Griffin was in the front row. Even Roseanne

Goldberg, who never came to these things, was seated on a recliner facing the doorway. Luckily, she was too engrossed in conversation with the pregnant woman next to her to acknowledge him or the swamped-with-family-demands-let's-chat-soon e-mail he'd sent her.

Everyone seemed to be there.

He scanned the accent furniture and bar stools.

Except for Hope Jordan.

He glanced at his watch. The party didn't officially start for another ten minutes.

"I'm going to pick up something and get out of here," a woman he didn't know whispered to her friend as he walked by. "I need to get to the grocery store before preschool pickup."

"Know what we're buying?"

"Laney's been hush-hush," the grocery shopper's friend said. "But I thought I heard something about spices."

"I heard toys," Samantha Torgenson said from a nearby recliner.

"I guess we'll find out soon enough." Will spotted an open seat that didn't face the window overlooking the playground construction. "What's to munch on?"

"So far, we've only been offered mimosas."

Peeking into the open pass-through, he spotted assorted platters covered in plastic wrap and aluminum foil on the breakfast table. "I think I'll check out the food before things get rolling."

"Let us know if there's anything interesting."

"For sure." Will tossed his sweatshirt across two empty chairs. If Hope showed up, there probably wouldn't be an open spot for her otherwise.

He slid through the kitchen door.

One glance through the pink, purple, and blue Saran Wrap and his rumbling stomach fell silent. A coffee cake, baked in the shape of a penis, complete with iced testicles and scrotum, sat next to a plate of muffins, iced pink and topped with raspberries. Other platters held unpeeled bananas in neat rows between facedown kiwi halves, cocktail weenies skewered to pearl onions, and grape-accented peach slices. Circles of goat cheese lay on round crackers, topped with Craisins.

Sarah Fowler, wearing a leather skirt, black top, and crimson lipstick identical to Laney's, appeared in the kitchen via the dining room. She put a hand on his shoulder and guided him back toward the swinging door. Before she pushed him back into the great room, she handed him an anatomically correct piece of white chocolate, complete with milk chocolate shavings groomed into the shape of a pubic hair heart. "Vagina to tide you over?"

* * *

Hope slid her patio door open and ambled out to her deck at 10:05, exactly as planned. What Tim didn't plan on was her sheer pink blouse, or the view of her legs in wedge heels and an above-the-knee jean skirt. The inherent pleasure was bittersweet. Since yesterday's chance meeting at Home Depot, he'd done little else but fantasize about her, dressed in a tight tank top and loose overalls, eager to spend an hour planting with him.

He crossed his yard toward their shared fence. "You look nice and ready for spring."

"I wish. Try a home shopping party at Laney Estridge's."

"I didn't realize you'd be going." It hadn't occurred to him that she'd have anything to do with a Mother's Helpers party. "I mean, you didn't mention it yesterday."

"I generally try to avoid home shopping." She shook her head, but seemed otherwise nonplussed by his presumptive gaffe. "But it seemed like the thing to do at the time."

"I know Theresa was looking forward to the party."

"She's all but on bed rest, right?"

He nodded.

"Pretty much explains her enthusiasm." Hope shook her head. "Have you ever been to a party full of housewives clucking over housewares?"

"Can't say I have." He tried to cull the disappointment of losing already stolen time from his voice. "But I should probably grab my plants so I don't keep you. I dropped Theresa off over there almost fifteen minutes ago."

"Honestly, there's nothing I'd like more than an excuse to show up late."

"In that case," his pulse quickened with a revived sense of chase, "join me to dig around in the dirt?"

She smiled. "Wish I could, but I can delay the inevitable a little by helping you get the flowers into your place."

"You're not exactly dressed for gardening." He allowed himself a lingering glance that included her legs. "I'll just come around and—"

"Laney's family room window faces my house. There's a good chance someone from the party will see you in my yard."

Maybe she wasn't dressed for spending a stolen hour together, but her willingness to show up late, coupled with her attention to secrecy, was encouraging. "That would kind of defeat the purpose."

"Which is why I already loaded your flowers into my trunk."

His gardening fantasy was taking a potentially more interesting turn.

She dangled her car keys. "I'll just drive around the block to your house and you can unload them right from my car."

"Wow. Thanks." He didn't even try to moderate his shit-eating grin. "I'll be waiting with open garage."

* * *

Before Will could figure how to exit the now standing-room-only crowd, the living room doors flew open and disco music filled the room. In a scene eerily reminiscent of Frank's diorama unveiling, a middle-aged brunette, stuffed into an outfit matching Laney and Sarah's, pushed a drape-covered cart into the room.

She whisked off the cloth covering the rolling table, picked up a fur-tipped riding crop, and waved it over a table filled with every sexual aid imaginable. "I'm Kitty and I'd like to welcome you to Mother's Helpers!"

Hoots and hollers filled the room.

"I knew this was going to be a Fuckerware party," Roseanne Goldberg shouted.

"The politically correct term is Interpersonal Intimacy Enhancement gathering," Kitty said.

Will took a bite of the melting chocolate vagina he clutched in his sweaty palm. "Definitely not Pampered Chef, is it?"

"Concept's basically the same," said Stephanie from weights class, who'd commandeered the chair he'd saved for Hope. "Lots of gadgets you think you have to have and then don't really use."

Will eyed an ethnically diverse assortment of dildos on the table. They all eclipsed him in either length or girth, and mostly both. "Hope you're right."

Thank God Hope hadn't shown up.

He looked past a group of giggling women seated near Kitty's table and scanned the room for someone heading toward the door, or at least looking as uncomfortable as he felt. Maryellen Griffin had slunk into her front row seat, clutching her purse. That she made no move to leave was undoubtedly the result of shock, but if she wasn't leaving, he couldn't either.

Not without looking like some kind of total prude, anyway.

Stephanie patted his knee. "Relax and go with the flow."

As her hand lingered on his thigh, he had to admit the idea, and her newly bleach blond pixie cut, did have a certain appeal.

"Edible undies!" Lisa Simon, who was seated to his right, squealed. "I've been wanting those forever."

A cute brunette who was seated beside the side goodies table examined a set of Ben-Wa balls.

Fact was, if he weren't the only man in the room, he'd be enjoying not only a beer instead of champagne, but the delighted squeals of the women all around him.

As Kitty explained the one-on-one, ultra-private ordering and delivery process, Will settled into a calm, up-for-a-good-time expression. How often did a man get a socially acceptable opportunity to watch a room full of horny housewives giggle like schoolgirls over X-rated toys and products?

"Ready to talk birds and bees?" Over catcalls that would embarrass a construction dude, Kitty picked up a decorative tin from the table behind her. "Our first product is Honey Bunny." She reached for the hand of a woman seated closest to the front table and dusted the length of her forearm. "And it's the best body powder you've ever tasted."

"You're supposed to eat it?" Maryellen Griffin asked.

"What goes on between two people in the privacy of their bedroom is always better when it's 100 percent organic." Kitty dipped a feather duster into the powder. "Give me your hand."

Maryellen's face had to be as flushed as her neck. "Mine?"

"Don't worry," Kitty said. "It won't sting."

"She looks like she wants to die," Lisa mumbled.

"Or she's imagining her evening festivities," Stephanie said. "I hear the Rev. Frank's a big time dirty talker."

Will couldn't help but laugh at a rumor implying Frank had a not at all surprising predilection for hearing himself talk. "Ugh."

"Apparently he's a growler, too."

"Total TMI," Will managed.

Kitty ran the duster along Maryellen's forearm. "Taste it."

All eyes fell on poor Maryellen as she took a hesitant lick of her wrist.

"Best of all, it's calorie free!"

Maryellen ran her tongue toward her elbow. "Mmmm."

Sarah appeared in front of him and dusted his arm with powder.

Laney whisked Stephanie and Lisa.

"Honey Bunny is $11.95 and available in both Wildflower and Cherry Blossom," Kitty announced.

"The cherry's kind of tart," Lisa whispered. "Did you get the wildflower?"

Before he could lift his hand to his mouth for a taste test, she leaned over, smiled seductively, and licked his forearm. "It's yummy. Try it."

"Your wish is my command." He licked his wrist.

Wild honey flavor began to dance on his tongue.

"Don't fill up." Kitty reached into a bin marked Mummy's Yummys, pulled out a tube of red gel, and squirted a blob on her finger. "There's much more to come."

* * *

Beautiful in an old school, Grace Kelly way, Hope didn't seem the affair type. While angelic looks and unexpected sexual predilections were anything but mutually exclusive, the chance of a less-than-gorgeous-but-more-than-eager neighbor charming a woman like her into bed by impressing her with flower planting for his pregnant wife was less than zero.

The challenge alone practically made Tim hard.

He snuck a glance at Hope before setting a flat of flowers along the wall of his garage and headed back to her car for another armload. "Thank you again for making this so easy."

"Glad to help." She handed him a bag of plant food.

She wanted him.

"I have to admit I'm still in awe over what an incredible gesture this is for your wife."

Even if she didn't realize it yet.

His *aw shucks* look wasn't quite sincere, but Hope's admiration, combined with what he knew would come in the way of appreciation from Theresa, was enough to make anyone grin like a total fool. "I'm just lucky my business allows me flexibility to do stuff like this."

She turned away toward the open door leading into his house. "Theresa and the kids are awfully lucky, too."

"Don't know about that." He couldn't tell whether her angsty expression was from some internal thought or the dizzying black and red wallpaper lining the hallway. Either way, he'd probably poured the sappy family man shtick on a little thick. "I'm sure Theresa expects me around a lot with two new babies and all the work she wants done to the house."

Hope took a step closer to the back hall. "Did you put up the wallpaper or is that the work of the former owners?"

"Here when we moved in."

"I've heard the Smithers had some out-there taste," she said.

"Theresa calls the wallpaper brothel chic."

Hope graced him with that low, throaty giggle.

"You've never been inside?"

"They invited us over one night, but it didn't . . . It wasn't . . ."

Somehow, asking about the swapping rumors he'd heard about them, even given his not entirely pure intentions, seemed tawdry.

"I always wanted to see this mural of Paris everyone talks about," she said.

"Wish you could, but Theresa insisted we paint over it right away."

"Probably a good idea." She looked slightly disappointed.

Not as disappointed as him. Luckily, there were plenty more Smithers touches for an interior decorator to marvel over. "We're so overwhelmed by the rest we don't know where to go next."

At least Theresa was.

"From everything I've heard, I can only imagine."

"Don't have to." Tim smiled at the opportunity that fell like a plum in his lap as he grabbed the last flat of peonies from her trunk. "Come on in and I'll show you."

* * *

"The Electrician, The Handyman, and Pool Boy are in stock so you can take them home today." Kitty spritzed the air with a spray bottle. "And all Household Helpers over $50 come with a complimentary bottle of antibacterial Clean'm up."

Laurie, who lived three streets over and had triplets, wrinkled her nose. "I can't imagine cleansing spray alone can clean that stuff up properly."

"You don't want to use anything else." Kitty caressed a metallic dildo with ROTOROOTERMAN tattooed along the shaft and handed it to the woman on her left to pass around the room. "Regular soap can crack plastic and latex, harboring nasty little germs. "

"Just like the real thing." Jane, sitting two seats to Will's left, shook her head. "That Roto Rooter scares me almost as much as a real Roto Rooter man."

"I'd be scared of men if I were Jane too," Lisa whispered. "With her ex-husband becoming her ex-wife and all."

"Can't even imagine." Distasteful as the current toys sounded, Will couldn't help but appreciate the social lubricant inherent in edible shaving cream and crotchless lingerie, if not dildos named after workmen.

"I don't know what's worse, finding your husband in bed with another woman or having your husband turn into one."

"Hard to say," Will said. "At least for me."

"Anyone here ever wonder about your spouse's whereabouts from time to time?" Kitty set The Cable Man, a black dildo with rotating balls, back into a silk-lined carrying case. She reached into a plastic tub marked His Pleasures. "Especially when he's out of town or off on an extra-long business lunch?"

"Or she!" Will said.

Kitty held up a hot dog bun–sized gel-filled equivalent of a toddler arm floatie. "It's called the Love Slave."

"Never mind," he added.

Giggles erupted around the room.

"You laugh, but send him off with one of these and some strawberry Love Him or Lube Him and he'll come back head over heels." Kitty squirted a blob of lubricant into one end. "And you'll know exactly who, or, should I say, what he's in love with."

Kitty stepped around the table, headed across the room, and handed the lubed sleeve to Will.

He ran his hand through his already mussed hair. "Pour moi?"

"Put your fingers inside and roll the casing back and forth over your hand," Kitty said.

"Here goes nothing." He plunged his fingers into the hot pink tube.

Felt his face erupt in a goofy smile.

* * *

"Theresa's going to love your advice about removing those poufy curtains and repainting in a neutral color," Tim said, taking in Hope's depth and breadth as he followed her up the stairs.

"The more natural light, the better." A ray of sunlight punctuated her point by reflecting off the gold in her hair. "It can be a real challenge to transform someone else's idea of a dream nest into your own."

Or successfully seduce the dreamy woman who lives on the other side of the shared fence.

"The master bedroom is relatively tame compared to some of the other rooms in the house," he said, reaching the top step.

They started down the hallway together.

"Is this . . . ?" Hope stopped and turned to look inside the gold-papered former guest bedroom. "The nursery?"

Before he could take a step in his intended direction, or at least away from the potential emotional minefield inherent in showing her the nursery, Hope disappeared into the room.

She looked toward the window. "You might want to move the cribs against the opposite wall. With the angle of the winter sun, light will flood onto the babies at an ungodly hour."

"Crucial observation," he said, noting the light in her smile.

"Especially with the reflection off that wallpaper," she said.

"Theresa mentioned something about taking down the paper and painting lavender in here."

"Benjamin Moore has a color called Pale Iris that would be amazing in this light." Hope eyed the pastel patchwork crib bedding sets. "That or Easter Bonnet would complement the bedding perfectly."

"You can come up with colors that specific off the top of your head?"

She picked up a comforter and ran the silky border through her fingers. "Designing nurseries is sort of a specialty."

Despite what seemed to be genuine enthusiasm for baby decor, his inclination to comfort her, tell her he was sure her attention to detail would pay off soon in shades of both pink and blue, could still lead down the wrong slippery slope. An appeal to her business savvy, was, well, infinitely more savvy. "What do you think it would take to get this room pulled together?"

"Money-wise or time-wise?"

"Both, I suppose."

"Depends on what you're thinking in terms of budget."

"Theresa already blew that on the cribs and bedding." He chuckled. "So I guess as cost effectively as possible."

"If she buys retail and picks in-stock furniture and accents—"

"Or I do," he said.

"Or you do." She paused. "Sorry, I didn't mean to presume—"

"You presume correctly." He smiled to relieve any embarrassment, but more in recognition of the brilliant idea that had begun to percolate. Instead of the birthstone necklace Theresa had been hinting about, he might as well capitalize on the opportunity of a dual-purpose gift that allowed him to avail himself of Hope's services in the process. He'd hire her to decorate the room. Despite, or, with any luck, because of the complications, she'd eventually succumb to his charms. They'd have their affair. Before things got dicey, her husband would knock her up and things would necessarily have to end.

She'd move on to motherhood.

He'd move on.

"Thing is," he said. "I need to deliver big this Mother's Day."

Hope nodded. "I suppose you do."

"Can it be done?" he asked.

"I've always wanted to try one of those While You Were Out remodeling jobs." Her voice trilled with an almost sensual enthusiasm. "The only thing is, I'd need two days—a full day for wallpaper removal and priming and then another to paint and get the room set up."

"I can get her out of the house for some kind of an outing two days in a row, but once she smells primer, she'll know what's up."

"Good point," Hope said, looking around the room once more.

Neither said anything for an overlong moment.

"You know what we could do, though . . ."

"Hmm?" he asked, struggling to keep his eyebrow from rising enthusiastically.

"Design a mock-up nursery, complete with furniture and accessory choices, paint colors, swatches, and window covering options she can pick and order from herself."

"And I give her that for Mother's Day?"

"I'd love it. I can only imagine she will too."

He loved the cost-benefit analysis of not having to go all out that much more.

"All I'll need to do is get in and do some measurements."

"I think we can arrange that, say, on a Sunday morning when she's at church?"

"Sure." She looked wistful. "But . . ."

"But what?"

"I didn't come in here intending . . ." Her cheeks colored. "One minute I'm standing in your garage, and the next, I've not only talked my way into your house and pointed out everything that needs work, but I'm decorating your babies' room."

"Clearly you're a relentless mercenary." He smiled broadly. "The least you can do is offer a good neighbor discount."

Her blue eyes sparkled with possibility. "For a nursery, I'll give you better than my usual neighbor discount."

His eyes had to sparkle that much more. "You're hired."

* * *

Will licked cinnamon lubricant from his fingers and stared at the device Kitty nestled lovingly in her hand.

"The Mini-Mixer has seven fully adjustable speeds." She lowered her hand toward her waistband. "Just place it in your panties, dress as usual, and go about your day."

"You're saying it gives you an orgasm whenever?" Sarah Fowler asked.

"And wherever. Use it in line at the grocery store or on the way to pick the kids up from school." She held up a palm-sized remote control. "Just pick *pulse* or *blend* and the next thing you know . . ."

"I've gotta have one of those," Stephanie whispered in his ear.

Never again would he think about standing in a long line at the grocery store or sitting through an arduous PTA meeting in the same way.

Kitty pressed a button. "Or give it to your partner to control."

With the whirring sound, Will shifted to readjust his boxers, leaned back in his chair, and enjoyed the sound of hash marks as women marked their order forms.

Stay-at-home fatherhood definitely had its advantages.

* * *

What would Frank do?

Maryellen quickly passed the quivering Mini-Mixer to the woman next to her and took a calming, calorie-free taste of the wild honey body powder sprinkled along her forearm.

Would he believe, like she had, that accepting an invitation to a Mother's Helpers party meant socializing with friends and neighbors over clever must-haves for homemakers? She didn't want to think about what he might have said or done had Laney answered the door for him in high heels and a skin-tight skirt, apologetic about the *silly* fun they were about to have. Was there any way he'd have listened to his intuition and turned for home because of the way things were shaping up or made a scene at an event to which he was specifically invited by a parishioner?

Question was, what did he expect her to do?

Once they'd hugged hello and she'd assured Laney she *loved surprises* and was looking forward to such *a great time* she'd taken the day off work, what else was there to do but take one of the few remaining empty seats in the front? Maryellen had heard about these kinds of parties, but never imagined anyone she knew would put her, a minister's wife, on the guest list.

"Bring it on," Laney, seated behind and to the left of Maryellen, said in response to whatever unspeakable item was making its way down her row.

Only Laney had both the nerve and the verve.

Apparently, more so after reading *Bring It On*, which had just made its way back to the library return bin. Maryellen didn't buy into the nonsense of wishing something into reality professed by that kind of self-help book, but for someone like Laney—attractive, fearless about going after what she wanted, and forced to be a breadwinner due to Steve's health—a message like that could make an event like this seem almost sensible.

"Smell this." The woman next to her said, passing what turned out to be a pleasant citrus-scented body wash.

Truth be told, Maryellen sort of appreciated being included, feeling like one of the girls at something that, for once, wasn't G-rated.

As long as Frank didn't find out.

"We won't have time to showcase everything," Kitty said. "But here on my table, there's an assortment of pleasure ware, from anal balls to the Zipper Zapper to check out after the presentation."

She was also counting down seconds until appetizers and her best chance for a graceful exit. No one would mention a sex toy party to Frank unless she caused a scene by getting up. If she did, she was afraid she might inadvertently spearhead an exodus of the surprised, horrified, and merely uncomfortable. There was no telling who might feel compelled to brag to Frank about *Maryellen's leadership in getting them out of Satan's clutches.*

And there was no telling how Frank would react.

Would he be mad she'd made a spectacle of herself?

Mortified she was there in the first place?

Maryellen spotted a muzzle in a bin marked Assorted Pleasures.

Or, worse, make her recount every detail of the party and role-play the highlights.

Laney and Sarah, all matching cleavage and leather, appeared beside Kitty, picked up matching baskets, and proceeded to toss assorted samples into the crowd.

Maryellen couldn't help herself from thinking about the rumor she'd overheard concerning just how close of friends Laney and Sarah really were. She managed a quick pinch to her forearm before a small bottle of Lord knew what fell into her lap.

Laney sneezed.

"Bless you," Maryellen said.

"Thank you." Laney noted the product she'd just tossed and winked. "And you're welcome."

Maryellen flashed a cursory return smile and avoided eye contact by sliding the sample into the pouch of her purse where she kept gum wrappers, useless receipts, and all other ready-for-the-nearest-trash items.

As she looked back up, a flash of silver reflected in the morning sun from out the side window.

Over on the next cul-de-sac, a Volvo inched out of the Trautmans' open garage.

Hope Jordan's Volvo.

Tim Trautman, tucking in his shirt with one hand and waving his cell phone with the other, ran to meet her car before she exited the driveway.

Instead of feigning interest in the various uses for the latest cream Kitty held in her hand, Maryellen watched them key numbers into their cell phones.

If only she'd had Hope's good sense to do something other than show up at the wrong place at the wrong time.

* * *

"If you don't buy anything else today, Second Honeymoon is the stuff happy, satisfied memories are made of." Kitty held up a tube and waved it for effect. "Use it on him and he'll last longer." Her crooked smile promised equal parts mischief and rapture. "Use it on yourself and plan on multiple, multiple O's."

"I know a certain Quick-Draw McGraw who could use a tube," Samantha Torgenson said from the recliner.

"My wham-bammer won't try special creams."

"Tell him it's a lube," Terri from Aerobics class answered. "That is, unless he considers lube insulting to his arousal abilities."

"My husband's very arousing. I just close my eyes and pretend he's George Clooney."

"I'll toast to that!"

The clink of champagne glasses filled the room.

Someone behind him said, "George Clooney doesn't do it for me, but that Robert Pattinson in *Twilight* . . ."

Leslie Johnson, whom he now knew to have a husband gunning for anal said, "I still have a warm spot for Tom Cruise in his *Top Gun* days."

Will eyed the $9.99 price point beside Second Honeymoon. Despite a sneaking feeling that a few of the products sounded far too good to be true and enough TMI to keep him from making eye contact with almost any husband he chanced upon mowing his lawn this summer, he was enjoying the wide world of sexual aids more than he could have anticipated. "I guess I'm more a Brad Pitt man, myself."

Kitty squirted some cream on a handful of Q-tips. "I need a couple of volunteers."

Stacy Simon, whose predilection for tea-bagging had him willing to follow her just about anywhere, grasped his hand and pulled him with her toward the front of the room.

Kitty waited with three Q-tips for her, and him, four. She pointed them in the direction of the front hall and basement bathrooms respectively. "Rub it on all the cracks and crevices, hang out for three minutes, then come back and give us the report."

The next thing he knew, Will found himself in a windowless bathroom, cream-covered Q-tips in hand, looking at the mildewed bottom edge of the plastic shower curtain.

Catcalls and laughter echoed from upstairs.

Will swabbed his left testicle.

He was about to play demo stud for a room full of hopped-up women.

He swabbed his right.

A fantasy he planned to relive in detail, again and again.

He cinched up his jeans, opened the door to the bathroom, and headed across the brightly lit, but strangely doggy-smelling rec room toward the pool table. With three minutes to kill before he was the center of rapt attention, he decided to hit some balls while he waited for his own to do whatever it was they were guaranteed to do.

He picked up a stick and cued up.

After a quick sneeze, he took a shot.

The red ball went into the right corner pocket.

His balls began to tingle. So did the back of his throat.

He took another shot.

Missed.

Unsure if the light-headed sensation accompanying his now definitely tingling balls was his imagination or the effects of the champagne on a nearly empty stomach, he took another shot.

The green-striped ball stopped a millimeter from the edge of the center pocket.

Sweat erupted on his upper lip.

He tapped the ball in and checked his watch. Still a minute and a half before he was supposed to reappear at the top of the stairs.

Had he put on too much cream?

His dick felt simultaneously cold and sweaty.

Maybe he could wipe the excess off before he went back up to give his report.

He was headed back toward the bathroom when a familiar giggle traveled through the cracked door at the top of the stairs. "You're having a sex toy party?"

His already tight throat went dry. The voice, which sounded like Hope's, but he prayed was anyone's but hers, reverberated down the stairs.

"Sorry I'm so late. I had a landscaping issue to deal with."

He needed water, but couldn't get his legs to propel him the ten steps to the bathroom.

"As in the playground?" Laney asked.

The playground?

Her response was muffled.

"Frank told me you were consulting on the final plans," Laney's voice carried down the stairs like she was using a megaphone.

He waited for the person who sounded like, but couldn't be, Hope to say, *No way!* or at worst, *he asked, but I'm afraid I had to decline.*

"I'm really excited to be part of the finishing touches," she said.

Will's tingling crotch went numb.

"I'm excited Frank didn't keep you too long. You're here in time for the grand finale."

"Can't imagine."

A throaty giggle followed.

Couldn't be her. Couldn't be her. Couldn't be . . .

"Will and one of the other gals are about to give us a report on a very special cream we had them test drive."

Before he could form a coherent fight or flight plan, the door flew open and Laney peered down the stairs. "Ready, Will?"

The last thing he saw before his legs buckled under him was Hope.

CHAPTER FIFTEEN

*Restrictions: 4.8. Antenna and Satellite Dishes: All antennas/
dishes shall be installed with emphasis on being as unobtrusive
as possible to others in the community. All antennas/dishes shall be
screened from view from any street and nearby lots to the
maximum extent possible.*

*A*fter Will came to, downed some Benadryl, and agreed to be checked out at the urgent care where one of the MOPS moms happened to work, Laney was sure the party was ruined. She couldn't have been more wrong. Of the thirty-five party attendees, all but, understandably, Will, still ended up ordering something. Twenty left with stock on hand, including Maryellen, who went home with both edible body powder and strawberry shave gel.

Another sign Laney's business success was meant to be.

If she could get herself and the girls into and out of the allergist's office by four, there'd be time to drop off the fourteen sealed, brown bags in her car to her other customers before they kicked off their weekends. Then, she'd have all day Saturday to plow through the Memorial Weekend details before her dinner planning meeting with Frank.

"Are we going to see that one freaky doctor we saw last time?" Libby glanced out the window down into the Melody Mountain Medical Plaza parking lot.

"He's one of the best in the city," Laney said. She'd expected to have to list off her never-ending sinus symptoms and beg them to let her piggyback her referral appointment on her girls' time slot, but instead, willed the timing to work, and magically there was a cancellation.

"I *so* don't want to be here," Margaret slumped into her chair.

"Wrong attitude," Laney said. With $350 as a training stipend, four party attendees enlisted to throw Mother's Helpers parties as soon as she became an official facilitator, not to mention a bag of complimentary sex toys, negative thoughts about anything, financial or otherwise, were a thing of her past. "Shift your focus from what you don't want to what you do want and you'll get what you want."

"I want to see that one woman doctor," Margaret said.

"I don't want any more dumb allergy shots," Libby sniffled.

"How about something more along the lines of, *I look forward to confirming my health with whatever precautionary allergy treatments my doctor thinks necessary to ensure my safety and happiness this summer while I fulfill my dream of being a counselor-in-training at camp?*"

Margaret rolled her eyes.

"You should be thankful your allergies aren't debilitating enough to make you sick." She made a note by Will Pierce-Cohn's blank order line to give him this allergist's contact info. When she'd called to check on him, he assured her he was okay and that his doctor thought it was probably something he ate and not the hypoallergenic cream he'd sampled. He'd left looking so pallid, though, it was hard to believe he couldn't use a second opinion.

"Oh, my God, Mom!" Libby said. "That book you've been reading has turned you into a total freak."

"Oh, my gosh." She certainly wasn't as freaky as Julie Connors or Roseanne Goldberg, who, judging by the laminated code sheet in her facilitator's training notebook, had a twelve-inch Gutterman and anal balls coming their way, respectively.

"Oh, my gosh!" Margaret pressed her face against the window glass.

"Did you just see what I saw?" Libby asked.

"Oh my God!"

"It's bad energy to use the Lord's name in vain." Hopefully, it wasn't worse energy that she couldn't wait to report to Sarah just how many people had picked up Love Sleeves along with Love Him or Lube Him gel, or the number of butterflies fluttering into people's homes in the next twenty four hours via brown bags. After all, Sarah was practically her assistant and their training demanded they memorize not only what color and flavor constituted a TO123 or a LM432, but what items sold the best.

And to whom.

"I can't believe this!" Libby said.

"Can't believe what?" Laney looked where the girls pointed. A pair of teenagers walked hand-in-hand between parked cars at the edge of the business parking lot. "Isn't that Tyler Pierce-Cohn?"

"I know!" Margaret said. "Right?"

"With Lauren Trautman!" Libby added.

"Eva's gonna be pissed," Margaret said.

"I didn't realize Eva and Tyler were dating," Laney said.

"They're not," the girls said in unison. "But . . ."

Tyler slipped an arm around Lauren's shoulder, she around his waist, and they headed for the Cold Stone Creamery across the street.

"Sure looks that way."

"You got to admit, they do look cute together," Libby said.

"Their vibrational wants must be matching up," Laney said. Like her own. All the things she wanted, a best friend, business success, and community involvement were interlacing in perfect harmony. "So what they want has to be."

Margaret shook her head. "I wouldn't *want* to be Lauren when Eva finds out."

"Or Tyler," Libby added, already halfway through a text message.

CHAPTER SIXTEEN

Article IV. Meetings of Members: Special meetings of members may be called at any time by the president or by the board of directors or on written request of members.

At a regular restaurant, Maryellen could have had whatever she wanted—a salad with extra lettuce, a fish entrée, even a bite of cheesecake for dessert. Instead, she sat dreading the arrival of barely recognizable meat and sauce-drenched vegetable dishes.

"Try the Crab Rangoon." Laney reached across the table and popped a crab puff in Frank's mouth.

"Mmmm." Frank's Just-for-Men brown hair reflected clownish red under the crimson paper lanterns and pleather booths of the restaurant. "We just love Oriental cuisine."

"Chinese," Maryellen said. Watching Laney ply Frank with appetizers was that much worse.

He'd suggested they conduct their Memorial Weekend planning meeting over a dinner he could *expense to the HOB*.

Laney suggested the Shangri-La.

Having spent two days suggesting to Janet Jamison, Sue Perkins, and assorted MOPS moms that the party was meant to be in good fun and nothing to think more about, Maryellen suggested another restaurant on another night, when, she hoped, the details of her last party wouldn't threaten any conversation related to the details of the one being planned.

"The pot stickers are outstanding," Frank said.

"Told you," Laney purred.

The Shangri-La, on Laney's schedule, it was.

Maryellen took a calming sip of jasmine tea and looked down at the doughy won tons submerged in her soup bowl. At least the broth smelled half-decent, and contained a generous helping of baby corn, cabbage, carrots, and bamboo shoots. When chilled, though, there would surely be a film of congealed chicken fat to be skimmed from the top.

"I've scheduled the playground dedication to start at ten sharp," Laney said, pausing long enough from her flirtation to get down to business. "Speeches are slotted from ten to ten thirty, followed by the ribbon cutting and champagne toast at the Songbird Canyon Court playground. The pool will open immediately following at noon, close at five for party setup, and then reopen for the potluck and kickoff party at six."

"Timing sounds about perfect." Crab-tinged cream cheese filled Frank's front teeth like tub caulk. "I'll pass that schedule along to the kids."

"My girls said the youth group is all excited to help out."

"Doubled their budget in exchange for being on call all weekend." Frank smiled. "Eva said the vote to help out was unanimous."

"That's great." Maryellen extracted a lone water chestnut from her soup. Before biting, she sucked the liquid, savoring the nutty flavor and apple-like texture.

"Did the high school jazz band commit?" he asked.

"Confirmed them this morning." Laney's dark circles, which no amount of makeup totally seemed to erase, looked somehow softer under the reddish light. "And Sarah hooked me up with the guy who does all the party decorations for the Broncos."

Maryellen pinched herself for overthinking the words *Sarah* and *hookup.*

"Fabulous," Frank said.

"Wait until you see the cake." Laney gave her now telltale wink. "I found a baker who'll make almost anything you request."

Maryellen swallowed the halves of the water chestnut she'd bitten in two. "Egg rolls anyone?" Before either of them could nod, Maryellen placed two of the greasiest specimens on Frank's plate and gave a slightly crisper version to Laney.

"Maryellen, you should order an appetizer tray from here for the potluck setup committee and the early birds."

"The homeowner's association is already providing decorations, boxed wine, soft drinks, and a keg." Maryellen placed the last egg roll on the corner of her own plate where it wouldn't make contact with the decorative carrots she'd taken from the center of the Pu-Pu platter. "I thought I'd assign the northernmost Phase One households to come a little early with hors d'oeuvres so we don't exceed the food budget."

"Weng Fei caters almost all my parties." Laney waved to the Asian man standing behind the register and bit into an egg roll that, despite its phallic shape, would have been downright puritan amid the edibles at Mother's Helpers. "I'm sure he'll cut us a deal."

"But," Maryellen managed, "the Phase One homeowners—"

"Can bring appetizers at the regular time. That way the people who've volunteered to help will get a special treat for coming early to help."

"Sounds good to me."

"Treats and surprises," Laney said. "The key to a fun-filled, successful bash."

Frank lifted his wine glass. "Here, here!"

While he paused to pique the attention of onlookers from other tables, Maryellen dipped her spoon into her water, collected some ice cubes, and dropped them into her chardonnay.

"Maryellen!" Frank pointed to the bottom of the laminated wine list. "It's Beringer."

"Sorry." She wasn't. Ice made the wine extra cold and cut the calories in half. Besides, at home, she refilled a Kendall-Jackson bottle with whatever was on manager's special at the liquor store. In a pinch, she'd even added water and he'd never noticed the difference. She lifted her glass in Laney's direction. "To you."

"Here, here," he said, his voice growing louder and deeper. "On behalf of the Melody Mountain homeowners, I want to offer my heartfelt thanks for the outstanding job you do and are once again doing for this community." He smiled at Laney. "Memorial Weekend's sure to be the most memorable party we've had around here."

Maryellen felt the slight sting even before the wine glass touched her lips.

* * *

Eva took a hit from the ceremonial pipe, passed it to her left, and ran the tip of a crystal-handled wand over the candle flame. "Tonight, we praise the Goddess for the success of the diorama spell. To thank her for our future successes, each of us will make a personal sacrifice."

Tyler looked away.

Lauren looked down at her hands.

She should have known the second Tyler took Lauren's hand, or the first time Lauren, acting way too innocent, asked *if anyone's seen him yet.*

Eva had to hold her hands at her sides to keep from strangling them both. That they thought they could sneak around playing lovey-dovey without someone spotting them and telling her, showed how stupid they really were.

She picked up scissors from the table beside her, came around the ping-pong table, and stopped in front of Lauren. "In honor of your spell contribution, we'll start with you."

Before she grabbed a handful of Lauren's hair, she gave Tyler her most winning smile. He'd make his sacrifice next.

In private.

* * *

"Dear Heavenly Father, we thank Thee for this food. Feed our souls on the bread of life and help us to do our part in kind words and loving deeds. We ask in Jesus' name. Amen."

"Amen." Maryellen dropped Frank and Laney's hands and examined the steaming platter of Hunan beef beside her. The meat looked fried. The Sesame Scallops were battered and fried. The Kung Pao chicken, while not as oily, was swimming in a sea of hot peppers. The Happy Family looked anything but.

Maryellen shifted her attention to the next table where the diners dug into dishes of a batter-coated dessert.

"That green tea fried ice cream is to die for," Laney said.

"I'll try to save room," Frank said.

Maryellen's throat constricted with the thought.

Frank dumped overflowing spoonfuls onto his plate. "What are we thinking in terms of attendance at the ribbon cutting itself?"

"Hard to say, yet." Laney put a mound of rice in the center of her plate. "I have Sarah working on an Evite with RSVP's for both the morning and evening events."

Maryellen gave herself another quick pinch.

"I'll follow up with a separate reminder to the board so they know they need to be at the ribbon cutting."

Ignoring the mini-Matterhorn of scallops she'd heaped onto her plate, Laney clasped a piece of beef via chopsticks. "I'd hate to have anyone feeling like the celebration is mandatory."

"Considering the scope of the project and the impact on the community, it is," Frank said.

Maryellen allowed herself exactly two pieces of Kung Pao chicken, one spoonful of Mu Shu, and all the snow peas she could collect from the Lo Mein. "Maybe you could make the ribbon cutting be the May meeting?"

"No can do."

"Why not?" Laney twisted a tangle of Lo Mein around her fork.

"Covenants."

"Can't you invoke some special circumstances rule? I mean, when will we ever be having a neighborhood-affirming, community-building event like this again?"

"It's a thought." He smiled at Laney. "Problem is, Pierce-Cohn will have a field day."

"Probably right," Laney said. "Especially after his performance at Mother's Helpers."

"Mother's Helpers?" Frank asked.

"The home shopping party Laney had on Thursday," Maryellen said quickly and helped herself to an ice cube from her water glass.

"Eat, Maryellen," Frank said through a mouthful of scallops. "She's always watching her weight."

"I wish I had your willpower." Laney looked her over as though she were a department store mannequin. "You can't be more than a size two."

Size zero, she didn't say, but made a show of nibbling the broccoli flower from the stem instead as Frank took chopsticks to his Hunan beef.

"Home shopping, like Avon?" he asked.

"A lot like Avon," Maryellen said.

"Much more hands-on, though." Laney smiled like the Cheshire cat.

Maryellen scraped excess sauce from a piece of broccoli and prayed Laney would leave it at that.

"Can't imagine how Pierce-Cohn can go to those parties and be the only man," Frank said, post-swallow and pre-bite.

"Will's one of the girls," Laney said. "But I really did think he was going to die of embarrassment when he came back from putting on that cream and saw Hope standing there."

"Some sort of allergic reaction," Maryellen said.

"My doctor confirmed there was nothing in there that could have caused—"

"He's fine though," Maryellen said, weighing Laney's reaction to an under-the-table *shut-up* kick.

"If you ask me, his reaction was more from overhearing Hope tell me she'd just come from consulting with you on the playgrounds than anything else."

"Hope said that?" Frank put his chopsticks down.

"Hope's consulting on the playgrounds?" Maryellen asked.

"Never hurts to have another set of eyes on the plans before they're finalized."

"But I thought she was against—?"

"She was." Frank swirled the contents of his glass, and took a pull of chardonnay. "Until I gave her the opportunity to admire her own handiwork by looking out her front door."

"Brilliant idea, by the way." Laney clanked his glass with her own.

Why hadn't Frank mentioned to her that Hope was consulting on the playground?

"Sounds like Pierce-Cohn doesn't necessarily think so." Frank could barely contain his self-satisfied smirk. "But her involvement's already paid off. She moved a flower bed set too close to the basketball court and changed up some plantings that would have attracted bees."

"She certainly seemed jazzed up about the project when she finally got to the party," Laney said.

"Good to hear." Frank made a show of constructing a Mu Shu with the rolling skills he learned as a teen working at Taco Bell. "When did you say your party was again?"

"Thursday morning," Laney said.

He looked up. "And Hope said she'd just met with me?"

"Almost missed the whole shebang because of it," Laney said.

"That's odd," he said.

"Why's that?" Laney asked.

"We did have a meeting that day, but not until that afternoon."

"That is odd." Maryellen set down the teacup she was using to warm her hands. "Because I saw her pull out of the Trautmans' driveway just before she showed up at Laney's."

"As in, Tim Trautman's?"

"Exactly." Maryellen allowed herself the briefest of smiles.

* * *

Holding the black satchel of offerings containing everything from an opal ring to an off-campus lunch pass to a chunk of Lauren's hair, Eva turned to Tyler. "As bidden by the sacred *Book of Coven*, it is time for the Head Warlock to make his ritual sacrifice."

Pretending not to notice the *no worries* glances the two of them exchanged, she handed Lauren a shift sign-up sheet for Memorial Weekend and grabbed Tyler by the wrist. "While we're gone, tell Lauren when you can work the ribbon cutting and party and she'll try to give you the times you want."

Her father's favorite cliché, *keep your friends close and your enemies closer*, had never felt so apropos as she led Tyler to the laundry room, slid open the pocket door, and sent him through. Before following him to the open area beside the washer and dryer, she turned back and slid the door closed behind them.

Almost.

It was all she could do not to check and see if Lauren was still fingering the thinned spot in her hair and trying not to look perturbed watching them disappear into the laundry room.

Tyler reached past her and slid the door closed.

She untied her cape and tossed it over the washing machine.

"I need to tell you something," he said.

"What's that?" She could feel him squirm.

"It's about Lauren."

"What about her?"

"And me."

She kept her back to him, so her face wouldn't betray the casual in her voice. "Tell me something I don't know."

"That's why you cut so much of her hair?" he finally asked.

"You can hardly tell she's missing any."

"There's a chunk gone by her left ear."

"Lauren's the most powerful Dedicant. Her sacrifice is almost as important as yours." Eva turned and waved her scissors, which happened to be at about crotch level.

A look of panic crossed his face.

"Don't flatter yourself." She snipped off a lock by his left ear, and then did the same to herself, but from the underside of the back of her head. "It's not like I care all that much."

He ran his fingers along the side of his head. "So you're cool about Lauren and me?"

She pulled out two empty Baggies from the satchel, put Tyler's hair in one, hers in the other, and zipped them closed. "As long as you continue in your role as Head Warlock without getting distracted when your gf—she's around."

The most annoying look of relief crossed his face.

She dropped the Baggies into the satchel. "You also need to make your sacrifices tonight."

"Thought I just did."

She let the strap of her tank top slide down her left shoulder. "There's one more."

His eyes fell to the cup edge of her new Victoria's Secret strapless bra, exactly as she expected. "I don't think I should . . ."

She traced the outer rim of his ear with her tongue. "We have to praise the Goddess."

"I know, but—"

"But what?"

He stared at the door. "Lauren."

"You just got together with her."

"I know, but—"

She began to tug at his shirt. "You're not exclusive yet, right?"

"Not yet."

"Then no worries." She reached for the top button of his jeans and began to unbutton his fly. "It's for the Goddess."

He confirmed his agreement with a low moan.

* * *

Maryellen locked the bathroom door behind her, entered the stall, and took a deep breath. She wasn't sure what was worse, keeping Laney off the subject of

Mother's Helpers while she flirted with Frank, smiling while the woman took over everything about Memorial Weekend, or listening to Frank obsess over Hope? Finding out he'd hired Hope as a playground consultant from Laney was bad enough, but to know poor Will Pierce-Cohn's sweating, burping, dizziness, and rash might have been not only an allergic reaction, but his reaction to Hope's involvement in the playground project, was practically unbearable.

What was Will going to do when the church land was finalized?

At least she didn't have to worry about Frank asking anything more about the party now that the conversation had moved away from Will and onto a rundown on Tim Trautman, and what exactly *Laney* thought Hope was doing over at his house.

And why *Laney* thought Hope felt the need to lie.

Brassy, shameless Laney, who seemed to be able to say whatever she thought and do whatever she pleased.

Amazingly, her theories, at least where Hope was concerned, were logical—Hope was helping Tim plant flowers, but said she was with Frank so no one would overhear and give up the surprise. Laney knew the flowers were a surprise because she'd dropped off Theresa's party goodies on Friday only to be treated to a tour of the blooms overfilling the beds that Tim, *who knew nothing about flowers*, had planted for her. Other than fulfilling Frank's need to know everything about Will's reaction, Tim Trautman in general, and Laney's insatiable need to gossip, there really couldn't be all that much more to the story.

Maryellen got up and started for the restroom while the two of them busily, and pointlessly, continued to conjecture as to whether Hope had seen Tim putting in flowers and, because of her love of gardening, had offered to help, or that given their common backyard fence, Tim couldn't help but notice her gardening abilities.

And her.

Maryellen bowed her head, said a small forgiveness blessing for feeling angry and taking part in gossip, bent over, grasped her hair with her left hand, and, although she hated to have allowed herself to eat so much that she had to, stuck her right index finger down her throat.

With a quick flush, the Happy Family was reunited where they belonged.

After a thorough hand washing and a swish from her travel mouthwash, she reapplied her lipstick and ran a brush through her hair. Reaching for a paper towel, she twisted open the door, threw the paper in the wastebasket, and started back.

Frank, busy gesturing with his hands, didn't notice her until she'd almost reached the table. He waved his fortune cookie. "We were waiting on you, Maryellen."

"Sorry," she said, reaching her seat, where only her plate remained amid to-go boxes. "You two go ahead. I'll save mine for later tonight."

"No, Maryellen." Frank picked up the remaining fortune cookie from the tray and tossed it to her. "We're going to do this together."

At least she'd managed to avoid the prospect of green tea ice cream.

Setting aside her plate for the waiter to wrap for the next day's lunch, Maryellen clutched her cookie. She wasn't even hungry for something sweet.

Frank and Laney shattered theirs and grabbed their fortunes from the mess of shards and crumbs before stuffing them into their mouths.

She carefully separated hers into two even pieces.

"Mine says, a person's character is his destiny," Laney said.

"What you desire is always possible," Frank read.

Maryellen pulled at the strip of paper hanging from one of her cookie pieces.

"Maryellen, what does your fortune say?"

She forced a smile. "You live a charmed life."

* * *

Before her parents came home, Eva removed half the hair from Tyler's Baggie and tied it together with her own using a pink ribbon.

She reread the directions for spell number two once more:

Take a lock of hair from your lover and tie a pink ribbon around it. Light three pink candles and then place the hair in a hollowed out apple along with a pinch of ground cinnamon, seven rose petals, and a lock of your own hair tied with a white ribbon. Pass the apple through the flame of each candle while visualizing yourself and your lover.

A little tongue in the ear and a reminder she wasn't into a bf/gf thing anyway and Tyler was where she wanted him, totally into the spell to disrupt Benchmark Testing week. Not that the Tyler/Lauren thing would last much longer, anyway, but boyfriend or friend-with-benefits, she wasn't about to let some innocent-acting freshman whisk Tyler from under her.

Or worse, shift the coven balance in some way.

She pulled a long curly hair from an envelope. Substituting black ribbon and candles instead of pink and white, she entwined Lauren's hair instead of her own.

Following the remaining instructions exactly, she wrapped the apples in white cloth, walked downstairs, and headed out the back door. The pink ribbon apple was to be buried under the window where she slept.

She set aside a pile of pea gravel from the designated spot and searched for an appropriate site for the other apple.

With no burial instructions for the black-ribboned apple, she settled on an easy to dig spot in the center of the garden below her parents' bedroom.

CHAPTER SEVENTEEN

Melody Mountain Ranch Miscellaneous Use Restriction
7.8. Failure to Maintain: In the event that the owner fails to
maintain his Lot in a manner consistent with the requirements
of this declaration, the Association shall have the right, to repair,
maintain, and restore said Lot.

When they were newlyweds, Will couldn't wait to climb into their apartment-issue plastic stall shower to make love. So much so, that when the Henderson Homes interior accent associate offered the granite-tile, double-showerhead upgrade, he had to readjust himself beneath the table in anticipation of a lifetime of water-based sports.

Meg turned on the spigots.

Needles of water stabbed Will under the crosscurrent of water.

Could he even get it up?

Meg wrapped her arms around his waist.

Will reached for a sliver of Dial perched precariously on the edge of the built-in soap dish.

She rubbed her nipples across his chest. "Since when do you turn away shower sex?"

Maybe since Thursday's humiliating transformation from devoted-to-the-kids-and-his-wife's-exploding-career-stay-at-home-parent into the infamous househusband-who-collapsed-probably-from-a-reaction-to-arousal-cream at a sex toy party?

In front of Hope.

Traitorous Hope Jordan.

How could she have signed his petition and then turned around and agreed to do landscape consultation on the playground? Was it possible that, in his allergic stupor, he'd imagined, or somehow misinterpreted what she'd said?

"It's just been a long day and I haven't felt myself and I have to get up early and . . ."

"And I have brunch with the president of the Colorado Animal Rights Association." Meg's tongue entered his left ear. "No time like the present."

Meg might never paw him like this again if she intercepted one of the concern calls and someone filled her in on the details of his fainting spell. How could he ever show up at another party, much less a homeowner's board meeting, and not relive the look of concealed laughter on the faces of the women huddled around him? Hope was the only one who didn't crack a smile. The only one to rush off for the glass of water he needed so badly.

Out of guilt, no doubt.

"Earth to Will?" Water droplets slid down his wife's shoulders and breasts.

He didn't have the energy to tell her what Hope had done, then argue the finer points about why it was or wasn't irrelevant.

He sighed and ran his hands down her back toward her lightly dimpled rear. Not eager to add humiliation-induced impotence to his woes, he closed his eyes and tried desperately to place himself Grotto-side ready to service a bevy of horny Playboy Playmates.

He slid a hand between her legs.

She let out a low moan.

He remained Play-Doh soft.

The-sexy-traveling-saleswoman-flashing-a-peek-up-her-skirt-at-the-hotel-bar scenario only reminded him he didn't have a *real* job. The-female-boss-with-a-penchant-for-sexual-harassment-and-a-little-light-bondage was out of the question.

Meg's hand drifted downward.

He conjured up a flight attendant, blouse unbuttoned one button too low, beckoning him toward the galley, where two blond fellow flight attendants awaited him and his big hard . . .

Before he could fail in his bid to join the mile-high club, the fruit of a prior, much more successful, labor bellowed from down the hall.

"Daddddddyyyy!"

"Damn it." Will dunked his head under the spray to drown out the bullshit in his voice.

Meg leaned her head out of the shower door. "Daddy's busy."

"We can't sleep," Madison said.

"Read for a little while."

"We already did," Nicole said.

"Then go watch TV for a few minutes until you get tired."

There was a pause.

"Really?"

"Downstairs—on the big screen."

Another pause.

"But Daddy doesn't let us watch TV downstairs after bedtime."

"Dad says it's okay this time," she added, not looking to see if Daddy concurred. "We've definitely got to get a big condo in Orlando if we want any privacy this vacation."

"I'll work on that tomorrow," he said. Along with looking at the want ads.

In the silence that followed, Meg rubbed her breasts across his chest and down his belly. "Where were we?"

Deep in househusband Hell. "Maybe I'd better go and make sure they aren't scared to go downstairs without me or . . ."

"They'll be fine." Meg knelt down and rubbed the soap down the length of his not-completely flaccid, but hardly impressive, cock.

There was only one fantasy that could possibly work.

He closed his eyes.

The spaghetti strap of Hope's black negligee slipped from her smooth, soft shoulder and fell down her arm, exposing the top of her breast and a sliver of pale nipple.

He opened his eyes.

Meg tightened her hand around him.

He closed his eyes again.

Bitch needed to make it up to him for being a bad girl.

The spaghetti strap of her black negligee slipped from her smooth, soft shoulder and fell down her arm, exposing the top of her breast and a sliver of pale nipple. With no sign of the concern or pity he'd last seen on her face while she hovered over him with a fan and a glass of water, she smiled seductively.

He leered in disdain. "Do you still find the playground project *really exciting?*"

"I was only saying that." She dropped to her knees. "We both know there's something wrong with that playground land, but I couldn't prove it without accepting his offer to consult so I could look it over."

"You didn't ask me first."

"But I did it for you."

"What else are you going to do for me?"

"Anything." She lowered the remaining strap and her black silk nightie dropped to the floor. "I'll do whatever you want."

He bent her over.

"Yes," she said, lifting that amazing ass into the air. "I want you so badly."

"And you're going to have me," he said, his dick harder than he'd ever felt it.

"Yes!" she screamed as he entered her from behind. "Yes!"

* * *

As the evening news went to a post-sports commercial break, Tim glanced out the window at his garden handiwork.

"Every time I look outside, I feel so happy." Theresa kissed him gently. "And excited."

"Excited's good," he said.

She kissed him again, but a lot less gently. Then, without a complaint about how exhausted she was, suggesting they go upstairs and lock the door, or saying anything at all, she probed her tongue deep into his mouth and gave him the most appreciative kiss he'd had since she came home to the pink flower beds.

"I wish there were more planting I could do." For the moment, all he could do was wait for his proverbial seeds to sprout. With a practiced flourish, he unzipped his fly with one hand. Ignoring the too-familiar powdery bouquet of her perfume, and the weight of her girth against his legs, he gently pressed her face toward his lap with the other. "But I have an idea."

She reached behind the couch, produced a sealed brown bag, and handed it to him. "I have a better one."

"A present?"

"From Laney's party."

He looked down at the bulge in his boxers. "Any chance I can open this in a few minutes?"

"You won't want to."

Mildly annoyed by the interruption of whatever golf gadget or tool for his workbench couldn't wait until after his blow job, he opened the sealed bag and looked inside at what appeared to be a gelatinous pink sleeve that looked like a mini arm-floatie. "What the—?"

"It was a sex toy party."

His cock began to swell thinking about Hope, surprised but amused, when she finally showed up and had a chance to survey the unexpected wares. "Seriously?"

Theresa removed the plastic wrap, squirted some sort of gel into the neon pink tube, and slid the thing onto what was already a healthy erection. "It's called the Love Slave."

Tim looked down at his cock, which looked a little too much like a pig in a blanket. "Sounds like my kind of toy, but . . ."

She began to roll the thing back and forth.

The gel warmed and began to tingle.

He relaxed into the cushions and pushed toward Theresa's hand. The friction felt surprisingly realistic.

"Feel good?"

Almost as good as if he were being sucked off by a certain comely neighbor while they conferred over wall textures, light fixtures, and how good his cock felt in her mouth.

The sound of rolling latex and lubricant filled the room with a *thwoop*.

Almost.

* * *

"Tell me how much you want me." Frank rubbed himself against Maryellen's belly.

"I want you," Maryellen whispered.

"Say it like you mean it," he said, moving down toward her freshly shaved pussy.

"I want you," she said. Her eyes remained tightly closed.

"Say it louder."

"Eva might hear," she whispered.

"She's sleeping. Louder."

"I want you."

"Tell me you want my big hard manhood inside your tight, shaved cunt."

"I do," she mumbled.

It had taken him nearly a year to convince her to shave down there. "You want my hard manhood in your tight, shaved cunt."

"I hate that word."

"Turns me on."

"I want your hard m . . . inside my tight, shaved cunt."

"Yes, baby!" He spread her legs, took aim, and pressed her. "Am I making you wet?"

"Yes, Frank."

"How wet?"

"So wet."

As Frank pumped away, focused on pulling out just in time to enjoy the sight of his seed all over Maryellen's flat belly, a disquieting thought popped into his head.

Trautman doing the same thing to Hope Jordan.

***

If anything, Hope was flattered by Will Pierce-Cohn's admiration-from-a-distance. She truly appreciated Frank's almost fatherly concern. Flirtatious men like Tim Trautman, however, sent her running.

Usually.

Tim was a shameless flirt. Normally the kind of guy she'd steer clear of, but for the fact he was so unabashed in his love for the mother of his children that he'd taken the morning off work to surprise her by planting flowers. She couldn't deny the appeal of feeling desired but also safe knowing the desirer was more attracted to his wife and the life they'd built together to do anything about it beyond ask her to collaborate with him on a nursery for his twins.

As if there was much of anything she'd rather do.

She stared at the pink and blue shards of light reflecting off her Murano glass chandelier. "I can't believe how much great work I suddenly have."

"Busy is good." Jim kissed her quickly.

He entered her even more quickly.

Thanks to the serendipitously named Mother's Helpers lubricant she'd bought at Laney's, any lack of preparedness was no problem. She opened her legs and envisioned sperm slip-sliding their way toward her fallopian tubes, destined for a crash landing with her eager egg.

A new life is ready to come through very soon.

She never expected to put so much faith in the predictions of a walk-in-welcome psychic, but the images Renata saw in the tea leaves were materializing, and repetitively. There was no doubt the *awkward moment* and *party* related to Frank's call about the playground landscaping and Laney's home shopping event. Then, Will Pierce-Cohn had that awkward reaction at the party while she was mid–white lie about why she'd been late. With everyone crowded around to see if he was okay, she could no more tell him she was really talking to Tim about a secret nursery plan than she could explain she was consulting on the landscaping because of Renata's predictions.

How working on the projects made her feel so fertile.

She'd tell him what she could as soon as she had the chance.

Hope relaxed into the pillow.

A new life is ready to come through very soon.

"Not going to be around much this next month," Jim mumbled.

She lifted her head. "What?"

He looked up, over her breast, made eye contact with her chin. "Have to go to London."

"London as in England?"

The motion from his nod rocked her more than the movement in his hips.

"No," she managed.

"No choice." He reached around and cupped her bottom. "International retail chain facing significant restructuring."

Despite a jolt of impending doom, she pressed against him. "When do they want you there?"

"Looks like the thirteenth."

"But that's Mother's Day."

"Hope," Jim stopped for a moment, "it's not like I can help the timing, I—"

"I don't even want to hear it." She pulled Jim close, pressed her hips against his. Hadn't Renata seen the image of a wheel, signifying business advancement and some marital discord as an inevitable part of the process? Once he made VP, he'd control his travel schedule. He could pass the small jobs on to the lower-level associates. As soon as they had kids, he'd pick and choose where he was going. They'd have more time together. As soon as they had kids . . . *A new life is ready to come through very soon.* "How long will you be gone?"

He lifted her legs into the air. "Probably a couple weeks."

She rested her ankles on his shoulders. "But you'll be back by Memorial weekend?"

He didn't answer.

"So that's a no?"

"It's an *I don't know.*"

"I'll try and figure out how to move up the nursery project and the landscape installation so I can come, too."

"I need to figure out the lay of the land first, and you know the client won't pay for that."

"But if I'm not there and you're not here—" Tears filled her eyes and began to zigzag toward her neck. "You'll miss ovulation."

"Won't matter if we succeed this month." He pumped harder.

"If we don't?"

"God damn it, Hope, do you want me to lose my erection?"

CHAPTER EIGHTEEN

*This Community Patrols for Solicitors—Street Sign posted at
Melody Mountain Ranch main entrances.*

The scenario made sense—Trautman wanted to surprise his wife by
planting flowers. Having no idea what to plant, he'd asked for help from his
backyard neighbor, whose garden was already awash in spring bulbs. That said
neighbor happened to be uncommonly helpful, and even more attractive, simply made the plan's implementation all the more palatable.

Frank shut the French doors of his home office, stepped over to the desk,
and picked up the phone to check messages.

Why did it bug the hell out of him, then?

He dropped the handset back into the cradle and powered up his computer.

The fact that Hope used their playground meeting as an alibi, particularly
in the company of Will Pierce-Cohn, meant she wanted to let people know she
was working on the landscape project. It could even be seen as a statement to
the community about her new allegiance to him.

Frank clicked on his e-mail.

He'd planned to schedule a landscape design meeting when he saw her at
church. While they compared calendars, he'd have mentioned he heard she was
talking about the playground. Hope would blush while she explained away her
white lie, gush about the flowers she'd helped Tim plant to surprise his wife, or,
if he and Laney had miscalculated the story somehow, fill him in on what it was
she was doing over there. Were he so inclined, Frank might even reconfirm his
nonsuspicions with a *way to show up the neighborhood husbands* pat on the back
for Trautman when he came through the greeting line.

Had either of them shown up at church, he might have.

Had either of them shown up, the *Dangers of Coveting* sermon he'd dug
from the back of the file cabinet and subbed for *Give to Receive*, wouldn't have
fallen on deaf and otherwise irrelevant ears.

But the commandment, as handed down by our Lord, expects that within the community of faith, the drive of desire will be displaced by the honoring of the neighbor, by the sharing of goods, and by the acceptance of one's goods as adequate.

His inbox materialized on the screen.

There were three new e-mails; none of them were responses to the *missed you at church* or *need to get a meeting on the schedule* messages he'd left Hope by phone yesterday afternoon and by e-mail later in the evening.

And again before bed.

She should have left a late-night message. Could have . . .

He skipped a deposit due e-mail for a Men Who Pray workshop, and the next, an escrow installment reminder for the church land, which would only serve as a reminder to never again put the possible spiritual needs of one, possibly two parishioners, above the long-term best interests of the whole community. He was about to double-click on his Association of Colorado Communities newsletter when a new message popped into his inbox.

From: Hope Jordan.
Re: Missed you at church.

Finally.

He opened the e-mail.

Hi Frank,

Yesterday morning went in a completely unexpected direction. Not only did I have to miss church (unfortunately) but I'm just getting back to returning messages. I really do want to meet to finalize the plans. Do you have time today?

He instant messaged a quick, *Are you there?*

Before he could add, *I'm working from home this morning,* her return *Hi* popped up in the dialogue box.

He added and sent, *Come on over and let's chat.*

His questions and her answers never seemed to catch up from that point on.

Great! Appeared on one line from her.

He wrote, *See you soon.*

How about a little later?

Meaning great, she would stop by a little later?

She answered by adding, *I have to be somewhere soon.*

Your exercise class?

Her *No* arrived a second after he added and sent, *If so, we can meet at my rec center office afterward.*

How about this afternoon like around one?

I assumed you'd be there this morning like usual.

One should work, he wrote back.

The confusion both dissipated and increased with her final out of synch comment.

Can't this morning. I have a coffee date.

* * *

Even in a gray turtleneck and ass-flattering, but otherwise unremarkable, black slacks, Hope's hello wave sent a rustle of desire through Tim and a rustle of disappointment through the male contingent of the Starbucks line. Bypassing the less lucky admirers, he took his place next to her and further marked his territory with a hello kiss to her cheek.

"Hi there," Hope said, not seeming to mind the familiar greeting.

Or, his simultaneous touch to her upper arm.

She was too pretty to be unnerved by a little touchy-feely, but the fact that Hope decided to cap off her otherwise professional ensemble with spiky boots reflected positively on the stolen hour they'd shared during church Sunday morning while she measured out the nursery.

And he assisted with the tape measure.

Tim looked up at the drink menu. "What can I get for you?"

"A tall, nonfat latte would be great," she said.

"A tall nonfat latte," he said to the pierced, tattooed barista who looked less than thrilled to have him eclipse her moment with Hope. "And I'll have a caffé Americano, tall."

"Thanks." Hope graced him with her smile again. "I'll go set up."

I'll watch, he didn't say, but did as her floral scent dissipated into the fog of slightly burnt coffee that would stick to his clothes for the rest of the day.

Remind him of her.

She considered a table for two, but continued on toward an overstuffed love seat nestled in the front window.

Yes.

Would she be a one-timer or more of an aficionado of the regularly scheduled marriage break? He'd have put money on her going the entitled-to-whatever-fancied-her-because-of-her-looks route had she not begun to unload the contents of her briefcase onto a long coffee table, which if he had to be honest, was the most viable workspace in the place.

"Tall, nonfat latte and a caffé Americano." The barista placed two cups beside each other on the pickup counter.

Tim grabbed the coffees and headed for the cozy niche she'd set up for them. "For you." He reached over the binders to hand her the latte. "I assume all this is for me?"

"It's not as bad as it looks," she said. "Since your nursery measured out the same as my guest bedroom, I thought we'd use a book of babies' rooms I've worked on for our dimensions, at least as a jumping off point."

He joined her on the love seat. "Jump away."

She took a sip of coffee and picked up an oversized black binder. "I have to tell you, you're the first man I've worked with on a babies' room."

"And so you figure I have some sort of design fetish?"

She laughed. "Actually, that didn't occur to me."

"Even worse."

"Why's that?"

"Means you've been dreading the prospect of remedial design 101 with *the husband* when we both know the wife is the real decision maker."

"Not at all," she said. "I brought along everything on babies' rooms I have just in case you weren't totally up on the gory details of nursery design."

"I think I can handle enough of the legwork to get something pulled together for Theresa to change up."

"Good." She scooted close enough so he could enjoy the fresh, citrusy undertones of her hair. "Because there are a couple motifs in particular I'm thinking will work well with your color scheme and the modifications needed for twins."

He brushed his arm lightly against hers as he opened the notebook. Resting the back cover on his left thigh, he let the front fall open toward her right leg.

She didn't move away.

"This is a princess-themed room I did for a client," she said pointing to a photo of a nursery made up of pale gray furniture, lace, and some sort of integrated play castle.

"Interesting," he said, mostly in response to the unexpected turn-on of her warm, coffee-tinged breath.

"I don't see this as the way I'd necessarily go for your project," she added. "But I did include some info in case you're interested in a similarly fanciful effect."

"But you wouldn't recommend it?"

"It's a little frilly for the cribs and bedding Theresa already has in there."

"Gotcha," he said, doing a cursory leaf through the fabric swatches, curtain styles, and furniture spec sheets tucked into the pocket folder behind the photo. His eyes were already starting to glaze over. "Did you collect all this extra paperwork since yesterday?"

"Only what I didn't have up-to-date info on, so depending on how you decide to proceed, we're ready to roll."

If they weren't in a crowded Starbucks, he'd be hard pressed not to knock all the paperwork off the table and show her how ready to roll he was.

"You're even more efficient than I expected," he said instead, and for the sake of propriety, turned the page to a tropically themed nursery complete with a rainforest's worth of stuffed animals sitting in a brown-and-green plush tree. "And even more talented."

Their eyes met.

She looked down and added a little too quickly, "Something like this could work if we modified the theme to accommodate the lavender."

He bit the inside of his cheek to keep from smiling. "A definite possibility."

He hmmed his way through a mock-up of a cowgirl room and a few fairy nurseries before stopping briefly to admire an ingenious pink camouflage design.

"It's a little on the edgy side," she said.

"Cute though," he said.

"I found that little play tent and matching camping chairs and couldn't resist pulling something together."

He flipped forward to the next page. The same room was done in an alphabet theme. "Is this your actual guest bedroom?"

"If I can see the room setup, I know if I've succeeded at what I was going for."

"Must cost a fortune."

"Only the paint is nonreturnable. Everything else goes back to the store." She looked away. "Or seems to find its rightful home."

"Truly amazing," he said, continuing to *ooh and aah* over farm-, ocean-, and whatever-themed nurseries as though he cared. Then, he turned the page to a design entitled, The Garden. With a background theme of flowers, bees, and butterflies, the room looked exactly the way he pictured a twin nursery would look.

Assuming he'd actually ever picture such a thing.

"I like this one," he said.

Her expression belied something he couldn't quite make out. "Really?"

"You don't think a garden theme would work?"

"I think it would be beautiful."

"But you seem surprised."

She took a drawn out sip of coffee. "I guess I didn't expect this one to be your favorite."

"It's bright and happy, and, for lack of a better word, hopeful."

She smiled.

"I think that's what I like best." He leafed through the previous page or two and flipped back again. "Definitely my favorite."

"Mine too." A tear, which he hoped was of gratitude and he would have preferred to encounter in a more intimate context, slid down her cheek. She grabbed a napkin and dabbed her eyes. "So unprofessional. Sorry."

He touched her on the shoulder. "No need to apologize."

"It's just I thought I might use this one for myself if . . ."

He could practically hear the explosion he'd triggered by stepping on one of the emotional land mines he knew were set all over his chosen field of play. "Hope, the last thing I want to do is take the nursery you're planning for yourself."

"It's okay," she said.

He flipped back to the farm theme on the previous page. "We can just as easily design the room like this or maybe—?"

"Once we adjust the furniture for twins and make the modifications necessary for the color change, the room will take on its own personality," she said. "And I really do think the lavender palette will be as pretty as the yellow I have on my walls."

"You have your nursery designed like this right now?"

She put her hand over his. "It's really okay."

Despite the instant lack of cogent brain function from the electricity of her touch, he managed a weak, "You sure?"

When their eyes met this time, her gaze lingered.

"The ends justify the means."

"I'm glad you feel that way."

"And knowing me, I'll have two or three new favorite girl nursery plans when and if . . ."

"Not if," he said. "Only when."

"Thanks," she said, pausing for an extra long beat. "*When* the time comes, I'm sure I'll have a new favorite."

"If not?" he asked.

"I guess we'll have a nursery in common."

* * *

Frank's hunch was right on.

Even parked three spots to the right of the Melody Mountain Plaza Starbucks, there was no missing Hope and Tim seated together inside the front window.

On a shared love seat.

That their coffee *date* looked to be on the up and up had Frank feeling slightly more stalker than concerned clergyman, but did little to mitigate his concern. He couldn't allow Hope, or Trautman, for that matter, to reap the disastrous results of what could be their worst impulses.

Hope reached for a briefcase propped beside the couch and pulled out a yellow legal pad.

Trautman's, anyway.

Frank rolled up his window to block the temptation of freshly roasted beans, pushed the auto recline button on the door panel, and relaxed into the bucket seat of his Prius. Trautman merited a watchful eye, but what woman in her right mind would even entertain the idea of a dalliance with a man whose wife was expecting?

Hope placed a hand on Trautman's shoulder and allowed it to linger while seemingly pointing something out with the other.

Frank was out of his car, past Tim and Hope's window nook, and standing in Starbucks pretending to scan the drink board before either of them looked up from her yellow pad.

Hope's laugh clattered like shattering glass in the vaguely charred air.

Amid the whir of espresso making and Starbucks' jazz CD du jour, Frank heard Hope uttering something that sounded suspiciously like *my guest bedroom*.

Tim's reply of *how about now*, or whatever it was that a supposedly Christian husband and father-to-be responded to such an offer, was drowned out by ice being pulverized into a Frappaccino.

Before he managed a conversation-halting clear of the throat, or took a step closer to see what else he might overhear before he did, a barista appeared from behind the pastry case. "What can I do you for?"

Frank moved toward the counter and lowered his voice to avoid compromising whatever was left of his anonymity before he could fulfill his obligation, mandate even, to stop any entanglements taking root. "Grande, half-caf, skinny caramel macchiato."

"Whipped cream?"

"Please, and a receipt." He handed the barista the church Visa.

Hope's voice rang through the crowded coffee shop, but with perfect clarity. "Frank!"

He tossed a quarter of his own into the tip mug, turned, and pretended to be surprised to discover the two of them seated too close, but slightly further apart on the love seat.

Hope waved.

Tim looked wolfish.

Both had managed to erase any telltale guilt from their body language.

With a perfunctory return wave, he headed toward their cozy nook.

"Hey Frank," Hope said as he reached the table. "If I'd known you were coming by, I'd have brought the playground plans with me."

"Your mention of coffee had me craving something I just couldn't get at the rec center coffee machine," he said, directing his attention to Tim.

Trautman raised his drink. "That Starbucks craving's about impossible to ignore."

Touché?

Had Frank not spotted the notebook of nursery plans, he'd have been tempted to deck the guy right then and there.

"Don't tell my wife." Trautman smiled.

He still wasn't sure he shouldn't punch him as a warning.

"Tim's having me plan out the twins' nursery as a Mother's Day gift for Theresa." Despite the touch of emotion in her voice, Hope's expression was luminous. "Isn't that about the nicest surprise you can imagine?"

Planning a nursery to surprise his wife. Planting pink flowers in advance of the birth of daughters. Was it possible the guy was just some kind of super-husband? Tempered by a clear view of Hope's yellow pad of design notes, Frank decided it best, for the moment, to direct any aggression or suspicion into a spirited high-five. "Dude, you're making the rest of us husbands look bad."

"Easy to do." Tim grinned at Hope. "Considering the expert help I've had."

"So I assume that yard rumor must be true?"

"Couldn't have picked all those beauties myself."

Hope smiled.

With confirmation of her role in the planting, Frank felt the muscles in his neck and face relax. Besides, whatever she was doing for Trautman paled in comparison to the job he'd given her. "Wait until you see how she's transforming the playgrounds."

"I've only been fine-tuning what was already a spectacular project," she said.

Spectacular sounded that much more so from her lips. Frank tried not to smile too broadly. "I'm afraid it's going to take up a lot of your time in the coming weeks."

"I'm just enjoying being a part of the process," she said.

"I'm just amazed at how smoothly this playground business evolved from what seemed to be a contested proposal to near completion with full community backing," Tim said.

"You and me both," Frank said.

"From my HOB experience, balancing best interests and specials interests like that takes real finesse."

"Thanks," Frank said, as humbly as possible and starting to wonder if he hadn't partially misjudged the man and his motives. He was undeniably solicitous to his wife, taking an active interest in the community, and clearly understood the ongoing challenge that was P-C. "I do my best to make sure our most impassioned and outspoken community members walk away from these situations knowing their opinions are valued even when, as with Will Pierce-Cohn, the community voted overwhelmingly otherwise."

"Which reminds me," Hope said. "There is a detail I should probably run by you so I can make necessary changes to the plans before our meeting later."

"What's that?"

"I think we need to talk more about the landscaping behind the skate ramp at playground number three. Where it abuts that—"

"Grande, half-caf, skinny caramel macchiato," echoed across the room.

"Hold that thought," Frank said, "while I grab my drink."

"I should probably run." Tim looked at his watch. "Have to, actually."

"Nice chatting with you, Tim," Frank said.

"You too, Frank." Tim met his shake and added an arm pat. "See you on Sunday."

Had he not felt pushed, ever so slightly, in the direction of the front counter, he might not have hesitated or felt the need to amble a little more slowly to retrieve his beverage, just long enough to hear Tim ask, "What day next week works for you?"

Or, to hear Hope answer, "How about Wednesday?"

"Ten o'clock?" rang through Starbucks like the chime of a clock.

Frank picked up the beverage with X marks beside *half-caf*, *whipped cream*, *caramel*, and *nonfat*. Even if Tim's motives were above board and Hope's mind was solely on business, with Jim in and out of town, the responsibility to make sure continued to fall firmly upon his shoulders.

While the two of them finished up, he took his drink from the pickup counter, and took his time sliding a protective cardboard sleeve around the cup.

Frank made his way back to Hope and eased into Tim's abandoned spot on the love seat. "Talk to me."

* * *

Will spent the hour he used to spend at morning aerobics, that he'd never spend in an exercise class full of housewives again, composing a reply to the message sitting in his inbox.

> *Will,*
> *Checking in to make sure you're feeling better.*
> *Allergic reactions are the worst.*
> *Look forward to seeing you soon!*
> *Hugs,*
> *Hope.*

He wanted to write back: *Anaphylactic shock, in all its painful and potentially fatal glory, was far preferable to what I think I may have heard just before I passed out.*

Followed by: *Please tell me it isn't true.*

Or even something simpler along the lines of:
Part of me was already dead before I collapsed.

Instead, he sat in front of the computer typing and deleting woefully inadequate responses, until, all but accidentally, he pressed send on what turned out to be the final version:

> *Hi Hope,*
> *I'm up, about, and back to normal, but still not at all sure what happened.*
> *Thanks for your concern,*
> *Will*

A true statement of not much and, somehow, everything he could bring himself to say.

After three hours waiting to see if she answered, three Advil, and, finally, a jog to the rec center for whatever escape the mostly housewife-free afternoon spin class might provide, his head still throbbed. Avoiding the main staircase so as not to be stopped by a stray attendee of Laney's now notorious party, he headed down the administrative wing for the back stairs.

As soon as he entered the hallway, a sneeze echoed down the hallway.

At least Griffin, who kept avoidably consistent hours by combining church and state with his 9–12 open-door policy for both his spiritual and secular constituencies, would be long gone.

"Bless you."

Or not.

The blessing, slightly patronizing and familiar, came from behind Griffin's door.

Will was about to turn back for the lobby and the far preferable reality of having to explain, for the eightieth time that, *Yes I'm totally fine now, and no, the doctors still aren't sure what exactly caused the reaction*, when the feminine *thank you* that floated into the hall sent a paralyzing icicle down his spine.

"You sneezed on the truth, as they say," Frank said, his words just audible through the crack in the door.

Will took an agonizing step toward the office.

"I really think you should also consider adding an extra drainage channel," Hope said.

"The erosion resistant plants you're suggesting won't be enough to do the trick?"

Even with his heartbeat throbbing in his ears, their words jarred his brain like cymbals.

"I thought so, but I was reading the *Farmer's Almanac* to figure out the best day to schedule the planting," Hope said. "Did you know heavy rain's predicted for June?"

There was no denying her involvement in the project now.

"Which may or may not mean anything."

"But got me thinking . . ."

That the playground could end up looking like a multicolored, nonfunctional fountain in the middle of a lake?

That this whole satellite playground idea was appealing in theory but not so much in reality?

That Will was right?

"Given that hill, extra drainage really should have been written into the original blueprint," she said.

Clearly, she'd given serious thought to some of the problems he had about playground site number one. Was there any possible way Hope really could have signed on because she believed there was something wrong with the playground land too but couldn't prove it without accepting his offer to consult?

For the briefest of seconds, Will felt lighter, allowed his imagination to drift.

I did it for you.

What else are you going to do for me?

Anything.

Frank's voice exploded his fantasy:

"With Pierce-Cohn so worked up, maybe I overstressed the first site and overlooked the second and third."

"Understandable," Hope said. "Given the scrutiny you faced."

They shared a chuckle.

"The first playground's got to be over-engineered at this point," Frank said.

"I hope this one won't be such a headache to correct, last minute and all, but one big rain and—"

"And I'd have been flooded with *I told you so's.*"

They both groaned.

"Will means well," she finally said.

"Maybe where you're concerned."

Will felt anything but well.

"I'm afraid this change is going to wipe out any fudge room," Frank said over the shuffle of papers. "But we have to do what we have to do."

"Maybe we can figure out something to offset any delays or unexpected costs," she said.

"I really appreciate how enthusiastic and on top of things you've been."

"Thanks," she said.

"Thank you," Frank said. "You've been just great to collaborate with on this."

Will felt like he couldn't handle another word even before she added, "This opportunity has meant more to me than you know."

Her words hung in the air as he tiptoed away down the hall and scrambled down the back stairs. Rushing past the cardio room, eyes straight ahead to avoid anyone else's, he stopped at the spinning studio. Hoping that somehow an hour of physical pain might numb the mental, or at least ensure he wouldn't run into Hope on the way out, he stepped into the spinning studio. As he adjusted to the low lighting and the moist heat of moving bodies, he scanned the small room for an open bike, but every one was taken except for the broken one in the corner with a missing saddle.

CHAPTER NINETEEN

*Meetings: 1.6. Posting of Notice. The Association shall cause
a notice of a members meeting to be posted in a conspicuous place
within the community. The Association may also send notice of
meeting via website, e-mail, or other accepted means.*

*T*here was absolutely no way Laney should have gotten up and gone to
Rise and Shine yoga. Not after spending half the night awake, rapid-cycling
over how she could reschedule an afternoon of showings with an out-of-town
buyer to finish her Mother's Helpers' training class so she could make it out to
Highlands Ranch for her first party as a paid MH facilitator. That was, assuming Sarah found a babysitter or Randall's last-minute meeting got cancelled so
he could watch the kids and she could fill in for Laney at the May homeowner's
board meeting she'd promised Frank she wouldn't miss, but had to if she was
going to make her party.

Make the money she needed to make . . .

Laney pulled away from the community mailboxes and headed for the
house.

She should have been home, working to clear her schedule, while she
awaited responses to the *just-in-case-she-didn't-make-it-to-the-meeting* report
she'd sent Frank at 4 A.M., and the e-mails she'd sent to Sarah, Kitty, and her
potential buyer. Not that the buyer had all that much potential, since he was
the husband half of a couple relocating to one of four cities including Denver,
but whose wife already had her heart set on Phoenix.

But all was cool.

The second she twisted her key in her mailbox and pulled out a commission
check from Avon, Steve's third-to-last severance check—the potentially
negative significance of which she'd deal with later—and a customer loyalty
coupon for $10 off at Old Navy, she knew the *Somehow It All Has to Work Out*

plea she sent to The Universe over Sun Salutations was the only way to have handled her impossible day.

She pulled into the garage, grabbed a cup of coffee, and marched directly to her computer to see what else The Universe had in store.

Laughed out loud when she opened the first message:

TONIGHT'S MMR HOMEOWNER'S BOARD MEETING RESCHEDULED!!

Coffee cup raised to The Universe and Frank Griffin, she settled in to scan the details of problem solved Number One:

> *Dear Melody Mountain Ranch Board Members, Committee Chairs, and Property Owners,*
>
> *In accordance with our by-laws, I hereby give 12 hours cancellation notice for tonight's regularly scheduled monthly board meeting. Please be advised that this meeting is hereby rescheduled and will take place "ceremoniously" at the official playground dedication on Saturday, May 26th, at 10:00 A.M. (with 9:45 board sign-in) so our hardworking board members can not only fully participate in the upcoming celebration and summer kick-off, but also enjoy the benefits of a job well done.*
>
> *I submit the following brief report in lieu of a formal meeting and have re-calendared all nonurgent business for the June board meeting. Any matters needing immediate attention should be submitted directly to me at President@mmrhob.org.*

How Frank had circumvented Will Pierce-Cohn to pull off an online meeting and offer the board the more enjoyable obligation of attending the ribbon cutting instead, became clear with the first item in the report:

> *It is with regret I enclose the following announcement:*
>
> *Dear Fellow Members of the Melody Mountain Ranch Homeowner's Board,*
>
> *I hereby tender my resignation as Community Violations Chair, effective immediately.*
>
> *Thank you for the opportunity to serve.*
> *Sincerely,*
> *Will Pierce-Cohn*
>
> *On behalf of the board, I would like to wish Mr. Pierce-Cohn all the best in his decision to focus his volunteer efforts on an expanded role in the Melody Mountain Elementary PTA.*

Laney lifted her cup once again, but to Will, whose anger over the playground, and not entirely surprising resignation, clearly provided the catalyst for her quickly realigning day.

> *Assuming the Community Violations Chair, effective today, will be Tim Trautman of 35424 Wonderland Valley Court. Mr. Trautman's experience as both Treasurer and Vice-President in the Eagle's Nest Vista subdivision makes him more than qualified to step into the position. We welcome Tim and look forward to getting to know him, his wife Theresa, and their soon-to-be expanding brood.*

As Laney skimmed the current budget, tabled-until-June business about upcoming road repairs, and the proposed directory of property owners, she couldn't help but marvel over the sheer synchronicity of it all. How interconnected. She'd shown a home, using, as Frank called them, *soon-to-be completed mini-Eden playgrounds, sure to make more complete that little slice of heaven we call Melody Mountain Ranch* as selling points, only to have those playgrounds result in a resignation that freed up her wildly overscheduled day.

Not to mention a position on the homeowner's board for Tim Trautman, her buyer.

If she hadn't sold the house to the Trautmans which eventually led, even if indirectly, to Will's resignation, she wouldn't be looking at the word-for-word report and hour-by-hour schedule, now entitled, *Our Upcoming, Not-to-be-Missed Memorial Weekend* she'd submitted, but prayed she wouldn't have to give in person.

Frank's, Tim's, and her own intentions heard and answered, en masse, by The Universe.

With his *Thanks to Laney Estridge, her committee, and the Melody Mountain youth group for their work*, Laney drained her coffee cup in toast to herself.

She was about to double-click on Compose Message to let Sarah know she was off the hook when she spotted the droplet of blood on her desk.

Sensing moisture from her nostril and just ahead of the gush, she reached for the Kleenex box, and had a wad of tissue pressed against her nose before the bleeding could damage the keyboard.

CHAPTER TWENTY

Improvements: A homeowner may proceed with improvements
without advance approval by the Architectural Committee
if the homeowner follows stated guidelines. ANY OTHER
IMPROVEMENT NOT SPECIFICALLY LISTED REQUIRES
COMMITTEE REVIEW AND WRITTEN APPROVAL.

*A*fter begging the last woman he'd hooked up with not to absolve her extramarital guilt by blabbing the details of how they'd gotten it on in the back of her husband's newly leased Lexus, Tim all but lost interest in the need for a little strange.

Until he spotted Hope, bent over her oven in black lingerie.

He couldn't be entirely delusional in thinking she might be willing to re-create the scene for him in the near future. After all, she'd invited him into her nearly identical but infinitely more tasteful home for a meeting in her guest bedroom.

"Can I get you anything before we get started?" Hope asked.

If her invitation weren't offered under the pretense of baby nursery planning for his wife, Tim would have taken his chances, leaned in, and kissed her then and there. "I'm good, thanks."

She started up the stairs in a tight-ish top and appropriately short skirt. "Follow me."

Anywhere, Tim whispered silently, falling in behind her.

Given the less-than-ideal circumstances, she'd have to make the first move, but he'd get to give that first, and only, *no for the record.* Something along the lines of, *the attraction is undeniable, but the action is nothing to take lightly* whispered quietly, with the proper expression of intensity. Afterwards, when the glow still colored her cheekbones, but the guilt waterworks began, he would hold her, assure her what had happened was not her fault, but inevitable. He'd whisper that everything was truly okay as long as they kept this moment, and any others that might ever or never happen again, to themselves. His promise, to never let anyone else feel their shared pain of knowing how they felt about each other, would be that much more poignant.

Especially if it turned out to be true, which was a distinct possibility, given the glimpse he got of upper thigh as she started up the stairs.

"I understand congratulations are in order," she said.

Or, fingers crossed, would be sooner, rather than later.

"Thanks," he said in answer to what she was actually talking about. "I got the call from Frank asking me to take over Will's position on Monday night and by Tuesday morning calls and e-mails were already rolling in from covenant violators."

"Seems weird Will resigned like that."

"Apparently he's been thinking about it for a while."

"Oh," she said, reaching the landing at the top of the stairs.

"He said he's been asked to cochair the PTA at his kids' school or something."

"I was worried he quit over the whole playground issue."

"Not according to him."

"That makes me feel better," she said. "I'm sure volunteering in the best interest of his kids has to be a more gratifying work than trying to reason with irritated homeowners, anyway."

"Maybe I should have given that a little more consideration before I said yes."

"I'm sure you'll be great," she said.

He simply smiled, followed her down the hallway, and stepped into what he could only call a truly beautiful nursery. Awash in the warmest shade of yellow he'd ever seen, Hope had somehow managed to capture the absolute peace of standing in a colorful garden under a shade tree enjoying a gentle cooling breeze. No detail, from the baby furniture to the accent flowers painted along the base of the walls to the insect-themed curtains, matching bedside lamps, and throw rugs, was overlooked. The place was baby Eden.

Squared.

"Wow," he managed.

"You like it?"

"Love it, but I'm back to feeling guilt-ridden over commandeering your nursery."

She pointed to a daybed covered in lavender swatches of paint and fabric that, despite not being pulled together, was already beginning to look like a purple version of her existing nursery. "Honestly Tim, working on this plan for you makes me feel like I did when I put the design together in the first place." Her eyes, already a liquid blue, sparkled. "Hopeful."

"I'm glad you feel that way," he said, hopeful himself that somehow, the emotion of it all might have her feeling the need to whisk all that crap off the bed and replace it with him.

She walked directly over to the bed like she'd read his mind, but instead of doing the improbable, or even slightly more plausible act of removing everything gingerly and moving it neatly elsewhere before attacking him, she picked up a binder with *Trautman Nursery* scrawled across the front in lavender pen. "And as I said the other day, once you pick the tones, fabrics, and finish accessories the room might have a similar feeling, but it'll have its own look."

"It's looking like I may be in over my head."

"I'll go easy on you," she smiled.

Now they were getting somewhere.

"For example," she pointed toward the opposite wall, "ignore the book shelf and changing table and picture an interconnecting shelving system with a storage bench that goes under and around the window." She opened the notebook and handed him a tear sheet. "You'll have all the storage you'll need but still have room for a double dresser with changing stations."

His head was already spinning.

"Which leads me to window treatment options."

"As in curtains?"

"Sheers or panels." she stepped across the room and tugged on what were apparently sheers. "I'll put a few different styles, including valances and roller shade choices, in the binder for you and Theresa to pick from."

"Sounds like a plan."

"As for lighting," she handed him something she'd printed off the Internet. "This one with the butterfly and flower motif would be perfect."

"Sounds good," he said, meaning it, particularly when he spotted the red Target tag and a price point of $24.99.

"I think you should consider this chair-and-a-half so one person can comfortably sit with both babies. We can order it with a lavender petal ribbon stripe that pulls in colors from the comforter. If not . . ."

Tim felt himself drifting off somewhere after *blue vs. gray* lavender and *hand-painted baby wipe dispensers* and didn't quite tune back until he heard *hand blown.*

"So that's a yes?"

"Sure."

She smiled and noted something in her binder. "Have I lost you?"

"No way," he said.

She raised an eyebrow.

"Maybe just a little decorating overload."

"I have pretty much all the information I need to get the plan pulled together," she said. "One more thing."

"What's that?" He smiled.

"What about doing some flowers like I have running along the base of the walls?"

"As in a mural?"

"Given the history of murals in your house, I'd normally advise against that." She giggled. "But widely spaced three-dimensional flowers at the baseboard could be really cute." She paused. "Especially if we mix in some birds and bees."

Their eyes met.

Hope's cell phone chirped.

She grabbed the phone from its pole position in her back pocket and looked at the display. "I'm afraid I have to take this."

The bad timing was so perfect, he was sure it had to be her husband.

"Hi, Frank," she said.

Or Griffin.

CHAPTER TWENTY-ONE

*3.0. Right of Appeal. If a Committee denies or imposes
conditions on a proposed improvement or homeowner, a homeowner
may appeal by giving written notice of such appeal within
twenty-one days.*

*H*ope's new aquamarine and silver bracelet caught a ray of morning sunlight and sent refracted blue light dancing across the dashboard as she turned off I-70 and onto the Pena Boulevard airport overpass. "It's really beautiful, Jim."

"Glad you like it," he said.

More a token *sorry I'm leaving on Mother's Day* than *soon to be a Mother* gift, there was no denying the bracelet's significance. Jim knew she loved blue and any blue gemstone. What he didn't know was that aquamarine was April's birthstone. She touched her left breast to reconfirm the tenderness she'd been feeling for the better part of a week. The tenderness she felt every time they'd had sex, which was every day since day fourteen, just to be sure.

The gift was another of the undeniable signs that continued to present themselves. It couldn't just be coincidence that Jim gave her an aquamarine bracelet on a Mother's Day that would be all about completing her nursery layout for the Trautmans and finalizing the playground plans.

Both of which projects were foretold by Renata.

A new life is ready to come through very soon.

All she needed was confirmation from the pregnancy test sitting on the counter awaiting tomorrow's first-morning urine from the first day of her missed period.

"Cop ahead," Jim said.

Hope slowed and watched the needle drop below sixty-five.

"British Airways is east terminal, I think," he said, scanning the signs directing Denver International traffic. "No, no, west."

If she could get him dropped off by 8:40, she'd be back home loading her car by 9:15 and over at the Trautmans to set up by 9:45. Ten at the latest, depending on when Tim could get away from church to help her get the car unloaded. She'd felt bad having to run off after Frank called to deal with the plant mix-up at the nursery, but Tim was satisfied by her offer to come over to his house during church again and not only lay out the nursery plan, but arrange the room so the various options they'd discussed from paint color to fabric swatches were set up for Theresa.

She'd be done by noon at the latest, giving her time to relax before she was due to meet with Frank.

Maybe even take a little nap.

Had she really just considered taking a nap between work on the two projects that made her feel unbelievably happy and energized?

"Hope! It's the west terminal!"

"Oops," she said, veering out of the far left lane.

Her text message alert buzzed before she'd completely corrected her almost mistake. "Can you check and see who that is for me?"

Had to be Tim calling to confirm timing.

Jim took her phone from the center console. "Frank Griffin."

Or Frank, who'd put her on speed dial judging by the amount of calls and texts that had been coming in, would likely continue, until the playground was done and set up.

"Need me to read it to you?"

"I'll get back to him after I drop you off."

"'Kay." Jim half-nodded.

"He tends to check in more if he knows you're going to be out of town."

"Be sure and thank him for me when you do," Jim said rechecking the outer pouch of his briefcase for his passport and tickets. "Nice to know someone's looking in on you for me."

Would he be so blasé if she admitted Frank's interest in both her professional abilities and her well-being had her feeling more appreciated than she had since—?

Her text alert buzzed again as she made her way past long-term parking. "Frank again?"

"Nope," Jim said. "Tim Trautman."

Since she ran into Tim at Home Depot?

"Read it?" Jim asked.

Since she'd be calling Jim tomorrow with the best, most commitment affirming of news, there wasn't any harm in sending him off across the Atlantic with one of Tim Trautman's flirty texts to mull over. "Read it."

Hope ur morning's been happy so far, Jim read. *Theresa wants 2 blow off church for a mom's day family outing. Totally bummin but im afraid i won't be able 2 sneak away n meet up with u this AM at my house. I left u a key.*

"Interesting," Jim said.

He'd seen the lavender fabric swatches all over the nursery, seen the schematic she'd been trying to make self-service for Theresa, and knew she was supposed to set up the Trautman nursery. But, shouldn't he also be wondering, like she did, if Tim really was a little more interested than he should be? "Why's that?"

"He texts like a teenager," he said.

And, if she had to be honest, had a way of making her feeling like one. Not having him there to help her set up, to be there to stand back and admire the project unfolding in his nursery, felt a little more disappointing than she might have expected.

"There's British Airways right up ahead," he said.

But, not as disappointing as Jim's distracted nonreaction.

"I see it," she said, pulling up to the curb and stopping the car in front of the skycap.

Jim handed over her cell and unclipped his seat belt.

"I really wish we could have booked a ticket for me. I mean—"

"I know honey, but we've been over this."

"But you'll try to be back by Memorial Weekend?"

"Do my best."

She pushed down any pointless questions and what ifs about next month's ovulation by checking her breast for the comforting tenderness.

"Love you." He kissed her.

"Love you, too." She kissed him back.

"Call you when I land." He pulled his suitcase and briefcase from the back seat.

Her text alert buzzed again as he closed the door.

* * *

So far, Mother's Day had been one of the nicest Maryellen could remember. Frank and Eva had gotten up early and prepared all her favorites, from black coffee in bed to a breakfast spread of cantaloupe, egg whites, turkey bacon, and even the banana pancakes she nibbled on to show her appreciation.

She slid the cool opal along the chain of her new Mother's charm necklace, finished unloading the dishwasher, and watched Frank open the shed, pull the outdoor chair cushions from storage, and begin to beat the winter dirt out of them. That he'd taken on the job of getting the patio furniture out and cleaned without having been asked was one of the best presents of all.

She slid open the screen door and joined him on the back deck. "Thinking you might like to have an early dinner out here tonight?"

"Hadn't thought about it." He draped a cushion over the railing and began to spray it with the hose. "We certainly could."

"Let's do. It's so beautiful out today."

"Sounds like a plan," he said.

She turned back for the kitchen to look up a recipe for an appropriately outdoorsy dish he might be willing to throw on the grill to cap off his day of above-average husbandry. But, before she stepped through the sliding doors and back into the house, she stopped and turned back around. "I figured you were hosing off the cushions because you wanted to eat out here."

"Hope's coming over in a little while to finalize the plans for this week." He pointed the sprayer at a chair cushion leaning against one of the deck posts. "I thought she might enjoy sitting outside."

CHAPTER TWENTY-TWO

Section 6.2A. Notice of Completion: Upon completion of improvement to property, applicant must give written notice to improvement committee for review and final approval.

No matter how faint, Hope was sure she saw a hint of pink running down the results window. If she hadn't woken up practically every hour and diluted the results by peeing twice, she'd have screamed the good news into the phone to Jim when he called to say he'd landed safely. Instead, she decided to hold her urine all afternoon and evening to take the "bonus" test for absolute confirmation. Once she saw the line again, she'd ring Jim right away and give him the good news. There'd be no tension between them about how long he thought he might be gone, or the details of his job, only excitement, unadulterated joy, and his promise to be home as soon as he could to witness the process of watching her bloom.

In the meantime, she was having the most picture-perfect day ever.

She'd woken up to wonderful, indescribable probability. Floated down the stairs to *not* have coffee. Opened the front door to get the paper, only to discover a loosely tied bouquet of lilies on the front steps. The thank you card, along with a check for the invoice Tim insisted be left on the desk in his office, was as gratifying as she could have imagined.

> Hope,
> *Wonderful doesn't even begin to describe the presentation that awaited us when we returned home yesterday. Paint swatches lined up and number coded with coordinating fabrics and curtain choices, accessories printed up and organized by price, totally self-explanatory design notebook, and that sample of the flowers along the baseboard blew me away. Theresa is beyond delighted.*
> *Thanks SO much,*
> *Tim*

The day only improved from there.

After carefully watching her heart rate at muscle conditioning class and a lunch she capped off with ice cream, she headed out to check on the plant material deliveries at the various playground sites. Under the bluest of skies, replete with puffy clouds and a cool breeze, she oversaw the nursery people as they set the trees, shrubs, and larger plants exactly where they were to be planted the next morning.

The youth group teens arrived right after school to plant the flowerbeds. Any concerns she might still have had about Will Pierce-Cohn being angry with her for getting involved with the playground or quitting the HOB because of her actions vanished when his son, Tyler, showed up with a winning smile and a willingness to do whatever she asked—especially when it meant working alongside that darling Lauren Trautman.

Lauren had rushed over to tell her how totally adorable the nursery plans were, what an amazing surprise it was for her mother, and how her own bedroom was on the list for Hope's next job. Frank stood beside her under the gazebo while Lauren gushed, nodding approval, but remained mesmerized with the emerging view of their soon-to-be-completed project. The rest of the afternoon was a happy blur of planting, imagining which of the teens her own someday teenage son or daughter would most resemble, and watching her plans morph into a beautiful, blooming reality.

By six, after checking off on all the sites and sending the kids to the rec center for a pizza party, she simply stood for a few quiet minutes and admired just how beautiful all the playgrounds, but especially the one directly opposite her front door, truly were.

A playground outside her front door.

By six-thirty, she was at the rec center standing beside Frank once again and inhaling a slice of gooey, cheese pizza.

Craving more as she ate.

She gobbled her second slice trying not to count down the thirteen minutes until seven, when her urine would definitely be concentrated enough to reveal the distinct pink line. Frank patted her lightly on the back, stood beside her, and whistled to get everyone's attention.

The room quieted down to a rustle of chewing and soda swilling.

"How about a round of applause to Hope for her landscaping brilliance and to the rest of us for a job well done?" Frank paused for the clapping. "I really want to thank you all for today and I want to thank you in advance for your continuing efforts for Memorial Weekend."

The kids clapped for themselves again.

"I made two promises in exchange for your help. The first, extra funds for your operating budget, which have already been deposited in your account." Over the wolf whistles, he reached into his pocket and pulled out a piece of paper. "Rec center jobs will be filled by the following youth group members: Facilities—Garrett Dines, Sports and Rec—Erin Cohen, Hannah Hunt, and for lifeguards—Heather McDaniel and Lauren Trautman.

"What about me?" Eva Griffin asked.

"I have one more very special announcement," Frank said.

Hope wasn't sure what was more telling, his beaming smile or the expectant look on his daughter's face.

"I am extremely proud to announce that Eva Griffin was nominated and accepted to Young Crusaders for Christ Summer Institute, perhaps the preeminent young Christian Leaders Camp in the country."

* * *

"We were starting to think you ran away or something," one of the twins said as Eva finally made her way into the girls' bathroom.

"Practically did to get away from my effing lame father." Eva choked back an angry tear, dipped her finger in Hannah's pot of Hard Candy lip-gloss, rubbed her lips together, and checked her reflection in the mirror. "I had to tell him I got my period to shut him up from going on about the *honor* of getting to go to that bullshit camp. Then, my mom followed me halfway down the hall babbling how everything is going to work out, as though she believes it or something."

"You okay?" Hannah asked.

"He can walk all over my mom, but he's not gonna step on me." The fact that Lauren chose that moment to emerge from the center stall and head for the trough sink without daring to look up didn't help matters any. "I know our next spell."

"What's that?"

"We're going to get rid of my dad."

Libby's eyes grew annoying huge. "Kill him?"

"A riddance spell, not a death spell."

"My bad," she said. "But isn't that like a totally advanced spell?"

"We're skipping the third spell and doubling our power into the fourth."

"What happened to the second one?"

"Did it myself," Eva mumbled.

"Tyler's not going to go for that." Margaret looked at Lauren for confirmation, like she was his official mouthpiece now. "Is he?"

"He doesn't have a choice," Eva said before Lauren could answer.

"What if the spell doesn't work?"

The door to the bathroom squealed open and next thing she knew, Hope Jordan was standing next to them looking like she'd been part of the conversation all along.

"Cover-up." Eva looked into Lauren's makeup bag. "Do you have any? The lights in here make me look dead."

"Think so," Lauren said, digging in her purse.

Hope smiled, but disappeared into a stall without a word.

Margaret flashed the *Oh, shit* look.

My dad must have sent her, Eva mouthed.

"It's all cool. She's cool," Margaret whispered over the sounds of a purse zipper and the rustle of jeans coming down or whatever. "I was watching the door."

A pained sigh came from Hope's stall.

"Lauren, your eyeliner is so awesome!" Eva said quickly in her most normal, carefree voice. "What kind is it?"

"Stila." Lauren still looked stunned but managed to play along. "The color is . . ."

"Hey," Hope's voice cracked as it filtered through the room, like she was super pissed or about to say she'd heard what Margaret claimed she couldn't possibly have heard.

"You sure?" Eva whispered to Margaret.

"Do any of you have a spare tampon?" Hope asked.

Part II

DEAD
RABBITS

CHAPTER TWENTY-THREE

General Provision 9.6. Common Property: Certain areas are designated as common property intended for the common use and enjoyment of the owners for their recreation and other related activities.

Hope celebrated day fourteen of her cycle and the start of Memorial Weekend with a bottle of Gatorade, a ride on her spinning bike, and an unopened ovulation predictor kit for company. Like every morning for the past two weeks, the length of her indoor journey was indefinite.

Jim called an hour and a half into the trip.

"Things are going amazingly well here," he said.

She twisted the tension knob on her bike upward.

"The president of the company took me out for drinks and confided there are some additional issues he thinks only I can straighten out."

"Quite a compliment," she said.

"Tell me about it." Jim's excitement was palpable. "Thing is, I'm going to have to push my return date out a little, so I can tour two of the distribution centers."

She gave the knob another half-twist higher. "What do you mean by a little?"

"I rebooked my flight for the eighth."

She sighed, partly with relief. He'd still be back long before her next ovulation.

"Honey, I know the timing of this job's been really hard on you, but if things go the way I'm thinking, my recommendations may help this company keep from laying off anyone but obsolete employees." He paused. "I could end up as the go-to guy for economic downturn restructuring."

"That's great. Really great." She took a calming sip of Gatorade. "It's just—"

"Why don't we plan some kind of getaway together the weekend I'm back? Maybe drive up to Aspen or head down to Santa Fe? Whatever you want."

"Won't you be too jet lagged to want to go anywhere else?"

"I'll have to run to Dallas early that next week to do some number crunching with the officers of the stateside parent company." He paused. "So there's no point settling in."

"I don't like being apart so much," she said.

"You have to keep in mind how lucky we are that I even have a job with all the downsizing going on."

"I know," she said, "and, I've been working my ass off to fill the time and keep my mind off . . . It's just that once I got my period . . ."

"Honey . . ."

She loosened the tension knob to a flat spin. "Just come home and make me pregnant."

The whir of the spinning wheels beneath her filled the silence that followed.

"Hope," he finally said. "The job's been extended."

The dreaded butterflies fluttering in her stomach mixed with the adrenaline rushing through her system and settled in her thighs.

"I promise, this isn't going to be as bad as it sounds. You'll come here. I'll be back and forth. We'll figure it out."

She pulled the brake on her bike and put her head on the handlebars. "For how long?"

"Possibly end of the year."

She began to cry.

"Hope, I'm going to be home at least one week a month."

"Ovulation week?"

"If not, I stipulated they have to fly you out every other month."

"So that's a yes?"

"Assuming I can schedule around what's going on at the job site and the home office."

"You have to."

With his pause, a bead of sweat traveled from the nape of her neck down her spine. "Starting when?"

"I need to be back in London on the seventeenth."

"But I'm not ovulating until the following week."

"I have no choice," he said.

"No, you don't," she said.

"Hope," he exhaled heavily. "I can't make the job of getting you pregnant get me fired from my real job."

"Then I'll fly back with you."

"I'll be working fourteen-hour days."

"And I'll be there to make sure you eat and rest and—"

"And get you pregnant?"

"Yes."

"One month isn't going to change anything."

"Feels like everything."

"Damn it, Hope. Why does this have to be so damn hard?"

"I ask myself the same thing almost every day." The lump in her throat dissolved into another sob.

"Can't we do the best we can, and if nothing happens, start up again first of the year?"

"I thought you wanted a baby, too?"

"I want less stress about the whole thing. I'm starting to wonder if that's the reason you're not pregnant yet."

"I'm starting to wonder why you're not more stressed."

"Can't you be a little more patient?"

"I've been patient for years."

"I want to feel like having a baby isn't a total obsession."

"I want to be pregnant so badly."

"I want to feel like sex isn't a job. I want to be able to enjoy it again."

"And I don't want, can't, talk about this anymore, right now." She hung up and slid off the bike.

She crossed the basement, stopped at the wet bar, and pulled the Gray Goose from the shelf. The phone was already ringing again before she'd finished filling her half-empty Gatorade bottle with vodka.

* * *

Turn lemons into lemonade.

All Frank thought while Laney, whom he'd just hung up with, raged over Randall Fowler's last-minute ribbon cutting cancellation. He'd been looking for the right opportunity to call Hope for almost two weeks and suddenly had it.

"I have nothing more to say to you right now," Hope said by way of hello when he did.

She'd shown up the morning after the pizza party and fulfilled her duty to oversee the final stages of the planting, then turned back for her house and all but disappeared. He'd called, had Maryellen stop by with candy, went so far as to question Tim Trautman, who reported getting the same vague *doing fine, thanks* message she'd left for him. He'd about run out of ideas for trying to connect with her until Laney called about Randall's ribbon-cutting bailout.

Turn lemons into lemonade.

"But what would you say if I told you I have an offer you can't refuse?" he asked.

There was an extended pause, presumably where Hope checked her caller ID. "Frank?"

"Sorry if I caught you at a bad time."

"I'm sorry. I was expecting, thought, you were Jim."

"I suspect I'm glad I'm not—at the moment, anyway."

Hope started to cry.

"Anything I can do to help?" he asked after a respectful pause.

"I don't know how anyone can help," she said through intensifying tears. "Jim's job in London's been extended."

"For how long?"

"End of the year, maybe."

"I see," he said, processing the implications and, despite her opinion to the contrary, opportunities to help.

Her sobs sounded animalistic with pain.

"Hope," he said after letting her cry it out. "I know it's hard to imagine at the moment, but the most impossible situations have a miraculous way of working out."

"Not if Jim doesn't even want to try to get pregnant until his job's over."

"That what he said?"

"If I'd known this was how it was going to be, I'd probably be in L.A. or San Francisco or . . . maybe not even married."

"You are where you're supposed to be."

"Waiting for nothing to happen?"

"The Lord always has a plan," Frank said.

"That's what I'm afraid of."

He waited until the crying that followed eased up.

"From my experience, the more challenging the situation the more magnificent His larger plan."

"I'll believe that when I see it."

"Maybe you already are."

"Meaning what?"

"The timing of my call."

She sniffled. "How's that?"

"Randall Fowler had a last-minute meeting and cancelled out for this morning."

"Isn't the ribbon cutting in less than two hours?"

"An hour and forty-five, to be exact," he said. "Which is why I called you to do the honors."

"You want me to ribbon cut?"

"Considering how many compliments I've already gotten about the playgrounds, I should have asked you in the first place."

"I'm flattered," she said.

"Can I take that as a yes?"

She took what sounded like another sip of whatever she was drinking. "After Jim's news, I don't know how I could possibly—"

"Miss the chance to be recognized for your landscaping skill among appreciative neighbors, many of whom are obligated by covenant to complete their yards by summer?"

"I'm afraid growing my business isn't my biggest priority."

"If Jim has to be out of town for the rest of the year, filling unwanted down time may well be."

He couldn't take her silence as agreement, but at least she seemed to be considering what he'd said. "Hope, I know The Lord guided both the timing and purpose of my call."

"Even if that's true, I don't know if I can get myself together enough to—"

"Her sentence was interrupted by the telltale blip of a call waiting on her end of the line.

"That's Jim."

The phone blipped again.

"Don't you need to answer?"

"I can't face talking to him right now."

Another blip.

"I need to get my head around things a little."

Instead of switching over to talk to him, she began to cry softly.

"Will he keep calling until you answer?"

"Most likely."

The call waiting tone blipped once again.

"You won't hear the phone if you're across the street enjoying a calming sip or two of champagne."

* * *

Eva set aside one bottle of champagne, combined the partially full case with a half case of kid-friendly Martinelli's sparkling cider, and loaded it atop the other boxes on her dolly. "Where's Heather?"

"Bathroom," Libby said. "She'll be back in a sec."

"Better be. We have to have all this loaded into your mom's car and over to the playground in fifteen minutes or—"

"Or my mom will flip," Margaret said. "She's been pissed off and bat shit crazy all morning."

Heather reappeared in the rec kitchen by her dolly.

"Back just in time." She glanced sideways at Tyler. "What about Lauren?"

Before he had a chance to fake nonchalance, Lauren rushed through the door, a noisy blur of red lifeguard uniform and jangling *official* whistle. "Staff meeting just ended."

Annoying as Lauren's new getup was, together as she and Tyler still were, Eva smiled anyway and popped the cork.

Everything was falling into place, exactly as planned. The spell called for a full moon, attendance by all coven members, and, along with some tricky-to-locate ingredients, like Thieves Vinegar and Black Water, *an evening of significance.* When she checked the lunar calendar she couldn't believe the next full moon coincided with Memorial Weekend. Her mom tried to smooth things over by promising to talk to her dad about rethinking his decision, or at least make the torture worth Eva's while by looking at new cars when she got home, but both of them knew it would never work. Didn't matter. The Goddess was with her, wanted her to do the spell to get her dad out of the picture before that stupid camp. So with her, Heather's family decided to push back a trip to California so they wouldn't miss the party, and then Lauren and the others who'd gone for rec center jobs were all assigned day shifts before she had a chance to tell them they had to be off by nighttime. Heather even got ahold of some spell-enhancing hash and baked it into brownies for them to have on the walk back to her house. The irony of her dad's latest edict, making the evening party mandatory for all youth group members so they could set up and clean up, was almost too cool to be believed. All she had to do was get her mom to let everyone off by about 8:45 so they could be at her house by 9:30 and doing the spell at exactly 10:03.

Eva raised the open bottle.

"To my dad's new ministry in Africa or wherever it is the Goddess sees fit to send him." She savored the sting of bubbles in her nose. "May there be enough dangerous snakes and heathens to distract him until I leave for non-Christian college."

* * *

Tim enjoyed the beautiful day, the impressive balloon bouquets, and the fanfare unfolding around him. More enjoyable was the sight of his family, all of them already a part of the very fabric of the neighborhood celebration. Theresa, who he'd set up in an aptly named beach chair, complete with sun umbrella and plastic flute of sparkling cider, greeted new friends and commiserated about those last few uncomfortable weeks. The boys scampered around the play structure with their buddies. Lauren looked adorable in her lifeguard uniform, standing amid the youth group kids, and practically glued to the Pierce-Cohns' son.

He looked around for Will and/or Meg, with whom he'd already met in his new board member capacity. They'd shared an official hello, talked politics, and had the obligatory *our children seem to be spending time together* chat. All he needed to do was introduce both of them to Theresa so they could chat together about the kids and any awkwardness about having taken over Will's position would dissipate for good.

The move to Melody Mountain Ranch had been overwhelmingly good for all of them, but especially him. One dip into the new, much more upscale pond and any hesitations he'd had about leaving Eagle's Nest Vista were forgotten. He smiled, patted a fellow board member on the shoulder, and worked his way through the crowd. Stopping at the play structure, he placed the tray of half-filled champagne glasses he'd been passing around on a counter-height step leading up to the corkscrew slide. He picked up one half-full glass, poured it into another, and left the empty behind. Setting the full flute back on the tray, he continued on toward the gazebo and a conversation group that included Jane Hunt, Maryellen Griffin, and, until he'd stepped away a minute earlier, Frank Griffin. Before he reached the women, who were already poised to descend on his tray for refills, he removed the extra-full glass, took the spot vacated by the ever-present Frank, and handed the champagne to the event's unofficial guest of honor.

Hope Jordan looked that much more beautiful and ethereal framed by all the flowers and plantings. But even with *father figure* Frank at her side, next to her since she'd appeared at the edge of the playground, she'd taken an unusually tentative, shaky looking step into the crowd. As she accepted her well-deserved compliments and clandestine attempts to cheer her up in the face of her recent disappointment, she looked very much like she needed the drink she plucked from the first tray that chanced past.

Not to mention the double she'd accepted, and was now sipping, courtesy of him.

It was only 10 A.M.

If she was drinking this much this early, she'd undoubtedly be in high spirits by the time the potluck ramped into high gear.

As Frank, who seemed hell-bent on cock-blocking him, returned toward his self-appointed post at her side, Rod Stewart's oldie, "Tonight's the Night," began to loop through Tim's head like a cheesy champagne-enhanced soundtrack.

Tim smiled at Hope. Ain't nobody, particularly Frank Griffin, could stop him now, or ever.

* * *

Will reached behind Nicole's sock drawer, located Madison's missing bathing suit top, reunited it with the bottom, and tossed both pieces into the suitcase.

"We're out the door," Meg called up to him from the front hall.

"'Kay." He put Nicole's favorite bathing suit along with his best guess as to an acceptable spare into the girls' shared suitcase.

"You coming soon?" she asked.

"Just need a few minutes to wrap up some packing."

"Want us to wait?"

What he wanted was to have scheduled their trip, not around package deals on Disney Cruises, but to miss Memorial Weekend at home entirely. He sighed, took a deep breath of cool, fresh spring air. Or, at the very least, he wanted to wake up to the forecast of heavy rain instead of the ridiculously azure sky and clear views of the snow-capped mountains he would have otherwise relished.

The tinny circus music of an approaching ice cream truck filtered through the house.

"Ice cream!" the girls yelled in unison. "Mommy, we need money!"

Their impatient squeals felt like fingernails on a chalkboard as Meg presumably fished for whatever was the going rate for the dubious delight of purchasing vaguely frostbitten treats from a potential pedophile.

He sighed as he heard them take off across the street. At least he didn't have to worry about their safety with the mass of fellow parents, homeowners, and people he'd been actively avoiding since Laney's party. "Go ahead, Meg." He pulled the girls' terry cloth cover-ups from their closet. "You need to get over there so you aren't late."

"So do you," she said.

But not until after his wife kicked off the festivities with one of her *kudos on a successful completion of a community-based project* speeches to her fellow constituents. Admittedly obligatory on her part, wasn't it concession enough when her own husband had petitioned against the project? Or, that their son was helping out at the party as a member of the youth group? Never mind their daughters were probably already lapping up ice cream he was almost as much against as the playground. For him to sit there, struggling to maintain his political spouse game face, was above and beyond whatever call of duty he had to endure. Will threw a few pairs of socks into the open suitcase and reached for the zipper. "I just need to make sure we're basically ready so we're not scrambling around to finish up later."

"Okay." Her heels clicked across the front hall then stopped. "You are going to show up, aren't you, Will?"

He had to, that or face a rehash of the Mother's Day *discussion* that, despite his insistence he'd left the HOB to redirect his efforts in the direction of activities where his contributions might be better appreciated, like volunteering at the kids' book fair, collecting items for the school auction, and organizing field day, would end with Meg calling his resignation a cop-out.

At least she hadn't gone so far as to sucker punch him with any snide remark about his embarrassing incident at Laney's, or even chide him about being the spouse of a political figure at a sex toy party.

"No worries," he said.

"See you there." The door closed behind Meg with a cross-breeze thud.

Will headed for the three loads of laundry awaiting folding into piles separated by destination—a suitcase bound for Florida or the appropriate dresser to await post-vacation service. By his calculations, the timing of the separating and folding process would make him miss Meg's speech and just enough of whatever Frank Griffin had to say for him to amble across the street and catch Randall Fowler cut the ribbon.

Frank Griffin's amplified *Welcome!* rattled through the house.

Will separated the laundry into a going-to-Florida pile and a not-going pile.

Really, no one would notice exactly when he'd shown up as long as he managed to raise the conciliatory glass of champagne he'd need as social lubricant.

By the first round of clapping, he had all the key clothing folded into the suitcases he'd placed next to each other on the floor for him and Meg.

Her name rang through his closed bedroom window.

He folded the remainder of the clothing in the not-less-than five and not-more-than-ten minutes he knew to be the length of her speeches, left the rest in piles for later, picked up Tyler's clothing, and started for his room.

He set his stepson's clothing into what was supposed to be a mostly packed suitcase, but Tyler's setup and cleanup obligations, coupled with a teen lack of enthusiasm for a family vacation that included Disneyworld, guaranteed there was no way he was packing for himself. For once, Will almost appreciated the blow-off on Tyler's part.

Outside, the crowd clapped for his wife.

He started down the stairs.

Avoiding the front door, and with it, the increased likelihood of Frank or anyone else on stage noting his exact arrival time, he headed for the kitchen and slid open the patio door.

"It truly took a village to raise these playgrounds," Frank's voice rang through the crisp but quickly warming air.

Will locked the sliding glass door and started across the patio. Despite lingering concerns, there was no denying how nice the playground looked at the end of the cul-de-sac. The convenience was indisputable—a fact he planned to mention as soon as he ran into Hope. Before she could utter a cursory hello, before he had to pretend he didn't notice the vague guilt that had better be etched in her face, or suffer any half-baked platitudes she'd come up with to explain her thoughts about her partnership with Frank, he'd congratulate her on a job well done.

Frank cleared his throat. "I'd like to thank Henderson Homes for their commitment to our community, Playworld Play equipment for their willingness to work within our budget, the residents of Songbird Canyon Court, Warbler Way, and Hummingbird Cove Court for putting up with the construction noise, the Melody Mountain Ranch Homeowner's Board for doing what they do so well, and our Melody Mountain Ranch Youth Group for their hard work and superior attitude," Frank said.

Will neared his side gate.

"I would especially like to mention and thank the organizer of today's event and tonight's not-to-be-missed Memorial Weekend kick-off, party hostess extraordinaire, Laney Estridge."

Catcalls and applause rang thru the cul-de-sac.

"In watching this project evolve from an idea into today's reality, I was struck by how much more there is to a beautiful playground than swings, a monkey bar, and in our lucky case, a half-basketball court and mini-skate park. When green space is to be transformed it must become even more beautiful. I think you will all agree that we've accomplished that goal."

The applause grew more deafening.

"For that I would like to thank our fellow resident and landscape designer . . ."

Will took a deep breath and cracked open the gate.

"Hope Jordan."

Will stopped.

"For your truly innovative ideas for blending environmental concerns with our needs as a growing community, I'd like to ask you to stand next to me and do the honors."

Frank handed Hope the scissors.

Will closed the gate and turned back for the house.

CHAPTER TWENTY-FOUR

7.7.21. Hazardous Activities: No activities shall be conducted on any Lot, Common Area, or Licensed Property which are or might be unsafe or hazardous to any person.

*M*aryellen nibbled the corner of the most delicious, fudgy, chocolate-chip-filled, caramel-drizzled brownie she'd ever eaten.

Not counting the one she'd already devoured.

There had to be at least 400 calories of pure sugar, fat, and carbs floating through her system, but it wasn't like she'd had time to eat much of anything else since her morning half-grapefruit. From the second she'd arrived at the playground pavilion, she'd been too busy accepting compliments on behalf of Frank, pouring champagne, and handing out slices of playground replica cake to take a bite herself. An afternoon's worth of poolside streamer hanging and balloon tying left her starving, but she wasn't about to have any of the greasy dim sum Laney arranged for the volunteers—she being the primary and most voracious volunteer of them all, at least where eating pot stickers was concerned. Once the casseroles, not-quite-homemade buckets of fried chicken, bread machine loaves, and bowls of fruit salad began to arrive, she had too much to do to sample anything. She managed to munch on a veggie or two while arranging various incarnations of Chinese chicken, Greek, and green salad around the stunning Mediterranean salmon salad she had every intention of making her dinner. Would have, had Laney not forgotten to buy enough of the reusable plates and plasticware she was also insistent be worked into the budget.

By the time Maryellen returned from an emergency trip to Safeway, the salmon salad, along with her second choice, a simple tossed romaine with feta and raspberry, had not only been polished off, but cleared away by the youth group.

How could she complain about not getting exactly what she wanted to eat when the teenagers seemed to be taking their job so seriously? Even Eva seemed blissful as she directed the others around.

A leader, just like Frank said.

After Eva's initial fit of rage and Maryellen's attempts to mollify her in the face of Frank's *decision made*, Eva had been quiet. So quiet, ominous silence permeated the house in the same way that used to have Maryellen running to check on her toddler daughter to make sure she was just coloring and not on the walls.

Not tonight though. By agreeing with Eva that the kids deserved to be let off from cleanup duties by 8:45 so they could enjoy the party, there'd be no meltdown.

The word *meltdown* made her think of chocolate—and the dessert table, overflowing with all the pies, cookies, and cakes that had appeared, like magic, while she was at the store.

Maryellen broke her brownie, the best dessert of them all, and stuffed half in her mouth.

What damage could a couple of brownies really do anyway?

Meg Pierce-Cohn, who'd exited a dull-sounding conversation about environmental tax credits, appeared beside her and surveyed the array of offerings. "What do you recommend?"

"These brownies are to die for." She handed one to Meg from the platter beside her before setting some on a plate for Frank, who'd undoubtedly been too busy basking in the blazing success of his day to eat enough to counterbalance however much he'd had to drink.

Which somehow reminded her of Will.

Before she could remind herself not to say anything, not to ask any questions about how he might be feeling, how he felt knowing the community was celebrating a playground he was against, she blurted, "Haven't seen Will today."

"He should be here soon." Meg took a bite of brownie. "There's so much to anticipate for a two-week trip that includes both a Disney cruise and the Everglades."

"Can't imagine," Maryellen said, even as she pictured an alligator sidling silently across the smooth, silvery surface of the empty pool, stopping to train a menacing eye at her husband, whose hand rested on the center of Hope Jordan's back. "Poor thing."

"Excuse me?" Meg asked.

"Hope Jordan." Maryellen shook her head. "Hasn't been able to get pregnant and now she found out her husband's going to be in and out of the country until the end of the year."

"I don't think I've ever been more frustrated than when I was trying to get pregnant with the twins." Meg took another bite of brownie.

"Which is why I think he asked Hope to landscape the playgrounds in the first place."

"Her husband?"

"Frank." Maryellen said, stopping short of bringing the conversation back around to Will and how she was sure Frank asked Hope to do the landscaping to settle his grudge over the location controversy. He'd done nothing but obsess about the whole thing and Hope's mental state since he spotted her signature on the petition. "Frank's keeping an eye on her because the poor thing's been drinking away her anguish all day."

"Difficult situation," Meg said.

"Very." She finished her brownie.

"Well," Meg finally said, turning in the direction of a conversation cluster by the retaining wall beside them. "You've done a nice job with all this."

"Thanks," Maryellen said, reveling in her first compliment of the day.

As Meg stepped away, Maryellen tidied the half-eaten platter by popping a stray crumb into her mouth. No one could say she didn't deserve to savor the sweet melting chocolate on her tongue. The tea lights she'd strung along the security fence seemed to twinkle in agreement as she started across the pool deck toward the deep end, where Frank leaned casually against the diving board trying to make peace between Laney and Sarah, who'd been sniping at each other since the ribbon cutting.

Hope, his charge, stood directly beside him.

Other than wishing Frank didn't feel such a strong need to stand beside someone other than her, Maryellen felt happier and more relaxed by the moment. She wedged in on the other side of her husband and offered the plate around. "Best brownies I've ever tasted."

Frank picked the largest from the pile and took a big bite.

"I know, right," Laney said, like one of the teenagers.

"I'm more into the lemon bars," Sarah said.

"You'll change your mind if you try one of these," Laney said.

Maryellen coveted a large crumb clinging to the plate's border.

"Already hit my dessert limit," Sarah said.

"Your loss," Laney winked and helped herself to yet another before turning back toward the dessert table.

Had she not been so busy sampling everything as it arrived, she might have realized sooner that they only had a small stack of disposable plates left over from last year's party.

And no knives.

Maryellen pinched herself lightly for thinking what felt like free-flowing unpleasant thoughts. She offered the remaining brownie to Hope.

Hope held up her drink. "I'm good."

"I'm good, too," Frank said, grabbing the last one, splitting it in half and giving it to Hope. "But a little of this will only make you better."

The photographer appeared and pointed his camera in Maryellen's direction. "Can you scoot closer to the couple next to you? The three of you are so well-coordinated."

"So funny," Sarah said looking at Hope and Frank. "You guys really do all match."

Maryellen laughed along, even though she didn't find anything particularly funny about Hope's blue, yellow, and red floral dress coordinating with her yellow top and jean skirt and matching Frank's multistriped polo.

Frank put his arm around both her and Hope. "Have to immortalize this lucky moment."

The photographer snapped the picture.

"Got a problem that may not be so lucky." Larry Miller or Barry Stiller, she couldn't pull up the name and Frank usually referred to him as Mr. Know-it-all, appeared as the photographer turned for his next subjects. "Borrow your rec center keys, Frank?"

"For?"

"I thought I'd take a peek into the mechanical room."

"What's up?"

"I notice there's water pooling on the lower patio."

Frank glanced out toward the lower level and back toward Hope. "Can't it wait?"

"If it gets worse and someone drinks too much and slips . . ."

"Better go with you—restricted keys and all." Before following whatever his name was, Frank whispered, "Mel, keep an eye on Hope."

Maryellen nodded and watched him walk away.

Then she watched Hope head for the bar.

The next thing she knew she found herself headed back to the dessert table where Tim Trautman had materialized beside Laney.

"So the brownies are the ticket, you say?" he asked.

"Definitely." Laney stood so close to him, her cleavage was practically touching his shoulder. "That is, as far as dessert goes."

"I see." He helped himself to a peek at her goodies while she leaned toward the now almost empty platter.

"They're especially delicious," she placed the last three squares on a napkin and handed it to him. "If you know what I mean."

"Excellent," he said, turning toward the bar. "I'll have to keep that in mind."

* * *

Tim removed the plastic tumbler Hope held in one hand and replaced the icy remnants of her drink with a fresh vodka and cranberry with a lime.

"Thanks," she said. "How'd you know?"

"Exactly." He grasped her free hand and began to lead her away from the pool area.

"Where are we going?" Her eyes twinkled with alcohol-fueled enthusiasm.

"Somewhere I should have taken you a while ago."

She looked confused, but followed along willingly enough. "I was starting to think you weren't coming."

"No chance of that." Which, despite his best efforts, took all day. After keeping his distance while champagne restored Hope's nonmaternal but otherwise lovely glow, he'd taken the boys to the pool thinking maybe she'd be there. She wasn't. He'd texted her while they splashed around in the water and, once he found out she was going to the potluck, planned to feed the kids at the party and send them home with Lauren. When he got home, Theresa had pizza waiting for dinner. He finally coaxed her into bed and got to the party, but then had to convince Gerry Miller something was wrong with the sump pump to get Frank away from Hope's side. "Theresa wasn't feeling perfect, so I hung around until she was settled in enough for me to stop by the party."

"Such a good husband," Hope said wistfully, drunkenly.

"Better friend." He led her around the back of the rec center and stopped at a secluded picnic table set in a grove of pine trees.

"Here?" she asked with a slight slur.

The cocktail and half a brownie he'd downed before locating Hope already had him feeling pleasantly buzzed.

"Time to unveil my ancient Chinese fertility weapon." He held her hand, helped her climb atop the picnic table, and joined her. "One of them, anyway."

She looked down at her drink. "How did you know I wasn't—?"

He didn't have the heart to tell her he knew she'd gotten her period at the pizza party through Theresa, via Lauren, who, in atypical teenage fashion, decided to actually share a few details of that particular day and recount Hope's disappointed request in the rec center bathroom. Instead he said, "The cocktail I poured for you at ten in the morning was a dead giveaway."

Moonlit tears began to forge a path down her cheek. "Wasn't my first."

"Can't say I'm surprised."

"I'm surprised I'm still coherent." She took a drink and the strap of her sundress slipped, revealing a fetching pink lace bra strap.

And an even more attractive shoulder.

"I really do think I might be able to help."

"After the last two weeks, I'm open to almost anything."

Her bare upper arm brushed against his bicep and "Tonight's the Night" started up again in his head. "When Theresa and I were trying for Lauren, I finally came to the conclusion we weren't succeeding because we were just way too uptight about the whole process."

"That's exactly what Jim said." Hope took a gulp of her drink. "About me."

Tim reached into his sweatshirt pocket and pulled out the brownies. He owed Laney one for the tip-off that they seemed to contain ingredients more medicinal than just chocolate. Judging by her friendliness, the payback was going to pay off for both of them. "Can't believe I didn't think of it myself."

Disappointment clouded Hope's face. "Aren't those the brownies Maryellen was going on about with the chocolate chips and caramel and—?"

"Maybe hash."

Her eyes widened. "Hash?"

"Or really strong pot."

"That explains why I feel so. . ." She covered her mouth, but didn't try to conceal her throaty giggle. "And, oh, my God, Maryellen's been nibbling on them all evening."

"Explains why she was so reticent to let them out of her sight."

"Frank and Meg Pierce-Cohn are going to be—"

"Feeling fairly excellent by about now."

"Do they know that they've been eating . . . ?"

"If they don't, they should suspect something by now." The caramel drizzle glistened in the moonlight as he waved the brownie in her direction.

"Shouldn't we say something?"

"Nah, they're gone."

"Aren't you worried that—?"

"I'm only worried about you."

"You're sweet," she said.

"So are these." He handed her a brownie.

"I can't remember the last time I did anything like this. Isn't it supposed to be bad for fertility?"

"After Theresa's miscarriage, I had her smoke a bowl or two to help her relax." He tucked a hair behind her ear. "Next thing we knew . . ."

She took a bite and began to chew.

Swallowed.

"What if we get caught?"

"Eating dessert together?"

She giggled.

He took a bite of his.

"What if word is out there's hash in the brownies and someone sees us eating them?"

"In your case, they're medically necessary."

"Can't argue with logic." She took another bite. "Really are delicious."

"No kidding." He licked stray caramel from his finger. "Mine always came out suspiciously sinewy."

"You've made them before?"

He smiled. "I make a killer mushroom pizza, too."

"Sometimes I wish Jim were a little more . . ."

Tim let his leg relax so his thigh grazed hers. "Handy in the kitchen and the garden?"

"Interested in my interests." She picked up her drink and took a sip, but didn't move her leg away. "Interesting."

"You know . . ."

"I know," he said.

She took another bite, chewed, and swallowed. "I don't usually do stuff like this—"

Tim broke the remaining brownie in half. "I'm not the judgmental type."

"But, I went to a psychic."

"Really," he managed, hoping he'd managed to temper the desperation from his voice.

"She read my tea leaves."

Did she see that once Theresa had the babies he'd be too tired from helping out with night feedings to even think about seducing Hope properly?

Hope's skirt rode up ever so slightly as she crossed and uncrossed her legs.

At least until things normalized, anyway.

"Kinda ridiculous, right?"

"Not at all."

"I wouldn't have believed anything she said, but I swear within days of her telling me she saw an anchor and a garden in the tea leaves, Frank asked me to consult on the playground." She smiled. "And I ran into you in the garden section of Home Depot."

He gave her a pat, but allowed his hand to linger on her thigh. "And the next thing you knew, we were talking about a garden-themed nursery."

"So you don't think I'm crazy for thinking the signs were clear?"

"Not at all."

"Thing is . . ." A tear rolled down her face. "I'm still not—"

"Pregnant?"

He wiped her cheek with his thumb. "You will be."

"Promise?"

"Even if I have to offer myself up for the cause." He gave his best just kidding smile so she wouldn't have to worry that he wasn't.

Unless she wanted to.

"You're funny." She smiled back. "And fun to be around and cute and . . . Theresa's so lucky to have you."

"I am a happy, lucky man," he said. "But . . ."

"But, I'm dying for something salty," she said.

That, he could definitely provide.

"I'm dying for—"

For? For him to take her off to a secluded corner and ravage her?

"Bugles." She put her head on his shoulder.

He reached into his pocket and pulled out his newly minted key to the rec center. "Your wish is my command."

"Guess I'm the lucky one, too," she said.

He ran his fingers through her hair.

Confusion crossed her face then disappeared in the deep blue of her eyes.

She leaned toward him, or maybe he leaned in first. One way or another, their lips neared each other's at exactly the same time . . .

* * *

Frank looped around the pool area checking every conversation cluster. He didn't necessarily expect Maryellen to be standing right next to Hope, but why couldn't he find either of them?

Maryellen was probably cleaning up.

With all Hope had to drink, she was probably in the bathroom.

Hungry and far more lightheaded than a few cocktails usually left him, he grabbed a macaroon from the picked-over dessert table.

He couldn't remember the last time alcohol left him feeling so disconnected. Not in charge.

Why hadn't he just opened the damn door to the mechanical room and let Gerry Miller play sump pump expert by his lonesome? Instead of five minutes away, he played audience for forty-five while the man detailed intricacies of the system, pondered possible causes for malfunction, and ultimately decided the thing worked fine.

Now Hope was gone.

He'd managed to keep an eye on her from that first tentative step out her front door. Hope had perked up, like he knew she would, with all the accolades. He'd counted her champagne refills—three—and distracted her from finishing Trautman's contribution of a fourth, even if the plastic flutes were equal to less than half a drink. He escorted her home afterward for a nap and confirmed she didn't need a ride to the evening party since she was only planning to make a cameo.

He glanced over the fence, out toward the parking lot.

Her silver Volvo was parked safely in the lot.

"Have you seen Hope Jordan?" he asked on his way toward the pool bathrooms.

"Not for a while," someone said.

"Nope," someone else said. "But I've been standing here talking for some time now."

He tapped Jane Hunt on her way into the restrooms and asked her to see if Hope had somehow slid by unnoticed.

She hadn't.

"How about Maryellen?" he asked Jane before she headed back toward the bar area.

She pointed to an out-of-the-way nook. "Over there."

Maryellen was standing with Laney where Jane pointed, but blocked from view by Roseanne Goldberg. He didn't see Hope, but maybe Roseanne was harboring her behind that ample backside.

He started across the pool deck.

"You really should set up an appointment with my naturopath, Laney," Roseanne's phlegmy voice bubbled in his ears as he joined them, standing together by the lost and found. "You never seem to be feeling right these days."

No Hope.

"He's great with nonspecific—"

"Frank," Maryellen sounded slurry. "Laney's not feeling so well. Overdone it, maybe."

"Go on home, Laney," he said, and hopefully with less impatience than he felt. "Maryellen and the kids will finish things up."

"But I let the kids off early so they could enjoy the party," Maryellen said.

"Shouldn't have," Frank said. "Where's Hope?"

Maryellen looked guiltily past him toward the other side of the pool. "She was right over there last I looked."

"There's no one over there now," he said.

Maryellen looked confused. "Must have disappeared."

"She did." Laney did look pale, especially under the pool lights. "With a fresh cocktail and Tim Trautman."

* * *

Bitch.

How could that bitch pick up those giant scissors without ever saying a word?

Meg certainly had a word to say when she came back from the ribbon cutting. Two of them: *Man up.*

He'd rolled that little phrase around all afternoon along with how disappointed she was he'd quit the HOB, that no one respected a quitter, that his brooding was *anything but sexy.*

Long after she left for the potluck to break bread with her constituents, recongratulate Griffin on behalf of not only the community, but the Pierce-

Cohn family, and go on to make excuses for her husband's *glaring, embarrassing* absence, he still couldn't figure out why Hope never bothered to mention she was consulting on the playground.

Why she was kissing up to Frank Griffin like he really did have a direct line to the Big Guy upstairs?

One thing Will knew for sure, Bitch needed to provide some answers.

He polished off his beer.

He didn't deposit the empty bottle in the recycle bin, or even rinse it out and leave it in the sink. He didn't even bother to clear it from the coffee table.

Time to man up.

* * *

Frank found her on the bottom step of the main stairwell by the vending machines.

She was glassy-eyed and clearly intoxicated, but alone.

"I've been looking all over for you."

Hope readjusted the strap of her sundress atop her shoulder. "Here I am."

"I was worried that you—" He looked down the hall, but didn't see that slime Trautman.

He hadn't seen him at the party, but the guy must have been lurking, watching, waiting for him to let his guard down and leave Hope's side. For all he knew, Gerry had gone to him first and, knowing the keys weren't supposed to be out of a board member's sight, pretended he didn't have his and sent him on to Frank to take the bait. "I'm just glad you're okay."

Glad Trautman wasn't by her side. Or worse.

"I needed something." Hope straightened her skirt. "To eat."

"There's food out by the pool." He tried to, but couldn't completely focus on what exactly was left beyond half-eaten pies and soggy chips.

"What I wanted—" She dropped some quarters into the machine, fumbled with the buttons. "Not Doritos." She watched intently as a bag of something twisted and fell with a dull thump. "Bugles."

"Bugles?"

She tore open the bag, popped one into his mouth, and popped one into her own.

The waffle-y, salty, oily, never-realized-how-delicious-they-were-ness of them was momentarily distracting until the hum of the vending machines grew too loud to ignore. "This area was supposed to be locked up."

"Tim let me in." She popped a Bugle in her mouth.

"Tim." The bright red of the Coke machine reflected his anger.

She scrunched her face. "You're mad."

"Tim wasn't supposed to open this area. Leave you down here alone."

"He's sorry." She giggled. "He just wanted me to give me some . . ."

"Some?"

"Bugles." She smiled. "He gave me change."

"Nice of him."

"He's a good friend."

How good? "You know—"

"Know what?"

He paused for the right words. "Men like Tim sometimes have ulterior motives."

"Usually."

He felt his face flush. Of course she knew. Women as beautiful as Hope always knew. "I just wanted to make sure—"

"I'm sure . . ." Hope licked salt from her lower lip. "Sure you take such good care of me."

"Wouldn't have it any other way," he said.

She seemed to be trying to focus her thoughts.

He couldn't seem to either.

"Jim said to say thank you," she finally said.

"For what?"

"Being there for me."

"I am absolutely there for you." Frank's smile couldn't possibly reflect his pleasure. "Which is why I had to make sure everything was kosher. When Tim took you down here and—"

"Tim's going to have a baby, you know."

So sick of hearing that name. "More than one."

"I want to have a baby, too." She began to cry.

He put his arm around her and tried to come up with the platitude or proverb that would comfort her, give her the faith and guidance he knew she depended on him to provide. Maybe he was feeling the effects of that last cocktail or maybe something about the citrusy freshness of her hair kept him from thinking clearly, but nothing seemed to make enough sense to say.

Patience is a virtue.

All good things come to those who wait.

Have patience.

"Tim promised."

Frank's mouth felt cottony. "Promised you what?"

"A baby."

"Tim promised you a baby?"

"When?" She buried her head in his shoulder. "When is it going to be my turn?"

Frank closed his eyes, willed himself to focus on saying something poignant, something to overshadow whatever meaningless promise Trautman had offered. "To lose patience is to lose the battle," hopped on some obscure neural pathway and floated past his lips.

She looked up at him.

He wondered where he'd heard the quote before and how he knew the author was Gandhi, but never for a moment questioned the hand of the Divine as his inspiration. "Come with me." He wiped her cheek and grasped her hand. He was suddenly sure of exactly what she needed; what he was being called upon to do to make her feel comforted, encouraged, and supported in a way that Trautman felt free to promise, but only he could provide. "I want to show you something."

He led her toward the back staircase, up the stairs, down the hallway, and unlocked the multipurpose room. As soon as they stepped inside, he flipped on the light, closed the door behind them, and led her to the walk-in art supply closet. With the light from the outer room to guide his way, he grabbed a box sealed with packing tape and marked FRANK GRIFFIN HOB USE ONLY. To make sure no one felt inclined to mess with it, he'd also added FRAGILE.

He placed the box between them on the small work counter.

Hope leaned against him. "What is it?"

He pulled a penknife from his pocket and sliced through the tape. "My baby."

"Oh!" she said, looking into the box. "Is this—?"

"For five years, I prayed my heart out and endured watching practically every minister I know break ground on their church." He sighed. "I finally hid my dream here where it wouldn't remind me of what I didn't have."

As she ran her finger lightly along the bell tower, her face lit up with recognition of the similarity of their desire. "Your baby."

"The baby I've never lost faith would eventually be mine." He glanced at the artist's rendering of the Rose Window replica that would grace the Melody Mountain Community Church. "After more prayers, pleas, and patience than I thought possible, Henderson Homes called about switching out the location of the playground and like that, what seemed impossible fell like a plum into my lap."

"You're going to have your baby?"

He put his hand atop hers. "We are."

Her brow furrowed in confusion.

"All I need is a few more bucks to close the deal and your help to bring the Melody Mountain Community Church to life."

"You want me to—?"

"Collaborate with me."

"Baby," she slurred.

"That you and I will bring into magnificence together."

"Wonderful." She threw her arms around him. "So wonderful."

Frank found himself holding her, inhaling her floral scent, the warmth of her words sending exhilarating warmth through him.

"Thank you! Thank you! Thank you. I would love to. I want . . . I would love to do it with you." She fell slack, her breast pressing against his forearm.

His hard-on pressed against the inside of his khakis.

"It's all going to be so perfect, so beautiful, Jim."

"I'm not Jim," Frank said.

"Oops," Hope whispered, her breath warm against his neck. "I meant Tim."

* * *

Maryellen squirted dish soap, paused to admire the delicate, rainbow bubbles floating past her face, and turned the hot water on the plates Laney wanted washed and stored for the next community event.

While the sink filled, she collected platters, utensils, and serving bowls piled up along the counters of the rec center kitchen. With everything that still needed rinsing and drying, she should have been mad at Laney for the timing of her latest bout of the *vapors*. She should have been madder at Frank for enlisting her to finish up while he ingratiated himself with everyone from Laney to Hope. Mostly, she should have been mad at herself for allowing Eva to talk her into letting the kids off when she knew they couldn't possibly have finished the job.

She should have been mad, probably would be, if she hadn't spotted the platter that had eluded her earlier in the evening.

Mediterranean salmon salad.

Wiping a clean-ish fork on her shirt, she stabbed at some stray greens and topped them with a nice-sized flake of salmon. Olive tapenade danced on her tongue as she polished off the last pieces of lettuce, picked up the platter, and collected a couple others to slide into the running water. While they soaked, she turned back for a chip-and-dip that had an unbroken Frito Scoop nestled in the crumbs. She obliged the Frito, which was practically begging for a plunge into some brown-edged, but otherwise palatable guacamole, by filling it to the fluted edge.

And then eating him.

Or her.

After a barbecued chicken wing, some carrots dipped in ranch, and two quesadilla triangles, any irritation she could ever feel toward her daughter for leaving a half-finished job gave way to a bliss she hadn't felt in forever.

Eating.

Anything.

Everything.

She couldn't believe how insanely hungry she was, how lucky she was to have the run of the leftovers, and how much she wanted a bite of the lasagna clinging to a casserole she was about to dump into the sink. Setting the dish aside, she turned off the water, pulled out a handful of plates to make room, and tossed them into the trash.

They fell to the bottom of the steel can with a liberating swoosh and a thud.

Another thud followed from down the administrative hall.

Maryellen heard the hum of voices.

She glanced at the clock—9:07. If whoever was coming by could bring a few things out, she'd have plenty of time to get everything that needed washing back out on the tables for people to take home with them. She grabbed a small stack of wet but otherwise clean platters, headed for the kitchen door, and peeked into the hallway. The empty hallway.

From behind her, the thuds grew more rhythmic.

She expected the warm feeling that crept into her cheeks, but not the giggle that escaped her throat, that she practically watched float through the back wall toward whoever had snuck away from the party for some unsanctioned alone time. She thought of grabbing her cell and calling the covenant violation hotline to report the animalistic grunts that, were Laney not long gone, she might possibly worry sounded something like Frank.

Or, Laney and Sarah.

Or, Laney and anyone, really.

She ignored the shudder of something and headed back toward the sink, set the platters on the drying rack, and turned the water back on. Before dunking the lasagna pan, she peeled a mostly dried noodle from the corner, stuffed it in her mouth, and relished the combination of spongy give and dry crunch.

She turned the water off again.

Heard shuffling from behind the wall.

She turned the faucet on, pulled the plug, and left the water running.

On her way to collect more items for rinsing, she stopped to admire the neon pinks and oranges of a small vase of Gerber daisies, rescued two lonely celery sticks from some threatening-looking mushrooms, and dunked them into seven-layer dip.

Ate them.

Ate the mushrooms.

By the time she made it back and turned off the water, the noises behind the wall had stopped. With no one nearby to give her a hand, she dried a load of clean platters and headed out toward the pool area.

Frank stood at the opposite end of the pool talking with Scott Marsh, Lloyd Levis, and a group that didn't include the long lost Hope Jordan. He waved her over like he'd been looking for her, waiting for her to join the conversation.

Like he wanted her beside him.

She laid the platters out on a table then looped around the pool.

"How's it goin' hon?" Frank kissed her cheek.

Pinched her bottom.

"I need to get a few more serving plates cleaned and back out here before everyone starts to head home."

"My girl's been working her tail off today," he announced to the group.

Maryellen felt herself blush, couldn't quite think of exactly what to say in response to his unexpected acknowledgment. "Find Hope?" she asked instead.

"Trautman," he said.

"She was with Tim?"

"She's in the ladies' room now. Suffering the effects of some over celebration last I heard," he said. "You should check on her when you head back inside."

Maryellen was about to say yes, or sure, or no problem, but belched instead. "Oops," she giggled. "Excuse me."

Frank gave her a sideways glance. "What were you eating?"

"Nothing," she said.

"Your breath smells like cheese dip."

Her throat tightened. She hadn't had any cheese that she could remember, but the realization of what and how much she had eaten began to burble up.

"Would you mind checking on Hope, please?" Frank asked, turning back to Lloyd Levis. "I really do like your idea about starting an intra-subdivision table tennis round robin."

Dismissed from the conversation, she grabbed a few plates from the dessert table and turned back for the kitchen. Dropping the plates on a counter, she helped herself to lemon bar crumbs and headed for the lobby bathroom.

"Hope?" she asked.

"Nope," whoever was in the stall answered.

Nope Hope.

Two more women walked in.

Her stomach had begun to ache, but she couldn't possibly relieve the pain with so many people around. She made a point of washing her hands before leaving the ladies' room. She turned back toward the kitchen planning to finish the dishes while she waited for the bathroom to clear out, meant to, but saw the moon, huge, yellow, and full through the plate glass front doors.

Full of cheese.

* * *

"Where's Lauren?" Eva asked.

Tyler kicked at imaginary pebbles. "It's just that . . ."

"It's just that what?" The chirp-hum of the locusts was deafening while she waited for his answer.

"I think we're going to have to put the spell off."

Cold rushed down Eva's spine. "Say what?"

"Lauren had to take off."

"What the fuck do you mean, Lauren had to take off?"

"Her mom's having the babies."

"Like right now?"

"Her dad called and said they needed to go to the hospital."

"It takes forever to have babies. Get her. She needs to be—"

"She left from the party with her dad to meet their mom at the hospital."

"No," Eva said. "No. No. No."

"It's not her fault her mom's having the babies right now," Tyler's voice cracked.

"Did I say it was her fucking fault?"

"No, but . . ."

"But we're doing the spell without her."

"We can't."

That bitch may have sashayed in and charmed everyone with her dimples and her fake innocent act, and she may have turned Tyler's questionable brain to mush by shaking her tits for him, but no matter what the excuse was, she wasn't going to mess this up. "We have to."

"What if we wait until I get back from Florida, then we can try again with—"

"No full moon and both of the Estridge twins at camp?"

"Shit," he said.

"Tonight is the only night we can do it before I'm supposed to be leaving for that stupid camp." She paused to catch her suddenly ragged breath. "You know the Goddess is with us."

Or was, until the hash brownies disappeared from the cabinet where she'd stowed them in the rec center kitchen. By the time they discovered someone had found the tin and brought it out to the dessert table, only crumbs were left.

Now, Lauren's mother was in labor.

"I don't see how we can do the spell tonight without a thirteenth—?"

"Every other detail's lined up."

"Except our thirteenth. The outcome's too unpredictable."

"What does it matter if my dad gets called to convert jungle natives or be the head minister in Antarctica? I'm cool with whatever, as long as he's gone before I'm supposed to be."

"Eva, you know everything has to be right if we have any chance of this thing working."

"And you know I've gotta do something about my dad. He's going to ruin my life."

"What if it doesn't work?"

"Gotta try."

"And when it doesn't?"

"Then it's your girlfriend's fault."

"This isn't her fault."

"No need to go defending her."

Tyler looked shaky, teary even. "You expect me to still do the spell with you, right?"

"What the fuck do you mean by that?"

"I won't. Not unless I know for a fact you're not going to make Lauren pay for something that isn't her fault."

"You must really like her."

His nonanswer felt like a scream.

"I see," she said.

"If I hear you've said or done anything to her while I'm away. . ."

"I promise, I won't do anything to Lauren while you're gone," she said.

"Swear?"

"I'll be too busy dealing with whatever happens to my dad."

* * *

"Better late than never," Meg whispered, and not entirely unkindly, before turning back to the group of neighbors/constituents circled, as usual, around her.

Will couldn't have agreed more. He scanned the pool deck for Hope, but didn't see her anywhere.

He was going to find her, and when he did there'd be no pleasantries. He'd just ask exactly how the fuck it was she signed his petition and ended up cutting the fucking ribbon? No matter what lame excuse she came up with, he'd let loose with just how pissed he was. How much she'd hurt him by saying nothing at all.

"You look like you could use a strawberry Margarita?" the neighbor/bartender of the moment asked from behind the makeshift bar.

"Think I'll stick to beer." Will grabbed the keg hose and made a point of tipping his plastic tumbler against the foam, frat guy style. Watching for Hope, he pretended to listen to Meg justify what they both knew was pork in a construction bill the homebuilder's lobby had been on her case about for weeks.

"Builders *loooove* to provide bells and whistles; they want to, but they can't without some sort of tax incentive that . . ."

For a second, he considered taking her aside, telling her to cool it, and that she sounded kind of defensive and also slurry. If he didn't know better, almost stoned. He almost did, when a flash of light reflected off the pool and caught his eye.

He spun around in time to see a woman in a floral dress exit the front of the rec center.

Hope.

She made a serpentine path toward her car.

"Homebuilders *looove* profit," someone said. "They don't need tax incentives to figure out how to charge us for those extras we love."

"Hope Jordan looks like she's had too much to drink," Will interjected and pointed toward the parking lot.

"I think we all have," Jane Hunt said.

"She seems to be headed in the direction of her car," he said. "Be right back."

He flew across the pool area, out the gate, and arrived at her car just before she did.

Hope sidled up and stood so close, the alcohol on her breath intermingled with her perfume. "Will." Her eyes looked red-rimmed under the street lamp. "I'm glad you're here."

"I don't think you should be driving," he said instead of what he planned to say, but only because her safety was more imperative than what he needed to say, would, once he made sure she wasn't driving.

"Probably not," she giggled. "After those—"

"How 'bout I take your keys?"

Her sundress rested slightly off her shoulder, revealing a peek of pink satin.

"You know," she said, "it's really good to see you."

He took her keys. "Why's that?"

"I feel dizzy." She leaned unsteadily against her car, took a deep breath. "Don't remember the last time . . ." Confusion crossed her face. "Don't remember."

"What?"

"Where's Frank?"

"Frank?"

"You know," she straightened up a little, "I really didn't want to look at that damned playground every time I opened my front door."

His heart began to race. "What?"

"You were right," she said.

His blood pressure either shot up or dropped. Either way, he thought he might pass out. "About what?"

"The bunnies." She shook her head. "Felt bad when they trapped all those bunnies."

"I'm sure they're okay," he found himself saying. "Relocated."

"To heaven," she said.

"Did they?"

"And you were right about the land. Too marshy to support . . ."

Hope hated seeing the playground out her window? She'd implied the bunnies had been more than simply displaced? To top it all off, she stood there, albeit drunk out of her mind, telling him he'd been right about the land all along? Could he be so drunk he was imagining things? "Are you saying?"

"Frank fixed it. All better now."

"Not for me," he said.

"I know." She put her head on his shoulder. "So sorry."

Her hair tickled his neck.

"I knew you'd understand," she said.

"Why didn't you tell me you were consulting on the playground?"

"You're the kind of man who's nice and kind and understands."

Her apology pained and tickled his brain. "Understands what?"

"I couldn't just ignore the cosmic message of both nursery and playground jobs coming my way." Her eyes sparkled. "Not after Renata saw an anchor and a garden in my tea leaves."

"Renata? Tea leaves?"

"I thought if I didn't . . ." Sadness darkened her face. "No baby."

He couldn't begin to understand what she was talking about, but whatever it was . . .

"So sorry, Will." She went slack in his arms. "I really am."

"It's okay," he said. Whatever it was seemed to somehow explain her reasoning.

She kissed his cheek.

At least to her.

He glanced back toward the pool to see how much Meg could see of him. "We should get you home," he said, holding her up.

"Wanna go to bed." She nodded. "Crazy day."

Crazy didn't begin to describe it. A *sorry* and an admission he'd been right all along?

He put an arm around her toned, yet soft shoulder, carried her to the passenger side, and opened the door. As he tucked her into the passenger seat, the fabric of her sundress bunched, revealing the orb of her right breast.

He shut the door, but not before an admiring glance.

On his way to the driver's side, he reached into his pocket, grabbed his cell, and dialed Meg. "I need to drive her home."

"Who?" Meg asked.

"Hope."

"You okay to drive?"

Despite an afternoon of drowning his bitter bile with beer, he'd never felt more sober. "I'm good."

"By all means, safety first. Please drive her," Meg said loud enough so not only he could hear her over the music, but whomever she was standing around chatting with. "I'm sure I can catch a ride."

"See you at home," he said, opening the door and sliding into the driver's side.

His good fortune felt almost too ridiculous to imagine as he rolled down the street, pulled into her driveway, opened her garage door, and parked inside.

He reached her side of the car in time for her to open the door, stand, and slide into his arms. "Let's get you up to bed."

"Thought you'd never ask," she slurred.

"Alarm on?" he asked nearing the door from the garage into the back hall.

"Code is my birthday," she said. "Twelve twenty-nine."

He put the key in the lock.

"Gonna change it to my baby's birth date," she said.

He pressed the numbers into the keypad and opened the door.

"When I have one."

"Good idea." He led her across the house toward the front hall.

"You want to get me pregnant?"

He stopped. "What?"

"I'm ovulating."

"Hope, you're very drunk." He definitely had to be too.

"And high," she said.

"You were smoking pot?"

"Eating brownies."

"At the party?"

"Don't know who brought them," she said in a singsong voice. "But they were delicious."

"Even more reason to get you up to bed."

"Exactly," she said as he lifted her into his arms and carried her up the stairs.

He had to be imagining that he held Hope Jordan in his arms and was carrying her to her bedroom where, at her suggestion, they were to procreate, get it on, fuck. . . . Was there even a word for a drug-, alcohol-, and infertility-driven once-in-a-lifetime opportunity to make love to the woman of one's dreams? "Hope, I don't think you mean what . . ."

"I know you're attracted to me."

"Impossible not to be, but—"

"Tim wants me to be pregnant."

"I'm sure he does."

"So does Frank."

"I'm sure he does."

"I need a baby," she said.

"I know you do," he said, flipping on the light as he reached her bedroom.

"Jim doesn't."

"Jim doesn't want to—?"

"Jim doesn't want it to be so hard." Her hand dropped from around his neck and flopped to below his belt where she attempted a drunken grab. "Are you?"

"Hope, you're not in your right mind," he managed, fighting the impulse to rip off her clothes and show her just how hard he was. "You should sleep."

"Not yet." She pulled her dress up and over her head. "Shower time."

There was no point concealing his erection as she grabbed his hand and led him toward the bathroom.

* * *

Unsure if the hot bath was helping her come down or enhancing what she was now sure was her high, Laney blew out the sandalwood scented candles. She sat up and reached across to the window to let in some cool air. As she opened the blinds, motion caught her eye from the window directly facing hers.

Hope's bedroom light was on.

The curtains were open.

Hope was naked, heading toward the bathroom.

She wasn't alone.

Was she with Tim Trautman?

Laney had given him a brownie thinking they might enjoy the effects together, only to have him rush off the second he spotted Hope.

It was always about Hope.

Laney turned to see if her glasses were anywhere nearby, instantly regretted the effects of the quick movement on her equilibrium and resorted to squinting.

She had to be imagining things, definitely shouldn't have had so many cocktails, because the man who followed Hope wasn't Tim. He looked like, had the same gait, and prematurely salt and pepper hair as, but couldn't be . . .

Couldn't be Will.

* * *

Maryellen just meant to take a little walk in the moonlight, enjoy the cool air on her face, and clear her head while she waited for the bathroom to open up. She'd meant to circle back, run in, and get a finger down her throat so she wouldn't have a belly ache all night. Then, she'd finish cleaning up and join Frank out by the pool.

She would have, had the moon not been so bright and inviting, bidding her to follow the warm, white glow where it led.

Which happened to be home.

Frank had probably found Hope again and was too busy playing savior in shining armor to his perturbed parishioner to notice she wasn't in the kitchen washing dishes. Even still, she should have called him to let him know where she was, would have, but couldn't find her phone.

She went around to the side gate, fumbled for the key, and let herself in the back door.

She needed to tell him she was home safe.

Needed to use the bathroom.

Needed candy.

Not necessarily in that order.

She flipped on the light in the kitchen, picked up the phone, and dialed his cell number.

Got his recorded voice.

Hi, you've reached Frank Griffin. I'm not available right now . . .

Please leave a message.

"Hi, it's me," she said. "I'm at home, so see you when you get here, I guess."

She hung up wishing he wouldn't hurry.

And then she wished something she'd never allowed herself to think ever before—she wished he wouldn't come home at all.

She headed for the bathroom, stopped at the pantry on the way, and opened the door.

Licorice.

She tore open one of the bags she kept stocked for Frank, grabbed a Red Vine, coiled it like a snake, and stuffed it into her mouth whole. Bag in hand and thoroughly enjoying the soft, sinewy, sugary strawberry-ness, she stepped out of the pantry and headed for the powder room.

On her way, she noticed the low, shadowy candlelight coming from the basement that signaled Eva was already home with her friends.

She cracked the door wider and crept down the first two stairs.

"And now it is done," Eva's voice rang out into the hazy air.

Maryellen peered around the blind corner and saw her daughter in what looked to be a purple cape.

She was craning to see more when the stair creaked.

"You hear something?" someone asked.

Before she heard the answer, Maryellen rushed back up the steps and stationed herself at the center island. She was nibbling a second piece of licorice when the basement door opened.

Eva, back in her normal black, appeared first. Tyler Pierce-Cohn, the Estridge twins, and what looked to be the rest of the youth group emerged from behind in a fog of incense and she hated to even consider what else. "Mom?"

"That's me."

"What are you doing here?"

"Eating."

"I see that."

"Red Vine?" She offered one to her daughter and then all around.

"No thanks." Eva narrowed her eyes, tilted her head slightly. "You're eating candy?"

"So good." She took another bite. "So fresh."

"We all decided to come home and hang in the basement," Eva said.

"The incense was a dead giveaway," Maryellen said.

"I . . ." Eva looked at the kitchen wall clock. "I didn't know you were here."

"Surprise!" she said.

"How long have you been here?"

She tried to look stern, tried not to laugh by telling herself that whatever Eva was worried about probably wasn't funny. She looked down at her watch. 10:08 P.M.

"I don't know, maybe ten minutes."

CHAPTER TWENTY-FIVE

All recreation center users are to treat the facility with respect,
demonstrate good sportsmanship at all times, and eat only in
designated areas—From the Melody Mountain Ranch Recreation
Center Guidelines.

"You there, Hope?" Jim, but not exactly Jim, yelled.
He was shorter, darker haired, more interested in her.
"Ready or not, here I come!"

More interested in their game.

As Jim, but not really Jim at all, disappeared into a candle-lit room filled with exercise equipment, Hope crept out from her hiding place beside a vending machine stocked with toy babies. She dropped a quarter into the slot and closed her eyes, letting her fingers choose between the pink and blue stork buttons.

A baby dropped into the cradle/receptacle to the theme music from the game show *Jeopardy.*

As Hope reached for an edge of the pink blanket swaddling her plastic newborn, a telephone rang from somewhere in the recesses of what she knew was the rec center.

"I wish you'd pick up," not Jim said.

Hope scampered down the corridor lined with vending machines, stopping briefly in front of a beverage machine. She pressed F9 and watched the machine drop ice, vodka, and some sort of incandescent purple liquid into a cocktail glass docked behind a plastic door.

Before the door slid open, a warning flashed across the top of the machine: *Pregnant and nursing mothers should avoid consumption of alcoholic beverages.*

She kissed her doll and reached for the drink.

As she took a long but unsatisfying sip, the phone rang again.

Hope hurried over to a new hiding place behind a machine vending home-baked desserts before Jim, but not Jim, appeared in the hallway. He looked around and disappeared into another room filled with half-drawn plans for playgrounds and churches she was supposed to design but had forgotten, abandoned, or been distracted from finishing.

"I didn't mean for things to go down this way," he said.

"Me neither," she whispered.

"I'm coming," his voiced echoed. "I'm coming soon . . ."

The machine beside Hope began to churn and buzz.

Hope looked through the pink-tinted glass and into the machine. Amid the homemade cookies, lemon bars, apple pie slices, and brownies available for purchase, a Blondie caught her eye and an intoxicating aroma, like warm brown sugar, vanilla, and chocolate chips, wafted through the air.

She reached into her pocket, grabbed some change, slid around toward the coin slot, and listened to the quarter roll into the machine.

Her finger was on F9 when a hand covered hers.

"Gotcha." Jim, but not Jim's, golden wedding band glimmered in the neon of competing vending machines. He helped her press the buttons.

"Thank you," she said.

"I know how badly you want this."

"So badly."

He reached in to retrieve the brownie. "I'm here for you."

She turned to face him and looked deeply into his blue-brown eyes. "You don't know what this means to me."

He fed her a bite of brownie.

Took a bite himself.

They chewed and swallowed in perfect time with each other.

"So good," she said.

"These are very special, you know?"

"I know," she said.

"So are you." He wrapped his arms around her. "And you deserve to have what you've wanted, needed for so long."

Not Jim leaned toward her as she leaned toward him.

Tim?

They shared a long, slow, brownie-flavored kiss.

They were still kissing when the real Jim's voice carried in from the other room. "It's just I feel kind of overwhelmed by the pressure I'm under to do something amazing here and—"

"I don't want, can't, talk about this right now," she said in the direction of his voice. "Trying to relax."

Not Jim kissed her more deeply.

Pipes began to squeal and water flowed from showerheads affixed to the ceiling and walls of the giant industrial shower into which they'd somehow been transported.

Their clothing disappeared.

He, whoever he was, licked the water from her neck, her breasts, worked his way down toward her belly.

"Should we be—?"

"No worries." He kissed just below her hipbone. "It's all by design."

"You mean?"

He stood and pulled her close. "I'm going to be a daddy."

"Oh." She pressed her hips against his. "Yes!"

The room filled with steam.

A door squealed open. She couldn't see who'd entered, but his voice was unmistakable: "You shouldn't be in here. You shouldn't be here. You shouldn't be . . ."

"No!" Hope heard herself scream.

She opened her eyes.

Cold sweat dampened her chest, back, and the Restoration Hardware ticking-stripe sheets she'd just picked to complement her Italian Vintage Floral duvet and dark maple four-poster bed. Hers and Jim's.

Her head pounded, her mouth was cottony. Her stomach more so.

Not in the rec center shower.

Not making love to a man other than Jim.

She was alone. At home. In her own room.

She tried to sit up in bed and instantly thought better of it.

"I hope the party was fun last night," Jim's amplified voice came through the answering machine. "Wish I could have been there."

Hash brownies.

Had she really eaten those brownies?

"Please call me back when you're up, honey."

With the click of the phone, she sat upright.

Regretting the quick motion, she managed to lean over to Jim's side of the bed and pressed play on the answering machine . . .

And realized she was naked.

With matted hair, and no memory of how she'd gotten there.

She had no memory of much of anything, beyond eating brownies with Tim Trautman.

How had she gotten home?

She slid back under her covers.

"You there, Hope?" Jim's voice tumbled her halfway back into the dream. "I'm sure you're still sacked out but I wish you'd pick up." The answering machine picked up his sigh. "Listen, I didn't mean for things to go down like they did yesterday." He paused. "I'm sorry, it's just I was feeling kind of overwhelmed by the pressure I'm under to do something amazing here. And, honestly, at home, too."

The tightness began to ease in Hope's chest.

"Thing is," Jim, the real Jim, continued, "I know how badly you want this, have needed this, for so long. And I know you might not believe this after our conversation, but I do want and plan to be a dad."

She'd had way too much to drink, ingested drugs, and was probably still not entirely sober when Jim's apology message played while she slept.

"Thing is, I gotcha about at least shooting for the right timing."

Played into her dream.

"I just want to try and be a little more relaxed about the whole process while we are trying. Call me when you get this and let's try and work out a schedule where you're here or I'm there at the right time until this job's over. You deserve, we deserve, to at least give it a try."

Relief flooded her head and then, her heart. Could what seemed to be a nightmare really be a dream coming true?

"I hope the party was fun last night." The kindness and understanding in Jim's voice flooded the room. "Wish I could have been there."

All just a bad dream.

She needed to call him back and thank him for the apology. Apologize to him for ignoring his calls all day yesterday while she wallowed in her misery.

Her guts burbled.

And drank too much.

Before she called, a cup of coffee to totally sober up and some toast to settle her stomach were probably in order.

A trip to the bathroom was a necessity.

Careful to hold her head as still as possible, she slid out of bed. Bypassing her slippers in favor of the cool hardwood and the cooler tile beyond, she started toward the bathroom. On the way, she glanced through the open window at the gray, drizzly sky. An incongruous sliver of hot pink caught her eye. She stepped over to the southernmost window and peered through the sheers at matching pink storks planted in the corner edge of the Trautmans' front yard.

Instead of the jealousy she'd already felt in anticipation of this moment, she smiled. Much as she couldn't believe she'd eaten a hash brownie, there had to be something in Tim's relaxation theory.

Hope padded across the room and entered the bathroom, focused only on the coolness of the tile radiating into her feet and up her legs. She opened the door to the water closet toilet and sat on the equally cool seat.

Peed.

All was well.

Wiped.

Reminded herself to get new, more padded cycling shorts to prevent the saddle soreness before the outdoor season got into full swing.

Flushed.

Jim was sorry. He was willing, wanted, to try and make sure they were together for ovulation in the coming months. What more could she ask for, besides the baby their argument had him that much more invested in trying to conceive?

She made it back across the bathroom to the double vanity and almost turned on the water before she saw the note in the basin propped against the spigot.

A wave of panic rumbled through her as she reached for the note and glanced at her name jotted across the front in unfamiliar handwriting. Her hand trembled as she unfolded the paper, torn from the pad on her bedside table.

Hope,

I'm afraid you'll be somewhat unclear about a few details when you wake up. Since I'll be on my way to Florida for vacation when you do, I thought I should clarify a few things. First off, your car is parked in the garage and I left your keys on the table in your back hall. Second, and much more importantly, please don't feel awkward about last night's unusual circumstances. Like I said before I left, no worries.

XO,

Will

* * *

It wasn't like Eva expected him to instantly drop dead or anything. Not after Lauren, or her mother, or both of them, messed everything up anyway.

"It's raining cats and dogs out there," her dad announced.

But did he have to be so, so alive?

He thudded down the hallway like Bigfoot, passing the powder room where she'd ducked inside the second she heard the rumble of the garage door. The last thing she felt like dealing with was his party-hangover, pre-church funk she'd have done anything to sleep through.

So unfair she had to be a freaking minister's daughter.

A pain shot across her uterus.

With freaking cramps.

"I can't believe you're already up and out in this rain." Her mother's voice floated down the hall and through the ridiculously thin door.

"Someone had to make sure the rec center was back in order," he said in that totally irritating, pointed way. "The kitchen was covered in plates and rotting food."

"I'll go back after church."

"Already taken care of."

"Sorry."

Eva could feel her mom cower. She could hear her sigh. At least they were only fighting. It was utterly revolting to have to cover her head with a pillow to drown out what she usually overheard. Being this close to the two of them while he rambled on about anything more than the potluck would be suicide worthy.

"I meant to finish things up, I really did. It's just—"

"It's just you let the kids go early."

"They'd worked so hard, I wanted to let them have some fun, too."

"I see," he said.

"And Laney was supposed to help."

"But got sick," he said.

"And left me alone to do all the work," she said.

Eva felt a twinge of guilt for her mom. They had to leave when they did or there would have been no spell—even one that didn't seem to be working.

"So you just decided to give up and wander home?"

Not yet, anyway.

"I . . . the moon was so bright I just . . ."

"Very weird, Maryellen."

For once, Eva actually agreed with her dad. Finding her mom standing in the kitchen gobbling candy was more than weird.

Like she'd had one of the missing brownies?

Her father exhaled dramatically. "I found your phone by the sink."

"Oh, good. Can't believe I—"

"Me neither."

"I don't know what happened. I just felt so . . . like I wasn't sure what was happening."

On the one hand, Eva felt totally weird about maybe getting her mom high.

"I told you never to drink on an empty stomach."

"I ate," she said. "Plenty."

On the other, her mom normally ate so little, the munchies weren't exactly a bad thing.

"I made sure I not only ate enough, but limited what I had to drink," he said.

"I thought I saw you drinking beer."

"I nursed one or two," her dad said.

Eva doubled over against another wave of cramps.

"I need to look over my sermon before church," her dad said.

"I'll leave you to it," her mom said.

With the sound of footsteps heading toward the kitchen, Eva stepped to the vanity and grabbed an Advil. Checking to make sure both of her parents were safely away from the path to the relative safety of her room, she slunk out of the bathroom. As she tiptoed across the tile and rushed up the stairs, the nasty bellow of her dad's *I nursed one beer* farts echoed out into the front hall.

* * *

"I missed you in my sculpt class this morning," Sarah said.

"Can barely get out of bed," Laney said by way of answer, her head still ringing from the sound of the phone. "I feel like someone clobbered me with a brick."

"Bet I know why," Sarah said.

If she hadn't been so pissed about Randall's last-minute ribbon cutting bailout, she'd have clued Sarah in about her own brownie suspicions soon after sampling the dessert tray she found in the corner cabinet of the rec center kitchen. "Why's that?"

"There was quite a rumor floating around eight A.M. stretch."

An image of Hope, through the open blinds of the Jordan bedroom, leached from the recesses of her liquor and drug-addled brain. "Involving Hope?"

"Did she eat those brownies you were chowing last night?"

Could Will Pierce-Cohn have really been in Hope's bedroom? "I'm thinking she must have."

"Then she ought to be feeling much the same as you."

"Because they had hash or something in them?"

"You knew?"

"Strongly suspected," she said.

"Why didn't you say anything?"

"You wouldn't have eaten one anyway." Laney paused. "But, oh my God!"

"Oh my God, what?"

"Maryellen."

"Definitely ate them!"

"Probably all she ate." Laney started to shake her head, but thought better of it when she felt what seemed to be her brain rattling inside. "She's going to be horrified when she finds out."

"Especially since she was like a pusher with those things," Sarah said.

"Even worse."

"Seriously, didn't you see her give one to Roseanne, Jane Hunt—?"

"And fed one to Frank."

"The Rev. did seem otherwise enlightened."

With their shared gallows laugh, a day's worth of anger and irritation began to dissipate.

"You know," Sarah said, "I really am sorry about Randall and the ribbon cutting."

"I just wish I'd known sooner," she finally said.

"His agent made us swear to silence, or you know I would have told you."

"Promise?"

"Swear."

"I guess I should probably ask how his meeting went?"

"Good," Sarah said. "For a minute I was worried we might be moving to somewhere awful like Pittsburgh or Cleveland."

"Thank God," Laney said. "Promise you won't leave me here alone."

"And have you reap all the Mother's Helpers infamy and glory?"

"I'll take you back on as my assistant if you'll do the dirty work of calling Maryellen and telling her she was dealing hash brownies last night."

"I owe you that," Sarah giggled.

"I'll contact Roseanne and Jane Hunt."

"What about Hope?"

With the name Hope, the whole scene from her bedroom window came back, in psychedelic, but no-way-was-it-a-dream Technicolor. "I'm thinking she already knows."

"Why's that?"

"You're never going to believe what I think I saw last night . . ."

CHAPTER TWENTY-SIX

Section 3.4. Hot Tubs. Hot tubs must be installed in "side" or "rear" yard with appropriate screening so as not to be immediately visible to adjacent property owners.

*H*ope alternated water, fruit juice, and virgin sports drinks with Alka-Seltzer and Advil until she knocked the wind out of the most brutal hangover she'd ever had. A series of harmonious e-mails with Jim resulted in plans for back-and-forth visits over ovulation week for the next four months and the official end to her day-after blues.

Without worrying, her memory of Saturday night extended to arriving at the potluck, a delicious tuna casserole, and *medicinal* desserts. Hope relaxed in a bubble bath. While she soaked, she didn't allow a single thought about what she thought she was doing eating hash brownies, what happened in the gap of time following, or the awkwardness of finding out she'd been brought home by Will Pierce-Cohn. She climbed into bed early and enjoyed the steady patter of rain on the rooftop. Instead of bad dreams about kissing a morph image of Jim, Tim, Frank, Will, and whoever else had worked their way into her subconscious, she dreamt of Piccadilly Circus and Trafalgar Square, both of which she'd see for real, soon.

After another indoor morning ride, courtesy of the rain, but accompanied by the *Today Show*, where Matt was coincidentally broadcasting from London, Hope almost felt like herself again.

Just like herself after a long steam shower.

The surreal quality of Sunday faded for good when she checked her Monday morning e-mail and found no less than three inquiries about landscape design services. A fourth e-mail was from Toni Thompson (a referral from Theresa Trautman) who wanted to schedule a more in-depth meeting to discuss the nautical nursery they'd chatted about on Saturday.

Had they talked at the ribbon cutting or over hors d'oeuvres at the potluck? She closed her eyes and tried to remember their discussion.

Fudging whatever it was they'd talked about couldn't be hard, especially when it came to nursery design, but weren't alcoholic blackouts only supposed to happen to alcoholics? Why had she let herself drink so much? She hadn't allowed herself to let loose like that since one troubling morning in college when she'd woken up with a similar lack of memory. Of course, that time, Jim was next to her in bed.

Not in London.

Hope took a deep breath.

Before responding to Toni Thompson or any other work inquiries, she fired off a quick appointment request to the fertility doctor. With her husband on board and all her reproductive ducks in a row, there would be no falling into a desperation free spin like that again.

As she finished, a message popped up in her inbox.

From: Rev. Frank Griffin.

An image of the two of them eating chips together popped into her head.

RE: Did you get my voice mail?

She glanced at the message alert flashing on her phone. After waking up from her dream early Sunday morning, she'd turned off the volume to avoid noise or further bad dream catalysts.

Then forgotten to turn the ringer back on.

Everyone else must have been nursing their hangovers as well, because she'd only missed three messages all day. She turned up the volume and pressed play to listen to messages from Frank Griffin, most likely Jim, and . . .

"Hope, it's Sarah Fowler. Sorry to be the bearer of weird news, but if your Saturday night was more unusual than you might have imagined, blame it on the brownies."

No need for more details there. She moved on to the next message.

"Hey it's me . . ."

Wasn't Jim.

"Tim."

No way he'd spent Sunday recovering with the telltale storks on the front lawn.

"I haven't had a chance to check in until now, but I wanted to make sure you're feeling okay after all of last night's festivities."

She remembered eating brownies with him. Sitting on the picnic table. Laughing.

"Sorry I had to run off like that." He paused. "You enjoy the Bugles?"

He'd lent her change for the vending machine.

"All's well here at the hospital."

Then must have left for the hospital.

"I'm the proud father of healthy, beautiful girls—Kayla Rose and Mackenzie Grace."

She smiled at the names and the satisfied exhaustion in his voice.

"I'm headed home to crash."

She could only hope he hadn't gone to the hospital as high as she was.

"Theresa is finally getting some well-deserved rest, too."

However he'd shown up, and in whatever condition, clearly all had ended beyond well.

"It's going to be out of the frying pan around here for a while," he said, his voice dropping. "But, I'm sure I'll see you soon."

Not for a week or two, anyway. Much as she wanted to see what Theresa had done with the nursery, they'd need to settle in before she turned up with matching gift baskets.

The message changed over.

"Hope, are you there?" Frank Griffin's deep voice nudged her out of her daydream imaging the twins' beautiful, completed nursery.

"I hate to have to leave a message of this nature on your voice mail, but there's a situation of which you need to be made aware . . ."

With the word *situation*, she was back in her kitchen, trying to ignore the tap of Saturday night's hazy reality on her shoulder.

"Unfortunately the brownies a number of us enjoyed last evening, including you, may have been . . ." He paused. "Were, probably laced . . ."

She should have told him herself, certainly would have, had she seen either him or Maryellen once Tim said his good-byes.

Had she even rejoined the party?

After all the kindness he'd shown her, listening to him labor over the word *hashish* made her head pound with intensity on par with yesterday morning's wake-up call.

She pushed fast forward, but lifted her finger from the button almost as quickly.

"You were very out of it when I found you by the vending machines in the lower level of the rec center. Unfortunately, we both were under the effects, and for that I'm sorry." He paused. "Given your mindset yesterday morning, I wanted to . . . to make sure you had a good time, but keep an eye out all the same. I'm afraid I failed miserably." He paused again, for even longer. "But I'm confident Tim Trautman provided sufficient distraction before I arrived." The timbre of his voice changed slightly. "And when you slipped from my grasp, I'm glad it was into Will's, so he could get you home safely."

Awkward as it was, she was glad it had been Will, too. She couldn't imagine showing up at church week after week knowing Frank had seen her . . .

*Please don't feel awkward about last night's unusual circumstances.
Like I said before I left, no worries.*

"Once again, I'm sorry about Saturday night and am praying you'll be back on track soon."

If Tim had taken her home and his wife had gone into labor while he was tucking her into bed, she'd be even more horrified.

"And one other thing," Frank said. "In my altered state, I may have done or shown you more than I should have." He paused. "Can I ask you to keep things—about the church—between us?"

She pressed reply and began to type, the words flowing with little if any direction from her blank brain.

Frank,
*Crazy situation, but at least we all seem to have been in it together.
I'm afraid the combination of alcohol and everything else left a few holes
in the evening. I'm glad to know you were there with me during some of
those moments. As for whatever you told or showed me, your secret remains
safe with you.*
Hope

* * *

Maryellen clicked on the Denver library website and pushed the job listings tab while she waited for the photographer's party pictures to download. Before Sarah's call, she'd looked so forward to creating a collage for the front hall of the rec center.

Would she be able to tell who was high by their expressions?

Who looked guilty of spiking their dessert?

She felt somewhat vindicated for her unusual behavior that night, but not enough to overlook the shame of not only eating so many brownies herself, but having served them around.

She'd expected Frank to feel much the same, or at least flip out that they'd used drugs.

And so publicly.

"Not our fault," he'd said. And while he finally admitted to feeling loose and disconnected, he was more proud he'd been able to *maintain his faculties—keep an eye out for those who couldn't resist temptations.*

He was calm and unflappable while they prayed on it and prayed for whoever felt compelled to serve a plate of drug-laced treats to their neighbors, then set about contacting anyone they knew or thought might have consumed the brownies. They went on to church and Frank remained collected and dignified standing at the pulpit while she could practically hear the hushed whispers as the rumor, which wasn't a rumor at all, spread like wildfire.

Marijuana in the brownies.

I thought I saw her feeding one to Frank.

They were high as kites, all of them.

She'd looked straight ahead, not daring to look at anyone who might have provided or partaken, or, God forbid, Jane Hunt, Tess Miller, or anyone else she'd practically force-fed a brownie. While Frank diffused tension by waxing eloquent on temptation, intentional and otherwise, she'd spent the hour trying to forgive herself for her unintentional, but no less mortifying, gaffe.

The week's library job openings somehow only served as a reminder.

Part-Time Barista—Branch Coffee Carts Multiple Locations (15 hours).

Job description includes preparing beverages, sandwiches, and baked goods.

Her stomach clenched with the thought of what she'd unknowingly ingested, then eaten in the aftermath.

Circulation Security Clerk—Pauline Robinson Branch library (30 hours).

After Frank's sermon, no one dared mention anything in the social hall beyond the usual and expected *great party* or some slightly more telling variation along the lines of *good times were had by all.* The what-can-you-do-shrugs that followed said enough.

If Frank hadn't been so downright clear-headed, she wouldn't have made it to the safety of their car before bursting into tears.

"No need to feel shame when it wasn't your fault."

He was right, of course, and everyone did get home without incident and no real damage seemed to have been done. Still, she couldn't help but draw comfort in the fact he lay awake beside her the last few nights, dozing off just before her, an hour or so before dawn.

She let her gaze drop to the final listing.

Coming soon:

Senior Librarian—Central Library.

Heart thumping, she looked again to make sure she wasn't imagining things.

She exited the website.

Better not to imagine.

Better to set her mind on the grim reality of the party picture download that had begun to populate the computer screen:

Laney putting a tablecloth on the main course table.

Daisies floating on the surface of the lighted pool.

Various neighbors arriving with their contributions to the potluck.

No pictures of a culprit, platter of brownies in hand.

She took a deep breath. Really, there was nothing to suggest the event wasn't entirely on the up-and-up.

Page two was much the same: An effusive Frank greeting various partygoers. Jane Hunt mugging for the camera. She leafed through a few more pages and began to agree with Frank that people would start to laugh it off and eventually forget about it.

Until the shot of the dessert table popped up on page three.

The following picture was of her, eating a caramel-drizzled brownie.

She deleted both photos, then recoded each .jpg that followed so there'd be no discernable break in the number sequence.

Frank looked a little confused two pages later while he gave directions to Eva and a cluster of teens, but not enough to get rid of one of the few photos she'd seen of the kids.

The taste of licorice filled her throat every time she thought about what the kids were doing in the basement. Had they eaten the brownies too?

That might explain why it sounded like they were chanting when she opened the door.

Maryellen edited out a red-eye photo of Jane Hunt and another of Roseanne Goldberg looking suspiciously squinty.

Then she turned to page ten.

Every photo seemed to put the filmy reality of the evening into clear focus: a group of glassy-eyed neighbors, including Laurie Owens and Anne Thompson, Laney, Frank, and Hope Jordan admiring the small plate of brownies she held in her hand. Frank, his hand placed protectively on Hope's lower back, just above the waistline of her coordinating floral dress.

She erased the entire page except for a shot of the three of them beside the diving board.

On the next page, Tim stood at the dessert table talking to Laney.

They're especially delicious. If you know what I mean.

Sarah said Laney had found the brownies in the kitchen and put them out. She thought someone from the Melody Manor patio homes brought them, which made sense since quadrant three was assigned to bring dessert, but no one seemed to have any idea who.

Maryellen flipped quickly through the remaining pages of pictures to see if there were any more potentially telltale pictures.

There were, but not that shed any light on the hash situation.

Hope and Tim sat huddled together on a picnic table in the first photo.

In the second, they were standing together, behind and to the right of a group party scene just outside the rec center.

They appeared to be kissing.

CHAPTER TWENTY-SEVEN

Meeting Agenda: Meetings of the board shall proceed on issues as generally set forth in the agenda distributed prior to the meeting.

The doc at Southeast Suburban Family Walk-In was new, or at least new to Laney, and older than she tended to trust, but intelligent-looking with deep-set eyes and a widow's peak.

"I thought I wasn't feeling well because, well to be honest, we had this party in my neighborhood, and in the midst of some mild overindulgence, someone thought it would be clever to add hash brownies to the dessert spread."

Thunder rattled the room.

"I see," he said, looking at her chart. "But you do indulge recreationally?"

"Almost never."

"Almost?"

"I'm really not a drug user." Other than the occasional hit off Steve's *prescription* pot, the Ecstasy she'd tried twice with Sarah, and the occasional line of coke she'd love to indulge in more often.

"Nosebleeds are consistent with inhalant use," he said.

"My nosebleeds started with this asthma inhaler the allergist prescribed for my sinus issues," she said.

He put the stethoscope in his ears to hear her heart.

"Vomiting?"

"Just the morning after the party."

"Cramping, diarrhea, or bloody stools?"

"Some diarrhea, but generally I just feel weak and lethargic."

The cold flat edge of the stethoscope found its way to her back, stomach, and kidney area.

"Any night sweats, heart palpitations, unexplained bleeding?" the doctor asked.

"Other than the nosebleeds, not really."

"How's the joint pain you reported when you were in a few months back?"

"Advil seems to help."

"Is this nausea similar to the nausea you reported in the appointment before that?"

"That was more sporadic."

"But your congestion has improved with the inhaler?"

"I haven't been using it all that long," she said. "But after that young doctor in your office said he thought my stress levels were affecting my resistance, I read this book that taught me how to visualize good health and other stuff that has totally changed my life. I even have my husband reading it because he has Chronic Fatigue, although getting ready for the Memorial Weekend party, which I chaired, was pretty stressful so I've had a hard time maintaining my attitude." She paused to take a breath. "So I'm not totally surprised that my health has kind of fallen off."

"Hmm," the doctor said, leafing through the chart. "I do notice you've been in seven times in the last four months."

"I've gone from sinus infection to flu and back again since last fall, so naturally I hoped this was from *accidentally* overeating those brownies."

He grabbed a tongue depressor.

"And, I didn't want to come in today, but my pharmacy couldn't refill my antibiotic."

"Standard protocol." He put the tongue depressor in her mouth and flashed a light toward the back of her throat. "Excessive over-prescription and misuse have caused a sharp spike in antibiotic resistant infection."

"Oh." She swallowed away the taste of sterilized wood.

He pressed his latex-covered fingers along the base of her neck.

"Do you think I have an antibiotic resistant strain of something?"

"Doubtful."

He moved the stethoscope on her chest. "Breathe normally."

The room filled with the sound of her congested breathing.

"Chest is clear." He lowered the stethoscope, picked up her chart, and began to jot notes onto the blank first page.

"It's mostly my guts that are bothering me."

He palpated her stomach.

"Do you think maybe I picked up some salmonella or something at the potluck?"

"Not in the absence of uncontrolled vomiting, diarrhea, or bloody stools." The doctor notated something. "It's possible you ate something a little off at the potluck in addition to those brownies."

"So, maybe not a food thing?"

He leafed through her chart again. "I'm more concerned about the sheer frequency of your visits for recurrent symptoms."

The sound of crinkling paper drowned out the rain as she shifted on the exam table.

"Your blood workup in April was normal and ruled out most anything of concern . . ."

Laney broke out in a cold sweat. *Except for possibly a strain of leukemia so rare only certain doctors in the country including myself have been trained to put together the seemingly unrelated symptoms?*

"But there's no harm in running another chem panel for comparison's sake."

"I've wondered if the different illnesses I've had may be related." Her heart thumped in her chest. "You don't think I have some sort of unusual immune—?"

"Unlikely."

Despite his reassuring smile, Laney didn't feel reassured at all.

"But I do think it's worth a look through your file to see if we can come up with any ideas going forward to improve your overall resistance."

"I'm all for that," she said.

"Imodium for the diarrhea and I'll send you home with a sample of something stronger you can use as needed."

"Thank you," she said.

"Log in to our website at the end of the week. I'll post your results and any further recommendations in your patient profile."

CHAPTER TWENTY-EIGHT

*No boats may be stored in such a manner as to be visible
from any other property for longer than 72 hours in a seven-day
period. Periodic movement to circumvent this rule
will be considered a violation.*

*E*va glanced at the rain beating on the *safe egress* basement window and then at Lauren, who was sitting on the couch, pretending not to text *Tylerpoo* or whatever stupid-ass pet name she probably already had for him.

"This weather sucks," someone said.

"Didn't have to work at the rec barely at all this week though," a Goth said.

A bolt of lightning sent an illuminating flash through the darkened room.

Lauren the lifeguard, who was still a nice pasty white, practically jumped out of her chair.

Eva resisted the urge to taunt her for being a scaredy-cat, imitate the way she twitched in her seat, or otherwise threaten to wring her neck. Just like she'd promised.

Instead, she reloaded the bong and passed it left.

"Can't believe our parents like ate the hash brownies."

"Totally classic."

"Sign from the Goddess."

Eva couldn't deny the freaky fortune of finding out her mom had gotten wasted and was too distracted by candy to think anything much about what they were doing in the basement. Things weren't close to how they were supposed to be, though. Her dad was very much around, camp was looming way too large, and Tyler and Lauren were still going far too strong.

A crack of thunder shook the room in agreement.

"I hope it's not raining like this up at camp," Margaret said.

"No using the C word," Eva said.

"My jeans are wet on the butt," Libby said.

"Gross," someone said.

"I think it's from your carpet, Eva," Libby said.

"Whatever." Eva sighed.

"I was planning on wearing these to . . . away tomorrow."

"I'm so screwed," Eva said.

"When are you supposed to leave for cam—?"

"I told you, no C word."

"Maybe it won't be that bad," Hannah said.

"Right." Eva didn't even bother to give her the evil eye.

"The spell could still work," Heather said.

"It wasn't supposed to work immediately," Margaret said.

"Something should have happened by now." Eva barely restrained herself from leering at Lauren as she checked her phone for another text. "What does Tyler think?"

Lauren looked up nervously. "Couldn't we maybe try again when he gets back?"

"This is a good-bye party for the twins." Eva held up her end of the deal with Tyler by trying her best not to sound bitchy, despite how desperately the situation called for it. "And we're having this little good-bye because they leave for you-know-where in the morning, so when Tyler's back, we'll have only eleven members."

"Right," she said looking appropriately dissed.

"What are you going to do?" Heather asked.

"Try to pressure my mom to get me out of going, I guess."

"Will that work?"

"Yeah, right." She stared directly at Lauren who wasn't even pretending not to furiously text her bonehead comment to Tyler. "Which is why I'm also working on a Plan B."

* * *

Hope had exactly a million errands to run before Jim came home Saturday night.

She opened the car door to a blast of wet.

A million errands that had to be done in nonstop, driving rain.

Hoping London would be as unseasonably sunny as Denver was rainy, she made a run for it across the parking lot, into the foyer of the library, and into a blast of cold air that sent a chill through her rain-soaked skin.

Or, maybe it was Maryellen's icy expression as she looked up from the book she was reading.

"*Bring It On,*" Hope said brightly. "That's supposed to be a great book."

"It's interesting, anyway," Maryellen mumbled.

They'd exchanged e-mails where Maryellen apologized for serving the offending brownies and Hope assured her there was nothing to apologize for. Still, there was the awkwardness of not having chanced into each other since the potluck. Hope focused on rubbing water droplets out of her hair. "I can't believe it's just nonstop rain out there."

"In here, too." Maryellen pointed to a bucket placed to the right of the circulation desk. "Supposed to continue through the weekend."

"I've already got a few hairline cracks in my basement."

"We have a wet spot in ours."

"I feel like we're going to have to get around in boats soon."

"If it keeps up like this, you may be right."

The conversation was so stilted Hope knew Maryellen still felt terribly uncomfortable. "Which leads to the reason I'm here," she said, hoping to relieve some of the tension. "I'm looking for books on boats, sailing—general nautical stuff for a nursery project I'm working on for a friend of Theresa Trautman."

"I see." Maryellen looked down at the computer screen and pushed a few keys. "Looks like there are a number of things we can order from other branches."

"If we have to," Hope said.

"All we have here are a few children's titles."

"Depending on the photos and illustrations, they could be even better."

Maryellen stepped out from behind the desk. "Follow me."

Hope fell in behind her as she headed over to the children's corner.

"It really was clever of Tim Trautman to have you plan out the twins' nursery the way he did," Maryellen said.

"For Mother's Day no less," Hope said.

"Such an incredibly nice gesture."

"Wonderful," Hope said. "I'm dying to see the finished product."

"You haven't yet?"

"Thought I'd give the Trautmans some time to settle in before I show up on their doorstep."

"Good idea."

"Thing is, I have these gift baskets with the girls' names in wooden letters shaped and painted to look like flowers. They're so darling I can barely wait to see them in the nursery."

Maryellen stopped in the kids' section. "I'm having one of those *On the Day You Were Born* charts made up for the girls."

"Great idea," Hope said.

"All I have so far is the birth date." Maryellen turned and scanned an upper shelf. "Can't forget that day."

"I suppose not."

"Wish I could."

Hope pretended to look at a nearby row of books during the awkward pause that followed. "Wish I could remember much of it."

Maryellen looked surprised. "You don't?"

"Very, very little. I rarely, if ever, have more than a glass of wine, but that whole day . . ." Hope somehow managed to swallow back the bubbling ache she'd managed to keep at bay. "The evening is largely a blank."

"You did have quite a bit to drink over the course of the day," Maryellen finally said.

"Embarrassing to admit."

"I saw you making a plate of food and talked with you by the diving board." The taut lines around Maryellen's mouth seemed to soften. "And I recall you were chatting with Tim Trautman."

"I do remember sitting with him at the picnic tables." Hope nodded with the vague memory. "And the next thing I remember I was eating chips from the vending machine, but not with him."

"We were really worried about you," she said quickly. "Frank was trying to keeping an eye out to make sure you were safe."

"I really appreciated that," Hope said. "Along with Will Pierce-Cohn getting me home." Hope felt her face redden. "Which I know because he left a note."

The pain etching Maryellen's face felt like a reflection. "I can't believe anyone would be so evil as to put out those brownies for all of us to eat without thinking—"

"At least we were all among friends."

Maryellen didn't say anything, but patted her arm, turned, and reached into the bookcase.

Within seconds, Hope held copies of *A Sailor Went to Sea, Sea, Sea*; *Sailboats!;* and *Ahoy Landlubbers*. "I'm afraid that's about all we have."

Hope opened the first book. "Maybe all I need."

"One more thought," Maryellen said. She was halfway across the room, swerving around another bucket before Hope could leaf through the next book.

Hope followed her to the adult side of the library and into a narrow stack, stopping at the base of the ladder Maryellen had already scrambled atop.

Maryellen handed down a coffee table book called *Yachts of the World*.

"Perfect," Hope said.

"Oh, and there's this." She pulled a pamphlet-thin book and tossed it down.

"A nautical knot manual?"

A droplet of water fell from the ceiling and plinked into yet another bucket sitting at the end of the stack.

"Might come in handy. You never know."

* * *

Laney logged on to the Denver Family Medical website and keyed in her name and password. Before she double-clicked on Patient Inbox, she called Sarah. "Swear to me you don't think there's something terribly wrong with me."

"We've been over this ten times," Sarah said. "A patronizing bedside manner doesn't mean the doctor thought you were terminal."

"Just very sick."

"Laney, read the test results."

"I'm scared."

"Positive thoughts, remember?"

A cold chill rattled down Laney's spine. "Don't have any."

"You're not sick," Sarah sighed, "but if you are, you'll ask yourself how you allowed yourself to get away from the good health you desire and deserve. Then you'll work on getting back into the proper mode of appreciation so you can receive all the blessings you're blocking with your negativity."

"Okay," Laney took a deep breath, "but if I have to have chemo or something, promise you'll run the Mother's Helpers parties I've scheduled for the next few months."

"Jesus, Laney, read the damn report already."

"Okay." Laney's temples, which hadn't bothered her since her second cup of coffee, began to throb.

A sound, like a box being pushed across the floor, filled Sarah's end of the line. "What are you doing?"

"Cleaning assorted crap out of my rec room," she said.

"While I'm reading my death sentence?"

"Obviously, I'm not terribly worried."

Laney calmed her skyrocketing blood pressure with the deepest breath she could take, and double-clicked:

Ms. Estridge:

Her imminent need to pass out disappeared with the first four words of the doctor's note:

I am pleased to report . . .

"Laney?" Sarah asked. "What is it?"

Laney took a deep breath and read the first sentence aloud:

I am pleased to report there were no abnormalities in your blood work, nor any significant changes in your levels relative to your last two blood workups.

"Told ya," Sarah said over the sound of cardboard sliding across concrete. Nearly blind from relief, Laney scanned the next paragraph:

In consulting my colleague, and the primary practitioner in charge of your care, J. Marc Fendelman, MD, we concur that the symptoms you reported on your two most recent visits are the combined result of a food-borne gastrointestinal irritant and seasonal allergy symptoms. Please complete the course of prescribed allergy medications as indicated by your allergist, over the counter digestive aids as needed, and 400 mg Motrin every 6–8 hours for headache symptoms.

"I'm waiting for my, 'Sarah's the most intuitive, smart, and beautiful friend ever,'" Sarah said.
"You are," Laney said, her eyes dropping to the paragraph below.

As a secondary note, we examined your chart for signs of underlying pathology to connect your most recent symptoms with complaints of sinus pain, respiratory issues, fatigue, and irritability reported during the unusually high number of visits you've sustained in the past eight months. Any connections do in fact appear to be circumstantial and unremarkable.

"I don't know what I'd do without you," Laney added.
"That's a start," Sarah said.

That said, in the absence of concrete pathology, it is my experience that chronic minor illness symptoms are best tackled in the long-term using a team approach. As you have already sought advice from an allergist and have a referral for a gastrointestinal specialist, the next step, in my opinion, will be to seek the help of a psychological professional.

As in, his diagnosis was Fucking Looney?

Please refer to the list pasted in below of preferred providers.
Health and Happiness,
P. L. Williamson, MD

"Shit!" Sarah said, as if reading her mind.
"What is it?" Laney barely managed.
"My laundry room floor is cracking."
According to P. L. Williamson, MD, so, apparently, was her best friend.

* * *

"That wet spot Eva found in the basement carpet seems to be spreading," Maryellen said.

Frank didn't turn from his computer. "I'll call the warranty repair line later."

"Do you need me to call?"

"What I need is a way to come up with eight grand by the end of the month." He looked out the window at the downpour. "Rain's killing church attendance."

"Everyone seems to be suffering the effects of this weather," she said.

"I doubt they stand to lose the land they've been dreaming of for years."

"Maybe you can get some sort of extension on the closing?"

"I come up with the money or they sell it out from under me." He put his head in his hands.

"But—"

"But nothing."

When he didn't say anything more, she turned to leave.

"Wait," he said before she could. "Did Lisa Manning ever say what they made at the Harmony Hills church rummage sale?"

"Around five," she said.

"Hundred?"

"Thousand."

Frank looked up.

She didn't bother to mention that Lisa Manning tended to exaggerate more than the average minister's wife.

"How soon do you think it would take for you pull something like that together?"

"Me?" The part of her that felt put upon was silenced by a proverbial hand to the mouth by the part of her that wanted nothing more than a chance to run something, maybe even save the day with a huge, successful yard sale. "I'm in the middle of a library cataloging project that's probably going to have me working late and I need to get the party picture montage finished and up on the bulletin board before I can even—"

"When were you planning to put it up?"

"I hung part of it today."

He spun his chair around. "Why didn't you tell me the photographer e-mailed the pictures?"

"You've never wanted to see the pictures before."

"I did this year." He looked down. "For obvious reasons."

In light of what was either a clear conscience, or no memory on Hope's part, Maryellen went into her computer trash and reexamined the deleted photos one after another, re-scrutinizing the photo of Tim and Hope. They weren't definitely kissing, only looking suspiciously like they could be. Meaning, they probably weren't. And if something did transpire, even though Hope had been drinking, she'd also eaten those hash brownies. By association wasn't Maryellen herself partially to blame? "Just like you said, there was really nothing to see but people having a good time."

"And you double-checked?"

His righteous indignation would blind him to just how circumstantial the picture was. "Triple-checked. There was nothing."

"I want you to forward everything to me before you put anything else up."

"No problem."

"Good enough, then." Frank glanced at his desk calendar. "How about the twenty-third for the Melody Mountain Community Church yard sale spectacular?"

"That's not even three weeks from now."

"Way the weather's been, we've gotta allow for a possible rain reschedule."

"I can't possibly . . ."

"Sweetie," Frank flashed the charming smile she'd only seen directed at Laney, Hope, anyone but her, in years. "With your yard sale know-how, you're the one person who absolutely, positively can."

CHAPTER TWENTY-NINE

Restrictions, Rules and Covenants: 5.7A. Garage doors. Garage doors may only remain open a maximum of one (1) hour.

*H*ope awoke to the sound of the garage door rolling open.

She'd bathed, brushed, and dabbed DKNY Delicious Night behind her ears. She'd turned down the sheets, climbed into bed, and turned on *Saturday Night Live* to stay awake while Jim made the drive from DIA.

Then nodded off anyway.

Given the twelve-hour days she'd been putting in, exhaustion was no particular surprise. But, she should have been able to stay awake while her husband, whom she hadn't seen for nearly a month, made the drive from the airport.

The garage door rumbled closed.

She hurried out of bed and ran into the bathroom to brush her hair and take a swig of mouthwash. There was no time to wash off the perfume that smelled bitter with her soap, shampoo, or whatever blip in her body chemistry caused it to smell like bitter almonds.

Hope smiled with the sound of his suitcase rolling over the hardwood in the back hall. The familiar click of wheels transitioning to the tumbled stone front hall tile.

She stepped onto the landing to greet him. "Welcome home, honey."

Jim abandoned his briefcase and suitcase, took the stairs two at a time, and scooped her into his arms.

His clothes smelled of airplane.

"Missed you," he said, and kissed her passionately.

His breath smelled of way too long a flight.

"Missed you, too." She held her breath and kissed him back as he carried her into the bedroom, deposited her on the bed, and began to tug at his belt.

She'd been waiting for this moment for two long weeks, but the promise of the pillow was somehow more appealing than his not-quite-shower-fresh body atop hers.

Hope closed her eyes along with her nose, ignored the heat of his breath in her ear, the mildly cloying tickle of his chest hair against her nipples, and the uneven edge of his right big toenail against the bottom of her foot.

"You feel so good," he whispered.

The unexpected friction when he moved inside her.

"Mmm," she whispered back, fighting the urge to doze off.

Pretended to come so he would.

CHAPTER THIRTY

10.5. Yard Sales: Yard Sales must take place only in the yard, garage, and/or driveway of owner. Items for purchase must sit no closer than one foot from sidewalks or common thoroughfares.

"Loved the Noah's Ark theme." Bruce Winters shook hands with Frank and turned to accept one of the donuts Maryellen offered.

"And I love Maryellen's marketing panache," his wife, Lynne, added, reading the tag hanging from the ribbon tied around one of the cellophane wrapped donuts Maryellen spent the better part of Saturday night putting together. "Melody Mountain Ranch Community Church Rummage Extravaganza!"

"Just wanted to make sure everyone knows so they can donate, sign up to help, or both."

"Mark me down to work sale day."

Maryellen took a satisfying breath of coffee infused air, wrote Lynne's name on her committee clipboard.

"Not so rainy today," Stan Flint said.

"I'm hopeful the storms have passed," Frank said.

So was she. Despite a little light drizzle, or maybe because of it, church was as well attended as Frank's sermon was well received. With every greeting and subsequent plink of collection plate change, Frank's good spirits improved. Better, Maryellen's *info donuts* had them smiling together for the first time since . . .

The potluck debacle already seemed to be fading from collective memory.

"You had me at cream-filled," Samantha Torgenson said. "Put me on the pricing committee so I get first dibs on anything good."

"What if we sell coffee in the morning and then cook up hot dogs?" the Orsons offered.

"Let me know if you want to print up posters," Katherine Powell, who owned a Jiffy Print franchise, said.

"Bless you for your contribution." Maryellen's growing joy grew that much more watching Eva work her way through the crowd, handing out the donuts she'd not only helped wrap, but had done without a single obligatory sigh, eye roll, or hint of teenage apathy.

To top it all off, Hope and Jim approached the greeting line, hand-in-hand, looking their usual relaxed, perfect selves.

"Great to have you back, Jim." Frank appeared at Maryellen's side and offered his handshake and his extra-friendly voice.

"Great to be back," Jim said. "If only for a few days."

"You've certainly been missed around here," Frank said to Jim.

"Plan to spend the afternoon planting grass and whatever else Hope needs me to do to make up for my extended absence."

Frank patted him on the back. "Gotta keep your girl happy."

Hope smiled, picked up a donut, and read the info tag. "Where's the sale going to be?"

"Here, in the parking lot."

"Won't that be logistically difficult?" Hope asked Maryellen.

"Setting up and taking down in one day's definitely going to be tricky." Maryellen smiled at Jim, allowing herself to appreciate for the briefest of seconds how Norse-god handsome he was. "But I think we can pull it off with a few strong volunteers."

"If everyone's supposed to bring donations to your house, why don't we just have it on our cul-de-sac instead?" Hope asked. "Jim will be gone again, but I'll volunteer my yard and garage for storage, and I'm sure Laney will let you use hers."

Eva appeared with a nearly empty basket. "Donuts are decimated."

Maryellen put a hang-on-a-second arm around her daughter. "Doing the sale on our street would be ideal, especially with the playground, but the covenants don't allow for—"

"Have Daddy change them," Eva said, watching her father accept a check from Mr. Jordan.

"Doesn't work that way, honey," Maryellen said.

"It is his yard sale," Eva said.

"But everyone knows your mom is the brains behind this operation." Hope smiled.

"True that," Eva added.

Hope's compliment was more than enough, but Maryellen beamed from Eva's endorsement. "Ready to refill our baskets, honey?"

Before she had to add a *Now, please* or any of the catch phrases typically required for a response, Eva smiled. "Sure, Mom."

Jim slipped his arm around Hope and they headed for the cafeteria.

Maryellen and her daughter started for the kitchen together. All was well.

"It's true, you know," Eva said as reached the double doors.

"What's true?" Maryellen put the key into the lock.

"I mean, Dad tells you to have a yard sale and, like, the next minute, you start organizing committees and have info donuts made up."

"You know I love yard sales." Maryellen was beyond touched to have Eva acknowledging her hard work. "And your dad only needs a few more dollars and he'll finally have the down payment money for land to build a real church." She even had a lump in her throat. "Great, huh?"

"Great we won't have to have a bake sale every five minutes."

Maryellen clicked open the door and let her daughter in first. "Amen to that."

Eva flipped the lid on a donut box and began to refill her basket. "Mom?"

"What, honey?"

"Don't you ever get sick of all the stuff he makes you do?"

Maryellen didn't dare look up for fear of what might show in her face, starting with exactly how sick she was of running bake sales. How much she hated wearing Sunday clothing to complement whatever Frank wore. . . How much she hated the way he made her talk. *Tell me you want my big hard manhood inside your tight, shaved pussy . . .* "What do you mean by that?"

"I dunno," Eva said. "Like this camp thing."

The sigh she'd anticipated from Eva fell from her own mouth instead. Why hadn't she known from the first missed eye roll opportunity that altruism might have little to do with Eva's unexpected *spirit of service*? That her compliments were likely as calculated as they were heartfelt? "You're still anxious about going?"

"I never wanted to go." Tears began to run down her face. "I don't want to go."

Could she blame her? It wasn't like Frank had ever discussed other possibilities, asked Eva for her input, or so much as considered any of Maryellen's own trepidations before writing the essay, filling out the paperwork, and signing his daughter's name to the application. "You know," Maryellen said, "I do understand."

Eva, whose face looked open and hopeful in a way she hadn't seen since before Frank announced his big surprise, practically fell into her arms. "I knew it!"

Frank was wrong to sign Eva up for camp without consulting her. More wrong for forging an essay in his daughter's name. At times, his neglect of her feelings and needs could even be considered criminal. But, as she stroked

Eva's dark hair, the crystals shimmered on that odd charm necklace she always seemed to be wearing.

Had taken off her first communion cross to wear it.

"Mommy," she sobbed, "you have to get me out of going to that camp."

Maryellen had cracked the door to the basement, smelled the burning incense, and taken a couple steps. Spotted Eva. Saw her eyes sparkle in the candlelight that bathed the room in shadowy light. "Eva, I don't think I can—"

"You're the only one who can."

"You know as well as I do that once your father makes a decision . . ."

"I hate him."

"Eva!"

She pulled away. "I do."

"Honey, he loves you and he's looking out for you in a way that someday you'll be grate—"

"Why don't you look out for me?"

Maryellen felt like crying herself. If only Eva knew how much she did to shield her daughter from the full force of Frank's righteous convictions. It nearly broke her heart to take Eva's pet stray to the pound to spare both of them from Frank's plan to mitigate certain rabies by putting a can of spiked tuna under the deck. "He's promised me he'll take you shopping for a car as soon as you get back."

"Like I really believe that."

Frank was wrong for signing his daughter up for a camp she had no interest in attending, but so right, even if he had no idea why. Their daughter needed the support, influence, and redirection of a Christian youth community away from home.

"So, you're going to just let him send me off?"

If only she hadn't seen Eva wearing that cape and holding that strange knife. "You never know. Camp could end up being a million times better than you ever expected."

"Or a million times worse."

The buzz of outside noise filled the otherwise silent room while Maryellen figured out how to clarify what was clearly not what Eva wanted to hear. "Sometimes, when I find myself in a situation where I'm uncertain or don't think I'm going to like it, I force myself to smile."

"You're kidding, right?"

"I know it sounds kind of hokey, but things don't seem so bad when you're smiling."

"Like in *The Sound of Music*?"

"In a way. It's how I deal with tough situations."

"And starving yourself."

"Eva!"

Any remaining glimmer of openness or possibility in Eva's face fell away and was replaced by a steely emptiness. "You know, your smile didn't seem forced after the potluck when you were gobbling up those Red Vines."

Maryellen swallowed a shot of licorice-flavored bile and with it the fear of what she might say in the face of exactly this conversation. "Yours did."

And now it is done . . .

"Wasn't forced at all," Eva finally said.

"What was going on in that basement, with your friends?"

"We were hanging out."

"Hanging out doing what?"

Eva's face contorted into a smile, but one Maryellen hoped never to see again. "Seemed like you were really, really high, Mom," she said.

"I . . ." Maryellen managed to say. *Little Witch*, she couldn't.

"Whatever." Eva grabbed her donut basket and started for the door. "I'm not going to camp."

CHAPTER THIRTY-ONE

*Henderson Homes has contracted with Star Warranty to
perform warranty work on your newly constructed home. Please
contact Star Warranty directly to assess and perform all covered
maintenance work—From Henderson Homes Five-Year Gold
Warranty.*

"This is Will Pierce-Cohn," he said, enunciating his last name. "I live at
46923 Songbird Canyon Court and my home warranty number is 532122 A
as in apple, Z as in zipper. I came home from vacation last night and discovered
a large crack running across the interior side of my family room exterior wall. I
need to get someone out here right away to take a look."

* * *

Tim Trautman pulled the closing documents from the file, located the
warranty fulfillment information, and dialed the number.

*You have reached Star Warranty Fulfillment Inc. Please leave your name,
number, builder, and purpose of your call. Due to the large number of recent
claims, you may experience a delay in response time, but a representative will return
your call as soon as possible. Please do not call the emergency line unless this is an
emergency. Be patient. We will get back to you.*

"Hi, this is Tim Trautman at 35424 Wonderland Valley Court. I'm calling
about some cracks around my living room bay window that should be covered
under the home warranty transferred into our name by the Smithers family
upon sale of the house. If someone could please call me back I'd appreciate it."

* * *

Hope typed in the e-mail address for Star Home Warranty Fulfillment, *Request for service* in the Re: line, detailed the particulars in the body of the e-mail, and pressed send.

She put a check mark beside call about cracks on her to-do list and moved on to plant materials she needed to review.

* * *

"Frank Griffin, president of the Melody Mountain Ranch Homeowner's here. I'm calling in both official and personal capacities. Seems we have floor tile cracking in some of the north-facing men's and women's poolside shower stalls. When you send your guys out, I'd also like to have you look at a damp area of carpeting in my basement I left you a message about last week. I figure it might help your backlog if you can double up and check both out together."

* * *

U back? Eva keyed into her phone.

Yep. Popped up from Tyler almost instantly. *Got in late last nite.*

Cool.

I guess if you can call a Disney cruise with parents who never stopped fighting cool.

Glad you are. She took a deep breath and typed the sentence that she'd been rolling around in her head for days. *Need to talk. Meet me at the playground in ten?*

Can't. Parents are at it again about some crack in the family room wall or something and I have to babysit for my little sisters until they quit fighting.

Have to talk to u.

Really can't.

Eva took a deep breath. *It really can't wait.*

CHAPTER THIRTY-TWO

9.1. Retaining Walls. Retaining walls may be used to accommodate or create abrupt changes in grade. Such walls should be properly anchored to withstand overturning forces and all retaining walls must incorporate weep holes to permit water trapped behind them to be released.

"Maybe I am crazy in the head." Laney lay face down on the examination/adjustment/massage table of Dr. Sebastian, chiropractor, acupuncturist, massage therapist, and naturopath. "But before I give in to insanity, I thought I'd see what you have to say. Roseanne Goldberg swears you're a miracle worker."

"I do my best." Bastian, as he asked to be called, placed a meaty hand on her left shoulder and another on the side of her face. "Hold still."

If she didn't feel so crappy, she'd definitely be appreciating his strong touch as he pulled, twisted, and cracked parts of her she didn't know could make quite those sounds.

"Any better?"

"I still can't breathe out of one nostril." She moved her head from side to side. "But whatever it was you just did to my back definitely helped."

"Hmm." He reached for her hand and helped her into a sitting position.

She took a deep breath of calming patchouli and God knew what else while Bastian turned to face the computer on the desk behind him. After a few minutes of typing, he turned back, reached for her left foot, and placed it on a pillow at the end of the exam table. He reached for a small metal prod that attached to his PC via USB port.

"What's that?"

"Tests your acupuncture points."

"By computer?"

"In part."

"What does it do?"

"Measures your energy imbalances." Bastian poked her heel with the end of the prod.

By allowing some pony-tailed practitioner of seemingly everything but actual medicine to prod her with a metal cursor, wasn't she simply confirming her diagnosis of crazy?

Music, like a rising violin scale, emerged from speakers mounted beside the computer.

"Liver is a little low."

He poked her big toe.

Another rising scale followed by a low beep.

"So are your adrenals."

She watched and listened to the machine hum, beep, work its way through scales in major and minor as he pressed points on both of her feet and moved toward her hands.

"Thymus isn't bad."

"So that's good?"

He tucked a gray strand of hair behind his ear and pressed the prod between her right thumb and forefinger.

A mini fire alarm went off.

"You are way out of balance."

"That's what I've been told."

He spun around on his chair and fiddled with the computer for what felt like forever. "I think I know what's going on here."

"What's that?"

He pressed on her thumb.

The machine not only did a scale, it began to whine and ring.

"What was that?"

"The *a ha* moment."

"As in you know what's wrong with me?"

"Mold."

"Mold?"

He nodded. "You're full of mold."

"Okay," she said, her heart suddenly heavy with yet another nondiagnosis. "What exactly does one do for that?"

"Supplements," he said.

"Supplements?"

"And . . ." He began to tap away on his computer again.

"And what?"

"If that doesn't work, we send you on to a specialist."

CHAPTER THIRTY-THREE

Section 2.5. Additions and Alterations. An addition should look like the original structure with matching architectural style and rooflines. Any alterations to the home will require submission of three sets of detailed plans.

*H*ope wrote JORDAN in black sharpie on the side of her urine specimen, sent it through the pass through, and joined the nurse for the obligatory weigh-in.

"Step on," the nurse said pointing to the scale.

She slipped off her shoes and hopped on the scale. Things were great with Jim. He'd been sweet and accommodating the entire time he'd been home and checking in constantly since he'd left first thing Monday morning. She never said anything related to fertility, babies, or that she was counting down days for this appointment so she could get her relaxed but proactive plans for getting pregnant under way.

"Down almost four pounds from last visit," the nurse said.

"Excellent." She'd have some wiggle room she'd hopefully need soon. "My husband's been out of town on business a lot, so I haven't been making much of anything for dinner."

She'd been so busy, breakfast and lunch had also become something of question marks.

Hope eyed the collage of baby photos lining the walls as she followed the nurse down to an examination room. "Actually, my husband's in and out of the country for the next six months. He's managed to rearrange his schedule so he can be here or I'm there during ovulation, so it's really important that whatever the doctor may want to prescribe is timed so my fertility peaks when we're together." Hope paused for a breath. Why was she bothering the nurse with all this?

The nurse merely nodded. "First day of last menstrual period?"

"Friday, May thirteenth."

She looked down at her chart and up at a wall calendar advertising Yaz. "And your cycles have been consistent at twenty-eight days?"

"Give or take."

"By my calculations you were due for your period on Monday, then?"

"Don't have it yet, but my husband was out of town until Saturday night, so there's really no chance—"

"I'm sure it's nerves." The nurse's tone was both bedside sympathetic and rote.

Hope nodded. "Or the stress of having him gone when I need him around."

"It all has a way of working out how it's meant to in the end," the nurse said, wrapping the blood pressure cuff around Hope's arm and sealing the Velcro fasteners.

"I'm not worried," Hope said over-brightly as the nurse pumped air into the cuff.

As the cuff squeezed her arm, her lungs began to feel almost as tight.

"No need to get into a gown." The nurse wrapped the stethoscope around her neck. "The doctor will be in to see you in a minute."

* * *

"I'm sure the nurse noted my husband is working out of the country until the end of the year. I'm trying to stay relaxed because it will help the process, and really, otherwise, I'll lose my mind, but I came in today so maybe we can figure out what's the highest safe dosage of Clomid, or whatever you think will work best to make sure I'm ovulating on schedule for the visits back and forth." Hope paused to take a breath. "I've been researching on the Internet and . . ."

The doctor smiled as though he was about to pat her on the head.

Hope's blood began to pound in her ears. "I know I sound intense, but you promised that if I didn't get pregnant in three months and it's been three months and now I'm dealing with the additional issue of having to time things accurately as though that's possible. The thing is, my husband wants to try and be relaxed about all of this, which I'm trying to do, but I don't want to have to approach him about artificial insemination or in vitro until—"

"Hope," the doctor put a hand on her shoulder. "There's no need for Clomid now."

"But I . . ."

"You're already pregnant."

"What?"

"Urine tested positive for HCG."

She leaned back against the wall alongside the examination table. "I'm pregnant?"

The doctor nodded.

"But, my husband and I just had sex—"

"Once is all it takes."

"But he's been . . . We couldn't even try until—"

"Apparently the right night."

"I can't believe it." She leaned back against the cool wall of the exam room, closed her eyes, and tried to control the racing, spinning feeling. "What do I do?"

"I presume you've continued to take the prenatal vitamins?"

She nodded, rubbed at the goose bumps suddenly lining her arms.

"Set an appointment three to four weeks from now." He stood and started toward the door. "We'll do the initial prenatal blood workup and maybe even hear the heartbeat."

The sound of her own heartbeat filled the room.

Part III

MORNING
SICKNESS

CHAPTER THIRTY-FOUR

*All Recreation Center Facilities are designed for safe and
enjoyable recreation. Violations of stated rules are taken seriously
and may result in loss of rec center privileges.*

*P*regnant.

Hope set the rec center elliptical machine for the doctor-recommended
max of thirty minutes and the intensity at seven to keep her heart rate and
painfully tender breasts in check.

She ran her fingers lightly across her belly.

Baby on Board.

She was dying to share the unexpected bliss with Jim every time they'd
talked, texted, or e-mailed. She couldn't wait for them to marvel together over
how, with all the testing and planning, they'd somehow managed to time her
fertility incorrectly for so long. She could barely stop herself from slipping up,
but there couldn't be a more poignant, unforgettable moment than telling her
husband he was going to be a father, face-to-face, in London, over a romantic
dinner.

A romantic vegetarian dinner.

The thought of consuming chicken, beef, or anything that once sported a
face sounded utterly revolting.

Knocked up.

Hope smiled, and set her iPod to the new playlist she'd created by typing
baby into iTunes search. Dave Matthews, Ludacris, U2, Lyle Lovett—everyone
seemed to have a song to contribute about their baby, infant or otherwise.

Mommy to be.

She warmed up to "Isn't She Lovely," Pharrel and Nelly's "Baby," and was
humming along with Britney to "Baby One More Time," when she spotted
someone in the cardio room doorway.

Her heart-rate monitor blipped upward.

Will Pierce-Cohn.

Whether it was the exercise funk that hung thick in the air, or the nonmemory of him tucking her into bed, which hung even thicker, Hope felt queasy.

She pretended to look at her workout stats display.

He looked around for a minute and then disappeared.

She took a deep breath to make sure she stayed below 140 beats per minute.

He reappeared.

She lowered her resistance to 6 and took another deep breath.

He headed in her direction.

She paused the music.

He stopped in front of her machine.

"Oh," she said tugging out her ear buds and hoping she looked more surprised and casual than she sounded. "Hi!"

"Hey." He wiped his forehead with the back of his hand.

"Finishing up a workout?"

The slightly ashen, first-awkward-meeting-since-that-night base beneath his holiday tan gave way to a hint of color. "I was just about to get started."

"Thought you might have jogged over here or whatever." She could only imagine the cast of her own skin. "No Sarah's class today?"

"More into cross-training lately, I guess."

"That's good."

"You didn't go, either?"

"Felt like a shorter workout today."

Across the room, a barbell clunked.

"I was planning to catch spin class, but I got here too late." He grinned wryly. "Unless I wanted to ride that one bike without a seat."

Her forced giggle evaporated into the hum of cardio machines.

"So." He pulled at the ends of the towel wrapped around his neck. "How're you doing?"

"Great," she said too quickly. "How was your trip?"

"Really great." He eyed a row of treadmills. "Just trying to readjust to life as usual."

"I'm doing the same in the opposite before I leave for London end of next week."

"Meaning you and Jim have gotten things worked out with schedules and stuff?"

"We have." Her smile felt natural for the first time since she spotted him standing in the doorway. "He'll be here or I'll be there for ovulation day until the end of the year."

And the best part, which she couldn't say, was that the timing didn't matter at all.

"That's great," Will said.

"It really is."

An overlong moment passed between them.

"I've been wanting to talk to you," he said.

She took a sip from her water bottle. "Me too."

They looked past each other.

"Don't know what happened that night," she finally said. "I barely ever have more than one glass of wine."

"Pretty much seems to be the common sentiment all around," he said. "But, like I said, *no worries.*"

"I guess I was just so angry and frustrated about the whole pregnancy thing, I—"

"No need to explain. As you know, our twins were in vitro."

"I don't think I did know that."

"I mentioned it to you when . . . when I was helping you get settled in upstairs."

"About that." She felt herself blush. "Thanks for being there for me."

"My pleas—" he said. "No problem."

Across the room, two unfamiliar women standing beside the weight rack looked over in their direction and began to whisper.

"Listen," they both said simultaneously.

"Thank you," he said first.

She shut off her heart rate monitor before he could hear it blip out of control. "For?"

"For everything you said that night."

Did she tell him she didn't remember a word? That the evening was nearly a total blur? Sweat broke out at the nape of her neck and rolled down her back. What had she said?

"Especially about the playground land."

"The playground land?"

"Too marshy to support . . ."

"It was." Cool relief rushed through her.

"I really appreciated your candor," he said. "Meant a lot."

Her heart rate plummeted back down toward normal. Had she said or done anything more troubling than whatever it was she'd admitted, likely that she'd jumped on Frank's bandwagon in large part because of the advice of an eerily accurate roadside psychic, there was no way the playground would be the first thing on his mind. "No problem."

No problems at all.

CHAPTER THIRTY-FIVE

4.30. Birdbaths. Committee approval is not required for
one birdbath that is less than three feet tall, including pedestal.
Placement of additional units requires Committee approval.

*L*aney reclined on the therapist's ultra suede chaise and tried not to break down the cost of his Roche-Bobois furniture in $175-an-hour, can't-submit-to-insurance increments. "So depending on who you ask, I'm sick with the crazy or—"

"Or allergic to mold," the therapist said.

"According to the naturopath I'm so full of it, I not only needed $250 of herbal snake oil but a referral to yet another specialist." She had to be crazy thinking she'd get answers from a "doctor" that specialized in practically every form of pseudo-medicine. "At least the *full of it* part of the diagnosis seems consistent across the board."

"But the good news is your health checks out with your MD."

"I guess." Laney reached for a Kleenex from the art glass tissue dispenser on the cocktail table beside the chaise.

The therapist leaned into the arm of his zebra-print chair. "What exactly feels bad?"

"I don't know, everything. I'm achy, foggy, forgetful, tired."

"Feelings of worthlessness or guilt?"

"Of course—I'm a wife and mother."

"How do you sleep?"

"Great until I actually lie down and try."

"Sleeping pills?"

"Make me feel like I'm in the *Wizard of Oz* poppy fields."

The therapist noted something on his pad. "How's your appetite?"

"Depends."

"Weight loss?"

"Eight pounds," she may have said with a little too much pride. "And counting."

"Are you able to enjoy hobbies, pastimes, and social activities?"

"When they make money."

"Do you enjoy sex?"

"Not with my husband," slipped out before she could stop it. "I mean, he has chronic fatigue, so he's not really ever in the mood lately, anyway."

"And how do you feel about that?"

"I make the best of it." Any meaningful discussion of extracurriculars was probably best left to a later conversation, imminent, judging by the way he began to scribble.

"You're on a hundred twenty-five milligrams of Zoloft?"

"Is that enough?"

"Getting the right dosage is key to optimal mental well-being."

"Clearly, I'm not optimized."

"I also think a course of talk therapy is key to getting to the root of some of the physical manifestations of your mental state."

"As in I have hypochondria?"

"As in it's worth talking over."

Laney gazed at the glass reproduction of *The Thinker*. "Like maybe once a week?"

"I was thinking more along the lines of three times a week."

CHAPTER THIRTY-SIX

4.56. Playhouses. Committee approval is required for playhouses more than 24 square feet and/or over 6 feet high.

*N*erves.

Hope set one of the matching gift baskets down, took a deep breath to relieve the jittery feeling, and rang the doorbell. Had to be nerves about the good news she couldn't yet share.

Tim opened the door with a sleeping baby nestled in each of his arms.

"Oh my God," she said. "They're absolutely gorgeous!"

His face was pure joy.

Picturing Jim with the same blissful expression over his son-or daughter-to-be had her blinking away that jumpy feeling.

"This is Mackenzie." Tim rocked just enough so the baby pursed her little rosebud mouth. He turned to the sleepy beauty in his right arm. "And this is Kayla."

"Blond curls," Hope said.

Tim twisted a tiny ringlet with a free pinkie. "If I wasn't cradling her while Theresa delivered her sister, I'd have sworn there was a mix-up at the hospital.'"

Kayla yawned.

"And this one looks just like her momma when she sleeps." Tim smiled down at the baby. "Come on in."

Hope picked up the second of the rain-dampened raffia and cellophane baskets she'd set below the doorbell and followed him into the house.

"I'd take those from you," he rocked one of his double blessings, "but—"

"I wouldn't put those little dolls down for anything, either." Hope stepped into the front hall and set the baskets on a table. "They're just beautiful."

"Speaking of beautiful, life seems to be agreeing with you," Tim said. "You look great."

She felt her cheeks color. "Thanks."

"Happier than last we talked."

"I feel good." It was far too early in the process and she'd been too nauseous to attribute any change in her appearance to *the glow*, but the fact he'd recognized something, even if unknowingly, had her glowing all the more. "I'd probably be happier if I hadn't volunteered my yard, garage, and now front hall for Maryellen's extravaganza, but everything's so well organized . . ."

"Ya think?" He looked at a box marked *yard sale* by the back door and shook his head. "I can't believe she actually has people delivering their crap to different houses by category."

"Maryellen's nothing if not organized."

"And about to pull off the most anal retentive rummage sale of all time."

They both laughed.

"Considering our last community event, I suppose I sort of understand her need to keep things under control," he said.

Hope took a deep breath to quell a sudden wave of the queasies. "Still can't believe we ate those brownies."

He winked. "Relaxed you, though, right?"

She remembered drinking vodka, eating brownies, and talking pregnancy, psychic predictions, patience. Was there, couldn't possibly be, the haziest memory of a kiss? "You know . . ."

"I know that was an utterly amazing night."

That jittery feeling returned.

Mackenzie's eyes fluttered briefly.

Tim kissed her tiny forehead.

"I just can't imagine how you went off to the hospital like that."

"Nor can I," he said.

"Hope!" Theresa appeared at the top of the landing.

"Congratulations!" Hope said. "Your daughters are absolutely gorgeous!"

"And thankfully, they're still sleeping," Tim said as Theresa came down the stairs and joined them in the front hall.

They kissed.

Hope flashed back to sitting with Tim at the picnic tables. She remembered walking alone down the hall toward the vending machine. So high.

There was nothing more.

That fuzzy memory she had of some sort of kiss had to be from the dream with *not Jim*.

"Look at those baskets!" Theresa peered through the cellophane at MACKEN-ZIE and KAYLA in letters shaped and painted to look like flowers. "I can't imagine how cute their names are going to look above their cribs."

"There are also tree decals and 3-D butterflies," Hope said.

"You didn't need to go to all that trouble."

"It's kind of ridiculous, but I've actually lost sleep picturing how it's all going to look on the wall above their cribs." In fact, her nagging memory felt no more real than the aching but false familiarity one had after a romantic dream with a celebrity or distant friend.

Kayla began to coo and Tim broke into the broadest of grins.

No matter how stoned and drunk she was, she wouldn't kiss a man other than her husband, couldn't kiss a man whose wife was pregnant, much less in labor with his two beautiful new daughters.

Mackenzie made a much more inauspicious sound.

They all laughed.

No way she could ever have kissed Tim.

"Do you have time to take the baskets upstairs?" Theresa asked. "I'd love to see what you've been picturing."

"Thought you'd never ask." Hope smiled.

If even a hint of anything had happened, wouldn't there be full-fledged horror if not profound awkwardness between them?

"I'll keep an eye on my girls while you do," Tim said.

Instead, there was easy friendship, a relaxed atmosphere, and joy. Hope rubbed what would soon be her own little bundle as she followed Theresa to the stairs.

Pure joy.

CHAPTER THIRTY-SEVEN

14.3. Notice of Complaint: Complaints shall contain a statement of charges in ordinary, concise language and clearly state the acts or omissions with which the homeowner is charged.

The dull throb of the flat-screen TV reverberated through the garage as Laney weaved around the Little Tykes play sets, cast-off lawn equipment, and worse-for-wear patio chairs that had usurped both of their parking spaces. She entered the house and set her purse on the table. "I'm home."

Her voice echoed through the empty front hall that was supposed to contain the boxes of Mary Kay, Pampered Chef, and assorted home shopping samples Mother's Helpers had deemed obsolete and had been earmarked for the yard sale.

"Hey." Steve lay beached on the couch like a steadily growing whale, inhaling Doritos like krill.

Accept that he's been diagnosed with Chronic Fatigue.

The therapist's words infused her sigh.

Expect him to be unwell, not going to accomplish much, if anything, from a honey-do list until he starts to feel like himself again.

The therapist warned her not to henpeck, but was a polite entreaty to bring three boxes up from the basement when he had nothing else to do so wrong? It wasn't like she was going to suggest he call Scott Connors, who was hiring insurance agents at his *booming* agency, at least according to that show-off Julie, when she'd called to schedule a Mother's Helpers party for next month.

Expect nothing.

As expected, nothing had moved, including him, since she'd left for the therapist.

"How did it go?" emerged from his blowhole.

"Apparently, I'm still depressed and have over-high expectations for the ones I love." She headed for the refrigerator for a Diet Coke. "But my hypochondria seems to be improving."

"How's that?"

"The therapist didn't hesitate to offer me an Advil for a tension headache." She shook her head. "Can you believe that?"

He pointed the clicker toward the TV. "You're not going to believe this."

"I don't exactly have time for ESPN. Randall Fowler's on his way over with yard sale stuff right now."

"Then we'll get to be the first to congratulate him." He upped the volume.

In off-season trade news, Randall Fowler inked a sweet deal that has him trading in his Broncos jersey for the Silver and Black.

Laney felt her knees weaken beneath her. "Meaning what?"

"Meaning your *bestie* is headed to Oakland."

CHAPTER THIRTY-EIGHT

*7.4.12. Garage Sales: The Owner of any lot may conduct a
yard, garage, or lawn sale if the items sold are his own furniture
and furnishings, not acquired for the purposes of resale.*

7*:04 A.M.:*

Despite the prediction of rain, the sky was a uniform blue. The only hint
of white came from the last few still-snowcapped peaks rising up behind the
houses dotting the hillside. Baby birds chirped like circus barkers. Summer
was in full swing, but having spent the better part of the week pulling together
the biggest yard sale Melody Mountain Ranch had ever seen, Maryellen felt
nothing, if not springy.

She attached balloons to the last of the neon-painted signs directing
traffic from Parker Road, along Melody Mountain Parkway, and through the
development to their cul-de-sac.

> *MELODY MOUNTAIN RANCH COMMUNITY CHURCH*
> *RUMMAGE SALE!*
> *TODAY!!!*
> *ONE DAY ONLY!!!!!*
> *SATURDAY, JUNE 23*
> *8–3*

Before the sale got going, Maryellen took a moment to admire the sea of
clothing, outdoor equipment, household items, toys, and furniture dotting
the lawns and driveways and flowing into the street itself. Since her first blast
e-mail, plans had fallen into place like clockwork. Parishioners, neighbors, even
random people who'd heard about the sale, began to drop off their prepriced,
separated-by-category items. Considering how much had come in, she was
amazed at how little pricing and sorting there was to be done. So little, in fact,
the Pricing-and-Sorting committee had morphed into the Night-Before-Prep
committee.

Thanks to Hope and Laney's generosity of both yard space and storage,
the loaders and haulers who would still have been unloading at the Melody

Mountain High School parking lot were enjoying coffee and bagels at the playground pavilion. Frank changed the covenants to allow multihouse yard sale permits upon approval of the board and then approved hers. And while the sale didn't officially start for almost twenty minutes, the first shift was in place with aprons on and change at the ready, awaiting the purchases of a Hispanic couple with a pickup truck, a consignment shop owner, and a smattering of early birds.

As she headed back down the cul-de-sac, Frank appeared from inside the house. Yard sale casual in a pigment-dyed T-shirt, Lucky jeans, and the sneakers he put on after helping with setup and running back inside to shower, he surveyed the scene, gave her the thumbs-up, and joined her beside the greeter's chair. "What do you need me to do, Mel?"

Maryellen smiled. "Just relax, mingle, and watch the money come in."

* * *

7:45 A.M.:

Hope kept her mug of peppermint tea in close sniffing proximity to ward off the no longer enticing aroma of fresh brewed coffee.

"I mean, I'm thrilled as hell Randall got traded, or whatever," Laney, who'd been on a stream-of-conscious rant about the Fowlers for the last ten minutes, continued, "but you can't tell me they didn't have any idea. I'm telling you, they knew all along."

Hope shook her head as compassionately and with as little motion as possible.

"And if one more person asks me how psyched I am about the *big news . . .*"

While Laney seemed content to vent about Sarah Fowler with little in the way of thoughtful response, Hope was happy to stand in one place and not try to track the conversation. She inhaled peppermint to quell morning sickness that, were there no sale as distraction, she'd be suffering in bed, or more likely, on the floor of the bathroom.

Not that she was complaining. She'd never been so thrilled to be so nauseous.

"Morning, Frank!" Laney said in a loud, too-chipper voice when Frank Griffin stopped at a table of books that was arguably outside shouting distance.

He responded to her wave with one of his official church smiles, but picked up a title of interest and began to read the back cover as though hesitating before heading over to say hello.

"He really does look cute when he does the dress-down thing. Don't you think?"

"Never really thought of him that way," Hope managed.

"Really?" Laney ran her tongue along her teeth, ostensibly to loosen rogue sesame seeds from the bagel she'd been nibbling. "How can you not?"

Hope belched.

"Morning," Frank said, making his way over, but not really zeroing in. His attention seemed to be on a transaction at the checkout table. "I'd love to chat, but Maryellen has me on a short leash this morning."

"I'm sure she does." Laney smiled.

"I'm glad I caught you both together, though," he said. "We can't thank you enough for the use of your yards and garages."

"No problem." Hope worked her lips into an upward curl.

"My pleasure," Laney said.

A woman who'd been milling through a nearby box of bedding came over with an unopened queen sheet set.

"The only price I see is the original tag from the store."

"Still in the package and originally $79.99," Laney said, examining the price tag. "Twenty-five bucks should be about right."

"How about twenty?" the woman asked.

"For an unopened Pottery Barn sheet set?"

The woman picked up a crystal vase from a nearby table. A $5 price tag hung from the base. "Throw this in and you have a deal."

"Should we do it, Frank?" she asked.

"I think that's a question best answered by Maryellen," he said, either missing or ignoring her double entendre. "Follow me."

"Thanks for your support, ladies," he said as the woman fell in behind him. "You're the best."

Two steps away, but a step before he was definitely out of hearing range, Laney said, "If he weren't a man of the cloth, I might be tempted to show him just how right he is."

With that thought, not-yet-digested peppermint rose in Hope's throat.

* * *

7:50 A.M.:

Maryellen watched Laney wave Frank over, conduct what she must have thought was a surreptitious g-string-liberating tug on the backside of her hot pink sweats, and break into a flirty smile. The day looked so promising, Laney's usual nonsense had no effect on her—not until a customer stepped over and she began to conduct what looked like negotiations. The sexual innuendo routine was one thing, but taking charge of the sale was another.

Maryellen stood and was on her way over to intercede when Frank started in her direction, customer in tow.

They met halfway.

"Laney suggested twenty bucks for this sheet set and vase," he said, showing her the items in his hand. "But, I wanted to get an okay from the big boss."

The *big boss* smiled. "Twenty sounds perfect."

* * *

8:31 A.M.:
"Yo, Laney," Steve Torgenson waved a lacrosse stick as he headed toward the checkout line. "Cool surprise about Randall Fowler, huh?"

"Fabulous!" she said. "Speaking of fabulous, you must just love that prolonging cream Samantha picked up for you at my Mother's Helpers party."

* * *

9:42 A.M.:
Whether Maryellen was greeting shoppers at the playground pavilion, refilling her coffee, or at the checkout table watching the exit parade of fondue pots, Little Tykes toys, and lamps destined for a new life as someone else's treasure, praise seemed to float in the breeze that had rolled in.

Excellent merchandising, items priced to sell . . .

I don't think I've ever been to such an attractive rummage sale . . .

Maryellen says a well-organized yard sale can bring in up to 30 percent more . . .

To that end, she stopped to straighten a rack of assorted coats.

Amid the hum of compliments, the distinctive cry of a newborn rang through the air and Maryellen turned to find Theresa Trautman standing beside her, double stroller in tow. "Oh, you're here!"

"We're all here."

She hugged Theresa and took in the heavenly tableau of rosebud mouths; plump, ivory cheeks; and blue eyes. "They're gorgeous!"

"The blondie is Kayla Rose." Theresa beamed, touching a little ringlet. "And our Mackenzie Grace," she lifted the pink woven cap, revealing adorable peach fuzz, "is darker like Lauren, but still sporting a mild case of cone head."

"I can't even imagine giving birth to two at once."

"There's barely time to think about it when they come two minutes apart and as quick as they did," Theresa said. "My water broke at eight-thirty. We were at the hospital by nine-thirty. I had Mackenzie by a minute after eleven and Kayla two minutes later."

"Absolutely amazing," Maryellen said.

"Isn't she though?" Tim appeared beside her and slid an arm around his wife. He glanced at his boys who had taken to digging through a table covered with assorted sports equipment. "So is your sale, by the way."

"Thank you," Maryellen said. "But everything pales in comparison to your beautiful daughters."

He smiled at Theresa. "Clearly, they take after their mama."

With the sound of a horn, one of the babies began to fuss.

"And apparently a little bit of daddy thrown in for good measure," he added, checking out the offending white van inching around the foot traffic. "That looks like Star Warranty."

The van approached and pulled into the Pierce-Cohns' driveway. The Star Warranty logo faced the central section of the yard sale.

"How timely," Tim said. "I think I'll go over and pester the technician about when we're on the schedule."

"Would you?" Theresa asked. "Those cracks beneath our bay window feel like they're growing."

"Why don't I take the babies with me so you're freed up to look around?"

Theresa eyed a table filled with toddler clothing. "Sure you don't mind?"

"Not if you don't mind that I'll get to show them off first." Tim beamed at his infant daughters.

"I think I'll make my way in Hope's direction. I promised Lauren I'd talk to her about doing her room as soon as the repair work is done."

"Sounds like a plan."

They kissed and he took off with stroller in tow toward the Pierce-Cohns' house and the workman who was unloading something from the back of his van.

"What a good husband and father he is," Maryellen said, giving herself a surreptitious pinch for any worries she might have entertained otherwise.

* * *

9:51 A.M.:

"Hey Laney," Warren Mickelson said, holding two matching art deco prints. "Fowlers all excited about their big move?"

"Very." She forced the most syrupy of smiles. "But housing's awfully expensive in California."

"With that raise, I'm sure he won't even notice," Warren said.

"And there's the diversity issue to deal with."

"The diversity issue?"

"Sarah is married to someone of color and all," she leaned over the table and stage-whispered, "but between you and me, I don't think she's all that comfortable living in an Oakland kind of environment, if you know what I mean."

* * *

9:55 A.M.:

People were busy shopping, socializing, and having fun all around her.

Frank, who'd just finished negotiating a 10 percent kickback from the ice cream truck in exchange for a parking spot beside the playground, parked himself on the pavilion and was chatting it up with the other fathers.

Hope looked downright blissful holding one of the babies as she talked not only animatedly, but utterly unselfconsciously, with Theresa and Tim.

Maryellen even saw Roseanne Goldberg smile, admittedly not over the sale itself, but her own conversation with the Star Warranty tech, whom she'd accosted at just about the same time as Tim on Will's driveway.

Best of all, Eva, who wasn't currently speaking to either her or Frank, appeared from inside the house. Her prolonged silence would have been much more concerning had she not come out of the house by nine, made a beeline across the lawn, and stationed herself beside the table filled with assorted mall baubles and Forever 21 castoffs she'd insisted on organizing, merchandising, and now straightening for the sale.

Maryellen smiled herself as she put a sold sign on a table and chair set bound for the first home of an adorable newly married couple who'd left to fetch their bigger car.

* * *

9:59 A.M.:

By letting the kids pay her instead of taking the crap they picked up in her *teen* section to the checkout tables, Eva figured she could pocket at least $100.

An hour in and she'd already siphoned off fifty, thanks in large part to Heather. No longer wanna-be African American, she'd tossed her hip-hop clothes, taken out her cornrows, dyed her blond hair black, and had snapped up pretty much anything at the sale that could pass as Goth.

Lauren, on the other hand, who'd shown up with her, fingered a bracelet or two, but her eyes never left Tyler's very closed front door.

"Haven't seen him yet today," Eva said.

Lauren's not-quite-lifeguard bronzed cheeks went splotchy. "He said he thought he might be playing golf or something."

Something like playing his unwilling part in Eva's Plan B.

On the night he got home from Florida, Eva had filled him in on the basics of her plan to run away. It was only after he refused to take part in a *passing of the Athame* hookup that she realized she hadn't thought things through enough. Not only had the spell to break Lauren and Tyler failed, he was like really in love.

Meaning she couldn't trust him not to rat her out to her parents.

If her dad found out, there was only one thing that would keep him from sending her to that damn camp.

"Probably better if we don't do anything," she'd said, thinking up an instant but crucial addendum to her plan.

"Glad you agree," he'd said. "I just can't. I mean, Lauren and me—"

"I'm late," she'd said.

"I should be taking off too," he'd said.

"No, I mean, I'm like late, late."

"Like you might be . . . ?"

"I'm not always on time or anything, so I'm not totally worried, but—"

"But what?"

The look on his face—a mixture of confusion, disbelief, and sheer panic told her he'd keep his mouth shut, at least long enough to get her plans finalized so she could take off.

"I'll keep you posted."

He'd been alternately texting to find out if she knew anything for sure and trying to avoid her ever since.

"Everything cool with you guys?" Eva asked Lauren.

"Every time I ask, Tyler says everything's good." Lauren sniffled. "He's acting weird though."

"Probably just having his boy period or something," she said.

"You think so?"

"I think these would look great on you." Eva handed Lauren a pair of skinny jeans she'd worn once but hated because they bunched at the knees. "They were mine."

"Totally cute," Lauren said. "I can't believe you're getting rid of them—they're Hudson."

"I loved them when I got them, but they're tight or something all of the sudden."

"That's a bummer," Lauren said.

Eva smiled. "Guess I'm getting kinda fat or something."

* * *

10:36 A.M.:

"I'm thinking she looks a tiny bit bloated," Stephanie Mitchell said.

"Hope Jordan would never retain fluid." Laney squinted and turned her head sideways. "Unless Will Pierce-Cohn somehow knocked her up after the potluck."

"What?" Stephanie asked.

"Laney thinks she saw Will in Hope's house." Lisa Simon shook her head. "You were high that night and you must be high now. Remember, we're talking

P-C here, so even if you did, what could have really happened? Besides, Hope's belly is flat as a board."

"Speaking of which, did anyone ever figure out who brought those brownies to the potluck?" Julie Connors asked.

"Nope," Laney said.

Stephanie raised an eyebrow. "Rumor has it, it was you, Laney."

"Wasn't me." Something about being credited with a night that would forever be part of neighborhood lore made Laney smile. "But, you know what I always say, treats and surprises are the key to a fun-filled, successful event."

* * *

10:51 A.M.:

"Great yard sale." A well-dressed, older woman, who was standing nearby, said to her equally well-dressed friend.

"They usually are around here." The other woman picked up a table lamp and examined the shade. "They all buy like they have money."

The comment might have bothered Maryellen had a sudden stir not filled the air.

"There he is," one of the kids yelled from the playground. "Hey, Randall!"

"Go Raiders," another kid yelled and a swarm headed in the direction of the Fowlers, who'd just arrived and were standing on Laney's driveway.

Randall graciously began signing autographs for the neighborhood kids.

"Who's that?" the woman holding the table lamp asked.

"One of our neighbors," Maryellen said sweetly. "He just signed a multimillion dollar deal with the Oakland Raiders."

* * *

10:52 A.M.:

Laney found a pair of earrings that looked suspiciously like the hoops she'd left at the Raymonds' after a particularly drunken hot tub party, and was headed over to ask Jen Raymond what she knew about them when she heard *Randall* ring out across the cul-de-sac.

About fainted when she saw him standing there with Sarah on her driveway, blocking her play—the run for it into her house she'd planned if they happened by the sale.

She searched for a nearby table piled high enough to hide behind, looked down, and pretended to examine jewelry she'd already milled through while she rummaged through her brain for an alternate escape route.

Carolina Herrera perfume warned her in advance of Sarah's imminent approach.

"Slumming it one last time?" she managed the second she spotted those perfectly manicured toes in gold-trimmed sandals she knew to be Prada.

"Laney, I've been calling and calling."

Laney looked up. "I haven't been answering."

"I'm sorry," Sarah said.

"I don't accept."

Neither said anything.

Laney pretended to look through a box of scarves.

"Laney, it's not like I can help my husband got traded."

"We've been through this once before."

"I'm really sorry."

"You should have told me."

"I didn't know."

"Lie."

"I'm not lying."

"You knew he was in talks."

"But I didn't know if anything would come of them."

She didn't want to cry. She couldn't let herself cry. She began to cry. "I shouldn't have had to hear it on TV."

"I know, honey." Sarah came around and wiped a tear from Laney's cheek. "I know."

"You don't know. I'm so hurt."

"I know, I know. I'll make it up to you, I promise."

"How are you going to do that?"

"For starters," Sarah said, "I'll come to visit and you'll visit me."

"And?"

"How about you list my house?"

* * *

11:05 A.M.:

"You like to play hardball, huh?"

"Depends on who I'm playing with." Emboldened by the success of her morning, Maryellen added a Laney-style wink, and then almost laughed out loud for doing so.

"I hear ya," the antiques dealer said. "I'll give you $125 for the standing mirror and the china."

"$150."

"Prime yard sale time's dwindling," the antiques dealer said. "And it's gonna rain."

Bright sunshine was preferable on paper, but too much heat cooled down sales. Best as she could tell, the scattered clouds that had rolled in were having the opposite effect, heating things up by providing the most optimal temperature for shopping Maryellen could have requested. "There are still lots of shoppers and it's not raining yet."

"When it does, your sale's over."

She glanced up at the cloud cover coming from the west. When she looked down, she couldn't miss Laney and Sarah, whose heated argument appeared to have evolved into a nearly as passionate, definitely as public, hug of forgiveness. "How about we split the difference?"

"Deal," he said.

She watched Sarah light a cigarette, take a drag, and place the cigarette between Laney's lips.

As she shook hands with the antiques dealer, Laney and Sarah walked together to the Estridges' side gate and disappeared into their backyard, hand in hand.

* * *

12:04 P.M.:

How she went from burping peppermint tea all morning to craving a condiment-covered beef product the moment the coffee and bagel sale transformed into a hot dog stand was a mystery.

Hope's mouth watered as she squirted mustard across the top of her steaming hot dog and took a bite.

A miracle.

Despite the on-and-off queasiness, the sale had been the perfect distraction. Maryellen wouldn't assign her to do much of anything, insisting the donation of her house and storage was more than enough, but work had found her. Not only did she and Theresa talk about more redecorating, three other clients had taken her aside about projects. One, a potential landscaping job, happened by chance when she came over to chat with Frank Griffin, who'd introduced her to the woman standing beside him and ducked out of the conversation to help an elderly lady carry a heavy kitchen appliance. When no one could find Laney to determine the price on some of her Tupperware, Hope stepped in with a catalog she happened to have lying around.

As she savored the second juicy bite of hot dog, she watched Will Pierce-Cohn say good-bye to the Star Warranty guy and drop his daughters at the toys.

He seemed to be whistling as he made his way over.

Once she knew he was way more interested in whatever she'd said about the playground than anything related to tucking her into bed, she'd all but let go of her embarrassment. Coming clean about the drainage problems, the bunny "relocation" site that was far too close to a highway for her comfort, and her agreement to work on the playground because of Renata's prediction seemed to have cleared the air between them entirely.

Renata's startlingly accurate prediction.

A new life is ready to come through very soon.

"Good as they look?" Will asked, joining her at the pavilion.

"Better." She took a bite. "I'm thinking I'll have to have another."

"Hold that thought." He headed for Larry Mitchell, who was manning the stand. "I assume you want it with everything?"

"You know it," she said.

* * *

1:18 P.M.:

Contrary to the antiques dealer's prediction, business was still brisk. Maryellen buttoned up her sweater. Unfortunately, the weather was getting a little too brisk.

* * *

1:25 P.M.:

Maryellen made the call to leave outdoor items on Laney's lawn, but dispatched the teardown committee to condense the remaining yard sale items and put everything on tables in her garage.

* * *

2:10 P.M.:

The rain didn't seem to distract or detract shoppers by all that much, if at all. In fact, people seemed to enjoy the cozy, indoor bazaar experience.

* * *

2:45 P.M.:

Maryellen called half-price among a rush of end-of-the-day bargain hunters who'd arrived sopping wet, but eager to load up on overlooked finds they knew they'd pay double for at the thrift store.

* * *

3:20 P.M.:

Maryellen sent the last shopper home with a box filled with two-for-ones on anything of equal or lesser value.

* * *

3:48 P.M.:
Thunder rumbled in the distance as the teardown committee braved the downpour to load outdoor items and the dribs and drabs strewn across her garage onto the Salvation Army donation truck that had backed into her driveway.

* * *

4:38 P.M.:
Overstuffed moneybox in hand, and backlit by a bolt of lightning, Maryellen took a deep, satisfied breath and closed her garage.

* * *

4:40 P.M.:
Laney let the damp cardboard box of unsold Kustom Kandle and Happy Chef samples she couldn't bear to see relegated to a thrift store drop to the floor of the garage with a thump. She pushed the garage door button. "*You* were embarrassed by *me?*"

"People were talking," Steve said.

"About?"

"Things you were saying." His voice was almost inaudible over the wind and the grind of the closing garage door as it closed. "That scene with Sarah."

"What do you mean, that scene? We were just making up."

"In front of everyone?"

"She's my best friend," Laney said.

"Hard to overlook that."

"She's moving away."

"Where did the two of you disappear to?"

"We needed to talk."

He shook his head.

"For your information, she asked me to list her house."

Steve passed the family room and headed for the refrigerator. "I need a beer."

Anticipating his next stop at the recliner, Laney headed for the family room and sat on the remote. "You know, we do need the money desperately."

"I don't have a problem with that."

"Then what do you have a problem with?"

"Shh," he said.

"Are you shushing me? Better not be, because I have every right to say or do whatever I want to do, particularly when I'm the one who's bringing in most of the—"

"Seriously, Laney." He put his index finger to his lip. "You hear that?"

"What?"

"That whooshing sound?"

"You mean the wind or the rain?"

He shook his head.

She resisted the urge to bolt across the room and shake him. "The house always makes weird noises when it's windy."

"You set the washing machine on delay for some reason?"

"No, but I ran a load this morning before I grabbed the last of the yard sale stuff."

"Did you hear it end?"

"Course not. I was already at the yard sale."

And then she heard it coming from downstairs, like running water . . .

Rushing water.

They moved together toward the basement door.

He opened the door.

She looked down.

Water filled the basement almost to the top of the first step.

* * *

5:34 P.M.:

Five thousand one hundred sixty-six dollars and twenty-nine cents.

$5,166.29!

$166.29 more than Lisa Manning *claimed* she brought in at her sale, and not over a weekend extravaganza, but in one not entirely dry day.

As rain pelted the windows in sideways gusts, Maryellen picked up the money she'd set across the carpet in paper-clipped stacks of like denominations. Starting with the hundred-dollar bills, she put the cash back into the strong box, rechecking her totals down to the pennies she'd spread out in twenty-five-cent piles.

$5,266.39.

Five thousand two hundred sixty-six dollars and thirty-nine cents!

She closed the money box, twisted the lock, and relished the sheer heft of so much coin on her way down the hall to Frank's office.

Couldn't wait to watch his slump-shouldered exhaustion give way to elation.

"Got a total," she said.

He looked up.

"And it's over five grand!"

"Great!" he said.

While it wasn't the enthusiastic *fabulous job* she'd expected and he made no particular move out of his chair to dance around the room with her like she'd hoped, Maryellen couldn't help but smile. "$266.39 more than Harmony Hills Church made in two days."

"Really great," he said.

His hangdog expression reflected otherwise.

"I know it's not quite the $7,500 you're looking for—"

"Need."

"Need," she said, a knot of disappointment forming in her chest. "If need be, we have enough left over to do a mini-sale."

"Not before next Friday," he said.

"You know . . ." The knot in her chest transitioned into a fiery anger that began to spread through her body. "It's not exactly easy to pull in $5,200 in one day."

"Not easy at all," he said.

"That's right."

"I can't imagine what could have been done better," he said.

"I hope you mean that, because I did this to help you, even though I—"

"Hope." He shook his head.

"Hope?"

"I heard a horrible rumor at the hot dog stand."

Maryellen's heart began to thump. "About Hope?"

"I just figured Larry Mitchell was talking about getting repairs done when he said, *some guys have all the luck.*"

"What?"

Frank's voice was barely audible. "Happened that night."

A jolt went thorough her. "What happened that night?"

"His wife said Laney saw them."

Maryellen was with Laney while Tim and Hope went off toward the picnic tables. She saw Laney leave with Steve via the pool gate. What she saw in the photo wasn't really . . . "Saw them where?"

"Apparently," Frank's voice faltered, "Hope was au naturel."

"At the rec center?"

He shook his head. "Her bedroom."

"Her bedroom?"

"Laney saw them through her window."

"Saw who?"

"She took off her clothes and he followed her into the bathroom." Frank paused. "Will."

Will? Maryellen tried, but failed, to swallow the bitter taste in the back of her throat.

"And I thought I only needed to worry about Trautman."

Not Tim?

Will?

CHAPTER THIRTY-NINE

Choose from six dazzling models in the Colorado Birdsong
Collection and revel in arresting architectural features like dramatic
foyers, standard-plus living rooms, and your choice of full or
partially finished basements.

"Mr. or Mrs. Estridge?"

"Yes?" Laney dared to look down the stairs for the first time since discovering the flood and addressed the head of Rising Tides Flood Control crew, not that she could tell exactly who was who beneath the masks and hazmat-type suits.

"We got the water up, the fans in place, and the furniture on blocks to prevent further damage while the carpet dries."

"How bad is the furniture?"

"I seen worse."

"What about the pool table?"

"My guess, it'll dry out fine with all the lacquer on the legs."

"That's a relief," Steve chimed in from the next room.

"Yup," the water damage guy said. "But I think you should come down here anyway."

The recliner squealed and Steve appeared beside her with a sneeze. "Smells kinda—"

"Probably ought to wear a mask," the water guy said, handing one to each of them before they made it to the bottom of the now unsubmerged stairs.

One look at the pile of gray, mottled drywall that had once been the lower twelve inches of the rec room walls and Laney had to grab the banister to steady herself. "Oh, dear Lord."

"Standard procedure," Steve said like he was some sort of remediation expert.

"We stopped cutting at the water line until your insurance people can take a look but . . ." The real remediation man motioned toward the laundry room. "I think we figured out what caused the flood."

"Washing machine?" Steve worked his way down the hall and looked into the laundry room. "Oh shit!"

"That's what I thought at first, too." The workman stepped aside so Laney could join them in the room.

What was left of it.

"Fuck," she said. Would have leaned against the wall for support, had there been anything left that still resembled a wall.

Shards of drywall, mottled with black, gray, green, and even purple spots lay in the corner. The pipes and wooden beams that remained, as well as the now-exposed concrete, looked like they were painted with a rainbow of fuzzy, furry splotches.

"Is that—?" Laney's throat felt like it was closing.

"Haven't ever really seen anything quite like it." The workman shook his head and pulled off a piece of drywall. "Your pipe basically fell out of the wall."

Steve began to cough.

"How can that happen?"

"Not sure. Your foundation's probably cracked." He shook his head. "Your walls are definitely rotted through. Molded through, I should say."

CHAPTER FORTY

Should a claim arise, it is in our best interest to address your problem immediately—From the Henderson Homes Structural Warranty guide.

*S*teve Estridge looked more worn out than Maryellen had ever seen him. Green, as though he could be any other color.

She shuddered with the thought of toxic spores, fanning out like enormous, slimy snowflakes, filling their basement until the walls rotted. "How're you holding up?"

"Been better," Steve said. "And I'm sorry to have to bother you."

"No bother." She opened her front door. "I can't imagine what you're going through."

"Neither can I." He shook his head. "Frank around by any chance?"

"He was holed up inside working when I left for my walk."

Confusion added to the distress already lining his usually smooth round face. "He isn't answering his phone."

"That's odd." She stepped into the house. "Frank?"

Her voice echoed down the hall.

"He may have said he had a meeting this afternoon." She motioned him to follow her down the hall and opened the garage door to his empty parking spot. "Must be."

Steve's eyes looked glassy, as though he was on the verge of tears.

"Is there anything I can tell him, or do to help?"

"I don't know if anyone can." He put his head in his hands. "Laney's tests and chest x-ray came back positive for Stachybotrys, Penicillium, and Aspergillus mold."

"Black mold," Maryellen said.

"We both have colonies established within our nasal passages and lungs. My Chronic Fatigue, Laney's headaches, illnesses," he paused. "Some of her more erratic behavior—"

"All from toxic mold," Maryellen said, before the poor man felt the need to try to qualify anything she'd said or done, particularly the moment she'd witnessed between Laney and Sarah.

"She's scheduled for an MRI and a battery of further tests to see where else the infection may have spread."

A sentence from one of the books popped into her head: *In milder cases a course of antibiotics, followed by medication, diet, and other treatment protocols may be effective in strengthening a compromised immune system. In the worst case scenarios . . .*

"Could be in her brain," he said. "It's been in our house, growing, probably since we moved in so there's no knowing how bad it's going to be."

"What are you going to do?"

"There's this clinic south of the border . . ."

"Terrible."

"Not as bad as the fact that mold isn't covered by my insurance."

"What?"

"According to the adjuster, mold is excluded from practically every policy in the state."

"They can't expect you to pay for the mold damage out of your own pocket."

Steve slumped against her car. "The adjuster suggested I take up the damages with the builder."

"I'm sure Star Warranty will handle an emergency like this . . ."

"Quickly?" Steve paused to collect himself. "According to the lady manning the phones at Star Warranty, Henderson Homes is over forty-five days late paying bills and the warranty company is refusing to do any more work until they get payment."

"But the Pierce-Cohns—?"

"Have some sort of enhanced policy or something."

Maryellen picked up the phone and dialed Frank.

Got his voice mail.

"Frank, I have Steve Estridge over here. He and Laney are sick from mold and his insurance company's refusing to cover mold-related damage and apparently Star Warranty is refusing to do work on any Henderson Home. He needs your help ASAP, so please call me, or better yet, call him—"

"On my cell," Steve said.

"On his cell when you get this."

"Thanks," Steve said as she hung up. "While Laney's in the hospital, I'm staying at the Embassy Suites. He can call there, too."

"You can't stay in the house?"

"The doctor says none of us can even go inside until they get rid of every last spore of mold."

CHAPTER FORTY-ONE

Stachybotrys chartarum and other molds may cause health symptoms that are nonspecific. At present there is no test that proves an association between Stachybotrys chartarum and particular health symptoms—From the CDC website.

"I guess I didn't expect the morning sickness to come on so fast." The paper crinkled as Hope lay back on the exam table against the current wave of nausea. "Or, be so all day long."

"Given the rapid rise in estrogen levels, persistent nausea is not uncommon," the Ob/Gyn said. "The good news is that significant symptoms are a healthy and positive viability indicator."

"That's what I've been telling myself, until I found out my neighbors had to move out of their house because of a mold problem." Hope took a calming breath, tried not to think about how batty Laney'd been at the yard sale. "I got worried when I heard the wife had a lot of nausea, too."

"I'd assume she has a number of other symptoms as well," the doctor said.

"Strange ones."

"Can be a tricky situation. Do you have a cough, sore throat, difficulty breathing?"

"No."

"Allergy symptoms."

"Nothing to speak of."

"Have you've found any signs of mold in your own house?"

"No," she said. "And as soon as I heard about the Estridges, I checked pretty much everywhere, including the small cracks I do have in my storage room."

"Keep an eye out." The doctor noted something in his file. "But I don't think you have anything to worry about where mold is concerned."

"That's a relief," Hope said. "In the meantime, I'm supposed to leave for London this weekend and I'm not sure how I'm going to be able to get on a plane."

"Throwing up?"

"At least four times a day."

"Eating small portions of bland, low-fat foods at frequent intervals?"

"But not always keeping even crackers down."

"I'm hesitant to prescribe an antinauseant this early, but some women have had found some relief with ginger pills."

"I'll give that a try."

"Start as soon as possible. If that doesn't help, I'll suggest some possible over-the-counter options."

"Do a lot of people have this kind of intense nausea?"

"When it happens, it usually hits around five weeks."

"I don't think I'm that far along yet."

"Sometimes when there're twins—"

"Twins?" The thought of the Trautmans' double stroller sent her heart racing. If pregnancy was going to make her this sick, it would be ideal to have her two kids in one go-around.

"The incidence rises with Clomid."

"I didn't take it last month though."

He looked down at her chart. "First day of last menstrual period was May fourteenth, correct?"

"I figured out my due date has to be March second."

"Huh." The doctor picked up a calculation wheel and began to spin. "First day of last menstrual period was May fourteenth. We add seven days. Subtract three months. Based on the forty-week model, that gives you an estimated due date of February seventeenth."

"For twins?" she asked. "I know they come early."

"We still calculate the date the same way." He examined the wheel again. "Taking the first day of your last menstrual period, due date is February seventeenth and a conception date of Saturday, May twenty-eighth."

"Memorial Weekend." The words fell out of her mouth like pieces of lead.

Part IV

COMPLICATIONS

CHAPTER FORTY-TWO

Architectural Addition Submittal Denial Process: If the
Architectural Board reviews and subsequently denies a submittal,
an appeal may be filed within twenty days.

ucked.

Figuratively.

Literally.

The conception in no way immaculate, and yet . . .

Tears streamed down Hope's face and dripped into the open suitcase she couldn't bring herself to pack or unpack.

How could she go to London at the end of the week? How could she not go and explain why she hadn't? Explain that even though she knew better than to encourage the attentions of a man with that telltale gleam . . .

Humiliation tightened her throat.

Three men.

And all she remembered was possibly a hazy kiss.

Followed by?

Tim Trautman, while his wife was in labor?

Pierce-Cohn in her own bed?

She'd assumed *no worries* meant nothing had happened, but Will could have just as easily meant not to worry about what *had*.

And Tim.

She knew from their first meeting at the rec center that Tim's flirtation was less than innocent, but really believed his commitment to his family meant he wouldn't try to cross the line.

Did she really believe she was that gullible?

And what about Frank?

There was no way in Hell that she and Frank could have . . .

In my altered state, I may have done or shown you more than I should have.

Hope ran to the bathroom.

I'm confident Tim Trautman provided sufficient distraction before I arrived. . . . And when you slipped from my grasp, I'm glad it was into Will's . . .

Which innocent wife and children would suffer the collateral damage of the substance-fueled seduction/rape/consensual God-only-knew what that had already forever changed everything?

She hunched over the toilet and vomited.

CHAPTER FORTY-THREE

Insurer reserves the right to exclude coverage for mold caused by or resulting from continuous or repeated seepage or leakage occurring over a period of time—from General Health and Home Policy Declarations.

"*W*ith so many questions, concerns, and bits of misinformation circulating through our community," Frank's calm voice rose above the nervous chatter and sour stress permeating the overcrowded multipurpose room, "I thought we should talk facts."

Roseanne Goldberg, seated to Maryellen's left, crossed her arms over her substantial bosom. "Like the fact the Estridges had to move out of their house?"

Maryellen shifted in her seat.

"I've been talking to Steve extensively," Frank said in answer to Roseanne, but addressing the group at large in his Sunday confident voice. "He and Laney are doing just fine."

Mold colonies established within our nasal passages and lungs.

Can't set foot in the house again until every last spore is gone.

Maryellen looked down at her lap.

The doctor thinks toxicity was behind some of Laney's erratic behavior.

Maryellen glanced at, but was careful not to make eye contact with, Will Pierce-Cohn. After talking with Steve about Laney's condition, she took some comfort in knowing that Laney wasn't in her right mind and hadn't been for months. If she did bring the brownies like people were saying, then she couldn't be held entirely responsible. Her reliability as narrator, particularly about seeing Hope and Will, was a huge question mark.

Despite it all, Frank was firmly back on *Pierce-Cohn* watch.

"For any of you who haven't heard, the Estridges did suffer a flood which, unfortunately, led to the discovery of a substantial amount of mold in their basement."

Someone in the row behind Maryellen sneezed.

"Bless you," she whispered.

"And while the effects of mold exposure continue to be very controversial," Frank said, "there is some evidence that long periods of exposure may be linked to health problems."

"Are linked," Roseanne said.

Laney's MRI showed signs of mold on her brain. My Chronic Fatigue, her headaches, illnesses—all from long-term exposure.

"While their kids, who thankfully have only suffered allergies as a result, are happy and healthy at camp, the Estridges will undergo a course of precautionary treatment and plan to recuperate in Mexico until their flood issues have been resolved."

Our best chance of curing her is at an experimental clinic just south of the border.

Frank looked out into the audience but seemed to avoid Maryellen's part of the front row.

"What exactly happened?" Julie Connors asked.

"The mold couldn't have grown overnight," Pam Davis said.

The insurance agent thinks there's a foundation crack that allowed water to seep in behind the walls. The heavy rain saturated everything until the walls started to give way.

"Great question." Frank scratched the side of his face. "Looks like an expansive soils problem exacerbated by the recent rains, combined with what may well turn out to be a construction issue unique to the Estridges' home."

"Meaning what?"

"Henderson Homes has already sent a structural engineer out to answer that question. We'll have the report soon. In the meantime, they've assured me that the Estridges and their home will be soundly restored."

"At least someone's covered," Craig Froam shouted from the back of the room.

Whatever calm Frank gained with his not entirely forthright explanation was lost in the chatter that erupted around the room. He cleared his throat into the microphone. "Which brings me to the primary reason I called this meeting today."

"Good." Larry Collins from Whipperwillow Way stood. "Because I'm glad for the Estridges and all, but I came here to find out why, when I call to get someone out for the leak in my window well, Star Fulfillment has *we are not currently accepting work orders on Henderson Homes Properties* on their outgoing message?"

Frank nodded sympathetically. "But only temporarily."

The rising din of voices began to escalate into a frenzied spiral.

"I asked almost the same question of Henderson Homes VP of quality control."

He waited until the room quieted to the point where Maryellen could hear the rustle of Roseanne Goldberg's blouse as she crossed her arms again.

"Melody Mountain Ranch is one of eight Henderson Homes developments in the metro area containing warranty-covered properties, and, it should be noted, one of the very few offered the gold-level, five-year, extended coverage."

"Which is useless if the warranty company won't take our calls," Larry restated.

"By show of hands, and not counting any damages since Memorial Weekend, how many of you have filed a work order in the last year?" Frank asked.

A smattering of arms went up.

"And how many of you have contacted Star Fulfillment in the last thirty days?"

Maryellen raised her hand, along with about two-thirds of the people in the room.

"Henderson Homes claims that they, along with all the other builders in the area, have had a 70 percent jump in claims *for the year* as a result of rain damage sustained in the last thirty days." Frank glanced around the room. "Which, as you can see, is consistent with our informal poll."

Despite simplifying both the Estridges' situation and the structural warranty coverage, which wasn't guaranteed until the engineer located the source of the moisture penetration, there was no denying Frank's ability to reason with a group poised to morph into an angry mob.

"If you've had work completed or been contacted to do so, please lower your hands."

About a third of the raised hands went down, along with Maryellen's.

"Which confirms their assertion that up until last week, their contract providers, including Star Fulfillment, have all been prompt to respond considering the unusually heavy load."

"Maybe if you're the Pierce-Cohns," someone whispered behind her.

"Work was done on a first-come, first-serve basis, with emergencies as priority," Frank said as though he'd heard from up at the podium. "Until Henderson Homes started scrambling to get the various subs paid up for so many claims in such a short time—Star Fulfillment in particular, whose payment terms are apparently the most strict."

"Which is great if you called early on," Susan Cole from Warbler Way said. "But what do the rest of us with covered damage do in the meantime?"

"Two options: One, wait for Henderson Homes to catch up with the accounting on the financial backlog and Star will once again be servicing those claims."

"How is that an option if I have a leak that's getting worse?"

"Exactly." Frank pulled out two stacks of paper he'd had Maryellen photocopy, and handed them to the front row. "I asked, and Henderson Homes agreed, to release copies of their negotiated billing rates for you to use to contract out work."

"So we have to find someone to do the work and pay out of pocket?"

"Ask your contractor about billing Henderson Homes directly. Given their reputation in the industry, I'll bet most will."

"And if we have problems?"

"Tim Trautman, our new Covenant Violations chair, has agreed to help troubleshoot."

A low mumble filled the room.

"Doesn't seem fair," someone said.

"Acts of Nature often don't," Frank said.

* * *

"You know that allergic reaction you had in the Estridges' basement was mold-related," Roseanne Goldberg said as Will passed by in the rec center hall, "don't you?"

He stopped. "Hadn't thought of that," he said.

"First thing I thought of when I heard about the Estridges," she said.

"At least it's going to be fixed," he said.

"Their house maybe, but I talked to a general contractor friend of mine. He thinks the Estridge situation is a huge red flag and needs to be looked into more closely."

Frank's booming voice echoed from the multipurpose room down the hall.

"That's his job." Will shrugged. "My house is fixed."

"Mine too," Roseanne said. "Because we both have lien warranties."

"I've never heard of a lien warranty," Will said. "Much less bought one."

"Was your wife a state rep when you bought the house?"

"Just elected."

"Then you must have gotten a little CYA gift from Henderson Homes. I negotiated mine into the contract to make sure future repairs would be covered." She shook her head. "They must have given you yours. You'd be surprised what those subs don't do on a building job."

"So you're saying?"

"I'm saying it's suspicious that so many houses, most of which seem to be on mine, yours, or one of the adjacent cul-de-sacs, have storm-related damages."

CHAPTER FORTY-FOUR

*Upon verification of an alleged violation, MMHA will send a
letter to the owner of the property setting a date when the violation
needs to be cured—from the pamphlet Melody Mountain Ranch
Covenant Violations and the Homeowner.*

*H*ope walked down a long, brightly lit hallway, toward the sound of a
cooing baby.

Her beautiful, blue-eyed, baby girl.

Lilly.

At the end of the hall she reached a white nursery so charming, so utterly
inviting she never wanted to leave.   Wouldn't have, but for the tug of her
newborn, who wasn't tucked into the eyelet and lace cradle, but behind one of
the four frosted glass doors at the back of the room.

She opened the first door.

"I'd love to give you your baby, but I gotta run." Tim gave her the gun
finger. "Catch ya later?"

She closed the door and opened the next one.

Frank was inside, reclining on a bench outside his newly built church.
"Collaborate with me, baby."

She shut the door.

"I've never wanted anything so much in my life," Will said as she opened
the third door. He pointed inside the fourth door which had swung open of its
own accord. "But, it's his job."

Jim, who was sitting on a glider rocker, and held a bottle, looked down at
the empty blanket in his arms. He shrugged and looked up at Hope.

"Where is she?" she asked.

"Waiting for you." He turned toward a hallway papered with words and
arrows pointing in every direction. *Frank, Will, Tim, Stay, Go, Silence, Truth,
Paternity, Maternity, Terminate, Procreate* . . . "Down there."

"I have absolutely no idea what to do," she said.

The baby cooed, "Mamamamama."

Jim gave her a peaceful, serene smile. "Just follow the signs, babe."

Hope awoke to brilliant sunshine for the first time in days. As soon as she processed the transition from dream world back to day-mare she couldn't help but wonder if the morning sun was a sign, in and of itself.

If so, the oversweet stench of the browning lilies on the table next to her sent a conflicting message.

So did the rest of the signs that began to appear all around her.

The answering machine blinked three messages, one confirming her afternoon nautical nursery meeting, another a front hall re-do, and the third, a backyard.

Did the sudden spike in her business mean *stay*?

She threw on a pair of sweats and headed downstairs to the kitchen for a stomach-settling piece of toast and a glass of the fresh orange juice she was constantly craving. On her way, she stopped to grab the newspaper, but spotted the Griffins' garage door roll open first. While she waited for Frank and Maryellen to back down the driveway and go wherever it was they were going, she broke into a sweat.

Frank?

She was about to open the door again when Will emerged from his side gate.

While he jogged up out of the cul-de-sac, she tried, but couldn't quite catch her breath.

Will?

How could she *stay* if she had to spend the rest of her life avoiding them?

She cracked the door, grabbed the paper, rushed back into the kitchen, and opened the paper to a full-page ad for Planned Parenthood.

Terminate?

After she'd stopped shaking enough to head back to the kitchen, she poured herself some juice, flipped on the TV, and went over to her computer. Two e-mails—a flight confirmation notice for her trip to London and a decorating question from Theresa Trautman—popped up at the same moment as the theme song for *Sesame Street* blared from the television.

Go? Tim? Procreate?

With her only clear chance of avoiding a chance encounter with Frank or Will, she headed out the door and down the cul-de-sac to grab her mail from the community mailboxes.

Amid the circulars, bills, and catalogs was a violations notice: *Dear Resident: Your property at 46919 Songbird Canyon Court is in violation of Homeowner's Covenant 6.2: Only approved sod shall be permitted for landscaping* *purposes. Please remove nonconforming ground cover by July 15 or face up to a $500 fine.*

She walked back down the street, onto her driveway, and glanced at a few tufts of sun-drenched fescue dotting her otherwise perfect Kentucky Blue Grass.

The wrong seed had indeed been planted.

Tears ran down her cheeks.

As she headed back inside to stare at the melted butter congealing on her toast, she prayed for a definitive sign, a message so clear, she would know exactly what the hell she was supposed to do about it.

CHAPTER FORTY-FIVE

To maximize safety, the following activities are prohibited in the pool area: running on the pool deck, standing or sitting on the shoulders of another participant, hanging on the safety ropes, and diving during open swim.

*E*va lingered in the shadows, waiting for the last two members of the coven to collect at the playground pavilion.

Tyler finally emerged from his front door and shuffled across the street.

"Tyler," she said.

He stopped beside her.

She looked down at her watch. "I said, nine sharp."

"Best I could do."

"Where's Lauren?"

"Not coming."

"I thought I'd made it clear this meeting was mandatory."

"I told her."

"So she knows she has to be here?"

"Eva," he looked straight at her for the first time since their last conversation at the playground. "I told her, told her."

"Oh," she said. In the darkness, there was no way he could see how hard she had to try not to smile. "Why'd you do that?"

"Didn't want," his voice cracked, "I didn't want her to hear it from you. Tonight. In front of everyone."

"I wouldn't do that."

"You practically did at the yard sale."

"How's that?"

"Telling her you're growing out of your jeans."

"I didn't mean—"

"Why did you call this meeting?"

"To let everyone know I'm taking off on the Fourth of July. I needed to tell everyone exactly what to say and how to say it so my parents can't find me before camp's over."

"And that's all?"

"That's it."

"So you're just running away?"

"That's the plan."

"You're not running away to some place for unwed mothers or anything?"

"I thought I might have to," she said.

"But you're not now?"

"Got my period, finally." She smiled. "Thank God . . . ess."

He looked like he was going to explode. "Why didn't you tell me?"

"I was waiting to tell you tonight," she said.

"You've put me through total hell."

"I'm sorry," she said.

"Like that's going to make it okay? Did you do this just to break me and Lauren up?"

"Why would I do that when I need you to take over while I'm gone?"

"Were you even pregnant in the first place?"

"Tyler, I . . ."

"Don't bother." Tears ran down his face. "I'm outta here."

She tried to grab his arm but he'd already taken off across the playground.

"Tyler, wait!"

He ran faster.

She tried to catch up, but tripped and fell. "Son of a bitch."

"What?" He stopped and turned. When he realized she was looking up at him from a big, mucky hole at the edge of the playground, he shook his head. "Karma's the real bitch and you've got a lot coming."

CHAPTER FORTY-SIX

Dear Resident: Your property at 46919 Songbird Canyon Court is in violation of Homeowner's Covenant 6.2: Only approved sod shall be permitted for landscaping purposes. Please remove nonconforming ground cover by July 15 or face up to a $500 fine.

A sinkhole on the playground.

There was no missing the symbolism there.

They—she—and the baby, had to go.

Why had she even bothered to ask for another sign when the violations notice said it all? *Please remove nonconforming ground cover by July 15 or face up to a $500 fine.*

A nervous cough escaped her throat and echoed off the vaulted great room ceiling as she reached for a pen and a sheet of stationery.

Dear Jim,
I've cleaned the house and paid all the current bills.

She'd had everything—a tall, handsome husband with an upwardly mobile career, a loaded-with-extras, semi-custom home, and the financial security to dabble in interior design when the mood struck her or there was a sale at the Design Center.

The joists of her house groaned with a sudden gust of summer wind.

She'd had nothing.

In truth, wasn't she really just a well-compensated employee whose job it was to play fair-haired corporate wife in an on-paper perfect union and tend to the details of a façade almost as flimsy as the sheets of brick lining the front of the house?

Hope rubbed her belly.

Still, *this* wasn't Jim's fault.

She swallowed hard to stem the rising tide of nausea.

If only she knew whose fault it was.

Tim Trautman was nothing, if not fertile. Will Pierce-Cohn was the world's most present, compassionate, involved dad. Frank Griffin had a direct line to the Son of all sons.

What had she done?

I'm sorry about any mistakes I've made, intentional or . . .

God forbid, had she done all three?

She scratched out *intentional or . . .* careful to cover her words until they were illegible. Instead she wrote, *I'm truly sorry.*

A tear rolled down her cheek and landed on the maple hardwood.

I'm afraid you'll have to deal with the violation notice. Given the circumstances, I think the homeowner's board will give you an extension. If not, you'll need to re-sod the lawn right away or fines will start to accumulate. If you have problems with anything, including the warranty coverage on the cracks in the storage room, just ask one of the neighbors for help.

He wouldn't have to ask. The minute she drove out of the subdivision, a line of eager-to-help-in-any-way neighborhood housewives would form at the door. Whoever eventually beat out the others for Jim's attentions could roll any additional basement repair costs into the Country French or California Contemporary redecorating budget that came with her marital trade-up incentive package.

I've come to realize this whole fantasy of marriage, suburban life, and domestic bliss was just that, a fantasy—at least for me.

She hated to put Jim through the inevitable pain, but she had to do whatever she could to minimize or possibly even avoid the collateral effects, not only on him, but the innocent wife and children of whomever it turned out was responsible.

Besides her.

Please try to forgive me for having to say good-bye like this.

What choice did she have?

I wish you only the best.
With love,
Hope

Hope took a deep breath of fresh air from the windows she'd opened before she closed the house up. She folded the good-bye note and put it atop the homeowner's violation notice, the warranty paperwork, and upcoming bills. All that was left to do was spray clean the chandelier and finalize the plans for the last nursery she'd decorate in the neighborhood—two jobs she could combine.

She picked up the length of rope destined to adorn the walls of the Thompsons' nautical nursery and opened the knot instruction manual sitting on the counter in front of her.

Pass the bitter end through the piece you are trying to secure. Form an overhand loop in the standing end, laying the loop on top. Push the bitter end of the line up through the loop, around the standing end, and back in the loop. Draw tightly and evenly. Make a hole. Take the standing end and slip it through the hole.

She slid off the barstool, walked into the front hall, grabbed the ladder from the closet, and left it below the chandelier. Rope in hand, she started up the curved stairway toward a landing designed to sweep light down the empty children's wing.

Careful not to lean against the oak rails, she swung the rope over the chandelier. A neighborhood kid had once broken through and tumbled onto a well-placed sectional in the great room of a Blue Heron model. It hadn't happened in a Lark Bunting like hers, but considering the circumstances, she couldn't risk a fall that might result in an eternity spent haunting her semi-custom as a ghostly housewife, not in flowing robes, but a shimmering sweater set and Capri pants.

Surely it was against the covenants.

She went back down the stairs and stepped up the ladder. The sweat of her palm smoothed the rough hemp as she tied the running knot.

As she took a test tug, Frank Griffin's too-familiar voice rattled the leaded glass panes framing the front door. "Go to Hell!"

She was already there.

Through the windows above the door she watched in horror as Frank, Tim, and Will materialized around the sinkhole.

"I'm not going anywhere you're going to be." Will's response drifted through the air and into her hall.

"There was no foreseeing this would happen," Tim said.

"What are you planning to do about it?"

"Not that big a deal.

"A huge deal."

"Just a hole."

The verbal arrows aimed at each other pierced her heart.

"I take full responsibility."

"Overzealousness."

"Lack of judgment."

"Another sign something's very wrong."

The most definitive of final signs, really.

Hope had prepared the house, she'd written a good-bye note, and she had a rope around the chandelier. Where she was going was undecided.

Or was it?

Hadn't she already sentenced herself to an eternity of slamming hollow doors and flipping the switch on the gas fireplace, anyway?

"More to the story than you're willing to admit."

"Don't look at me."

"Who should I look at, him?"

She could just as easily step down and add a line or two to her note: *The Spic and Span in the utility closet works well on the faux marble. Be sure to tell the insurance company it was an accident.* She'd climb back up the ladder and slip the rope around her neck . . .

Their voices fell, but their conversation looked more heated.

Will, Frank, and Tim Trautman turned toward her house.

Would the last people she wanted to see be the last people she saw on Earth? Even if she deserved the worst, she couldn't think only of herself. Not anymore. Heart pounding, she ducked, pulling frantically at the rope dangling in full view of the windows above her front door.

The rope snagged.

Her foot slipped.

CHAPTER FORTY-SEVEN

The Board may adopt the recommendation of a Tribunal or has the discretion to decline an enforcement action or grant a waiver, even where a violation exists, if the Board determines declining enforcement or granting a waiver is in the best interest of the community.

*M*aryellen stared at her kitchen computer and tried to ignore the heated debate unfolding at the playground by fantasizing about the impossible: *Senior Librarian, Denver Central Library, 40 hours per week. Required Education: master's degree. Experience: 5 years required. Languages: Spanish proficiency preferred. Benefits . . .*

The crash jolted her from her dream.

From that moment on, everything happened in both slow motion and double-time.

She ran out her open patio door, out the side gate, and into the street to meet Frank, Tim, and Will.

Will, smashing through the glass with his fist.

Rope.

Blood.

Hope, in shock, sprawled out amid the shards of chandelier glass that sparkled like diamonds.

The scramble for towels, first aid.

Paramedics.

Hope trying to explain how she was trying to clean the chandelier when it collapsed.

Emergency room.

The ER noise swirling around Maryellen, broken only by the sound of Will, Tim, or Frank dropping a coin into the coffee vending machine or unwrapping a candy bar.

Wondering out loud how long before they got word.

Sniping, ostensibly, over their interrupted argument.

"We can't sit back and pretend nothing's wrong anymore."

"Things may be much more serious than they seem."

"No need to overreact until we see."

All three men looking grim as the doors to the triage area opened and a doctor appeared. "Who here's responsible for Hope Jordan?"

"I am," all three said.

In unison.

CHAPTER FORTY-EIGHT

Homeowner Assessments are due the first month of each quarter.
Accounts not paid by the last day of the month will be considered
overdue and assessed a late fee.

"Jim," Hope said, the emotion of thirty-six hours' worth of both dreading his arrival and desperately needing him by her side filling her voice. "You're here."

"Came straight from the airport. I can't believe I couldn't get a flight from London any sooner." Jim scooped an arm beneath the pillow and hugged and kissed her with an enthusiasm that caught her off-guard.

As though she could ever be any more off-guard.

He handed her a bouquet that dwarfed the substantial arrangements already sent over by the Trautmans and the Pierce-Cohns. "Can't believe this happened."

"I'd learned some nautical knots for a nursery job and I thought I'd try one to help me keep my balance so I could clean the chandelier because I was trying to get everything done before I—"

"It's okay," he said. "We're lucky you escaped with just an ankle fracture."

"Didn't expect . . ." Hot tears ran their familiar path down her cheeks. "The chandelier to collapse."

So much she didn't expect.

"Everything's okay, honey. More than okay." His face was unadulterated happiness. "You're okay. We're going to have a baby!"

* * *

Maryellen exited the elevator on Hope's floor, a vase filled with flowers in hand. She rounded the corner, headed past the nurse's station, tiptoed down the hallway toward room 314, and peered inside.

She couldn't see around the curtain to confirm that Hope lay in the bed, but even in the darkened room there was no missing Jim Jordan's broad shoulders and wheat-colored hair.

Before she could knock on the doorframe, she heard the voice of a third person in the room. "How 'bout we give the daddy a look?"

After some rustling, whoever it was added, "There's the gestational sac and the yolk sac inside. We have a four-point-three-millimeter-long fetus," he said, "and I didn't think we'd be able to get it yet, but there's a heartbeat."

"Heartbeat," Hope repeated.

Maryellen set the flowers beside the door and tiptoed down the hall.

* * *

She'd slipped, broken her ankle, had shards of glass tweezed from everywhere, and the baby's heartbeat was still strong as could be.

"I really can't believe this is happening." Jim patted her cast gently. "I think I'm actually kind of nervous."

Hope cracked the car window, took a deep breath of fresh, nonhospital air, and looked out toward the mountains. "Me too."

No one knew.

No one wanted to know.

Wasn't it better in a way, if there was more than one *donor?* How would anyone, including Hope, know for sure the baby was or wasn't theirs?

"Do you have any feeling yet whether it's a boy or a girl?" Jim asked.

"I've dreamt about a girl," Hope said.

"A daughter would be really cool." Jim turned, headed down Parker Road toward the subdivision. "But so would James Jordan Jr."

Jimmy.

When he or she wasn't born a tow-headed blond, or even blond at all, she'd claim the dark hair and small stature came from some distant, long-deceased relative on her side of the family. Like the grass, details of house and home usually escaped Jim anyway.

"It's too early to start making plans, but if my job gets extended, which I should know here soon, we should look into renting out the house and have you come to London."

"Definitely."

"How great would it be to have my first child born in England?"

She couldn't tell him any more than she could hand down a marital death sentence to Maryellen, Meg, and/or Theresa. What would she even say? *There's a small addendum to the fabulous news? The baby is totally ours, but not exactly yours? I have no idea how it happened, but . . .*

They pulled into the cul-de-sac.

All she'd ever really wanted was a baby.

Maybe she just had to accept that she was getting her dream in a different way.

Wood covered the spot where Will must have punched through the glass.

An anything but normal way.

Jim pushed the garage door clicker and eased the car into his parking spot.

There was always a chance the baby could turn out to be blond after all.

"Let me help you inside," Jim said.

All she had to do was get the note that said otherwise, and life would simply go on in a new incarnation of normal.

"I'm good." She got out of the car, ignoring the zing of pain up her leg. "If you'll bring in the flowers, I'll get a broom."

"You sure?" he asked.

"I just wish I could have come home first to clean things up before you saw—"

"Honey," he hugged her. "Accidents happen."

While Jim headed for the trunk, she hobbled past the glass-filled front hall and into the kitchen. Stepping over the dishtowels splayed across the floor, she reached the counter and riffled through the toppled pile of paperwork that lay mixed in with odds and ends from her first-aid kit. She collected the violation notice, bills, and information for the warranty company. She picked up the towels, checked the floor, the first-aid kit, and the towel drawer.

Her good-bye note was missing.

CHAPTER FORTY-NINE

*The Melody Mountain Ranch Recreation Center is not
responsible for any accident occurring on MMRC property.*

"It's against company policy to touch, move, or otherwise disturb any item unrelated to an accident or assistance of the victim," the ambulance representative said.

"So they wouldn't have taken anything with them from the scene?" Hope asked, the word *victim* buzzing in her head.

"What day did you say the incident occurred?"

"June twenty-eighth."

Keyboard taps punctuated the silence.

"Report lists one dishtowel, assorted Band-aids, and glass shards from the chandelier in addition to any unknown items on the victim's person."

She'd checked every cabinet, rooted through the trash, gone through the drawers, even stuck her hand down the disposal.

No note. Anywhere.

"Nothing like a bill or a letter or anything?"

"Nope," the woman said. "Wish I could help you."

* * *

*The ideal Senior Librarian will have the ability to thrive in an
environment of constant contact with people from all backgrounds and
age groups. Essential is a positive attitude, excellent interpersonal skills,
cultural sensitivity, and a sense of humor.*

Maryellen shouldn't have sent in an application, especially when she couldn't ever really consider taking the job.

She did fit all the criteria, except for a single sentence that kept hanging her up: *Ability to creatively problem-solve, negotiate, and handle stressful situations in a positive manner . . .*

"Leaving for a meeting at Henderson Homes," Frank yelled from the back door.

"Okay," Maryellen said, not feeling that way.

While he somehow seemed to be taking the Estridges' misfortune, the playground problem, and Hope's accident in stride, she couldn't shake the unsettled feeling.

The Estridges were doing better and the structural engineer was in the process of preparing a report that recommended insurance coverage for their damage and medical expenses. The sinkhole would be fixed. And, Hope, thank God, was okay.

More than okay. Expecting.

If only she hadn't heard the ultrasound technician in Hope's hospital room. *A heartbeat.*

With the sound of Frank's car backing down the driveway, Maryellen reduced the job website and typed *fetal heartbeat detection* into Google Search. Seemed like she was further along with Eva before the doctor could detect a fetal heartbeat, but the technology had undoubtedly improved.

Via ultrasound, a heartbeat can be detected, at the earliest, by around 6–7 weeks.

Frank told her that Hope had gotten her period the Monday after Mother's Day at the rec center. The day after Jim left for London. If a pregnancy definitely "started" on the first day of the last period, two weeks before conception . . .

Not daring to look down at her desk calendar, or count back weeks in her head, she clicked out of Google and enlarged the library job website.

Must be fearless, flexible, and fun.

* * *

Will waited by his side gate for the forensic engineer he'd hired to come out the Estridges' back door, work his way through their rear gate, and meet him up the street beside his plain white van. "Sorry for all the secrecy."

"Not the first time I've had to investigate on the down low." The engineer handed Will the Estridges' spare key and began to unzip his hazmat suit. "But the first time in a while I've seen a house in this bad of shape."

Will wasn't going to get involved. Lien warranty or not, his house was fixed. He was no longer obligated by his role on the homeowner's board. No matter how much Roseanne urged him to call her contractor friend to hear for himself how suspicious the cluster of damaged homes were, or Meg egged him on about doing what they both knew had to be done, he wasn't about to set himself up for ridicule again.

And then the sinkhole opened on the playground.

"Foundation's seriously compromised in that house," the forensic engineer said.

"Is it fixable?"

"Anything's fixable."

"Expansive soils?"

"Are just the beginning."

"Meaning what?"

"A combination of under-engineering and possibly a bad concrete pour, for starters."

"Apparently the engineer from Henderson Homes agreed. The owners told me extensive repairs have already been authorized by the insurance company."

"Glad it's not my house," the man said.

"If it were your house, how concerned would you be about the surrounding homes with cracking problems," he pointed to the yellow taped area on the edge of the playground, "and that sinkhole over there?"

"Very," the man said.

"That's what I was afraid you'd say," Will said. "That area was something of a marsh before it was a playground."

"Not surprised," he said.

"Why's that?"

"Water table's pretty high around here."

"Would that cause these sorts of problems?"

"Given all the rain, it could definitely lead to the problem on your playground."

"And be related to whatever's going on with the Estridges' house?

"Under certain circumstances."

"Like?"

He opened the door to his truck and threw in the hazmat suit. "I want to check into a few things and I'll get back to you."

* * *

Hope waited for a call, a message, anything to save her from having to ask about the note.

For the answer.

No one stepped forward.

She collected herself and stepped out onto her front porch.

Will, who was talking to the driver of the white windowless van parked up the street, turned immediately as though he'd sensed her.

She began to negotiate the front steps, still adjusting to her walking cast, silently practicing the question: *Did you, by any chance, in the midst of all the confusion, happen to take any of the paperwork lying on the kitchen counter?*

She had the foggiest memory of him tucking her into bed.

Nothing before.

Nothing afterward.

If he said yes, he'd taken the note, what would she say? *Sorry, I don't remember, but guess what happened?* Or, *Thanks. Oh, and by the way, I'm pregnant with your baby.*

The van headed up the cul-de-sac and Will crossed the street and was waiting for her when she reached the sidewalk.

He looked perturbed. "Hope."

She was more than perturbed. "Hey."

"How are you?"

Mortified. Terrified. "Hobbling along," she said.

"You're so lucky it wasn't worse."

Or unlucky.

"I don't know what might have happened if you guys hadn't been there," she said.

He glanced over at the yellow tape beside the playground and shook his head. "I'm just glad you're on the mend."

"Thanks," she said, noticing the tiny cuts on the back of his hand from smashing his fist through her window. She took a deep silent breath. "Did you, by any chance, in the midst of all the confusion, happen to see or move any of the paperwork lying on the kitchen counter?"

Time stopped between her last word and his response.

"Was never in the kitchen," he said.

Their eyes met.

"I never left your side," he said.

She immediately felt both better and worse.

"I can't seem to find an important letter that was part of the stack," she managed.

"That's weird," he said, his attention shifting to the van that had just left as it headed back down the cul-de-sac toward them.

"I'm sure it's somewhere, it's just that—"

The van stopped beside them.

"Sorry to interrupt," the driver said through the open passenger window. "But, I didn't want to take off without mentioning something."

The man waited, presumably, for her to leave.

"I should go," Hope said.

"Glad you're okay." Will gave her a cursory hug. "Probably should check with Trautman or the Griffins."

* * *

Maryellen saw the caller ID and let the phone ring three times before she was able to answer. "Hope."

"Hi, it's Hope," Hope said awkwardly, having fallen into the caller ID etiquette trap.

"How are you?" Maryellen asked.

"Good," Hope said.

"That's good," Maryellen said. "Really good."

"Listen," Hope said. "I called because I wanted to thank you and Frank again for everything you did."

"It was nothing," she said, despite everything she wanted to say. To know.

"I also have a quick question," Hope said.

"Sure."

"In getting things back in order," Hope seemed to take a breath, "I can't seem to locate some paperwork."

"Paperwork?"

"There was a pile of bills and stuff—a violation notice and a letter."

"A letter?"

"Not a letter, really. More like a list of information I made for Jim."

"Oh," Maryellen said.

"I'm sure I misplaced it somewhere, and it's not all that important or anything, but I don't want to have to try and recreate everything I wrote down, so I thought I'd just check and see if you happened to have any idea what might have happened to it."

"No idea," Maryellen said. "I'm sorry."

She though she heard Hope sigh.

"Maybe you should check with Will?" Maryellen asked. "Or Tim Trautman?"

* * *

Tim walked into Frank's office, sat down in the guest chair, and tapped the door closed with his foot. "There's some stuff I need to run by you."

Frank stopped tapping his pencil on the edge of his desk. "'Bout what?"

"Henderson Homes."

Frank's air of tension seemed to ease. "Let me guess, Pierce-Cohn's crowing that the Estridges are going to get the short shrift on their repairs?"

"Been ignoring that stuff," Tim said. "But there's also concern that the barrage of claims is causing a lot more than a delay in getting Star Warranty and other subs paid."

"Meaning what?"

"Rumor is, Henderson Homes is in financial trouble."

"Where are you hearing this?"

"E-mails and inquiry calls on the troubleshooting line."

"From who?"

"The Connors, Scott Sandburg, not to mention my wife, who was talking to—"

"Let me guess. Will Pierce-Cohn."

"Actually, Roseanne Goldberg."

Frank shook his head. "Same difference."

"In any case, she has my wife all worked up about Henderson Homes going under from claims, the threat of litigation from the Estridges, and who knows what else."

"The structural engineer made a recommendation to Henderson Homes' insurance company to cover all expenses on their loss," Frank said. "So there won't be any litigation."

"That's a relief," Tim said.

"But no surprise," Frank said. "What's surprising is Henderson Homes' willingness to pay a crew holiday overtime to come out and fix the playground tomorrow so we're up and running for the Fourth of July—if they're going under, that is."

* * *

Dressed in sweats as though she could possibly work out and stationed at the bottom of the stairs where she couldn't miss Tim, Hope lay in wait like the stalker she was fast becoming.

The spinning studio door opened and three men and a woman clip-clopped past.

"Hope!" Larry Miller emerged and started past her. "Good to see you up and around."

"I can't believe a chandelier would give way that easily," Jane Hunt said. "So scary."

"Scary doesn't even begin to describe it," a voice said from behind her.

She turned.

Tim, whom she'd spotted driving toward the rec center and confirmed he was there by driving over herself to check, stood three steps above her, still in his street clothes, gym bag in hand. "But all's well that ends well, right?"

She could only pray that was true.

"Back to working out already?" He hugged her, his hands lingering at her elbows. "Or did you just come by to try and run into me?"

Had he seen her park two cars down from him and wait in her car until the class she presumed he was in was almost over? Where had he been if he wasn't at spinning?

"Actually, I do need to talk to you." She looked down toward her cast so he wouldn't see her face flush. "I have a question."

"Anything." His flirty smile made her stomach turn. "I'm sure the answer's yes."

God help both of them.

"Did you, by any chance, happen to see or take any paperwork on my kitchen counter?"

"Paperwork?"

She nodded.

"I grabbed dishtowels from the drawer, but I never saw or touched any mail."

"You sure?"

"Positive."

"Thanks," she managed.

They stood staring at each other for a minute.

"That it?" he finally asked.

"That's it," she said.

"Okay, then." His smile no longer reached his eyes. "Well, I guess that's that."

* * *

"Frank?"

"Not now, Maryellen."

"I just have a question I really—"

"And I have a problem I really need to deal with. The crew who's supposed to be here, who are getting paid double so we don't spend the Fourth fishing kids out of quicksand, is MIA." He picked up the phone, dialed, listened to what sounded like a message, and dropped the handset into the cradle. "And Henderson Homes already let everyone off for the long weekend."

"It's only eleven," Maryellen said.

"And they were supposed to be here by nine."

"Workmen are always late," she said.

He began to tap at his computer.

She waited for a moment. "It's about Hope."

He didn't look up. "How's she doing?"

How exactly did she answer that question? Keeping Hope's *good* news was difficult enough. Add in the possibility the math might not add up, that the baby wasn't . . . could possibly have been fathered *that night*, by someone other than Jim, left Maryellen feeling all but speechless. "Okay, considering."

"Good," he said. "Found an alternate number."

"You haven't had a chance to check in with her since the accident, have you?"

"I have to get all this under control first." He picked up the phone. "Why?"

"Hope seems stressed in the aftermath of it all," she said.

He dialed the number. "That what she said?"

"No, actually, she called to find out if we happened to see or pick up some kind of letter or list from a pile of bills she'd left in the kitchen."

"This is Frank Griffin, president of the Melody Mountain Ranch Homeowner's Board," he said in response to what was obviously another message. "I can't seem to get through any of my usual channels, but the crew that's supposed to be at work on our playground hasn't shown up. I need the job completed today. I need someone to call me ASAP."

He slammed the phone down.

"All I took from the kitchen was a first-aid kit," he said, flipping through the business cards he'd tugged from his wallet. "Don't know what happened to any note."

"Note?"

"Letter, list, whatever."

* * *

Will said he never went into the kitchen. Never left her side. Had anything happened between them, there was no way he'd say *no worries* after seeing that note. The worry would have filled his eyes when she asked him about it.

Tim said yes, but not to taking the note. She'd been wrong about his motivations, but not his interest in keeping any extracurricular secrets from destroying his beloved family.

Nothing had happened with either of them.

Which left Frank.

Two days had gone by since she'd spoken with Maryellen about the missing letter.

Two days with no response.

* * *

As dusk neared, Maryellen put the red, white, and blue frosted cupcakes she'd made into a basket and walked into Frank's office. He'd been in there all day, hiding, as far as she could tell, while everyone else was outside enjoying the Fourth at the playground, yellow tape and all.

"Fireworks are going to start pretty soon," she said.

"I'm aware of that."

"We should probably go out there so we have time to socialize before it's too dark."

"I'm waiting for a call."

She took a calming breath. "It's only going to make things worse if you don't show up."

"I'm aware of that, too."

"Frank?"

"Lay off, Mel."

She wanted to, might have, had her patience, which she'd overexercised in the last day and a half, at least where he was concerned, not begun to collapse. Had he not used the one word that she couldn't stop thinking about where Hope was concerned.

Note.

No one, including the emergency crew, seemed to think anything about Hope cleaning the chandelier using a rope and knot for safety. Of course, no one else who'd seen the accident knew about, had suggested, the knot book.

No one else knew she was pregnant.

And possibly left a *note*?

"Speaking of calls," she said. "I assume you got back with Hope while you've waited?"

"I told you I'd get back with her when I had the chance."

"It's been two days."

"Do I need this right now?"

"I think she may need you," Maryellen said.

He exhaled dramatically.

"Pregnant," she blurted.

Frank looked up. "What did you say?"

She hadn't meant to bear false witness, would never have normally, but wasn't Frank Hope's spiritual advisor and self-appointed guardian? Shouldn't he be privy to the burdensome secret she'd been carrying around? "Probably a rumor, but with the other rumors out there about Memorial Weekend, I thought she might need your ear."

"Jesus Christ."

"I'm sure she'll be out to watch fireworks. Maybe you can talk to her then."

Frank looked one-upped at best, ashen at worst.

He nodded.

"I'll grab a sweater," she said. "Will you be ready when I come back down?"

He nodded again.

As Maryellen went up the stairs, she pinched herself not only for being suspicious and gossiping, but allowing herself to revel, if only for a moment, in the horror on his face.

She crossed their bedroom and entered her closet. Her black sweater, the one that went with the striped top she was wearing, was missing from its spot on her sweater shelf. Eva must have borrowed it and either not put it back, or had worn it over to the Hunts where she was celebrating the Fourth with her friends.

Hoping it was the former, she went across the hall and opened the door to Eva's room.

Eva's unusually neat room.

The bed was made. Her desk, usually a war zone of pencils, paper, and class work from who knew how many semesters, had been cleared.

The trunk she was supposed to be packing for camp lay open.

Empty.

She opened Eva's closet and cold dread slipped down her spine, fanning out toward her arms and legs. The rack held only colored clothing. Everything black was gone except for Maryellen's cardigan, which was folded neatly atop last year's abandoned pastel sweaters.

"Frank!" She tore down the stairs.

He pointed to the phone at his ear she hadn't even heard ring.

"I think Eva's run away!"

"Can't be happening," he said.

"But it is," she said, not sure he'd even heard her. "Is that Eva?"

"No!" Perspiration dripped down his forehead. "What the hell am I supposed to do?"

"Who is that?" Maryellen asked.

"Can't be happening." Frank hung up the phone. "Can't be. Can't be. Can't be . . ."

"We need to call Eva!"

"Didn't mean . . ." Frank slumped in his chair. "Out of my control. Not my fault. It's—"

"How can you say it isn't your fault?"

Frank stared blankly past her.

"Maybe if you hadn't been so caught up in having her go to that Christian Leader's camp and listened to her, ever listened to what she wanted instead of what you want . . . ?"

"Sorry," he whispered.

"It's a little late for sorry," she said. "Eva's gone."

"Gone. Gone. Gone." Frank whisked a pile of papers from his desk into his briefcase. "Whoso diggeth a pit shall fall therein: and he that rolleth a stone, it will return upon him."

"Where are you going?"

He bolted for the front door. "Find Eva."

"But we don't know for sure where she is," she yelled after him. "We need to text her and her friends so we can—"

The door slammed behind him.

* * *

Hope was at the bottom of the driveway as Frank rushed down his front steps.

"Frank," she said.

He looked up.

Froze.

Their eyes met.

"Hope deferred maketh the heart sick: but when the desire cometh, it is a tree of life," he said, turned, and ran down the cul-de-sac and onto Harmony Valley Drive.

Before she could process what he'd said or what he hadn't given her the chance to ask, she heard the tinny jingle of an ice cream truck, the screech of wheels, and a horrifying thud.

Part V

BIRTH

CHAPTER FIFTY

14.1. Amendment of Articles and Bylaws: The Articles of Incorporation and Bylaws may be amended with the provisions set forth in such instruments.

*M*aryellen wasn't sure what a grieving widow was supposed to feel or think or notice, but how could she not notice what a truly beautiful, unseasonably temperate day it was? How could she not appreciate how fragrant the flower arrangements, particularly the enormous wreath of lilies and freesia sent by the Estridges, whom she had to beg not to interrupt their treatment to fly in? How unusually pleasant the breeze rustling through the Harmony Hills Neighborhood Church on what should have been a sweltering, stifling memorial service?

Somehow wasn't.

Somehow, as Roger Manning, Frank's fellow clergyman and biggest competition, described the rewards her husband was already enjoying in his *new home*, she kept thinking about how much she'd like a warm chocolate chip cookie, right out of the oven, from the home he'd left.

Along with a cold glass of milk.

"Rest assured a man as virtuous as Frank Griffin—a respected minister, a successful pharmaceutical sales representative, a loving husband and father—has bountiful pleasures waiting for him in Heaven."

A baby wailed from somewhere behind her.

Despite a vague sense of irony, Maryellen felt oddly free.

Had to be the shock.

She'd known before the first scream and then the knock on the door that something was wrong, but seeing Frank, lying there lifeless, his legs sticking out beneath the wheels of the ice cream truck, was too surreal to process. The last few days since, a blur of hushed condolence calls, casserole deliveries, and arrangements she'd helped make for others but never imagined orchestrating for herself.

For Frank.

His body just released from the hospital morgue.

Maryellen put her arm around Eva, who was now sobbing in great gasps. She felt a terrible ache for her stricken daughter, but somehow, nothing in particular for herself.

"And while we thank God for the happiness Frank is enjoying in the bosom of the Lord, one also has to feel righteous indignation. Why did He choose to take a man so ambitious, so full of future greatness, and so beloved from us?" Roger paused, the same way Frank would have. "So early."

The only thing she felt with the strength or conviction she thought she was supposed to feel, was that if it weren't for Eva, she might have come untethered.

Float away.

"I mean this was a guy who loved life, loved a challenge, a guy who didn't lose." Reverend Roger smiled the benevolent smile of one who'd not only beaten Frank in the great race, but was acing his dress rehearsal as heir apparent to the flock he'd left behind. "And while we always win when we join the Lord, I wish I understood why He chose to take him just when he'd accomplished his biggest goal. Folks, I was with Frank just last week and I will never, ever, forget his pure elation as we discussed the land deal he'd inked for the Melody Mountain Community Church."

Maryellen had to concentrate to not shake her head. It was just like Frank to tell Roger he'd completed a deal he was still $2,000 short of finalizing.

With the quiet rustle that filled the room, a certain peace filled Maryellen. At least Will wouldn't have to know exactly where that land was to have been.

Maryellen put her arm around her daughter as she sobbed that much harder.

Not that it mattered now.

The only thing that did matter was that Eva hadn't really run away, not out of text message range anyway, and wherever it was she had gone was far enough to miss the horror of seeing her father rolled off, covered by a sheet. Maryellen thanked God again Eva's missing clothing had reappeared in her closet sometime after that unspeakable evening spent in the same emergency room where she'd sat with Will, Tim, and Frank waiting for Hope . . .

Who's responsible here?

I am, they said.

All three of them.

"While we will all ask this and other questions, it's not for us to try, nor maybe will we ever understand His plan in all this . . ."

Didn't matter now.

CHAPTER FIFTY-ONE

Section 8. Drainage. For drainage purposes, the grades and low elevations as left by the Developer shall be considered the natural drainage.

*N*ever again would Hope hear the jingle of an approaching ice cream truck without conjuring the image of Frank running into oncoming traffic. She'd be haunted by the sight of his lifeless body for the rest of her life.

And yet, hadn't she been freed?

She couldn't look Maryellen in the eye and might never be able to again. She couldn't stop watching Eva sob at the funeral, nor stop herself from marveling at how pretty she really was. From the picture memorial it was clear she'd been fair as a baby. Even if the baby did end up dark-haired and Hope had to claim some sort of Black Irish throwback, who would be the wiser?

Hope patted the hint of bloat that had settled into her mid-section.

Her job now was to protect the secret and anyone who could be hurt by knowing the answer she herself wasn't totally, entirely sure of.

Hope deferred maketh the heart sick: but when the desire cometh, it is a tree of life.

Or, maybe she was.

* * *

"So unbelievably, incredibly tragic." Theresa handed Tim a cup of coffee. "I can't even begin to process how awful I feel for Maryellen and poor Eva."

"Terrible," he said, reaching for the sugar bowl. "Beyond terrible."

"I'm going to call over there later and see if there's anything I can do," Theresa said.

"Good idea," Tim said. "I'm headed over to the rec center to clean out the office for Maryellen."

"That's a great idea," Theresa said.

"I volunteered to take on the playground problem, too." Tim said. All he had to do was make a few calls, get things resolved, and he was a shoe-in for the presidential slot.

Theresa cracked an egg into the frying pan. "Really great."

* * *

"I can't believe Frank met his end at the hands of a drunk driver behind the wheel of an ice cream truck." Will stepped into the shower. "The *I told you so* of it all makes me feel almost responsible."

"Imagine how Hope Jordan must feel," Meg said. "She was coming over to talk to him and saw the whole thing."

Will turned on the spigot.

"She seemed almost as shaken up as Maryellen and Eva."

"Yup." He dunked his head under the warm, calming water and tried not to think about it.

"Will?"

He squeezed shampoo into his hand. "Huh?"

Meg opened the shower door. "Do I need to be concerned about Hope?"

"She does seem really distressed."

"About you and her, I mean."

He avoided that intense look he knew too well and couldn't deal with by lathering his hair. "Not at all."

"You do know there is a rumor floating around?"

"Rumor being the key word." He paused before rinsing to make brief eye contact. "Started by Laney, of all people."

"I know, but . . ."

"But nothing."

Will's cell phone rang.

"Let it go to voice mail," Meg said.

"I need you to check and see who it is first."

"But—"

"Could be really important, Meg."

She sighed, but turned for the phone. "Willams Forensic Engineering."

"Sorry," Will bounded out of the shower, simultaneously drying his head and reaching for the phone. "Got to take this."

* * *

Maryellen woke to the whoosh of something being dragged down the carpeted hallway. She flew out of bed and opened the door to her daughter tugging what appeared to be her now full trunk toward the top of the stairs.

"Ready to go," Eva said.

"Go where?"

"Camp." Tears ran down Eva's face. "Daddy wanted me to go to camp."

"Honey," Maryellen said. "You're not going, now."

"But I . . . Daddy wanted me to learn to lead and I'm a leader." Eva began to sob. "I was up all night packing."

"So we'll unpack."

"Daddy wanted me to go so badly—"

"It's okay," she said.

"Not okay. Not okay. Not okay," Eva said, sounding eerily like Frank.

"Let go of the trunk." She uncurled Eva's fingers from the handle and put her arm around her daughter's shoulder. "You need sleep."

"Can't. Haven't. Don't want . . ."

"Have to." Maryellen led her into the bathroom, took a sleeping pill from the prescription the doctor insisted she fill for herself, and gave one to Eva.

"Daddy's gone," Eva said accepting a cup of water. "And it's all my fault."

"Honey, it was an accident. A terrible accident."

"He was running to find me."

"Running," Maryellen said, uncertain where he was going, but sure it wasn't entirely to find Eva. "He wasn't looking where he was going."

"I killed Daddy."

"The ice cream truck driver was drinking and—"

"You don't understand." Eva trembled. "I . . ."

"I told your dad he shouldn't have signed you up for that camp without talking to you first, but he didn't listen," she said. "He didn't hear."

"But Mom," her voice wavered. "I . . ."

"I should have listened, too," Maryellen said.

"You did," Eva said. "That night."

The icy dread rushed through Maryellen. "You need to sleep."

"It's all my fault Daddy's—"

"It's not your fault." Maryellen guided her toward her (and not Frank's) side of the bed. As she settled her under the covers, the floral duvet accentuated the light blue of Eva's T-shirt. How long had it been since she'd seen her daughter in anything other than black, and at a time where she'd never expect to see her in anything else? "It's all going to be okay."

"Not okay," Eva said as she started to doze off. "Not okay."

Maryellen tried not to hyperventilate as she stroked her daughter's hair. The second she nodded off, Maryellen rushed downstairs to breathe into a paper sack. She settled in front of her computer to get whatever relief and distraction checking her e-mail could provide.

The first e-mail to pop up was a response to her application from the Denver Public Library.

She turned off the computer and breathed harder into the bag.

CHAPTER FIFTY-TWO

Section 1.5. Completion of Construction. Construction of a home on a Lot, once started, must be diligently pursued and completed within a reasonable time.

"The building plan filed with the city and county required perimeter drains, but there aren't any in our quadrant of the development." Will parked in the Tech Center high-rise lot. "Henderson Homes was apparently strapped from breaking ground on the MM Collection and a project in North Denver and decided to cut corners."

"Unbelievable." Roseanne Goldberg, who he'd invited along, shook her head.

"To cover their bets they offered enhanced warranties to those of us in the drainage *challenged* areas."

"And left a couple especially damp lots empty," she added.

"I told everyone there was something wrong with that land." Will shut the car door. "I'm not leaving until they admit what they've done and agree to make everything right."

"They're going to deny—"

"Which is why I didn't call or give them any advance warning," he said.

"I'm sure they'll have some excuse about the drainage system being unnecessary given their take on the soils report," Roseanne said.

"The Estridge house is a smoking gun," Will said "So much so, the forensic engineer left and came back to tell me he recommended their house be torn down and rebuilt."

"Which Frank dismissed summarily."

"But Laney and Steve didn't," Will said. "They're waiting on a revised report from the structural warranty people."

They entered the building.

Will pressed the button for the third floor.

They got on and rode up in silence.

The elevator doors slid open and they stepped into a hallway containing a single set of double doors.

Locked double doors.

The Henderson Homes sign was gone.

The HH logo left a ghostly imprint on the wall.

CHAPTER FIFTY-THREE

Section 5. Severability: Invalidation of any covenant or restriction by judgment or court order shall not affect any other provisions, which shall remain in full force and effect.

Frank wasn't panicking about Eva like he should have been.

He wasn't panicking about Hope like Maryellen suspected he might have been.

Whoever called Frank must have told him Henderson Homes had gone belly up, causing Frank to freak out and run out the door to escape.

Bad as it was, Maryellen felt sort of relieved about what it wasn't.

And then Roger Manning called.

Good thing you've got the deed in hand, he'd said.

She pushed away everything, including the thoughts the lingering smell of Old Spice conjured as she opened the door to Frank's office.

She powered up his computer and tried to open the file cabinet.

Locked.

A password popped up on his computer.

His desk drawer was also locked.

She picked up his office phone and checked the messages. All were condolence calls from pharmaceutical clients.

Tears, but of frustration, slid down her cheeks. Why hadn't she ever thought to ask him about passwords, where he kept keys, or anything about his system in case of an emergency?

Would he even have told her?

She leafed through a stack of correspondence and bills in his inbox.

Now, her inbox.

She found nothing and, at the same time, everything she should have been aware of all these years, but let Frank handle. To fight off the growing feeling that the floor was dropping out from beneath her, she closed her eyes. Where would he have put the deed, assuming there was one?

She stood still until she'd calmed herself enough to reopen her eyes. When she did, light reflected off the silver box he kept on the shelf above his desk.

She reached up and opened the lid.

A key.

She opened his desk drawer, pushed away the paper clips, spare pens, mints and found another set of keys.

She unlocked the file cabinet.

Riffling through every file, she found records related to the various medical devices and pharmaceuticals he'd repped until she reached a Pendaflex in the bottom drawer at the back of the cabinet.

It was labeled *Viagra.*

He'd never repped Viagra, much less worked for the company.

Inside was another key and an index card with the password for his rec center computer:

OVALOFFICE.

* * *

Maryellen opened the door to Frank's rec center office, locked the door behind her, and forced herself to walk across the room and slide the key into the file cabinet lock.

The click felt somehow reminiscent of Russian roulette.

More so when she started to leaf through the church files.

She skimmed myriad counseling records, overstuffed files filled with sermon, fund-raising, and community-building ideas until she came upon a Pendaflex marked DONATIONS. Inside, she found printouts of every donation, down to the penny, made to the building and all other funds since the inception of the church.

$38,0133.12 worth of donations were earmarked for the building fund.

She opened the file tucked behind and entitled, MELODY MOUNTAIN COMMUNITY CHURCH FINANCIALS, pulled the most recent profit-and-loss statement from the front of the folder, and located the line item, *Building Fund.*

$38,0133.12.

Her heart, beating frenetically, dropped back down and was almost normal by the time she went through the rest of the files and pulled the last folder.

Inside, like she expected, was a key and a three-by-five card with the password for the home computer: MELEVA.

For one emotion-fraught moment she thought she might shake the grip of her steely shock when she realized the password was a combination of his nickname for her and the name Eva had so desperately wanted to be called by him.

She might even have cried, had she not also found copies of three checks, one for twenty-three thousand, one for ten thousand, and one for five thousand, all written on an account entitled MMCC Building Fund.

The payee on all three was Henderson Homes.

CHAPTER FIFTY-FOUR

*Duty to Maintain Insurance: The Community Association
shall keep in force at all times, to the extent fully attainable,
comprehensive liability and casualty insurance.*

"They haven't declared Chapter Eleven?" the Melody Mountain Ranch Community Association lawyer asked.

"Not to our knowledge," Trautman said.

Under different circumstances, Tim's de facto step-in as HOB president would have pissed Will off to the same degree the spectacular view of the Front Range from the lawyer's seventeenth floor window would have buoyed his spirits.

Considering how bad the situation was, neither much moved him.

"They seemed to have closed up shop and disappeared," Tim added.

"In a way, that's better," the lawyer said. "If they had filed for bankruptcy, your losses become just another claim among what will inevitably turn out to be many."

"What about insurance?" Tim asked. "Can't we go after their builder's insurance?"

"If Henderson Homes didn't feel obligated to follow the building code," Will said, "what are the chances they felt like paying for builder's insurance?"

"How do we find that out if there is no Henderson Homes to contact to get that information?"

"Someone will eventually resurface," the lawyer said. "In the meantime, I'd hire a P.I. to run a skip trace and whatever else he or she thinks needs to be done to dig up the principals of the company as quickly as possible."

"And then?"

"You pray there's some money somewhere."

* * *

"I found receipts for payments to Henderson Homes from the Melody Mountain Community Church account and a stream of back and forth e-mails between Frank and the H.H. finance department on his personal computer," Maryellen said. "But I didn't find anything in the way of a deed."

"They haven't declared Chapter Eleven?" her lawyer asked.

"Not to my knowledge. And Frank was theoretically short $2,000."

"That's sort of worse."

"How could it be worse?"

"If they had filed for bankruptcy, you have a convincing paper trail to petition whoever's appointed trustee to deed the land to you as promised."

"But since they haven't?"

"I'd wait. If Frank did come up with the money, the deed could turn up. If not, someone from Henderson Homes will eventually resurface. At that point, either they'll file for bankruptcy and we go the trustee route, or we go after them for the money and/or the deed."

"What do I tell the membership of the church in the meantime?"

"To pray."

CHAPTER FIFTY-FIVE

*Section 10.2. Correction of Noncompliance: If the Board of
Directors determines a noncompliance exists, the applicant shall
remedy the same within a period of not more than 45 days.*

*M*aryellen's palms began to sweat as she twisted another key into yet
another lock and opened her mailbox. Before she looked inside, she bowed her
head: *Dear Lord, Please provide some resolution to this financial mess, if not for
me, for the members of the church who stand to lose so much more than just their
pastor. Amen.*

She pulled a single piece of correspondence from her box.

The Visa bill.

She sighed, opened the monthly statement, and looked over the charges
like Frank always did, but without the questions about the grocery tab or what
she'd spent $59.88 on at Macy's.

As always, everything checked out.

Everything, but a cash advance for $2,000, made on June 29, the day before
Frank had his last meeting at Henderson Homes.

* * *

"The best thing we can do right now is keep calm," Tim said over the angry
din of neighbors crowding the multipurpose room.

"First you tell us our builder disappeared," someone said from three rows
back. "Then you tell us to be calm?"

The last thing he wanted to do was step into power in the midst of disaster,
but the whole phoenix-rising-from-the-ashes angle did have workable upside
potential. "I'm saying cooler heads always prevail when the going gets tough."

"Are all of our houses going to rot and sink like the Estridges'?" someone
else asked.

"We're going to make sure that doesn't happen," Tim said.

"I'm selling," came from the back row.

"Not without disclosing the cracks and damage," someone else said. "The Fowlers took off for Oakland and their house is sitting there empty and not for sale."

"The situation is dicey, to say the least." Tim waited for the first lull in the spiraling hysteria. "But, we've hired a private investigator to locate the principals of Henderson Homes."

The room quieted ever so slightly.

"We will get the playground fixed and we will make sure that the affected homeowners and our community as a whole is made right." He paused. "I promise."

* * *

"Nothing?" Will asked.

"Not on the skip trace," the private investigator said. "But that's not entirely unusual considering they just closed shop less than two weeks ago."

"Where do we go from here?"

"Dig deeper," the P.I. said.

"Meaning what?"

"Depends on your budget."

"We used the last of the homeowner's board fund on your retainer."

"Afraid I can't much help you, then."

* * *

Maryellen grabbed a cookie and left the multipurpose room modifying the prayer she'd been revising and restating for days: *Dear Lord, I now realize the shock and, honestly, outrage I felt upon seeing Frank cash-advanced the last $2,000 for the land from our joint credit card was all part of your plan. I have faith the deed for your church was somehow processed because of his unusual, but ultimately well-meaning, actions and will find its way to me so I can make things right for the former members of Frank's congregation. Amen.*

"We're so fucked," Ron Hill said to his wife as they passed Maryellen in the hallway.

And please, please, please right this mess. Amen, she added before finishing her last bite of cookie and detouring into the ladies' room.

Closing herself into a stall, she wiggled her not entirely loose jeans down below her hips to pee. Somehow, in the midst of it all, her need to feed had grown, but she just didn't feel like putting herself through the purge anymore.

The door to the bathroom opened with the scrape of a stroller against the doorframe and accompanied by the sound of two screaming babies.

"Let me help you," a voice said.

Maryellen looked through the crack in the stall door.

Theresa Trautman pushed the stroller, followed by Meg Pierce-Cohn who picked up and began to rock one of the babies.

"Thanks," Theresa said over the wailing. "I never thought about them both being colicky at the same inopportune moment."

"My girls always fussed at the same time," Meg said. "Still do."

Both babies screamed louder.

"The colic, mixed with the lack of sleep . . ." Theresa said, tearfully.

"Is one of the toughest parts of having twins," Meg said. "Two weeks after having ours, I sent Will in for a vasectomy."

Vasectomy.

Will Pierce-Cohn was fixed.

* * *

"You an attorney?" the representative from the Estridges' structural insurance asked.

Will's idea, to advocate for the Estridges who were getting the runaround as to the ultimate fate of their home, and, at the same time, make inquiries into Henderson Homes' construction insurance coverage, seemed less brilliant by the second. "Not per se, but I am an authorized representative of—"

"Authorized how?"

"The Estridges asked me to, and—"

"And this is an open file. We are only authorized to speak with the Estridges or their legal counsel."

"I see," he said. "Can you provide any information on a non-open file, unrelated to the Estridges' loss?"

"What would that be?"

"Can you tell me if Henderson Homes also carried their builder's insurance with you?"

"Not unless you're an authorized representative of Henderson Homes."

* * *

Maryellen bowed her head.

Dear Lord, While I admit, it's growing more and more difficult to maintain a positive attitude, I am grateful You spared the Pierce-Cohns from what could have been unbearable shame. I pray that the blessing of overhearing the conversation between Theresa and Meg is Your way of telling me there is no reason to be concerned about Hope's pregnancy. Please, don't let . . . She couldn't figure out which name was better or worse to insert. *Please let Jim be the father of Hope's baby. Please also let the neighborhood situation resolve. And,* she paused. *Please, let the deed be in the mailbox. Amen.*

She turned the key in the lock.

Inside, she found a polite, carefully worded letter from the church brotherhood wondering how they might be of assistance in organizing and preparing the Melody Mountain Community Church for its upcoming merger with Harmony Hills.

And a 10 percent off coupon for Bed Bath & Beyond.

* * *

"Question?" Will asked.

"Shoot," the forensic engineer said.

"What's it going to cost to retrofit the drainage we need?"

"You don't want to know."

* * *

Maryellen got back in her car after another fruitless mailbox pass and drove down the street toward her house. She pulled into the garage and went inside to find Eva curled up on the sectional, weeping silently in the blue light of the TV. "I thought you had some friends coming over?"

"I don't."

"Why don't you call—?"

"If they came over, it would only be out of guilt."

"People don't know what to do in these situations."

"Especially when they feel guilty."

"Why would anyone feel guilty?"

"Mom." Eva looked up at her. "I know you heard, saw what was going on in the basement after the potluck."

"Oh God, Eva, I . . ." Maryellen saw herself looking at her daughter in that purple cape through a haze of candles and incense. "I'm not sure what I saw."

"Because of the hash brownies."

"I . . ." Maryellen said.

"My fault," Eva said.

"How is it your fault? Lan . . ." Maryellen stopped herself. "One of the parents—"

"Mrs. Estridge found the brownies we hid in the cabinet at the rec center. She brought them out but she didn't bring them to the party."

"Oh Lord." Maryellen felt sick.

Eva looked down. "They were supposed to enhance a spell."

"Experimenting," Maryellen finally managed, mainly because she couldn't figure out what else she could say. "Normal part of the adolescent process."

"The spell was about Daddy."

Fighting a horrific, aching revulsion, she forced herself to sit down and put her arm around her daughter. "Whatever it was you kids were doing couldn't possibly have caused what happened to happen."

"Tyler found this book. We thought it would be cool to form a . . . People were into it and when Lauren moved into the neighborhood and fell for Tyler and wanted to join we had thirteen people."

"Thirteen," Maryellen found herself repeating.

"When Dad said I had to go to camp, it just made sense to try a spell that would send him to Africa or something." Her voice was husky with anguish. "He wasn't supposed to . . ."

"You were play acting. You couldn't have—"

"Tyler said we shouldn't do it after Lauren took off because her mom went into labor. He said the results were too unpredictable. I thought maybe Daddy would go away, but somewhere close, or for less time. With only twelve we weren't strong enough to effect . . ."

And now it is done.

"And then I broke up Lauren and Tyler by pretending . . . I can't even talk about it. . . . Everything's ruined. And now everyone hates me, but none of it matters, because Daddy's gone." She buried her head in Maryellen's shoulder. "Daddy's gone."

Maryellen closed her eyes. She thought about asking Eva to join her in a healing prayer, but thought better of it. She began to recite the words silently instead: *Heavenly Father, in my present need, help me to believe that You understand my pain and will do what is best for me.*

She stopped.

Frank was not only dead, but had left her to deal with an emptied building fund, a sinking playground, a cracking home, and a question mark where Hope Jordan was concerned.

Eva's tears dampened her shirt.

Worse, he'd left her with a despondent, hash-brownie-making, teen witch for a daughter.

Could this really be what was best for her?

The built-up tears from the past days, weeks, months, probably even years finally erupted and streamed down her face. As she cried for how little she missed Frank, how much she wished he was around to deal with his mistakes, and sobbed that much harder over Eva, she couldn't get herself to recite the *Give me the strength to trust You and put the present and future in Your Hands* remainder of the prayer.

"Are you okay, Mommy?" Eva asked.

"Honestly?" Maryellen found herself looking up at her equally teary daughter. "Everything's really fucked up."

Eva looked way more shocked than Maryellen suddenly felt.

"And the only thing I can think of to do is just face it."

CHAPTER FIFTY-SIX

Unless property is contraband, hazardous, or illegal, every reasonable effort will be made by our police department to ensure the return to the rightful owner—from the Melody Mountain Ranch jurisdictional police policy manual.

"Sign here," the policeman said, pointing to the X on the paperwork he set in front of Maryellen.

With her signature, he unlocked the door beside the front counter and disappeared inside.

She'd left the hospital after the accident with Frank's wallet, watch, and wedding ring, never having given a thought to the now dead cell phone or the tire-marked briefcase that lay inside the clear plastic evidence bag the policeman reappeared with in his hand.

She'd let go of finding a deed, or anything else that might make sense of the mess Frank had left, resigning herself to making the best of what she could control—day-to-day life and helping to heal her daughter. Then, the letter had come from the police station releasing Frank's belongings.

She accepted the evidence bag, flew back to her car, and dumped the contents of the briefcase onto the passenger seat.

Two unlabeled files slid out.

The first held the purchase contract between Frank on behalf of the Melody Mountain Community Church and Henderson Homes. Finalized with $2,000 on July 1, courtesy of the Griffin family Visa cash advance, and following three earlier payments of $23,000, $10,000, and $5,000, the deal was originally signed by both parties on March 15, which she couldn't help but note was two weeks before the April board vote ratifying the new locations.

The deed was to have been processed and mailed following the holiday weekend.

Before Henderson Homes had closed its doors.

Before Frank had died.

At least she had a definitive answer as to whether it was ever coming.

Particularly when she opened the second file.

CONFIDENTIAL COUNSELING NOTES:
HOPE JORDAN

Maryellen pinched herself until she could force herself to close the file without reading the contents.

When she did, a monogrammed slip of Crane stationery flew out the bottom, and fluttered to the ground.

Dear Jim,
I'm sorry for any mess I've left behind . . .

CHAPTER FIFTY-SEVEN

Insurance obtained by the Community Association shall, to the extent possible, and without undue cost, cover each board member.

"Whoa," Will said, hanging up the phone.

"Who was that?" Meg asked.

"Maryellen," Will said, wondering whether he'd really heard what he'd just heard.

"What did she want?"

"She called to tell me she got Frank's briefcase back from the night of the accident." Will paused for a second to process what he was about to say. "Apparently, there was paperwork inside proving Frank signed the playground deal ahead of the board vote."

"Seriously?"

"Not only that, she thinks the fraud involved should activate the board Errors and Omissions policy and cover the repairs on the playground."

Even as the shock registered on his wife's face, he still couldn't believe the rest of what Maryellen had told him. "The playground switch happened in the first place because Frank was working his own side deal with Henderson Homes to buy the mandated playground land—"

"For his church?" Meg asked.

Will nodded. "Maryellen said she'd been trying to protect me from what Frank had done, but couldn't anymore."

"Why's that?"

He waved the piece of paper he held in his hand.

"A phone number?"

"From Frank's phone," he said. "Someone from Henderson Homes called him right before he ran out the door."

"This may be the break we've been looking for," she said.

299

"But may also have killed Frank," he said. "Maryellen said he ran out of the house right after the call came in."

"Wasn't he was running after Eva?"

"He may have been, but she thinks the caller knew Henderson Homes was shutting its doors and felt bad enough to call Frank and give him a heads-up."

"Holy shit," she said. "I'd have run off too if I knew Henderson Homes had gone under."

"Especially if you'd put down forty grand on your secret land deal, but didn't get the deed."

CHAPTER FIFTY-EIGHT

Community Center Rules and Regulations: Disorderly Conduct includes but is not limited to unacceptable loitering within the facilities or on the grounds as deemed by staff to be destructive or offensive.

*M*aryellen waited until the rec center was closed, and using Frank's keys she hadn't yet relinquished, opened the door, turned off the alarm, and headed straight for the kitchen.

It was against everything she believed in to read Hope's confidential counseling notes, but she had to. Hope's "letter" was a suicide note, that or the saddest good-bye she could imagine. Exactly the kind of note she herself might have left to spare a husband any pain beyond whatever he'd feel from her departure.

Like the pain of finding out he was to be a dad, but not a father?

Maryellen turned on the light and stood in the middle of the room, willing herself back to the night of the potluck, back into her hash brownie high surrounded by platters of food and the hum of voices in the next room.

The rhythmic thuds from behind her.

The bulk of Frank's notes didn't reveal much beyond Hope's misery over not conceiving, how the frustration led her to question her faith, and the prayers and psalms he'd offered to help her persevere while she awaited the Lord's ultimate gift.

They certainly didn't explain why he'd lied about having the note.

She walked to the back wall of the kitchen. As she rapped on the sheetrock she could practically hear the animalistic grunts like they were still happening.

The more troubling of Frank's comments began to swirl through her head: *Fertility hormones may be clouding Hope's better judgment. I've asked her to consult on the playground, in part to keep an eye on her. I have concerns about the*

underlying nature of Hope's working relationship with Tim Trautman. There's a
rumor afoot concerning Hope and Will Pierce-Cohn . . .

Maryellen ran out the door, through the darkened main lobby, around to
the administrative hall, and into the multipurpose room. The light she flipped
on reflected off the door handle of the walk-in art supply closet that shared the
south wall of the kitchen.

Normally locked, the room must have been open that night for access to
decorating supplies.

Or was opened.

She was about to unlock the door herself, but stopped. Even though the red
light wasn't on, the last thing she needed was to show up on the security camera
as she let herself into a supply closet after hours when she wasn't supposed to
be there anyway.

That familiar sensation of cold dread and adrenaline began to spread across
her chest and through her body.

The camera had to have been on during the potluck.

She rushed down to the security office, made her way inside, and unlocked
the cabinets until she found boxes of stored tapes. She located Saturday, May
28, INTERIOR.

Her hands shook as she turned on a monitor, put the tape into the machine,
and watched a black and white image of the empty lower-level hallway appear
on the screen.

The time flashing at the bottom right corner was 11:01 P.M.

The very moment the first of Theresa and Tim's twins had been born.

She pressed rewind and watched rotating images scroll backward in reverse
double time from the various cameras set throughout the rec center. At 10:15,
she paused to zoom in on a short, dark-haired man entering the rec center.

Will Pierce-Cohn.

If anything did happen between him and Hope, it wasn't at the rec center.

And, he couldn't be the father.

At the 9:35 P.M. mark, she slowed the speed to watch more carefully the
people exiting the bathrooms, walking backward toward the pool area. Another
short, dark-haired man stopped to talk to someone before entering the men's
room.

She zoomed in.

Frank.

He headed back toward the pool area and the tape switched views to the
closed door to the multipurpose room.

She'd almost caught her breath from seeing her husband, knowing he'd
been alone, when the empty fitness wing hall appeared on the screen.

Hadn't Theresa said her water had broken at 8:15 and they were at the hospital by 9:30?

Hope had definitely mentioned eating chips from the vending machine with someone.

Maryellen rewound the tape, stopping at 8:15.

She watched at normal speed as the camera changed views every five minutes, switching from the main entrance to the crowded pool area to outside the bathrooms.

At the 8:30 mark, the fitness center hallway appeared on the screen.

Hope stood beside a short, dark-haired man in front of a vending machine.

Maryellen zoomed in.

Tim.

He appeared to be talking on his cell phone.

Hope put money into the slot.

Maryellen's heart began to thump watching Hope make a selection and Tim head away from her toward the stairs.

The camera cut to the administrative hallway and a view into the multipurpose room.

Through the open door.

The pounding in her heart gave way to a sick ache. She forced herself to watch the next few scenes as they flashed before her, five minutes at a time.

Main entrance.

Pool area.

Outside the upstairs restrooms.

At 9:04, she took a horrified breath in preparation for what she feared she would see when the view switched into the open multipurpose room.

The empty fitness hallway filled the screen.

She looked at the time on the monitor. It read 9:10 P.M.

She rewound and pushed play again.

The tape skipped from the 9:00 view of the restrooms to the 9:10 view of the lower level.

9:05 to 9:10 was gone from the tape.

As she fast-forwarded to the 9:30 view of the multipurpose room, the closed-door view of the room, she remembered how early Frank was up and gone the morning after the party.

"Had to make sure the rec center was back in order," he'd said.

* * *

"Mom?" Things had gone from weird and horrible to weird and different, starting the second her mom had dropped that F-bomb. Waking to find Mom staring directly at her, a piece of paper in hand, was somehow, weirder still. "What is it?"

"I was very annoyed with your dad that night," her mom finally said.

Eva turned off the already-on-mute TV. "What night?"

"The night of the potluck."

"Oh." The lump that had permanently settled in Eva's throat began to throb.

"I thought it was the combination of him not appreciating how hard I was working and . . ." She paused. "And those hash brownies."

"I'm so sorry, Mommy. I—"

"I'm glad to hear that and I know." Her mom shook her head. "But, I woke you up because I need to tell you something."

"What is it?"

"I was the thirteenth person."

"What?"

"Your witch rules. Weren't there supposed to be thirteen people to do your spell?"

Eva's temples began to throb. "I don't ever want to think or talk about that, ever ag—"

"But I was there." She looked up. "Not downstairs with you, but in the house."

Eva wanted to, but couldn't avert her eyes from her mother's intense gaze. "Doesn't mean a thing. You weren't in the coven."

"I was angry with him that night. So angry, I wished as hard as I could he wouldn't come home."

There were only twelve of them in the circle. As they chanted the spell, Eva knew it wouldn't really work, which made her know for sure nothing serious would happen. But if her mom was standing in the room above them thinking she wished Daddy wouldn't come home . . . ? "Can't be true Mom. Can't be."

"Which is exactly the conclusion I finally came to," she said. "Because neither of us really wanted him to be gone. What we wanted was for him to be present with us, for us, and not just for how we reflected on him. I didn't want him to be so damn competitive."

Familiar hot tears began to roll down Eva's cheeks.

"Your dad ran into that ice cream truck not because we willed him to, but because he was so busy trying to run away from the disastrous results of his insatiable need to control and run everything and everyone, he wasn't looking where he was going."

"But I was one of the things he was trying to control."

"You can't control people, only guide them," she said. "Remember that, because you're a lot like him."

The words stung.

"Thing is, there's hope for you." She seemed to grimace with the word. "And me." She waved the paper in her hand. "See this?"

Eva managed a nod.

"I sent in my resume for a head librarian opening at the Central Library mostly to see what would happen. I didn't think I had any chance, but this is an e-mail with the response."

"What does it say?"

"I didn't allow myself to read it," she said. "I knew there was no way I could take the job even if by some chance this is a request for an interview."

"Why not?"

"That's the other conclusion I came to," her mom said. "Do you think it's a request for an interview or a thanks for applying, but?"

"You'd be a great head librarian."

"Thanks." Tears filled her mother's eyes. "I'm going to read it right now."

"Go for it."

"If they want to interview me and it's not too late, what should I do?"

"Go on the interview."

"And what if I get offered the job?"

"Take it."

"My commute will be almost an hour either direction every day."

"We could move," Eva said.

"I wouldn't want to uproot you so soon after Dad's . . ."

"If you got a job, or if you just wanted to move, I'd support you and go because it's what you really wanted," Eva said. "That's all I ever really wanted from Dad."

"Me too."

Eva grabbed her mother's free hand as she read the e-mail.

CHAPTER FIFTY-NINE

*Enforcement: The Association or any Owner, shall have the right
to enforce, by any proceeding at law or in equity, all restrictions,
conditions, covenants, reservations, liens, and Declaration.*

$\mathcal{M}$eg's invitation of lunch down at the capitol, clearly an attempt to lift Will from his funk, seemed doomed to failure.

Failure being the concept du jour.

The phone number Maryellen had given him paid off in that a disgruntled ex-employee of Henderson Homes answered the call. Will found out Henderson Homes was basically open one day and closed the next. The man had no idea how the company handled, or if they even held, insurance. He did know the aggravating details of Frank Griffin's land deal from inception to final payment, including the promise of a deed that was to be processed and mailed but never arrived. Will gave that info to Tim to handle. Out both a job and a final paycheck, the man was certain Henderson Homes pulled up stakes not because they were bankrupt, but to protect themselves from ending up that way after the unprecedented number of rain-related claims. Furious and certain Henderson Homes left with a pile of money to protect, he'd been doing his own investigating.

He had managed to come up with some vague information that one of the principals of the company had some sort of interests in California before his trail had gone cold.

Cold as Will's.

At least there was chocolate on Meg's desk.

Will opened the See's Candy and helped himself to a Kona Mocha. "A welcome surprise."

"Candy isn't the only surprise I have for you today," she smiled and closed the door.

"Here?" he asked. The last they needed was for her to be removed from office because of a sex scandal in her own office. With her own husband, no less.

Besides, he was hardly in the mood.

Meg picked up her phone and dialed some numbers. "Thought you might enjoy being part of this call."

She pushed speaker.

"You ready?" she asked.

"Ready," the man on the other end of the call answered before Will had a chance to ask what he was supposed to be ready for. "I'll dial, then patch you in."

"Perfect," she said. "Thanks."

"What's going on?" Will asked during the silence.

"I fed the situation with Henderson Homes through a few legislative and construction connections in California," she said. "I got an interesting call from a legislator who represents a suburban constituency north of Los Angeles."

"Interesting, how?"

"Representative Curtis," a speaker-enhanced voice filled the room from the other end of the line. "Pleasure to hear from you."

"I'm looking forward to having you break ground on your project."

"We're looking forward to becoming part of the landscape of your growing community."

What the? Will mouthed.

Meg smiled.

"Listen," Representative Curtis said. "I called today because an associate of mine is having an issue with a builder in her legislative district and I thought you might have an answer or two that could be of some help."

"My pleasure."

"I'm going to pass this call over to her."

"Hi," Meg said. "This is Meg Pierce-Cohn. I'm a Colorado state legislator and one of the Melody Mountain Ranch homeowners saddled with a cracking foundation from your failure to follow building codes by installing proper drainage. I've told Representative Curtis all about your abrupt pullout from our state to avoid paying for your mistakes."

There was silence on the other end of the line.

"I'm inclined to ask the city to put a temporary hold on approval of your plans," Representative Curtis cut in. "That way you'll have time to make right on this situation and have some engineers, at your cost, ensure we won't have a repeat performance of what Representative Pierce-Cohn has told me about your project back in Denver."

CHAPTER SIXTY

Section 10. Oil and Mining Operations. No oil drilling, oil development operations, oil refining, quarry, or mining operations of any kind shall be permitted upon or in any Lot.

The multipurpose room was full, but the only noise came from the rustle of paperwork.

"Please sign on the four X's located on the first, second, fifth, and sixth pages," the lawyer representing Henderson Homes, DBA Casa De Oro Homes L.L.C., of California, said.

Will's arm brushed against Meg's as he signed on the first X and handed the pen over.

She smiled.

He squeezed her elbow.

Hiding in plain view had worked well for the former Henderson Homes execs, but not as well as Meg's connections in both government and the media. Their eagerness to stay out of the harsh glare of the local media spotlight and continue to develop in California made for a true win-win. Maryellen was granted the deed to what would have been the Melody Mountain Community Church. The Estridges were getting a brand new house. Perimeter drains were slated for immediate retrofitting, warranty repairs were already being done, and the playground would be fixed starting Monday. Best of all, in a gesture of goodwill, every affected homeowner was being issued a healthy check, the amount of which depended on the depth and breadth of their pain and suffering.

"After you've read each page, please also initial the bottom right-hand corner," the lawyer said.

"I presume all repairs that haven't already been completed are guaranteed within sixty days?" Trautman asked.

"Except for the quadrant three and four cul-de-sacs which can't be completed until after the drainage retrofitting."

"And the new warranty will be good for five years from today?"

"Yes," the lawyer said.

"And how can we be sure they'll be honored?"

"They're backed by lien warranty against Casa De Oro Homes."

"What if someone comes down with mold sickness as a result of the cracking we already have?" Roseanne asked.

"Covered," the lawyer said. "Despite a lack of generally agreed-upon data on true toxicity."

"Not going there," she said. "What about the nondisclosure clause on the back page?"

The lawyer cleared his throat. "With your signature you are agreeing to the terms outlined, whereby you will not discuss with anyone, including the media, homeowners in unaffected areas, or prospective homeowners, the terms of this agreement or the cash settlement."

"What do we say if someone asks about the earthmoving equipment or whatever?" someone in the back asked.

"We've provided an FAQ of sorts with answers we'd like you to give," the lawyer said. "There are five other communities in Colorado who haven't been granted the same courtesy and my clients would like it to stay that way."

* * *

Tim opened the door to the art closet, pulled out the cart of champagne he'd set to chilling, popped the cork, and poured the first glass. "To Melody Mountain Ranch—Life once again in harmony with our dreams!"

The first round of *Hear! Hear!* was followed by countless toasts to perimeter drains, repair trucks, the Estridges' new home, Maryellen's deed for the church land, the playground he himself scheduled for repair, et cetera, et cetera. He drank to Roseanne Goldberg for her skill as a tireless watchdog, Maryellen for her attention to important detail, and to himself, as Jane Hunt so kindly put it, for his eloquence, grace, and *wartime* leadership ability.

"Thank you," he tipped his glass in her direction, but turned his attention, and with it everyone else's, to the Pierce-Cohns. "But I think we all realize that our lives and futures would be in a much bleaker place if it weren't for the tireless efforts of both Meg and Will Pierce-Cohn."

Over the thundering applause he made his way over to stand beside the two of them. "We wouldn't be standing here right now if it weren't for you."

"Thanks," Will said.

"Thank you," Tim said,

"Which of you is officially taking over as prez?" Roseanne asked. "Because there's something we should—"

"Talk to him," Will said.

"You're not going to run?" Tim focused on looking neither bristled by Roseanne's question nor too delighted by Will's answer.

"I have one more toast I'd like to make," Hope's husband said from across the room. Everyone quieted as he raised his glass. "Round about the time the Estridges are safely back in their new home, Hope and I will be having our first child."

Will raised his glass. "I think I've had my fill of neighborhood affairs for a while."

Tim gave Will a brotherly pat on the shoulder but smiled at Hope. "To neighborhood affairs."

***

Maryellen allowed herself a glass of champagne, and then a well-deserved refill.

Her house and the playground would be restored. The deed to the land was hers, at least until she sold the property on behalf of the Harmony Hills Church. Frank's life insurance insured her and Eva's comfortable future.

She looked over at Hope, standing beside her beaming husband.

And Hope was officially pregnant.

Maryellen first blamed Hope for seducing Frank, subjecting her to countless hours of imaginary interrogation and non-NATO-approved coercion techniques. *When you say you don't remember anything from the night of the potluck, what exactly don't you remember? Where the hell don't you remember being with my husband? Does the art supply closet ring any kind of bell?*

Problem was, every time she actually spotted Hope in her open garage or at the rec center, all she saw was strain and misery where there should have been glow.

Worse, everywhere she looked, from the sunken playground, to the empty lot, to Eva's troubled expression, all she saw was the *legacy* of misery Frank had left behind. Fallout from his need to conquer and control hovered like a gray cloud she couldn't attribute to Hope any more than she could blame Eva for the after-effects of the hash brownies that had been accidentally passed around.

Hope claimed not to remember that evening at all.

Frank clearly had, and had gone back to the rec center to erase the evidence.

Guilt stricken, he'd taken the note from Hope's house thinking she'd attempted suicide and worried she'd written something incriminating about him.

When nothing came of the "fall" he lied about having the note.

Whoso diggeth a pit shall fall therein: and he that rolleth a stone, it will return upon him.

Maybe it was the now-familiar shock, or the odd sense of justification that had led her to dip his toothbrush every so often, but she decided then and there to let Frank take it up with his maker.

Maryellen looked over at Hope, standing practically glued to Jim, and noticed her hand trembling as she raised a champagne flute of sparkling water to her lips.

If she did remember, she was suffering terribly.

And if she didn't, wasn't it that much worse?

* * *

"Interesting how you soft-pedaled Tim on the presidency issue," Meg said. "Are you really going to let him step in?"

Will steered the minivan toward the entrance to the cul-de-sac. "If I do, will you think I'm a pussy?"

"I'd hardly categorize what you did, have been doing all along, as anything akin to being a pussy," Meg said. "You saved the neighborhood."

"Aw shucks," he said, "I didn't do it alone."

"You certainly didn't do it with any help from Tim."

"He got the Errors and Omissions insurance activated."

"After you fed him the information."

Somehow, Trautman's pomp-but-no-circumstance routine didn't bother Will at all. "He kept the troops entertained while the battle surged around him."

"By spouting rhetoric."

"Making him perfect for the job." Will pulled up the driveway and pushed the garage door button. "As history has shown."

"Trautman's a sleaze," she said.

"Roseanne'll keep him honest." Will pulled in and turned off the engine.

"You know," she said, "I overheard your comments about Hope."

"Okay."

Both were silent for a moment.

"Will, did anything happen between you and Hope that night?"

"No," he said, tempted to say nothing more and enjoy the power a touch of jealousy always added. He couldn't though, not with the worry he saw in her eyes. "Meg, I would never compromise our marriage that way."

"You sure?"

"Can't say I wasn't tempted."

"Fair enough. She is beautiful."

"She's not you. Us."

Meg kissed his cheek. "Do you think anything happened between her and Tim?"

"Trautman wishes."

She put her hand in his lap.

Will pushed the garage door remote, sat back, and let her.

CHAPTER SIXTY-ONE

4.25. Greenhouses. Committee approval is required.

Hope felt beyond anxious as she passed the excavation equipment in front of the Estridges' house and started up Maryellen's front walk. She'd managed to keep a polite distance. Somehow, she'd even kept it together enough to accept a warm hug from Maryellen after Jim announced their pregnancy at the neighborhood meeting.

If only he'd kept quiet, she could have gone about finishing the last of her upcoming jobs, set up the holiday decorating in advance, and waited in peace for the relatively minor repairs on their home. Once everything was done, she'd have joined Jim in London, not returning until after the baby was born.

Fundamentally, the plan hadn't changed, other than forcing herself to smile through all the well wishes and jarring *I knew its*. In two days, she'd still be on a plane, free of any worry, at least where the neighborhood was concerned.

Perspiration broke out at the nape of her neck.

All she had to do was get through the tea she couldn't decline with Maryellen.

The front door opened before she could put her finger to the bell.

"Welcome," Maryellen said.

Hope smiled through pure, sick dread. "Thanks for inviting me."

"I wanted to have the chance to say a proper good-bye before you leave."

"So sweet."

"I won't be here when you get back from London." Maryellen opened the door to the boxes lining the back hall. "We're moving."

"Moving?" Surprise and, strangely, a tinge of panic tempered what should have felt like relief. "I had no idea."

"Neither did I until, well, until I just did." Her face hinted at a smile. "Truck's coming in the morning."

"I didn't even know you'd put the house on the market."

"I didn't," she said. "Laney and Steve are going to live here while their house is being rebuilt."

"Oh," she managed. "Where are you going?"

"I have a job prospect downtown," Maryellen said. "Whether I get it or not, I fell in love with this little bungalow in Congress Park."

How much less anxiety might she have suffered knowing Maryellen was leaving too? "I guess I'm just surprised by the suddenness."

"The hush money made the decision that much easier."

"I hate to think of it that way."

"I hate to think of the other people in the other communities whose homes won't be fixed," she said. "But I had my daughter and our future to think about."

How many of her own thoughts had centered around Maryellen, her daughter, and their future? She willed away the sting of impending tears. "I really am so sorry for everything you've gone through."

Maryellen nodded. "Everything happens for a reason."

"But sometimes so differently than you might ever expect."

"Have to agree with you there." Maryellen motioned her toward the kitchen. "Come. I have something for you."

"For me?"

The note lay on her kitchen table beside the teacups.

Hope stopped breathing.

"He had it with him when he died," Maryellen said. "In his briefcase."

Her heart couldn't have stopped, not with the way her brain was racing or the way words began to spill from her mouth. "Frank must have taken that note thinking it was a . . . If only he had known I wasn't trying to . . . I was having some marital problems he knew about, so he must have taken the note thinking he was sparing me from the aftereffects of doing something rash. Wasn't doing what it may have looked like." She took a breath. "I'd cleaned the house and was trying to clean the chandelier because I was thinking about, planning to leave Jim."

"I see," Maryellen said in response.

She patted her belly. "We worked it out, though."

"Obviously."

"I'm sure Frank didn't admit he had the note to—"

"To protect you," Maryellen said.

Hope nodded.

Maryellen smiled. "All that matters now is you're going to have the beautiful, healthy baby you've wanted more than anything."

With the hug that followed, Hope prayed she wasn't as clammy as she felt.

"You know," Maryellen said releasing her. "It's so hot today, I don't think I'm in the mood for tea." She opened the freezer. "How about an ice cream sandwich instead?"

As Maryellen led Hope to the back porch to eat their ice cream, Frank's last psalm began looping, probably infinitely, in her head.

Hope deferred maketh the heart sick: but when the desire cometh, it is a tree of life.

Part VI

AFTERBIRTH

CHAPTER SIXTY-TWO

Duty to Disclose: In connection with any possible conflict of interest the existence of said conflict, financial or otherwise, must be disclosed prior to any discussion or action on that issue.

Ten months later

*L*aney backed her new Lexus out of the Griffins' garage and reparked at a strategic angle to highlight both the for-sale sign featuring her professional glamour shot and the view of her nearly finished, already fabulous, house next door.

The Universe had come through in spades. She still had a standing appointment at Bastian's for mold-related chiropractic adjustment, but the bill for homeopathic supplements was nothing relative to the mortgage she'd never have again.

What she did have was everything she ever wanted.

Steve was healthy again and working for Scott Connors at his booming insurance agency. The girls not only had passing, if not stellar, grades, but also had enthusiastically stepped into the shoes of Eva Griffin as copresidents of the Melody Mountain Ranch Youth Group. Mother's Helpers was doing brisk business. Better yet, as soon as she sold Maryellen's house, she'd have the commission proceeds from both the Griffin and Fowler properties to help furnish her completely rebuilt, loaded with granite, hardwood, and crown molding, dream home.

She tucked a stray strand of freshly low-lighted hair behind her ear and straightened her cream-colored jacket. She'd managed to sell Sarah's house using the new ten-year warranty upgrade as a selling point and without arousing any suspicion as to why a pre-owned house would come, free of charge, with such a bonus.

A car neared the entrance to the cul-de-sac.

No reason she couldn't do the same for Maryellen's.

She hurried up the front steps, clicked open the lock box, and opened the door as though she hadn't been living there for nearly a year, waiting for her house to be done.

Closing her eyes, she took a Chi-balancing breath, willed these buyers not to ask too many questions about the house or neighborhood she was contractually unable to answer, and waved as a Toyota Sienna XLE approached the driveway.

The passenger window slid down and the wife, an attractive brunette, waved warmly.

Laney proffered a practiced, but authentic smile.

The husband parked and came out the driver's side. Forty-ish, five-ten or so, graying and wearing nice sportswear, he fell firmly into the more handsome than Tim Trautman category.

Of course, he probably didn't do that trick with his tongue Tim did.

Laney offered her hand. "Laney Estridge, Mountain Realty."

"Rob Fineberg."

And Tim's handshake was anything but clammy.

The wife made her way over. Her leggings and tunic top both hid and highlighted the beginnings of a baby bump.

"I'm Tara." Her sufficiently oversized diamond wedding set sparkled in the sunlight. "We were so excited to see your listing online."

"Isn't this a Henderson Home?" the husband asked.

"Better known these days as a Casa De Oro home," Laney smiled. "They've gone big time in California."

The wife looked past her at the roofers, laying sheets of shingles onto Laney's roof.

Laney prayed she wouldn't have to cough out a lie about the amazing warranty-covered job happening next door.

Instead, the wife pointed at the playground. "Look, honey."

"Saw that," the husband said.

"We love having a place for our little ones in this corner of the development."

"You live nearby?"

Laney nodded without elaborating. "Meg Pierce-Cohn lives on this block, too."

"The state rep?" Rob asked.

"And Tim Trautman, our HOB president, is over on the next cul-de-sac."

A bi-weekly convenience, in and of itself.

The wife scampered toward the open front door. "This house does look a lot like my sister's in California. Don't you think so, Rob?"

"This one's bigger," he said.

"This particular floor plan is somewhat unique." Laney's voice echoed across the oversized foyer as she stepped inside and pointed to the full-size living room. "There's also an enhanced great room."

"I love the space." The wife spread her arms out.

"Price seems a little on the high side," Rob said.

"The owner's willing to entertain a reasonable offer," Laney lowered her voice slightly. Her desire to play the heartstring card and tell the story of Frank's tragic accident and its emotional aftermath for both Maryellen and Eva was overridden by her business sense. Even though Frank hadn't died in the house, he'd succumbed too close for selling comfort. "She's a widow and doesn't want to hold on to the property indefinitely."

"I love the décor," the wife said.

Laney's heart skipped a delighted beat. "It is darling, isn't it?"

"We'll still need to factor some redecorating if we write a bid." She patted her tummy. "If only for the nursery."

"The neighbor across the street designs the most darling nurseries I've ever seen," Laney said. "And there's a waiting list to have her do Christmas decorating."

"We're Jewish," the husband said.

"Perfect," Laney said, relishing the quick save. "Congregation Beth El just broke ground at the corner of Wonderland Valley Way and Wonderland Valley Parkway."

"What about the schools?" the wife said, heading for the kitchen. "And the rec center?"

"First rate," she called after her, confident she didn't need to follow behind to point out the commercial style refrigerator and range or the granite Maryellen had the resale wherewithal to have installed from the beginning.

The husband ducked into the office.

"Everything's built in," Laney said following behind.

"Hmm." He didn't stop to examine the cherry desk or pull on a drawer. His attention was instantly focused on the window, or rather through the window and across the street.

More accurately, at the neighbor standing on her driveway.

Wearing a tank top and jean shorts, Hope Jordan was bent over her stroller tending to her infant daughter Lilly, providing an inadvertent peek at her voluptuous nursing chest.

"Who's that?" the husband asked.

"Hope," Laney said. "The interior decorator I was telling you about."

"Honey," the wife called. "You have to see the kitchen."

The husband's eyes lingered as Hope took her gorgeous, if unexpectedly dark-haired, daughter out of the stroller. She turned, and gave them a full frontal view of her slightly more curvaceous but equally as fetching post-pregnancy figure.

"Coming," the husband said.

100
290
——
390

400
420
——
820